A DREAM ACROSS TIME

A DREAM ACROSS TIME

Annie Rogers

BIVENS AND JENSEN PUBLISHING

Printed in the United States.

For information address:
Bivens and Jensen Publishing
P.O. Box 448
St. Michaels, MD 21663

A Dream Across Time / by Annie Rogers

ISBN 0-9770183-0-X
ISBN 978-0-9770183-0-7

Library of Congress Cataloging-in-Publication Data
Burt, Mala, 1943-

Library of Congress Control Number: 2005906961

Second Edition

10 9 8 7 6 5 4 3 2

Visit our Web site at
www.bivensandjensen.com

ACKNOWLEDGMENTS

Special appreciation goes to Patrick Elien, a wise and gentle St. Lucian of many talents, who was the inspiration for the character of Marcus.

A Dream Across Time is dedicated to the people of St. Lucia, proud of their heritage and modeling a democracy for developing nations.

PROLOGUE

France 1789

Their departure from the estate in Normandy had been hurried, the curtains in the coach had been kept closed. Now Anne-Cecile's curiosity overrode her fear, and she looked out. Through the curtain's narrow gap she could see piles of barrels and crates and crews of shouting men. She could smell the sea air. As the coach moved slowly forward, she saw masts.

Jean-Clair du Diamant supported his young wife down the carriage steps, her legs numb from the long ride.

"We have arrived at the docks, *ma chérie*," he said. The fresh sea air steadied her, but within moments the foul smells of the wharf reached her, and Anne-Cecile brought her scented handkerchief to her face.

"Husband, I hear only rumors from the servants, and you tell me nothing. Are you displeased with me? Are you sending me away?"

The question pierced his heart.

"Ah, no, *ma jolie*. But it's too dangerous for us to stay in France."

Stories were circulating about the terrible fate of aristocrats near Paris and now in the countryside. The unrest had spread to the local peasants. But Jean-Clair dared not share his fears with his wife.

He held the girl he had married out of expedience - a marriage to ally two powerful families. Children were the important thing, and the sons she bore him within a year of their marriage assured the Diamant line would go on. He had not anticipated caring for her, loving her with a growing passion.

"Henri and Elly will care for you and the children. I must see the bankers in the city to arrange the letters of credit. Then we will sail to my brother in the Indies."

Shouts from the wharf captured Jean-Clair's attention, and he felt the fear in Anne-Cecile. He moved her toward the coach.

"You will be warmer in the coach until they are ready to board us," he said, helping her re-enter the dim, stuffy interior. As he spoke he pressed a small parcel into her hands. "These are the children's christening gifts from the King and Queen. They may be the only legacy we can give our sons."

He pushed the fur-lined hood back from her face. She felt his warm hands as he threaded a stout cord around her neck and placed a small pouch between her breasts. His hands smelled of horse.

"For our future. Safeguard this as you would our children," he said, tucking the warm fur robe back around her. She swayed slightly as dread, cold and fear attacked her.

"Jean-Clair, please come with us now," she begged.

"*Ma chérie*, I promise to be back shortly."

He spoke reassuringly, knowing his young wife had an inner strength she must access now. He pushed her dark curls away from her cheeks, his fingertips trying to erase the anxiety that lined her face.

"All is arranged. Soon you will board the ship. I will join you in a few hours, and we will sail first to Martinique and then on to Charles in Sainte Lucie." Jean-Clair tried to settle her escalating anxiety.

"We will be separated for only a few hours. I would never leave you or the children."

"Then I will not be frightened," she said.

He kissed the sleeping children, memorizing their twin faces, the tiny chins with the distinctive Diamant cleft. Two joys beyond price.

"I shall return soon," he murmured as he exited the coach.

He spoke quietly to Henri as he watched the activity on the ships, listened to the shouts and noises of the wharves. "If I am not back by the time the ship sails, the captain is to sail without me. Take my family to Charles. They will be safe there until I can join them."

Henri climbed up next to the driver, then rapped on the carriage to indicate they should move ahead.

Anne-Cecile gazed at her husband from the carriage window, her faced etched in worry. The carriage moved forward toward the dock. He smiled reassuringly, then mounted his horse and raced toward the city.

Sainte Lucie 1793

Anne-Cecile sat up on the chaise-longue, her skin damp and clammy from the heat. Two dark-haired boys rolled in the long grass, pummeling one another in mock fury. Her sons were now four, sturdy and tall for their age, browned by the tropical sun.

They would have Jean-Clair's height. Perhaps his aristocratic bearing, even here in Sainte Lucie.

She fingered the pouch hanging from a frayed cord around her neck. As ill as she had been during the voyage and after, it had never been removed. When she grasped it, it summoned Jean-Clair's image, confident and strong, while danger had been all around them. She lay back on the chaise and watched her children at play. Her thoughts turned restlessly to the new danger now closing in on her.

Ships from France brought word to Martinique and then to Sainte Lucie - news that was months old and contaminated by rumors. The evil of the revolution had spread to the islands. Only last week, when Monsieur Delacroix, owner of a neighboring plantation, came to visit, the dinner conversation centered narrowly on the unsettled times.

"Four of my slaves gone this week alone," he'd said, sipping his brandy. "Off to the forest to become brigands. No doubt armed by sympathizers of the revolution. And before they went, two oxen down. Poisoned. I tell you, we are sleeping with the shutters bolted."

"Surely you do not think your slaves would harm you?" Charles asked. "I am sure ours are loyal." The table fell silent as a black woman entered the dining room to serve the stewed goat. When the last plate was filled, the slave left and conversation resumed.

"I do not know. But it was better before our people in France stirred *liberté, egalité, and fraternité* into this ugly mess. They have no idea what it takes to put a hogshead of sugar on the docks, nor do they care." Delacroix took a bite of the stew.

"Do you know what my overseer heard one of the field hands say last week? That the whites had loosed snakes in the forest so the slaves would be afraid to escape. What nonsense! Fear of the *fer de lance* doesn't seem to keep them from running, although where they think they can run is beyond me. They meet the sea at every turn."

Charles pushed his plate aside, his eyes on his wife, Yvette, and her troubled face. "Perhaps we should retire to the veranda for a *petit punch*. This conversation is frightening the ladies."

Anne-Cecile and Yvette stayed at the table.

"Are you afraid?" asked Yvette, after the two men had left.

Anne-Cecile smiled encouragingly. "I have felt safe at Les Jumeaux since the day I came. You and Charles welcomed us into your family. You know I am grateful. Jean-Clair would be also." She stared at the table, caught in flickering candlelight.

"But are you not frightened, Anne-Cecile?"

"Yes, but Jean-Clair always told me to have courage. I try."

Yvette clutched her serviette. "I am frightened for all of us, especially my children."

"I do worry about my twin boys," Anne-Cecile said quietly. "I am so glad to be here, Yvette."

"You are Jean-Clair's wife, the mother of his heirs. You belong here - doesn't half of the estate belong to Jean-Clair? And I am so glad of your companionship. You have been like a sister to me." She reached out to take Anne-Cecile's hand...

But that had been a week ago. Now thunder sounded, drawing Anne-Cecile from her thoughts. Or was it galloping horses?

As she rose to check on the children, a powerful dark-skinned woman appeared on the veranda. Anne-Cecile always drew comfort in her strength, more, in her spiritual calm.

"Mistress, best the children come in now."

"Oh, B'til, they are having such fun," Anne-Cecile protested. "It does me good to see them joyful."

"Mistress, you not be hearing the drums? Evil about. Best the children come in now." B'til insistently motioned with her large hands for Elly to get the twins. Elly moved at once, chasing the laughing boys.

"B'til, you are frightening me. Where is Mistress Yvette?"

"Master and Makus come riding just now. Horses lathered, 'bout to drop. Master talking to Mistress. He tell me get the children indoors and bring you to him. Sent Makus fetch Master Henri and bring fresh horses."

Anne-Cecile moved quickly to the urgency in B'til's voice. "Louis and Philippe, come inside now, pay attention to Elly. Elly, take them to their room."

"*Oui, Madame,*" Elly murmured, dipping in a slight curtsy. She took the boys' hands, pulling them in her wake. Philippe glanced back at his mother and glowered. His twin, Louis, the younger by a few moments, looked back and smiled.

Anne-Cecile hurried along the shadowed Jumeaux veranda. At the doorway of Charles and Yvette's bedroom, she saw him seize his wife's shoulders.

"The brigands have burned Jalousie Estate. All the family are prisoners. Probably dead by now. A guillotine has been erected in the Soufriere square. They are going to execute all French aristocrats."

"Oh, dear God..."

We must go to Martinique. Pack only what you can take in a small bag. We leave in minutes."

Seeing Anne-Cecile sag against the doorway, her face ashen, Charles moved to grab her.

"No time for fainting. Get some things for yourself and the boys. We will go ahead. Henri and Makus are bringing horses for you. I have told Makus the track we'll take. A ship is waiting for us."

Anne-Cecile fought down the nausea and hurried to the children's room and instructed Elly what to pack. She shushed the children, who cowered instinctively at the fear in her voice.

"Bring them to me in my room as soon as you are ready, Elly. Hurry, we only have a few minutes."

Anne-Cecile ran back along the veranda to her room, her hand going instinctively to the small pouch around her neck. Throwing open the doors of the mahogany armoire, she reached into its depths and withdrew two small psalters, prayer books which had been christening gifts from her Norman family, the Roches. Each miniature book was exquisite, the fine script on the vellum pages detailing each child's lineage. From a small carved box she took two intricately executed gold chains with crosses encrusted with tiny diamonds. She stared at them, held by their beauty. How proud Jean-Clair had been when these crosses had been presented by the King and Queen of France. A christening day for their sons beyond all imagining.

Elly stood white-faced in the doorway with the children.

Anne-Cecile took several rings and gave them to Elly. "Hide them in your bodice," she said.

"Listen to me carefully," she said to the children. "We are going on a journey. We must go quickly and quietly. It is important that you obey Mama and Elly."

As she spoke, she fastened a golden chain around each small

neck, buttoning their shirts to cover the small diamond crosses. Folding Philippe's psalter into a silken scarf, Anne-Cecile lifted his shirt and tied the book around his waist. "You are my first born, Philippe. Be strong, child." She motioned Elly to do the same with Louis. The children's shirts hung loose, obscuring the small bulges.

"These psalters are precious," she instructed the children, trying to keep her voice from trembling. "Do not take them off until I tell you to do so. And do not remove the chains. Keep them hidden."

"Come, Elly. I hear the horses. Take Philippe. I will take Louis."

Charles, Yvette and their children could be seen in the far distance heading down the track into the rain forest.

Henri finished saddling the horses assisted by Makus, the powerfully-built slave trusted by Charles. B'til hurried from the kitchen with provisions tied in a cloth. She pushed Anne-Cecile and Elly to the horses. "Mount! Mount!" She handed Louis up to his mother. Philippe was handed to Henri, who tucked the boy in front of him on the saddle.

Makus stood back, drawing his cutlass. "B'til, you and I lead the horses. If we meet brigands on the track we tell them our masters be prisoners, go to guillotine in town. Best tie Master Henri's and Mistress' hands."

Makus grasped a bunch of long grass by the side of the clearing, severing it with a quick swipe of his cutlass. B'til loosely bound their hands in front of them. The rough grass rasped at their flesh, but all submitted.

"Little Master, hold on to the horse's mane," urged Henri as he put his tied arms around Philippe.

Makus strode off, leading the first horse carrying Henri. B'til followed. Several times they stopped, listening to violent shouts echoing on the rain forest track. The sun would set soon, and all knew how quickly darkness descended in the tropics.

B'til wished the moon was not in its fullness.

Makus turned them onto another track.

"Master say ship to take you away be by Malgretoute. Cesaire wait there. A boat take you to the ship."

Her twins had been lulled into a restless sleep by the rocking motion of the horses, but Anne-Cecile knew they might wake at any time, hungry and fussy. Her hands ached and the grass had rubbed her wrists raw. Just as she was about to ask Makus to remove the bindings, the horses whinnied nervously. She caught the smell of unwashed bodies and something else, sickly sweet. Men armed with cutlasses, one with a flintlock pistol, emerged from the forest.

"Where you be going with these whites?" the man with the pistol demanded.

"No business but mine," Makus said.

"I be James from Jalousie. Our masters dead and we be free. We kill more just up the track." He waved his pistol. "We take the women. You take him to guillotine, unless you want kill him yourself."

"I be Makus from Jumeaux. No more masters. My prisoners now." He motioned to their bound wrists. "We go Soufriere, see their heads in the basket."

Makus began leading the horses forward. James, the leader, jumped in his path, but Makus pushed him roughly out of his way, his confident bearing and size not lost on the brigand.

"Go 'bout your business and leave us." Makus threatened James with his cutlass.

James hesitated, then stepped back. "You can join us later. We go Jumeaux. See what we find."

Makus led them along the track while Anne-Cecile, terrified, watched the shadows. Only Louis, cradled in her arms, kept her from screaming.

Dark descended quickly and the moon began to rise.

"Makus, hurry," B'til whispered.

Anne-Cecile could hear Henri talking quietly to Philippe, who had awakened. In her arms, Louis was beginning to stir.

"Mama, are you sick?"

"Hush, *mon petit chou*," she whispered as she stroked his hair.

"Mama, where are we going?" he asked, his voice husky with sleep.

"For a ride on a ship."

"In the dark, Mama? I will not be able to see the ship."

"You will see it in the morning when you wake. Now be still, Louis, and go back to sleep." She felt her son relax into the rhythm of the horse's movements.

When Anne-Cecile's horse reared up in fear, she grabbed at its mane and clutched desperately at Louis. The horse backed up, its ears flattened.

"Makus, what is it?" whispered Henri, trying to control his own skittish mount.

"B'til, hold both horses," Makus said.

Anne-Cecile watched him step ahead on the trail. He followed a twist in the trail, then stopped. Moonlight reflected from bodies jumbled in a heap. Grimly he pulled a woman away from the pile, her skirts over her head. He uncovered the face of Mistress Yvette. Her blood glistened in the moonlight, her children dead beneath her.

Where was his Master? He would not have let his family be killed without defending them. The glint of a buckle caught Makus' attention. Pushing aside the brush, he knelt beside Charles.

"Master. Best you be dead and not see what evil done your family."

"Makus?"

"Master, be you alive?"

"Makus, the Mistress, the children?"

In the moonlight Makus could see deep cuts in Charles' flesh.

Makus ran back to the others.

"Master Henri, you must come," Makus said, severing the binding on his wrists. "B'til, untie the women and stay with them."

Makus and Henri ran back up the track.

B'til handed Philippe to Elly. She motioned the women to silence as she tied the horses to a branch and moved ahead, disregarding Makus' order.

"What is happening?" Anne-Cecile asked, as B'til disappeared from view.

She could hear muted talking, then groans.

"What has happened?" she shouted, her voice tinged with hysteria. "Henri, B'til, where are you?"

Henri appeared on the path, carrying Charles. Anne-Cecile clutched her son tightly so he would not see.

"Monsieur Charles near death. Madame and the children dead." Henri spoke woodenly. He gently laid Charles beside the trail.

"B'til, stay with our master while I take the Mistress and the children to the boat. Then I will return."

Anne-Cecile summoned all her strength and more at this new loss. She must protect her children. Above all, the twins.

"Henri, I command you to come with us on the ship. It is what my husband would want."

Henri's hand left bloody marks on her arm.

"I will see you safely on the ship, Madame. Your husband would want me to keep you and the children safe. I am sure he would also be very angry if I left his brother and his family to rot in the tropical sun."

Anne-Cecile gave in to the obvious need.

"Tell me what I must do."

"Put on Yvette's shawl. Smear the blood on you." Henri handed it to her and it repulsed her. She started to retch. "Do it," Henri said. "If we encounter more brigands they will think Makus has been at you. Rub the blood on your face and arms and on the children."

Anne-Cecile was paralyzed.

"If you do not do this," Henri said quietly, "we may all die as well. Take the shawl."

Anne-Cecile took the shawl. She had helped Yvette choose the fabric, had seen her wear it.

She rubbed Louis' face and her own, the smell of her friend's blood drawing her closer to fainting. She held on, retching as she blindly shoved the shawl at Elly, who dabbed at Philippe, then smeared her own face and arms. When Anne-Cecile opened her eyes she witnessed Henri and Makus carrying the bodies into the bush, out of sight of the trail. B'til took Anne-Cecile's hands.

"I will stay here, Mistress. Think of nothing but reaching safety." She pulled several succulent leaves out of her pocket. "The children must chew these leaves. 'Twill keep them sleeping, make them forget."

Anne-Cecile pushed a juicy leaf into her son's mouth. She passed another back to Elly, who ministered to Philippe.

Makus led the horses down the dark trail. He stopped, calling out the sound of a night bird, then listened intently. The call was returned.

They moved forward. Again and again Makus stopped to make the night bird's song, waiting for its answer. Finally he could see the dark beach exposed before him, and he led the group to a stand of sea grape. From this place they would not be visible from the beach or the water. The call of the bird sounded and this time Makus answered. In a few minutes Cesaire appeared.

"Where be the ship?" Makus asked.

The small, dark man pointed, then curiously eyed the whites on horseback. "What you do here?"

"We meet up with some evil ones on the trail. An ugly bunch, rampaging. Dangerous times to be about."

Cesaire took charge. "Crossin' the beach, they be seen in moonlight. Must run fast. I not see anybody aroun' last little while. Go now to the boat!"

Cesaire's dark body melted into the shadows.

Makus supported Anne-Cecile and Louis, now quiet from the narcotic effects of the leaves. She slid down off the horse. The bloody shawl clung to her, ugly in the moonlight.

Makus instructed the others. "Cesaire's fishing boat just beyond where the large boulders be. He signal Captain to pull anchor when you in the boat. Master Henri take Philippe and you two mistresses take Louis. Run fast as you can across the sand. 'Twill be most dangerous time."

Henri gathered up Philippe in his arms and spoke urgently to Anne-Cecile. "Mistress, explain to the ship's Captain what has happened. He will take you to Martinique to your husband's family there. I must stay here with Monsieur Charles."

"You will die if you stay here," Anne-Cecile said, her voice trembling.

"I must stay. You will be safe with the Captain. Now, run for the boat."

A suffocating dread came over Anne-Cecile as a cold malignant mist arose, enveloping them. Makus looked around, foreboding etched on his face. Pushing the group on its way, he whispered frantically, "Evil be here! Run! Run!"

Henri and Anne-Cecile, hampered by the bodies of the drugged children, struggled to run in the soft, dark sand. Cesaire, watching from his fishing boat, saw the little group move ever closer to the surf.

Then dark figures emerged from the mist, rushing toward the fleeing whites, cutting off Makus and the women from the water. Evading outstretched arms, Henri reached the surf and plunged in, his grip tight on Philippe. Plowing through the waves, he got close enough to thrust the twin's limp body into the safety of Cesaire's boat.

"Go!" he shouted and then turned to face his attackers.

Henri struggled to maintain his footing. The blow of a stout club sent him to his knees, and he was dragged back onto the beach. In his last moments he clung to the solace of knowing Philippe was safe.

Anne-Cecile saw Henri fall beneath a torrent of cutlass blows, arcing metal glinting in the moonlight. She could not see Philippe! She clutched her throat. *Where was Philippe!* In the distance Anne-Cecile saw a fishing boat pulling away, making for the anchored ship. She strained to hear the sound of anchor chains, but then the mob was running toward her.

Cesaire pulled mightily on the oars, abandoning any hope of rescuing the others. He called out the prearranged signal to the ship. A lantern was lifted at the stern and a rope ladder thrown down into its light. Throwing Philippe over his shoulder, he began the climb. At the top the Captain took the boy.

"Where are the others?" he demanded.

"Attacked on the beach. Only had time for this child. Master Charles and his family be dead. This child look dead too."

The Captain placed his ear on the little chest. "His heart's beating." Turning to Cesaire, he ordered, "Be off. If any remain alive, tell them I have taken the child to Martinique as Monsieur du Diamant ordered."

Makus grabbed Anne-Cecile, Elly and Louis. He pushed Elly to the ground. Resting his foot on her back, he stood above the frightened captives, brandishing his cutlass with one arm, his other around Anne-Cecile, warning off the menacing figures who approached.

Makus roared out and the figures halted.

"These women be mine. And the child. I have bloodied them already."

Makus pulled at Anne-Cecile's bodice, ripping it and exposing her breasts.

Anne-Cecile fought against Makus, screaming in terror and fear. As he threw her over his shoulder, he whispered to her, "If you want to live, be still." Sharp thorns stabbed and scratched. Makus dragged them deeper and deeper into the dense bush.

Anne-Cecile's head crashed into an overhanging branch and she lost consciousness. Makus did not stop.

When Anne-Cecile regained consciousness, she was in a cave, dimly lit by flambeaux. B'til sat next to her. Elly was nearby playing quietly with Louis.

When the images of cutlasses and blood came back she moaned in anguish. "Philippe, where is Philippe?" Her moans escalated to a scream, and B'til covered her mouth with her hand.

"Best grieve quiet, Mistress. We be safe in the cave, but hear brigands in the forest."

B'til's hand pressed down until Anne-Cecile stopped struggling. She removed her hand. "Quiet now, Mistress."

"Where is Philippe?"

"Makus go find what happened," B'til said.

Moaning came from deeper in the cave. B'til made her way to a man lying on the ground.

"Who is it?" asked Anne-Cecile.

"It be Master Charles. The fever on him. Wounds turning bad. I do what I can. We not think he live so many days. Try to sleep, Mistress. Best you rest."

Anne-Cecile drifted away, hiding from the pain of loss that assaulted her. Hours later she awakened to find Makus kneeling by her side.

"Philippe? Did you find him?"

"Mistress, I find Cesaire. He too be hiding. He tell me he give Philippe to the Captain of the ship and it sail for Martinique."

"Oh, thank God." Relief surged through her as she clasped Makus' hand.

"Thank you, Makus." She wept then, unending tears, sobs drawn from days of pain. "When this nightmare is over, I will find a way to bring Philippe home."

"He be safe with relatives on the neighboring island," Makus said.

Anne-Cecile looked at her slave. How could she express her gratitude? "Makus, I will remember what you and B'til have done for the Diamant family. Your loyalty will not go unrewarded."

The torch flame fluttered on some errant current of air. Shadows danced on the walls. "Bring Louis to me," she said.

CHAPTER ONE

St. Lucia, West Indies 1980

At the airport's entrance magenta bougainvillea and yellow hibiscus rioted on the median strip, drenched in tropical sunshine. Jamie Elliott's green eyes widened in response to the lush foliage and pulsing colors. She smelled ocean, the salty tang overlaid with the diesel exhaust of tourist laden taxis careening away from the airport. She felt exhilarated.

"Oh, Paul. Isn't it beautiful?"

"Chaotic's more like it."

"Strange...it feels oddly familiar." The scene before her shimmered, turned dark around the edges.

"Don't go spacey on me now, Jamie," he said.

Paul caught the eye of one of the taxi drivers. "Omega," he called out. "We're waiting for a driver from Omega."

"Oh, sure, that be Emmanuel, then. He over there limin' wit' Portia." The driver waved to a small, dark skinned man in the corner. "'Manuel, these people waitin' on you." The first driver smiled, then moved on to the next group.

A young man hurried toward them. "Welcome to St. Lucia. I

be Emmanuel." He grasped their hands like they were old friends, just reunited. "I be takin' you up to the house in Rodney Bay. Mr. Wilkerson, he make all the arrangements so I take good care of you."

Jamie warmed to his open, friendly manner as he led them to his shining, yellow minibus.

"Mr. Wilkerson, he send this for you." He motioned to a small cooler. "I load the bags and you check it out. There be cold beers, soda and rum punch in that water bottle. Oh, and in the bottom, that one is water, Mistress."

Jamie flashed him a smile. "Perfect. I'm really thirsty."

Paul opened a beer and drained it in several swallows. "What is this pony bottle crap?" he said to Jamie. "You need three of 'em just to quench your thirst."

Jamie ignored him and took a long swallow of cold water. She lifted her dark, shoulder-length hair and wiped the cold, sweating bottle against the back of her neck, sweat sheening her pale arms.

"We loaded now, so best we start," Emmanuel said as he slid the van door shut.

"Paul," Jamie said, "your seatbelt."

"Lay off, Jamie. Stop acting like my mother."

"Sorry. Say, what do you think that customs guy thought we had in our boxes? He seemed surprised when he pulled out my sewing machine and painting supplies."

"Who knows?" Paul palmed another beer. "It was a pain in the ass."

As the van pulled away from the taxi area and left the airport, Jamie hoped Paul would fall asleep so she could gawk to her heart's content and ask Emmanuel a million questions. She couldn't remember when she had been this excited.

"This be your first trip to St. Loosha?" asked Emmanuel after they had been driving for a short while.

"Yes, it is," she said.

"Well, then, I be the first to show you the beautiful blue sea of St. Loosha before we go norf."

Turning the van off the road, he followed a dirt track which wound through a grove of coconut palms. He finally stopped the van on a stretch of golden sand.

Jamie was spellbound. The water was brilliant shades of blue and turquoise, and the beach seemed to go on for miles. Fishing boats in stripes of red, green and yellow were clustered under coconut palms, which stood like slender sentinels lining the shore. Men sat under the trees, mending their nets.

What an adventure, Jamie thought. *A great new job for Paul and a new start for us. Things'll be good again, like they used to be.*

Jamie's artist eyes drank in the colors and composition as she reached back and shook Paul out of his doze.

"Paul," she said, shaking him awake. "You have to see this, it's just too gorgeous."

They stepped out of the transport. "Those waves would be great for wind surfing." He slapped a gnat away from his face. "If it weren't for the bugs, I'd think we'd landed in fuckin' paradise."

Jamie ran down to the water's edge, mesmerized by the scalloped trails left by each receding wave. She couldn't get enough of the sea's greens and blues.

"Hey, don't take your shoes off, Jamie. Come on back." Paul glanced at Emmanuel.

"How long a ride to Rodney Bay? I'm beat." Paul's previous mood had improved with the cold beers, the bright tropical sun and a brief nap.

"Yeah, mon, we get to the norf in some couple hours. The road rough in spots. But Mr. Wilkerson, he say take care wit' you and I be doin' that. He be vexed if you not happy."

As Jamie walked back toward the van, a tiny, yellow-breasted bird swooped in front of her, its bright color reminding her of the parakeets she'd had as a child. As they sped up the road, the exotic landscape entranced her, lush vegetation simultaneously tropical and surreal. But most of all, she was mesmerized by the surging sea with its constantly changing blends of blue and turquoise.

"Do you ever get tired of looking at all this beauty?" she asked Emmanuel.

"Oh, no. God give us this island, and he want us to be givin' thanks for the gift. The tourists, they comes an' look for a little while, but us Looshans get to look every day, every day. Always the sea and the island. Different and always the same. We be blessed people, we Looshans," he said.

She glanced back at Paul, who had fallen asleep again. *He looks so vulnerable when he's asleep,* she thought, her former irritation sliding away. *He's probably as scared as I am.* She remembered customs. Those steely eyes glaring while grubbing hands searched the luggage, looking for Lord knows what. Jamie shivered, in spite of the heat. They'd never even traveled before, let alone lived in a third-world country.

As they left the sea, the road wound up into the hills, through acres and acres of banana plants. Jamie wished Emmanuel would drive slower so she could really look at the large purple flowers which hung from the bottom of what appeared to be the beginnings of a stalk of bananas. She had another unsettling flash of recognition. *Where have I seen that before?* She closed her eyes for a moment, pushing at the memory, trying to remember.

She felt the van accelerate and opened her eyes to see it passing a flatbed truck overloaded with telephone poles. Chains crisscrossed the load and workmen, perched high on the pile of poles, waved at her as the van pulled abreast. Jamie smiled and waved back.

Suddenly the yellow van swerved toward the loaded truck. She caught a glimpse of a red pickup truck coming fast around the bend.

The flatbed's top heavy load shifted as its wheels went into the ditch. Jamie watched in horror as poles rolled and banged to the ground. Men screamed. Emmanuel pulled onto the shoulder and jumped out. The telephone poles lay thrown across the road, like a giant's game of pick-up sticks.

Jamie saw bodies on the road. She jumped from the van and ran for the nearest man. He was unconscious, bleeding from a gash on his head, one arm folded unnaturally beneath him.

"Don't move him," she ordered as men began to lift the injured man. "His back may be injured." The men looked at her, spoke to one another in a language she couldn't understand, then lifted the unconscious man into the back of a pickup truck.

"What are you doing?" Jamie yelled. "Has anyone called an ambulance?"

"The nearest ambulance is forty minutes away, if it's available. And the closest phone is far down the road. The injured will get to hospital faster in the trucks."

Jamie turned to look at the good-looking man addressing her. "You were driving the red pickup," she accused.

"The injured need help," he said and strode off. Jamie followed, glancing around for Paul, who was standing by the van. She motioned for him to come and help.

A crowd had gathered around an injured man. *What's wrong with these people?* Jamie thought. *Why aren't they helping?* She pushed through and knelt down by the victim, pulling back a shirt sleeve to expose a spurting wound.

"We need some clean cloths," she said. If only Paul were nearby, he could get something clean out of their suitcases. Someone handed her a folded shirt.

"Thanks," she said, looking up. It was the man who had been driving the red pickup. "I'm Jamie. I could sure use some help."

"Andre. Tell me what to do."

"Do you know how to make a tourniquet? Otherwise this man will be dead before he ever gets to the hospital," she said. Andre spoke in rapid Patois. As they waited, Jamie glanced at Andre's profile. When he turned to face her, her artist senses took in his calm dark eyes, the distinctive cleft in his chin.

"Are you a doctor?" he asked.

"No, just a first aid course in college. You seem to know what *you're* doing...?"

"When you live here, you need to know some basic first aid."

A dirty rope and a stick appeared, quickly formed into a serviceable tourniquet.

Jamie was relieved someone was taking charge. She watched Andre move from one injured person to another, checking them, sending people on their way or telling them to stay. Then he motioned for her help. They worked well together, their movements graceful and coordinated. She watched the power in his muscular back as he helped lift one of the injured into a truck.

"I didn't expect this," she said, gesturing with bloody hands. "We just arrived on the island. My husband's signed on with Omega. Where will these people be taken? There *is* a hospital here, isn't there?" Jamie asked.

"Yes, quite a good one actually. But there are few ambulances on the island."

As Jamie stared at Andre, something stirred deep inside. She pushed it down. "Well, I hope I'm never in an accident here. People with spinal injuries can be crippled for life if moved improperly. What kind of a country is this, anyway?" Now that the crisis was under control, Jamie's emotions were taking over.

"A rather poor one, I'm afraid." Andre extended his hand to calm her. "I'm sorry this is your introduction to St. Lucia."

Jamie took his hand and looked quizzically at his face. "Do I know you? You seem familiar..."

The words trailed away as Jamie suddenly felt woozy. She swayed and began to slide to the ground. Andre caught her and pulled her into the shade, where he sat her down and pushed her head to her knees.

"You're awfully good in a crisis, but do you always collapse afterwards?" he asked when her vision began to clear.

"'Fraid so. I should have thought to warn you I'd be on the ground once things were under control." She looked at him again. "Are you sure we haven't met?"

Andre noticed the flush creeping up her neck. He knew the signs of heat exhaustion. "Let me get you some water from my truck."

"Thanks, but we have water in the van that's taking us to Rodney Bay. My husband's around here someplace."

"Let me walk you back to your van, then. Can't have you passing out in the road again." He took her arm as they headed toward the van, his touch reassuring. "It's a small island. We'll run into one another again. Thanks for helping. You made a difference. Next time we meet, I hope it will be under more pleasant circumstances."

At the van, Emmanuel was alarmed. "Mistress, you be covered with blood. You hurt?" His face showed concern as he handed her a wet rag. "Mr. Andre's truck get mashed up, for true."

"Do you all know each other?" Jamie asked with annoyance as she climbed into the front seat of the van. She scrubbed at her hands and arms.

Turning to Paul, she asked angrily, "Why didn't you help?"

"Why'd you jump into that mess? You don't know those people."

"Those people? They're people, Paul. They needed help, for God's sake. How could you just stand there? I kept looking for you, asking for you to come." Tears burned. "Oh, go to hell."

"Emmanuel, let's get going," Paul ordered, reaching into the cooler for another beer as the van started on its way.

Jamie looked across the road, where Andre was inspecting the fender on his truck. He glanced up and gave her a thumbs up sign and a smile, which turned quizzical when he saw her tears. She didn't see him watch the van until it was lost to view.

Blood had dried around the edges of her fingernails, and Jamie picked at it. She sat for a long time, knowing she would have to confront Paul, also knowing it would have to wait.

"Where do all these people live?" she finally asked Emmanuel, noticing people walking on the sides of the road. Men carried machetes, some entire stalks of bananas on their shoulders. She saw women who balanced boxes on their heads, baskets of laundry, even one with something that looked like a gas canister.

"Some live by the road or in the fishing villages. Some up the hills where they be growing some bananas or maybe vegetables for market. That why the men be carrying cutlasses," he replied.

"It's what I call a machete," Jamie said.

Apparently the accident had not fazed Emmanuel, and they swept around the curves, weaving in and out, avoiding one pothole after another.

In one village both sides of the road were lined with children of all ages, all dressed in blue skirts or pants and yellow shirts. Matching blue and yellow ribbons adorned the girls' braids. "Like a flock of little yellow breasts," said Emmanuel.

"Yellow breasts?" asked Jamie.

"Our little banana birds, we call them yellow breasts. You saw one at the beach. One build a nest just outside my front door. The mama let me know how vexed she be each time I go in and out. But I say to her, we can share this place."

The children called to one another, happy to be released from school. Even at the end of the day they all looked immaculate, most carrying book bags or small plastic bags. Only a few of the boys had shirts hanging out, shoelaces untied. Smiling faces lifted as the van passed. Emmanuel honked and Jamie returned the waves of the friendly, open-faced children.

"They're adorable. Do all the children wear uniforms to school?"

"Yes, and each school have a different color. You will see as we go up the road. Some red and white, some brown and blue, or green and yellow. All different. Just like our island birds."

"I had tropical birds as pets when I was a child. Always wanted a parrot. Maybe here..."

"Our parrots almost gone. They trapped for meat, for the feathers. Only twenty or so left, protected now in the rain forest. We hopin' they come back," Emmanuel said.

The van continued its climb into the hills. Views of the ocean were left behind, and the banana and coconut plantations swallowed the road. It was shadier here, the air cooler. Suddenly rain fell, glazing the vegetation. And just as quickly the rain was gone. To Jamie it seemed that the sun had not even been covered by clouds.

"A little blessing," Emmanuel said.

She looked back at Paul, who was again asleep. He looked so young. Her anger softened. She often wondered if their children would have that same open, unguarded look about them. The best part of Paul. Would they have his ashy blonde hair and soft brown eyes? His square jaw reminded her of Andre's cleft chin. Images of the accident came crashing back. *Oh, stop it,* she told herself as her stomach rumbled. *You just need something to eat and a bath.*

And we will be better here. A stable job for Paul. No money worries. He'll be more settled and I'll be the best wife, plenty of time for me to pursue my painting and designing. We can be happy again. I'll make it happen, she promised herself, remembering how she had relied on Paul's strength after her father's death. Before Paul had started drinking so much.

Jamie watched the sides of the road, taking in one impression after another: a boulder strewn river with women doing wash, clothes spread out on the rocks to dry, deep mountain valleys and hills shrouded in mist, little wooden houses with primitive decorative touches in the bright colors she'd seen on the fishing boats. And glorious flowers everywhere. Jamie, sated with the visual joy of the scenery and still reacting to the accident, was suddenly very sleepy.

"Mistress, wake up. We here." Emmanuel's voice reached through her foggy slumber.

The van had stopped in front of a small, one-story house. It was a drab gray, built of cement block with a porch that continued around three sides. Patchy grass and a few bushes with an untended look struggled to survive.

"Paul, wake up. Paul. We're here."

"Is this it, Emmanuel? Are you sure this is the right place?" Paul asked, looking around.

"Yes, Mr. Elliott. Mr. Wilkerson told me bring you to the Fricks' house around the gap from the St. Lucian hotel, and this be it."

The front door opened and a small woman walked out to the van. Her skin was the color of mahogany, her hair plaited in tight cornrows. Huge golden hoops hung from her ears. Dark eyes regarded Jamie somberly.

"'Manuel, what you do these people? My mistress bloody."

"Accident on the road. Mistress Elliott help."

"I thank you for helping our people. I be Delia. Your housekeeper."

"My housekeeper?" Jamie said, looking at Paul. "We didn't hire a housekeeper."

"Mr. Wilkerson, he want everyt'ing just right for your arrival, so he bring me round this week to clean and shape up the place. Even have some salt fish salad for your dinner. But first you best get a wash up."

Jamie looked around helplessly. Delia stood for a moment, her dark eyes assessing Jamie, then took charge.

"Bring the bags and all this stuff into the house, 'Manuel," she commanded. "And be quick or I get vexed. My mistress tired. She need a sit down and a cool drink."

Jamie allowed herself to be led to a chair on the porch. Once in the shade, she noticed the breeze and thought she could hear the sounds of the ocean in the distance.

Paul, still standing by the van, heard as well. "Jamie, I'm going to look for the ocean. I can hear the waves." He turned and walked away, oblivious he was leaving her to deal with paying for the ride from the airport. Her heart sank and she flashed back to the lonely nights in their little apartment, nights when Paul stayed out late, drinking with his buddies.

Delia put a tall glass in Jamie's hand. "You sit for a spell," she said and motioned Jamie to a chair on the porch. Then Delia turned back to the van. "Step up, Mr. Taxi Driver," she called out to Emmanuel, "work to do."

Jamie took a sip of the cold drink. Tart, sweet and wonderfully refreshing.

"This is delicious, Delia. What is it?"

"It be lime squash from your tree."

"I have a squash tree?" Jamie asked as she started to rise.

"No, Mistress, a lime tree. Now you sit," said Delia, a warm smile now in her eyes. Jamie decided the better part of valor was to allow herself to be bossed by this petite, dark-skinned woman who seemed to come with the house.

She took another sip of the pale juice. A small dark bird with a red breast alighted on the porch railing. "Hey, little guy. Come to keep me company?" The gentle breeze from the ocean caressed Jamie's skin, and she leaned back and closed her eyes. Everything here was different, yet so familiar, beguiling, enfolding - like echoes of old dreams resonating somewhere deep within. Even now a flash of a tiny yellow bird danced across her memory. I hope I dream tonight, she thought. This is an island for dreaming, and I haven't dreamed in a long time.

She started as a mahogany hand touched her shoulder.

"I be goin' now, Mistress. Clean towels in the bathroom for you. You feel better when you get washed up. Here some tea to help you sleep. I be back in the morning."

CHAPTER TWO

Andre and Emile Demontagne stood on the high rock outcropping, muddy and sweat-stained after clambering over boulders and hiking up rain forest tracks to reach this vantage point. They were looking for the orange blossoms of African Tulip trees, descendants of those planted by their forebears to mark the boundaries of land given their family by the King of France. From this height occasional bright flashes of color were visible, vague outlines of the original boundaries.

"I never get tired of looking at the land, Emile. Our family has been custodians of it for generations. Strong ties here between this land and our blood."

"And to Bertille and Marcus," Emile said. "Bertille's still flying around. Dreaming while she's awake. You ever do that?"

Andre shook his head. "Being in New York most of the time blunts the island experience, I guess."

"By the way, what the hell did you do to the estate truck?" asked Emile, the younger of the two brothers.

"Drove it off the east coast road yesterday into a boulder. It was either that or hit a transport or a truck full of phone poles."

Emile grinned. "Looks like the boulder won."

Andre gazed off over the craggy land, his dark eyes quiet.

"You've gone dreamy-eyed on me," Emile said. "What's going on?"

"Nothing's going on. I guess the accident keeps intruding. People got hurt. We pitched in to help."

"We?"

"Jamie and I."

Emile's eyebrows went up. "Jamie, who's Jamie?"

"You should have seen her, Emile. Got all sweaty and bloody helping these workmen she didn't know."

Emile's eyes twinkled. "And you helped, of course."

"I jumped in, yes. We saved a man with a tourniquet."

"Why, Andre, how romantic."

"We were helping, I tell you."

"Okay. Then what happened?"

Andre looked at the ground. "She fainted...in my arms."

"Is she good looking?"

"I guess so. We were busy."

"So...she's good looking. Why don't these things happen to me? You don't need another woman. You've got Taylor in New York."

"No, it's not like that. She's married. He's taken a job with Omega."

"Good, then they'll be here for awhile. Husbands never stopped me before."

"Leave her alone, Emile."

The tone startled Emile into a smile, a smile that faded as he watched the changing emotions on his brother's face. "What is it?"

Andre picked up a rock and threw it down the hill. "Something about her, like I knew her. Had met her before."

Emile shrugged, knowing when to leave his brother alone.

They gazed out at the landscape before them. Its majestic volcanic peaks and precipitous valleys had challenged the early settlers to raise sugar cane for the rum trade. Distilling rum, although no longer practiced, had provided the foundation for the Demontagne family's wealth. For the most part the hill country had not been farmed intensively until recently, when it was planted to bananas and other fruits that could be raised on its steep slopes.

Andre pointed to a faraway crescent of beach. "I haven't abandoned my idea to build a hotel on our land by the Pitons," Andre said as he surveyed the awe-inspiring landscape. "I've been thinking about coming back to the island permanently. New York is fine, but I really miss being here."

"We'd love to have you back, but don't get your heart set on that hotel," Emile said.

"The family has four thousand acres! I'm only looking for two hundred of them."

"Yes, but that acreage happens to be between the Pitons. Those mountains are the national symbols of St. Lucia, for Christ's sake."

"I'm planning to look at the Grande Anse land, too. No national landmarks there."

"You've forgotten the turtles who lay their eggs there," Emile reminded Andre. "Anyway, there's a terrible rip tide on that beach. You could always make money taking bets on how many tourists would be drowned."

Andre laughed, then turned serious. "I'd been hoping I had your support to help me convince Father. Sounds like I still have to convince you."

"True enough. Remember, this is virgin forest. We're just custodians, Andre, for the next generations."

"I know that."

"So...?"

Andre studied his brother's taut face. "Look, Emile, I just want others to have a chance to experience the island the way we've known it." He paused and looked out over the valley that spilled down to the sea and the crescent of dark volcanic sand. "I want visitors to stand under Diamond waterfall like we did. I want them to see the parrots fly again, flocks of parrots."

"Parrots won't mean much to them, not like they mean to us, especially to Bertille and Marcus," Emile said. "Look, Andre. If this hotel you're planning is anywhere near Bertille and Marcus' land, you know what will happen."

"They'll complain the spirits will be disturbed."

"Damn right. This idea of yours could set us all against each other. Mother and Father, Bertille and Marcus. I'm serious, Andre, you could strike at the very lifeblood of our heritage."

"Emile, we would not endanger the rain forest. I love it as much as any man. And we would protect the parrots."

"How? By caging them?"

"No! By protecting their habitat. And Bertille's and Marcus' six hundred acres."

"Do Bertille and Marcus know that? And our parents? What about them?"

"Look," Andre said. "I know the parrots are on the verge of extinction. And I also know, perhaps better than you, about just how sacred that six hundred acres is. Who talks to Mother most about how Marcus' family was given the land after they saved our Diamant ancestor from the guillotine in Soufriere?"

"Okay," Emile conceded.

Andre turned to his brother, his face serious. "You've got to realize the only viable option left for these islands is tourism. Slave labor was the only reason agriculture supported the island in the past. Farming alone can't support the economy."

Emile kicked the dirt. "I've devoted my life to the estate. I think what I've done is important."

"It is! You have a graduate degree in agronomy. You manage two large estates. The family and our people have benefitted greatly from your efforts. Emile, I'm not talking about abandoning the estate. I'm talking about making it possible to preserve our heritage."

Emile didn't respond.

Andre held up a hand. "Okay. Let's leave it alone. We need to get these boundaries sorted out or nothing's going to happen."
He turned to his brother. "Emile?"

"What?"

"I know there are going to be some unhappy moments during all this. But I promise you, we'll honor our obligation to protect all the land, especially Bertille's and Marcus'."

"Mother and Father will see to that. They view our heritage as sacred."

"Believe it, Emile, so do I. I imagine each generation has had its own take on the obligation."

"Maybe so. But it's such an unusual history. Off island, could we ever explain it with a straight face? Would anyone believe it?"

Andre allowed a grudging smile. "That Bertille and Marcus are descended from the Arawak and Caribe Indians? That over the generations they intermingled with slaves from Africa? What's so hard about that?"

"Not just that, Andre. The rest of the family history. Anne-Cecile Diamant, the lost twin."

"Well, it is a little preposterous. Hey, did you know Mother has some of the original records of slave purchases, even has most of the original land grant?"

"Where's the rest, d'you think?"

Andre shrugged. "Who knows. But I bet one day the lost twin turns up."

"There is no lost twin."

"You sure of that? Remember how the story goes? Mother's ancestor had the twin boys and one was lost when the French Revolution came to the island. And..."

"I know the story, Andre. And Marcus' and Bertille's family helped one of our ancestors hide a fortune in diamonds from France."

"Oh, yeah. That one. Just try to tell it off island, maybe to those New York lawyers." Andre laughed, a rich and open sound in the sunny quiet.

"Maybe they'd come down here and dig holes looking for diamonds, like we did as children." He put a hand on Emile's shoulder. "Will you go over the hotel proposal with me? If I satisfy your objections, I'll have crossed most of the hurdles Father is sure to raise. Can I count on your support?"

"If you keep in mind preserving and protecting the land, you'll have crossed most of those hurdles," Emile advised. "Father will never object to making money. But, hey, what about Taylor? Is she ready to give up life in New York for St. Lucia?"

"I'm sure I can persuade her if that's the way things fall out,"

Andre said. "Okay, let's finish what we came up here to do. How soon can we get a crew to start cutting the boundaries?"

"We'll talk to Father when we go back to the estate. Come on, it's getting late. Bertille is making breadfruit balls for dinner, and I'm starved."

Hiking back to the truck, Andre was quiet. Emile did not disturb his thoughts.

An hour later, Emile's muddy pickup negotiated its way down the winding entrance to their family home, Les Jumeaux Estate. A few minutes after fording a shallow river, its banks overhung with vines, Emile pulled the truck into the circular driveway. Beyond a lush planting of heliconia, Andre glimpsed the pale yellow, wooden estate house built more than two centuries earlier, the house of his childhood memories.

Andre reached the porch at the same time his father appeared at the door, barefoot and attired only in disreputable shorts. The broad roof of the veranda shaded the older man. In the dim light Andre noticed more silver at his father's temples than he'd remembered.

"Father, if I saw you on a street in town, I'd think you were a beggar. A distinguished-looking beggar, but a beggar nonetheless." Andre spoke affectionately, thinking how well his father's given name, Auguste, suited him.

"And if I saw you, I'd think you had been in the piggery. Ah, it is so good to see you, Andre. Go clean up and then come sit with me on the veranda."

After a quick shower, Andre joined his father.

"Can I get you something to drink?" his father asked.

"A cold beer would taste great," Andre said, sitting in one of the large rush-seated rockers that lined the veranda. "Emile and I've just been up the mountain talking about the boundary project. Actually, I got here a couple of days ago and have been at Mother's in Castries. I'll fill you in on all the details of my meetings with the hotel people."

Auguste sat down after calling to someone in the kitchen. "Remember, Andre, I am not yet committed to this resort idea of yours. I have yet to see a proposal."

"I know, Father, and when I'm ready, I'll make a formal presentation to the family. The solicitors in Castries as well as the venture capitalists I consulted in New York agree that having clear title to the estate is the first step."

Auguste's eyes restlessly surveyed the land. "Yes, recording the boundaries needs to be accomplished in any case, regardless of whether we decide to move forward with a hotel project."

Andre hesitated. "It may be most useful to work from the original document."

"From the land grant?" asked Auguste, accepting a tall glass of juice from a maid. "You'll need to ask your mother about that. She's the family historian."

Andre took a long drink of icy beer. "Emile and I talked today about the stories Bertille told us when we were growing up, about the Diamant brother's wife who came to the island carrying a fortune in diamonds."

"All families seem to have stories of lost fortunes and ties to royalty," Auguste said dismissively, sipping his juice. "Your Mother and I are in agreement, Bertille's and Marcus' right to their land will not be questioned when we are clearing titles."

"Of course not," Andre said. "Can you check with Marcus as to how soon he can put together a cutting crew? I can have a surveying crew here in a week."

"Let's go ask him. He's out in the sheds." Auguste slipped on sandals and a tatty T-shirt.

They found Marcus in a storage shed examining the wheel of a tractor. His nappy hair was cut short, and his full beard wagged as his face creased into a slow smile.

Andre went to him, embraced him.

"I've missed you, Marcus," he said.

"And you always come back. You come back to us."

"Yes. And also, I take you with me. And Bertille. You keep me anchored."

"Anchored in the ways of this spiritual place."

"Yes. And anchored in the memories of my boyhood, and being

with you and Bertille. You taught me so much."

"You and Emile were good boys. You honored our ways."

"We learned from your ways, were schooled in your ways."

Marcus wiped his big hands. "Have you been dreaming, perhaps?"

"No. Why do you say that? Emile asked the same thing."

"There is an aura around you, a presence. I can't quite define it, but it is good."

Andre smiled, feeling a little uncomfortable with this man who knew him so well.

Auguste stepped into the silence. "Emile and Andre have been out looking at the boundary trees. We are ready to begin cutting the lines. How many men can you spare from the estate, Marcus?"

Marcus thought for a moment. "I will make Etienne the crew chief. He is dependable, can read maps and use a compass. He can organize a crew. Part of the boundary goes around our own family's land, and other people don't like to be that far into the bush. We may have some problems getting the men to work that area."

"Bertille's magic?" Andre asked, his face serious.

"Yes. With gifts such as these it does cause concern. But no one need fear my Bertille. She flies with her parrot spirits to protect us. People without such gifts don't understand. It's a shame, but that's the way it is."

"They don't come close, Marcus, because they fear Bertille's magic, afraid she'll turn them into *loup-garous*," Andre said, chuckling.

Marcus did not return the smile. "A difficult heritage." His eyes were like agates. "As is your own."

"Our families will always be close, Marcus," Auguste spoke quietly, his words carrying an immutable truth. "My wife and I owe you and Bertille more than we..."

Marcus interrupted. "We will not speak of this, sir. Family cares for family." A smile softened the momentary sternness on his face. "Now, when do you want us to start?"

"As soon as you can. The rains may be a problem in a month, and we'll have to stop if we get heavy squalls."

"I will get it organized."

"Marcus, I want to say hello to Bertille," Andre said. "Do you know where she is? Emile and I were just talking about the stories she told us when we were small."

"And you would sit at her feet while she told them. I think your favorite was about the turtle who ate the mango moon."

"If I ever get married and have kids, I'll tell them at bedtime. They're better than any books."

"You will be married, Andre," Marcus said, looking into his eyes.

"Well, Taylor and I are..."

"You will be married."

Andre watched him, surprised. He wanted to ask more, but it was obvious that Marcus had said all he would say on the subject. "Just remember, when you tell our stories to your children, that they are sacred and ancient. Honor them."

"I will, Marcus."

"Your family and mine are entwined like a vine around a tree in the forest. They cannot part without the destruction of both."

The smile came again, and also a gentle dismissal. "I think Bertille is in the kitchen."

CHAPTER THREE

The scorpion in the bathroom was ugly and threatening, its tail curling up as she entered. Jamie stared at it, deciding how to get rid of it. Clearly paradise had a downside. She took care of the scorpion with a shoe and dumped the remains in the trash.

Through the window she heard the unfamiliar night sounds and wondered where Paul was. Wearily she went back to the kitchen and ate standing at the sink. When she finished she turned to survey the boxes - boxes holding her painting and sewing materials, her dreams in a way. And other things from New York, another world. She did not notice her tears as she bent into unloading the boxes. Finally she went to bed, leaving the door unlocked for Paul.

A bright sun did not wake Jamie the next morning. Paul did.

He nudged her. "Hey, it's me,"

Jamie lay still.

"Jamie?"

"I hear you."

"I was figuring on some coffee. You know, first day on the job, an' all."

"Where were you?"

"Me? With some of the Omega guys. Met 'em down at the beach."

"What time did you get in?"

The bed moved as Paul got up. "Hey, what is this, an interrogation? I don't need this, first day. I need coffee."

Jamie sat up slowly on the bed and looked at him. His good features were puffy, the eyes dulled. Not that anyone else would notice, but Jamie knew him intimately. All the things she loved. Had loved...?

"Our first night here and you walk away five minutes after we arrive. When are you going to grow up? Paul, I didn't know where you were. Does it ever occur to you that when you disappear like that I get worried and afraid?"

"Oh, God, Jamie. I didn't even think. I was having a good time, and you were here with Delia so I knew you were all right. I guess I lost track of the time." Paul's voice trailed off.

"Delia left an hour after we arrived. Then I was alone."

Jamie went into the bathroom. The door banged behind her.

"I'm sorry, Jamie. I really am." Paul spoke through the door. "Yesterday was hard for both of us, but it was good for me to connect with some of the guys I'll be working with. And you're so resourceful, I knew you'd be all right. I'm sorry you were worried and scared. Couldn't we pretend this is the first day?"

Jamie came out of the bathroom. "Just put yourself in my shoes, that's all I ask."

"Not good at that."

"I know. Look, we need to come first for each other. Wherever we live."

She put her hurt aside. "Okay, let's pretend that this is our first day, that yesterday never happened, not the long flight, the terrible accident on the road or the scorpion in the bathroom."

"Scorpion in the bathroom? What are you talking about?"

Jamie told him as she rummaged through boxes looking for the coffee maker. Paul followed her into the kitchen, opened the fridge door and spooned something into his mouth.

"Hey, this potato salad is really good."

"It's not potato salad. You're eating green bananas and salt cod."

"Oh, man. I wish you hadn't told me that. Green bananas and salt cod, huh? Oh, well, when in Rome," he said, taking another spoonful.

"Where'd the maid get to?" he asked.

"She's not the maid. She was quite clear with me that she's the housekeeper. There seems to be a distinction. I think she goes with the house." Jamie tried to put a good face on the new day.

Inside, anger smoldered. She wondered what she would do with it.

Jamie found the coffee maker but realized she couldn't fit the plug into the receptacle. An adapter went on the list she'd started last night. In the back of a cupboard she found an old metal percolator.

"I hope you won't mind boiled coffee," she said as she turned on the gas. The smell of the ground coffee brought to mind an image of her mother, standing by the stove in the morning while Jamie fed Snoopy, her green parakeet. She decided to call her later. Let her know they'd arrived okay.

"As long as I get my morning fix of caffeine..."

The coffee was just beginning to perk when a battered jeep pulled up in front of the house.

"Brian Carey, here," a man called out, waving to her.

"And Barbara. I've come to help you get settled in, and look you over."

Jamie opened the front door and watched a small woman with very curly blonde hair stride up the sidewalk, a bucket in one hand, a broom in the other. Setting her cleaning supplies on the porch, she extended her hand.

"Hi, hon. I'm Barbara. Brian is taking Paul to work with him, so you've got me for the day. It's probably sort of pushy of me, but I remember how overwhelmed I was when I arrived, so I thought you could use someone who's been standing where you are." Barbara rattled on. "Oh, here comes Delia. We'll make short work of it all."

Jamie was bemused by all these people taking charge.

Delia stood in the doorway, sunlight bathing her lovely mahogany skin, gleaming off her earrings. Her dark eyes regarded Barbara and her bucket and broom.

"Mornin', Mistress Carey. What you be doin' here so early?"

"Just helping out, Delia. Being a good neighbor. I know you've scrubbed out all the corners, so don't be looking at me that way."

A quiet smile touched Delia's eyes.

Barbara smiled back. "Go on now. Make up a big pitcher of lime squash before you start anything else. We'll need it later."

Delia picked up a basket and headed toward the lime tree.

"Keep an eye on Delia."

"Oh?"

"These islands are strange, Jamie. Once you get the exotic beauty of the place assimilated, you'll discover other things."

"Such as?"

"Oh, it's hard to put into words. Undercurrents, beliefs that haven't caught up to the twentieth century."

Jamie smiled. "Tarzan swinging through the trees?"

Barbara shrugged, poking the floor with the broom. "These are ancient islands, Jamie. The Carib and Arawak Indians. The African beliefs and customs that came with the slaves. The veneer is thin and cracks at times."

"Are you trying to scare me?"

"No, just saying things are different. There's a deep spirituality here. It's there in Delia. There's more to her than maid."

"Housekeeper."

"I stand corrected, hon. Housekeeper."

Paul had finished his coffee and stood by the jeep, an engaging smile on his face, the one that always made her heart turn over. He tossed her a kiss. Brian put the mangled jeep in first gear and ground down the road.

"Let's sit before we start," Barbara suggested. "Delia can be something of a martinet," she said, her head nodding toward the tree in the back. "But she's a terrific worker, honest and fiercely loyal, if you pass muster. Her cousin, Claudia, works for me. You're lucky to have her."

"It's just that we never even had a cleaning lady when I was growing up. I don't know how to treat her."

"Be fair, give her clear directions, pay her on time and remain the mistress. She'll be an enormous help, and if Paul succeeds at Omega, Delia will have a lot of status because she works for you. Housekeepers don't get paid a lot here, but it all contributes to the island economy. So don't feel guilty and enjoy having someone else do the dishes. By the way, how did you sleep?"

"Frankly, I was exhausted after the trip but had a hard time going to sleep. Noises I'm not used to, I guess," Jamie said, not wanting to elaborate on Paul's absence last night.

"Well, the tree frogs and cicadas are loud, but after two years here the night noises and the clacking of the palm fronds have become a lullaby," Barbara said reassuringly. "And if you continue to have trouble, ask Delia to brew you some sleeping tea."

"Maybe that was what she put in front of me before she left last night. I smelled it and threw it in the bushes."

"Some sort of local herb, no doubt. She knows what she's doing. Delia's related to the Deroche family. Well known on the island as bush doctors." Barbara glanced around her. "Henry Wilkerson rented this place for you, didn't he? I know it probably wasn't what you envisioned, but it does have some good points. The location is great and there's a breeze off the water. The Fricks lived here before. Not an imaginative bone in Elsie's body. I can't fathom painting this place gray. But, hey, maybe you like it. There I go sticking my foot in your business."

"Well, the gray is rather drab."

"You mean ugly as dirt."

Jamie chuckled. "Well, yes. Especially compared to the wonderful bright colors all around. I guess I'm most disappointed not to have a coconut palm in the front yard," Jamie said. "I had a fantasy of coming to a tropical paradise full of coconut trees. I think there'll be more to get used to than I thought."

"Well, if you want a coconut palm or bougainvillea or just about anything else, just stick it in the ground with some manure, hang around for six months and you'll be living in a fully grown garden."

Jamie smiled. "The air here just wraps itself around you, doesn't it. I haven't even been here twenty-four hours and it feels like forever. Familiar, comfortable." *Like meeting Andre and feeling he's been a part of my life,* she realized but didn't say out loud.

"By the way," Barbara said, "that dead-looking tree in the corner, the one with the pods on it? It's a spectacular flamboyancy tree. Come June, it'll be covered in brilliant orange flowers. Well, I'm here for the day. Where should we start?"

"I suppose we could begin by unpacking the rest of the boxes," Jamie suggested as they entered the living room.

"I know this furniture," Barbara said, looking around. "Every time somebody leaves the island we pass stuff around. Hey, I've got a lamp that matches that one on the end table. But seriously, hon, none of us worker bees at Omega are house proud. Mostly we live on our porches, and none of us has the money or the interest to 'decorate' our houses."

Barbara pushed her blonde curls behind her ears and started slitting tape on packing boxes.

"What is all this stuff?" she asked, lifting fabric out of a box.

"I collect fabric the way other women collect jewelry. Paul was definitely not happy with me for bringing it all, but I didn't know what would be available here."

"Not a whole lot, hon," replied Barbara. "Maybe you could give me some lessons. When buttons fall off, I send them out to be sewn back on."

"You're kidding," Jamie said, grinning. "I certainly can teach you how to sew on a button."

"Maybe," muttered Barbara, continuing to open boxes.

By lunch time all the boxes were unpacked and everything stored as best it could be, given the limited drawer and closet space. Items had been added to Jamie's growing list of things to purchase. Grass rugs for the living room and bedroom, straw mats for the door and beside the bed, curtain rods, metal containers for storing food.

They sat on the veranda to complete the shopping list. The little dark bird with the red breast joined them.

Jamie pointed. "What kind of bird is that?"

"Lesser Antillean Bullfinch. Very sociable."

"He visited me last night."

"Give him crumbs and he'll join you for every meal. He might even bring his wife around."

They sipped tall glasses of lime squash.

"This is good stuff," Jamie said.

"Nectar of the gods, all right."

Jamie smiled at Barbara.

"What?"

"Oh, I just feel good. A new found friend - but also how different we are."

"I'm the beautiful one from Baltimore," Barbara said. "You'll just have to manage."

"You're blonde."

"You're brunette."

"I'm tall..."

"Don't say it!"

"You're not that short. And you strike me as having things pretty well under control. You're nobody's fool, Barbara."

"This could be the beginning of a beautiful friendship."

"You stole that line."

"It's not stealing if it's a famous line," Barbara said indignantly. Jamie just smiled. Despite the morning scene with Paul, this day was turning out just fine.

"You asked what I wanted to do first. It's only my first day here, but I think I'll have to paint some of these rooms. And eventually the outside. This gray paint is depressing."

"Well, for paint we need to go into town. Do you think you can wait until tomorrow? Or, if you want, we can go this afternoon?" asked Barbara.

Jamie winced. "Actually, Paul went off and didn't leave me any money, so it will have to wait 'til tomorrow. I can't even think what else needs to be done."

Out of the corner of her eye, she saw a small animal scurrying around the corner of the house. Then a flash of metal as a cutlass swooped through the air.

"Did you get it, Delia?" Barbara asked as she jumped up and ran to the edge of the porch.

"Yes, Mistress, this one rat not trouble us any more." Delia picked up the carcass with the point of her cutlass and smiled victoriously before throwing it into the trash can and heading back to the house.

"If you ever get tired of housekeeping, there's a job for you at Rent-to-Kill," Barbara called out to Delia's back.

"What was that?" Jamie asked, afraid of the answer.

"Rat. Fact of life here in the tropics, hon. Keep everything put away, all the time. They'll chew through just about anything, plastic, wood, even screens. Put rat poison on the list. We'll get some at Stanthurs. Keep it around and it'll help control the rodent population," Barbara declared.

Jamie was not pleased to hear she would be sharing this tropical paradise with four-legged critters and made a mental note to double the amount of poison.

"What is Rent-to-Kill? Sounds like a Mafia assassin for hire."

Barbara chuckled. "It's the local pest control outfit. Look 'em up in the phone book if you don't believe me. They'll come and spray your house once a month for roaches and stuff. You don't need 'em as long as you've got Delia and her cutlass and you keep her supplied with Doom."

"Doom?" Jamie asked, suspicious that Barbara was pulling her leg.

"Yeah, Doom, you know, bug spray in a can," Barbara replied. "Hey, I didn't make this up," she said, responding to the incredulous look on Jamie's face. "Why don't we walk over to my house? We need to call the phone company about getting you a phone. They'll take your request under advisement, may show up tomorrow or next year. Never take things too seriously here. I'll call Brian when we get to our place and leave a message for him. He can bring Paul home with him and you can have dinner with us."

"Sounds great. What about the house?"

"Delia can close up. Delia, do you have a key?"

"Yes, Mistress."

"Good. Lock up when you go, please. Mrs. Elliott will expect you back at 8:30 tomorrow morning."

Jamie and Barbara walked down the street enjoying a comfortable silence. Suddenly Barbara stopped in mid-stride.

"You haven't seen the beach yet, have you?"

"Only when Emmanuel picked us up yesterday," Jamie said. "Down by the airport."

"Well, then, we are most definitely going in the wrong direction."

Barbara took Jamie's arm, turned them in their tracks and propelled them through the entrance to the St. Lucian Hotel. Jamie followed in Barbara's wake as the spunky blonde cut a determined path through the hotel lobby toward the sound of the waves, finally emerging onto a beach of golden sand. Shaded by the coconut palms lining the beach, Barbara pointed out Pigeon Point, the causeway and the hazy outline of Martinique, the next island to the north.

"Take off your shoes," instructed Barbara.

"Man, you're bossy,"

"Just take 'em off."

The women walked in the cool scallops of foam left by retreating waves and headed east on the sun-drenched beach. On the hotel's beach loungers, tourists were soaking up the warm sun. Jamie was shocked to see a woman slathering sun tan lotion on her naked breasts. They gleamed proudly in the sun.

"Don't gawk, sweetie. It's not polite." Barbara chuckled at the look on Jamie's face. "She's probably French. You'll get used to it."

Barbara waved to a slender man in a navy uniform. "Hotel security," she commented as they left the hotel property. "He tries to keep the Rasta hustlers off the beach, but the beach belongs to the Lucians so there's not much he can really do."

"What are Rastas?" Jamie inquired.

"Rastafarianism is a religion. They don't believe in cutting their hair, so it grows really long and wraps itself into dread locks. Gentle souls for the most part."

About a quarter of a mile down the beach, Barbara led Jamie

into a building, open to the breezes. The sign over the entrance read Calypso Bar. The two women sat on tall stools, grateful to be out of the sun. The bartender approached to take their orders.

"James, two of your best fruity, tourist drinks to welcome my new friend, Jamie Elliott, to beautiful St. Lucia," Barbara said.

James looked at her across the counter with eyes that had assessed many a customer. They were quiet and kind, touched with a calypso sense of humor, a lyrical gleam. Jamie returned his frank look with one of her own. They smiled, liking each other.

Soon orange juice, bananas, mangoes, rum and grenadine syrup were whirring in the blender with crushed ice.

"Hon, this is Mick's," Barbara motioned expansively. "An unlikely name, perhaps, but originally opened by some Irishman who has long since left the island. Each successive owner tries to change the name. Only the tourists call it by the name on the sign. Anyone who's been here awhile calls it Mick's. And James makes the best and deadliest drinks on Reduit Beach."

Barbara smiled as the bartender put two tall, frothy glasses of peachy liquid in front of them.

"These be on the house as a welcome to a friend of Barbara's." James' lilting Caribbean accent was as sweetly exotic as the drinks they sipped.

"You're smirking," Barbara said.

"No, I'm not. I'm just happy. When I woke up this morning I was ready to head back to the airport."

"Why?"

Jamie ignored the question. "Now I'm drinking this exotic watchacallit with a new friend."

"James, what do you call this one?" Barbara asked.

"St. Lucian Sunrise."

Jamie raised her glass and looked at it. "You know what?"

"I haven't a clue."

"This," Jamie said, swirling her drink, "is the color I want for my living room."

"Nice choice," Barbara said solemnly. "You're not a little tiddly, are you?"

Jamie laughed. "No, just happy. This has turned out to be a good day." But her thoughts flashed back to Paul, this morning's puffiness on his once-handsome features. She kept her smile in place.

Barbara glanced at her watch. "I'll have to call the phone company in the morning. They're closed now. Still want to come and have dinner with us?"

"Would you mind, Barbara? I don't have any food in the house."

"Love to have you. We'll hear about Paul's first day at Omega."

"Come again," James called out as they left. "I make a tab for you, Mistress Elliott. So any time you down this way, we 'ave refreshment for you."

Jamie linked arms with her new friend.

Barbara smiled. "We look like Mutt and Jeff, don't we, hon? I think we're going to be good friends."

Jamie smiled back and squeezed Barbara's arm.

"Yes, I think we will be."

CHAPTER FOUR

Two days later Jamie headed out with Barbara. Emmanuel sat in the back seat, getting a ride into town.

"You okay?" Barbara asked, noticing the strain on Jamie's face.

"Not now, okay?" Jamie said, a slight motion of her hand indicating Emmanuel in the back seat. "Later." *Later all right,* she thought, not ready to talk about Paul heading off to Mick's after dinner with the Careys the other night - and not coming home until two. Barbara was great, but Jamie didn't know how safe it would be to confide.

Barbara changed the subject. "Parking in Castries is awful," she grumbled as she maneuvered around pot holes. "If I find a spot on the square, I'll pull in and as soon as I'm stopped, get out and run," Barbara told Jamie and Emmanuel.

Jamie looked at her and laughed.

"Get out and run?"

"Yes, Mistress. Run!" Emmanuel apparently knew the drill. "'Manuel, get your van back from your brother and meet us in a couple of hours at Bridge Street, by the post office. I'll send you round to pick up what we buy."

Barbara cut between two vans, narrowly avoiding an ice cream vendor's cart. "The spaces around the square are rented, but everybody parks there anyway. If there's a policeman nearby, I keep circling, but if there's not, I park and run."

"Don't you get a ticket?"

"Jamie, hon, you're in the Caribbean. The concept of parking tickets hasn't made its way this far down the island chain."

Barbara pulled into a spot, glanced around and commanded, "Run."

Jamie ran as instructed, belatedly realizing that Barbara had not said where to stop. A block away she halted near a street vendor with a wooden tray full of cellophane wrapped candies. Barbara walked toward her, a grin spreading across her face.

"Ever run track and field?" she asked. "I'm going to recommend you to the island running club."

"Well, you said run," Jamie grinned back. "How come you didn't?"

"The police were all on the other side of the square. Besides, they know I can run faster than they can," Barbara boasted. "Come on, what's first on your list?"

"Paint," Jamie said. "Rosy peach for the living room. Same color as the St. Lucian Sunrise James made for me. And I have a fabric swatch with a really nice aquamarine. That's for the bedroom."

After forays into every store handling paint, she looked at Barbara in exasperation. "Okay, there's white, yellow, red and blue. Doesn't anybody mix paint on this island?"

"Not really, hon," Barbara smiled. "I didn't mean to put you through hell, but I thought it would be better for you to have a taste of the realities of island life. We improvise and cannibalize - mostly make do with what we can find."

"Is that why most places don't look quite finished?"

"You got it. And if you ever do get it finished, the tropical sun, salt spray and humidity ruin everything. Living here can be a battle."

"I had a battle of wills with Delia this morning. I tried to put some trash out and she brought it back."

"She's right. Material, broken fans, a cracked plate. You'll see. And then someday, you'll be glad to have some of that junk."

"Well, I'm not about to lose the paint color battle," Jamie said, determined. "I'll mix my own."

"Wow. I'm impressed. Try the Berger brand," Barbara advised. "What colors do you need?"

"Hmmm, I think if I have four gallons of white, a quart each of red, yellow, and blue I can come up with what I want."

"More power to you, hon. Now you know why my whole house is white...inside and out." She put her arm around Jamie's shoulder. "You're going to do just fine here. You're adaptable and that, more than anything else, makes island life work."

"I hope so. I've been here less than a week, and I already know this isn't the paradise pictured in tourist brochures."

Barbara laughed. "They'd never show Delia whacking a rat with a cutlass."

"But I have to tell you, Barbara, I have a curious sense of belonging here. Lots of things seem oddly familiar. Even some people I've met," she said, her thoughts turning, as they did often, to Andre.

Jamie paid for her purchases, and Barbara instructed the sales girl about who would be picking them up.

"Come on," Barbara said, glancing at Jamie's list. "The straw rugs and mats are at the market. We came past it on our way into town."

"That run-down building by the waterfront? It could stand a coat of paint."

"That's the one. Actually it was painted two years ago. It looked really spiffy - for six months."

"You're kidding. How often do you paint your house?"

"Once a year, but it always seems to need it. You stop noticing after awhile. Walk down the beach, look at the sea, the beautiful flowers. Faded paint doesn't seem so important."

"I'm not quite there yet. Besides, I really want to make our house a place where Paul'll want to hang out." *Spend time with me instead of drinking with his buddies,* Jamie thought. "We had a tiny apartment before. This is our first real house."

"Well, hon, you've got the energy and imagination. I can't wait to see it finished."

They made their way through the vendors clustered around the market building. Women sat under brightly colored umbrellas, surrounded by baskets of lettuces, spring onions, herbs. Others had tidy heaps of mangoes, knobby brown roots and strange green fruits covered with prickly spikes.

"Darlin', you need lettuce, seasonin' peppers? Look at this beautiful thyme." A vendor with a madras turban on her head thrust hands full of succulent, aromatic herbs toward Jamie.

"Chocolate, palm brooms, herbs for a purge." The melodic lilt of the vendor's sales pitch caught her attention. Her senses were bombarded by the colors, smells and sounds of the busy market place, and she wanted to look at and touch everything.

"What's all that stuff?" asked Jamie, seeing a vendor with small plastic bags, little bundles of twigs tied with twine, old bottles filled with liquids of various colors.

"Bush medicine. Delia probably knows what's in it." Barbara pointed to other bottles. "That's St. Lucian hot sauce. You could strip furniture with it." She grabbed Jamie's arm. "Come on," she said as she dragged Jamie through the market.

"Stop pulling. I want to look."

"We'll do a shopping trip another day. Right now we're headed for a vendor from Choiseul. Your straw rugs, remember?"

Jamie wiped her hand across her forehead as they entered the dim building. "What a relief to be out of the sun," she said as Barbara guided her toward the back of the market. A pale brown face, the color of café au lait, with friendly dark eyes, lit up on seeing Barbara.

"I've brought my friend, Jamie Elliott, to you, Serena. She's just come to St. Lucia and needs some rugs."

Serena's face, that of a black Madonna, was suffused with gentleness as she put the infant sleeping on her shoulder into a straw baby carrier.

Jamie looked at the child longingly. *Someday*, she thought. *If*

Paul doesn't blow this job. Because, she suddenly realized, she liked it here. She wanted to stay.

Using a long pole, Serena began pulling rolled straw rugs from the top of a pile. Each was different.

"Jamie, which one do you like?"

"What?"

"What do you think, Serena?" asked Barbara, wondering what was on Jamie's mind and distracting her. She'd ask later.

"Well, they all nice, but this rug last longest," Serena said, pointing. "Matilda make this rug - took three months."

"How much?" asked Barbara, then dickered over the price.

"That price okay with you, Jamie?"

Jamie nodded, embarrassed. The cost seemed insignificant for a three-month effort.

"Emmanuel will come for everything later, Serena," Barbara advised. "Mistress Elliott will also need small mats for the doors, mats for the dining table and baskets."

"You give me a great day, Mistress," Serena said to Jamie when she had completed her selections. "So I say thanks with a gift." She handed Jamie a pair of earrings made of iridescent feathers.

"They're beautiful. Thank you. What kind of feathers are these?"

"From our St. Lucian parrot," Serena replied.

"But..." Jamie looked horrified.

"Oh, we don't capture the parrot," she added quickly, reacting to the look on Jamie's face. "We find the feathers in the forest. No, our parrots precious. We be taking care of them."

Barbara looked at the earrings. "The earrings you gave me don't look like that."

"Because they from my rooster, Mistress," Serena chuckled. "Parrot feathers only for some." Her eyes grew reflective as she looked at Jamie. "Don't know why they jump into my hand."

Jamie slipped the earrings on. The green and gold feathers floated in the slight breeze. She turned to Serena. "They are special and beautiful. Thank you."

"Okay, what else?" Barbara asked.

Jamie consulted her list. "Where can I get a mirror?"

"Valmont's," said Barbara, waving good-bye to Serena. "Down the street and through the alley."

Entering the store through a shabby door, they picked their way through bins of nails, piles of tools stacked on the floor and rusty cans of paint. Barbara showed Jamie the various pieces of mirror.

"I was thinking of a mirror in a frame," Jamie said.

"Don't come that way here, hon. You get a piece of mirror and have someone make a frame. What size do you want?"

"What is the biggest piece here?"

"How about this piece?" asked Barbara. "Odd shape. Has a piece broken off."

"Actually, it's perfect. Will they sell it for less because it's a broken piece?"

"You're getting the hang of it. Let's give it a try."

Barbara walked toward the counter. She stood patiently while the shop girl stamped another customer's receipt. But when the girl sat back down on her stool, studiously ignoring Barbara, Barbara moved herself right next to the girl and leaned over the counter.

"Hello," she said. "You have a customer waiting, darlin', so perhaps you could get off your stool and sell us that piece of mirror."

The girl slowly came to her feet, her blank eyes masking sullen anger. "What you want?"

"Measure this piece of mirror and give me a price," Barbara said, her voice steely.

"It's okay, Barbara. I'll look at another store," Jamie said.

"Let me take care of it, hon," Barbara said.

Jamie stood back, perplexed by Barbara's almost rude behavior.

The girl picked up the piece of mirror to lay it on the counter. As she did so, Jamie caught a gleam of satisfaction in her eyes as the mirror slipped and shattered on the tile floor.

"No more mirror this size. All finish," she said, then turned her back on Barbara and Jamie and sat back on her stool.

"Your first introduction to the ugly legacy of colonialism," Barbara said angrily, as they left the store.

"Maybe if we had just waited?"

"We'd be waiting until Thursday. Look, I don't like being rude, but sometimes it seems the only way. Watch the locals and see how they get service."

Jamie kept her thoughts to herself. She didn't think she could talk to someone the way Barbara had just done.

"Looks like the mirror will have to wait. Valmont's is the only store that stocks mirror. Anything else on the list?"

"Yes, what kind of curtain rods can I get?"

"No real curtain rods here. Most of us use plastic-coated metal rods. They're at M&C. A couple of blocks over."

"Isn't there a store where we can get everything? I'm tired."

"Nope." Barbara grinned. "Takes stamina to shop in St. Lucia." She headed off at a brisk pace, leaving Jamie to follow.

Forty-five minutes later Barbara announced, "I don't know about you, but I've had it. Let's go home."

She and Jamie carried a bundle of long plastic-coated metal rods. They'd bought long pieces which could be cut depending on the need - towel bars, curtain rods.

Emmanuel and two of his brothers were waiting for them by the post office.

"You and your brother can hold these rods out the window of the van. They're too long to go inside," Barbara said as she fished around in her purse for a couple of red bandanas. "Tie these on either end. Then go around and pick up all the things we bought and bring them to Mistress Elliott's."

Barbara and Jamie started through an alley back toward the square and the car. Hearing a commotion, they looked back. A policeman stood by the van, waving and shouting.

"Oh, hell, what now?" Barbara muttered and headed back to the van in time to hear the policeman issue a verdict.

"You cannot travel with these poles hangin' out the window."

"How do you propose we get them home?" Barbara shouted as she shouldered her way through the gathering crowd.

"You cannot travel with these hangin' out the window. You in violation." The policeman huffed, turned on his heels and left. The crowd began to chuckle. Barbara looked around and chuckled, too.

"What will we do, leave them on the sidewalk?" Jamie felt helpless.

"No, darlin'," replied a woman in the crowd. "The guys hang them out the window and try not to kill anybodies on the way."

"But the policeman..."

"Eh, eh. He full of himself. How he goin' after this van? On his feet? By now he busy havin' a Red Stripe."

Barbara motioned Emmanuel on his way and the van lurched ahead, the bundle of poles projecting in front and behind. Jamie and Barbara headed back to their car. Soon they were out of town and flying down the road toward Rodney Bay.

Later they sat on Jamie's porch and watched the sun moving lower into the western sky. Jamie looked around with wonder.

"What in the world am I doing here?" she asked out loud.

Barbara nodded, her face serious. "I asked myself that twenty times a day at the start. Sometimes I still wonder. Things are different here, done differently. It looks like Paradise, but people here are like people everywhere. Some lovely, generous souls and some nasty sorts."

"Like everywhere," Jamie said.

"It's different. Strange, serious undercurrents leftover from slave days and before. These islands have long histories, old traditions."

"I think I know what you mean. But in spite of that, I'm liking it here."

"I can see that. I have that feeling about you. Some folks come down, think it's a hoot, like Gilligan's Island, the next thing you know they've fallen apart. Alcohol, easy access to drugs, affairs. Their lives just unravel."

Jamie wondered if that was happening to Paul. An almost imperceptible shudder ran through her - a cold wind. Her fingers found the feathers at her ears.

Barbara looked at Jamie carefully. "Hon, you okay? Look, what I'm trying to say is you need to keep your feet on the ground. Don't be too dependent on Paul. He's going to be very busy on the new

Omega project, and there will be early mornings and late nights. I'm not trying to scare you, Jamie. I just don't want you to get hurt."

Emmanuel honked the horn of his van as he pulled up to the house.

"They took their time. Must've stopped for a beer with the cop," Barbara said. "Looks like the poles are intact."

Emmanuel and his brothers carried everything onto the porch. Jamie paid them and they went on their way.

"Well, what has Delia fixed you for dinner?" Barbara asked.

"Fixed us for dinner?" Jamie repeated, feeling stupid.

"Yes, didn't you ask her to fix your dinner?"

"No, was I supposed to?"

"Only if you wanted her to fix dinner for you. She's quite a good cook, you know, along with her teas for whatever ails you."

"Yeah, well I'm not ready for bush medicine. Besides, I catch her looking at me weird. I don't think she likes me."

Barbara pulled open the refrigerator door and peered inside.

"Looks to me like she does. She fixed a great dinner... fried plantain, creole chicken, breadfruit balls..."

Jamie's face showed her dismay. "Breadfruit balls?"

"Try 'em, hon. They're addictive. I like 'em cold, but you might want to put 'em in the oven for ten minutes before dinner. Hey, I'm going home. You've got my number. Call me if you need anything."

"I don't have a phone."

"Right, I forgot. Try the coconut telegraph," Barbara called back as she strode down the road.

Placing the new straw mats on the table, Jamie added a bowl of flowers picked from shrubs around the house. She wondered when the phone would be installed. She missed being able to talk to her mom, hear her reassuring voice. Have her say, *You'll be fine, Princess.*

She had just turned off the oven when she heard Paul come up the steps.

"Hey, I'm home." Pulling her into his arms, he nuzzled her neck. "What have you been up to?"

"Oh, Suzie Homemaker stuff," answered Jamie, glad she couldn't smell beer on his breath, hoping he wouldn't head out to Mick's right after dinner. "Barbara and I went into town. I'll tell you all about it over dinner," Jamie said as they walked arm in arm toward the table. *Maybe he's settling in,* she thought, remembering Serena's baby and her own longing.

"Smells good. What is it?" Paul asked.

"Something Delia fixed. Don't know what it is, but you're right, it smells wonderful." Jamie put the food on the table, hoping nothing would spoil the evening that was starting out so well.

CHAPTER FIVE

Nearing Kennedy Airport, Andre watched the traffic back up. He glanced at his watch.

"What's the hold, Angel?"

"Looks like an accident, Andre. An ambulance is there and a tow truck. We'll get through."

"Have I told you lately how glad I am Jack Deroche married you? When are you going to give Marcus and Bertille a grandchild?"

"If Jack ever finishes grad school," Angel replied. "Hey, I really appreciate you getting me the paralegal job with your company. The extra money helps."

"Twofer...who would have guessed you had your chauffeur's license?"

As the limo passed the accident, Andre watched the well-disciplined paramedics and firemen, the police channeling traffic, keeping it moving. There had been none of this in St. Lucia. Andre smiled to himself, remembering the intense young woman - what was her name? - mucking in, getting bloodied, helping the injured. She'd been something, Jamie had. His smile broadened. *Jamie.* Like he could forget her name. *What was that all about?* he wondered, feeling a little guilty. *Get your act together,* Andre, he told himself.

You're meeting Taylor in San Juan, flying on to St. Lucia.

The limo picked up speed, leaving behind the flashing lights. Andre looked at his watch. He just might make it. A few minutes later, Angel pulled to the curb. Andre jumped out. "See you in a couple of weeks."

He dodged through a group of turbaned men and threw his carry on onto the x-ray machine. On the other side, he grabbed his things and kept running. At the gate, they quickly checked his passport and boarding pass. The stewardess stowed his bag and he slid into his roomy first class seat, grateful as always that his success meant he never had to ride in coach again.

Slow down, he thought, fastening his seatbelt. He took a deep breath, leaned back and closed his eyes. *I can't wait to see Mother's and Father's faces when they see the diamond on Taylor's left hand.* It was time to settle down, he thought. Raise a family. Taylor was perfect for him - bright, perceptive, beautiful. They had very different backgrounds, but their values were the same. Maybe he should have told them. He hoped Mother would make an effort to be welcoming. She could be cold and pretentious.

He rubbed his temples, a headache coming on. The engines roared as the plane sped down the runway, pushing him back in his seat. *Let's face it*, he thought. *I can't control Mother, or Bertille. She'll probably ask her parrot spirits if Taylor is the one for me.* The throbbing in his temples intensified.

As the plane lifted free of the runway, Andre mentally inserted Taylor's cool, blond elegance into Les Jumeaux Estate, wondering how she would handle the decidedly rustic accommodations. *With aplomb*, he decided. *She does everything with style.* He'd never really seen her ruffled. Always in control. Not like Jamie, who got her hands bloody, helped out, then fainted. *Jamie?* Why did he keep thinking about her? *Maybe we did meet somewhere we've both forgotten about. A dream maybe.*

Two worlds! He stopped himself, looking around the cabin at the expensively dressed executives. *I look just like them, but I'm not,* he reflected. *With them I'm the driving force, the focus, making money for my clients. On island I'm the descendant of old island families, full of dreams and island ways, ways calling for obedience and honor.*

A glance at his Rolex told him they were leaving a few minutes late. His city watch. He rarely wore a watch on island. With the city people he hid his island self. They needed a three-piece mirror image, someone like themselves.

He thought of Bertille's connection to the forest and its parrots, the seamless way she flowed between the physical and the spiritual. Most of the world saw the physical and the spiritual as very different; for Bertille it was all of a piece. He remembered Marcus' wise eyes and what he'd said on their last meeting - *you will be married.*

Once the plane leveled out, Andre reclined his seat. He'd been up late last night finishing a financial analysis. Wanted to have a clean slate for this trip where he would introduce Taylor to his family and his island, his heritage. Time she got acquainted with his island self.

He swallowed a couple of aspirin, hoping his headache would be gone by the time he landed.

In San Juan he waited at Taylor's arrival gate until she came into view. She walked toward him, her slender body clad in an elegant gray silk pant suit, her no-nonsense blonde bob tucked behind ears where diamond studs sparkled.

"You look gorgeous," he said, pulling her into his arms. Her strong, signature perfume enveloped him.

Andre took her carry-on, and they walked arm-in-arm to a nearby gate where the plane for St. Lucia was already boarding. Once they were seated, Andre leaned back and got comfortable.

"Andre? You going to sleep?"

"No, just thinking."

"About what?"

"Life. Us. Your meeting my mother."

Taylor laughed. "Actually, I was thinking about who would meet us at the airport. Darling, are you worried about me and your mother? We'll get on just fine."

"I hope so. She can be overbearing at times." Andre chuckled. "Just don't ask her about the family. I don't think I'm ready for you to hear where all the skeletons are hidden."

"Darling, stop worrying. Now, who's meeting us?"

"Father told me he was sending Marcus."

"The family chauffeur?"

Andre snorted. "Hardly. He's Emile's right hand. Knows more about the estate than anyone else. Our families have been connected for generations."

"Generations?"

"Since the French Revolution. They were slaves who helped our family survive a slave uprising. Afterward, my ancestor freed all the slaves and gave them land. Marcus and Bertille still have what their families were given. It's near the hotel site."

"So how do they feel about the hotel idea?"

Andre's brow furrowed. "I'm working on it." He took her hand, and for a moment Jamie's bloody, firm grip touched him, then was gone. "You know, there's always been some speculation that Marcus and Bertille - that their family mixed with ours over the centuries."

Taylor glanced around the cabin, watching a man munching peanuts. "So, Marcus is related to you?" Taylor asked, vaguely troubled that Andre might have a Negro ancestor, wondering how she would explain *that* to her mother.

"We don't think so." Andre pointed to his cleft chin. "But there are some of these scattered around the island, and it's pretty unusual."

"So, Marcus will pick us up and take us to the estate. Who will be there?" Taylor persisted, the term "estate" spinning in her imagination, antique-filled rooms, formal gardens.

"My father, of course. He lives on the estate. And Emile. And Marcus' wife, Bertille, will be around. She keeps house for my father. She'll want to have a look at you too. It was Bertille who raised Emile and me," Andre said by way of explanation.

"Where was your mother?"

"She was...sick a lot when we were little."

"Sick, what kind of sick?" Taylor wanted to know.

"Well, not sick exactly. Depressed, I think. Three babies all in a row. Nobody knew what to do back then."

"Three? I thought it was just you and Emile."

"We had an older sister. Elizabeth. That's a long story. Another time?" Andre said.

"Of course, darling. Tell me about Bertille, then."

"You know, when I read Jung in college, I knew he was talking about Bertille. Archetypal woman, plump curves, a lap with room to spare. She'd tell us stories and sing...I don't quite remember the songs but the melodies were compelling, primitive." Andre was lost in thought for a moment.

"What are you thinking?"

"I just remembered something else. Emile and I are in the forest some place. There's a waterfall and a big pool. Marcus is showing us how to make a trap to catch crayfish. I know that Bertille is in the little hut in the clearing, but we can't go in. Marcus won't let us. Odd. I wonder why I remembered that?"

"It sounds like you had an amazing childhood, Andre."

"Yes, but there were some pretty bad times. Marcus and Bertille were our constants. They have such strong connections to the land. It's inside me, too. You know, I can only spend so much time in New York - too much concrete. It's really why I come back to St. Lucia so much. I feel smothered in the city, can't breathe."

Taylor stared out the window, her frown hidden. "And your mother? Will she be at the estate?"

"No, she lives in Castries where her businesses are located. You'll meet her later this week."

"She and your father don't live together?"

"They decided years ago to live apart. One of the bad times. Told us Father preferred life on the estate and Mother wanted to live in town."

"Why didn't they get divorced?"

"Don't know. Probably because of the estate. Came from her family. It's like a sacred trust. She'd never divide it in a property settlement."

"It's just land. If she was unhappy..." Taylor stopped, reacting to the look on Andre's face.

"It's not just land, Taylor. It's our heritage, why we are who we are."

Taylor drew back.

"Look, I don't expect you to understand, at least not right now. The land sustains us, heals, protects us, it's our blood..." Andre waved a hand. "Sorry."

Taylor put her arm through his. She pulled him close. "I want to understand, Darling. I really do."

The plane dipped and began its descent. Andre leaned past Taylor, pointing out the twin Pitons, the mountains St. Lucia was famous for.

"That's all Jumeaux land - starts in the mountains and runs down to the sea. Emile and I were on that hill a couple of weeks ago." He stroked her hand, turned it, watching the diamond solitaire catch the light.

Taylor watched the primeval landscape out the window. "I'm sure I'll love it," she said, but feeling apprehensive for the first time. She wondered what sort of a reception awaited. Andre's mother, a matriarch, with a history of depression.

The view from the plane changed from primeval to small villages to cultivated fields. The plane touched down and rolled to a stop. On the tarmac Andre lifted his arms to the sultry Caribbean air. To the perceptive it was a gesture of homage, a spiritual offering, then it was gone. Taylor felt the blast of humidity. Her silk trousers stuck to her legs.

As they exited the airport, a porter followed with their luggage piled high on a hand truck. At the curb Taylor saw a middle aged man, his beard shot with grey, his skin the color of rich aged wood. He stood by a red Nissan pickup. His demeanor was so calm, so regal, she halted, unsure how to approach.

Andre pulled her forward and reached out his hand. "Marcus. It's good to be back."

"Welcome, sir," Marcus said, taking Andre's hand. He nodded to Taylor.

"Taylor," Andre said, "This is Marcus Deroche. Marcus, my fiancée, Taylor Whitcomb."

"My pleasure." Marcus dipped his head toward Taylor and raised his eyebrows at Andre, a question in his eyes.

Taylor smiled and said, "I'm happy to meet you. Andre's told me so much about you and your family."

Andre opened the truck door for Taylor, then climbed in beside her.

"Andre's parents are anxious to meet you, Miss Whitcomb," Marcus said, putting the truck in gear and pulling away from the curb.

Andre took her hand. "My parents seem to know you must be someone special."

CHAPTER SIX

It was late afternoon when Jamie completed the design she was working on, a sleeveless sun dress. She pulled boxes from under the bed and began rummaging through them, looking for fabric she would paint before she made it into the dress. *This piece drapes well,* she thought, *and the surface will take paint.* Satisfied, she picked up her sketch book.

Jamie's pencil made bold sweeps across the page, a hibiscus flower with a hanging stamen forming itself on lush curves, presenting well to her practiced eye. The flower was elegant, delicate, evocative. It would make a fine design for her sleeveless sun dress. And yet... Jamie thought about it, her mind distracted a little as she realized she would be late with dinner. *I don't even know if Paul will come home for dinner or just later, drunk again?*

Irritated, she turned to a fresh sketchbook page. The blankness of it stared back, waiting.

When the idea came, it thrilled her, welling up from some startling hidden place inside her, some fount of experience she had never found before. The pencil flew, animated across the page. A parrot formed itself, motionless in frozen rapid flight, winged beauty and energy. But then, as if bidden by some unseen hand, she superimposed a second parrot, wings curled in full swoop, both birds creating a lush rendering. First one bird dominated and then the other, in some primal piquing of the senses. Jamie stared, fascinated. The hibiscus was lovely, of course. This ... it echoed, resonated deep inside. Then she smiled, freeing herself of the odd mood. But would it resonate with others, this almost abstract jungle exotica? *Who cares,* she thought, *I'm the one who'll be wearing the dress.*

When Jamie looked at her watch again, it was 9:30 and three yards of fabric were painted and drying on the bedroom floor. She momentarily panicked as she realized she had totally forgotten about dinner. But just as quickly her panic turned to anger as she realized Paul was still not home.

It was after midnight when Jamie heard the sound of the front door opening. It had turned into an ugly and pathetic ritual. She lay still under the bed sheets, listening. Soft cursing as he stumbled in the dark. Why had she turned off all the lights? *Serves him right if he falls,* she thought. She tracked his progress to the bathroom, saw the slit of light under the door. At least he'd closed it. Then he was crawling into bed beside her. Jamie kept facing the other way, clutching at her pillow.

"Jamie?"

Slurred.

"Jamie, girl. I had dinner with the guys."

The pillow twisted in her fingers.

"What's that paint smell? Doin' a dress?"

"Go to sleep, Paul."

A hand touched her shoulder, descended to her breast. "I was thinkin'..."

She pushed his hand away. "You thought wrong."

"Oh, yeah?"

Jamie was up then, twisting around to look at him. "This is St. Lucia, Paul, not your college frat house. It's your new job, the place you work, make something of yourself."

"I'm in with the other guys," Paul protested, "we..."

"Do they drink like you? Does Barbara's husband get drunk?"

"I don't need this shit," Paul said.

Jamie felt the bed move as he got up. "And leave the goddamn lights on. I might step on your damned fabric. And wouldn't that be a tragedy beyond all description." He mumbled as he found the bedroom door. "I'll be out here tonight. I don't need your crap."

Jamie lay still. Her eyes grew wet and hot. *A baby? Here?* Her thoughts were cushioned in the darkness, but it offered up no answers.

A few days later, Jamie sat on her front porch thinking about Paul. The bullfinch joined her, looking for crumbs.

"Hey, Rufous. When are you going to bring the wife around?" She put some crumbs on the railing.

"I've got a husband, but he doesn't come home when he's supposed to."

The bird steadied a large crumb with tiny claws and pecked.

"You know what he said to me? Said maybe if I made an effort to meet people..." She slumped in her chair. *But that's not right,* she thought, *he's making this all my fault. I feel so helpless, wish there was someone who would tell me what to do.* She looked at the bird.

"And now I'm talking to birds. My husband already thinks I'm half nuts. We'll just have to keep this our little secret."

Jamie put some crumbs on the arm of her chair, wondering if the bird would come closer.

"And I can't tell my mother, she'd just worry. She and Daddy were so good together. I guess I thought all men would be like him."

Her morning reverie was interrupted by a cheery hello. The bird flew into the bushes as Barbara approached, garden gloves and a shovel in hand.

"I'm here to take you to Trim's for horse patooties," she announced.

"What are you talking about?" Jamie asked, hoping Barbara had not heard her talking out loud.

"You've been complaining to me for weeks about your garden, so I'm here to help you get it whipped into shape. Where do you want the flower beds?"

"Whoa, slow down." Jamie was laughing, pulled out of her bad mood, buoyed by Barbara's enthusiasm and energy.

"Now, tell me what you are envisioning?" Barbara asked.

Jamie stood in the yard and looked at the little house now painted a creamy pink, its trim enameled bright white.

"Something climbing up this support that I can train across the top of the porch. And something low and colorful, to edge the bed by the front walk."

"Hmm, jasmine, maybe, it has a divine scent. And maybe dwarf ixora for the edging, there's a dark, hot pink that might be nice. You have some cash? Nobody takes plastic."

Jamie's gloom evaporated under Barbara's sunny energy. "Where are your garden gloves? Do you have any boots or old shoes? It's apt to be mucky at the stables."

Jamie was incredulous. "We're not really going to dig manure?" Knowing Barbara, she thought it quite possible.

"No, not really. The guys do it. But I want to make sure we get well rotted patooties. Otherwise, the roots of your new plants will get burned. I tromp around the piles and tell them where to dig. St. Lucian men aren't very tolerant of being told what to do by a woman, but they know I tip well, so they suffer and dig where I want. Got everything? Let's get going."

At the stables, as Barbara inspected the piles of stable muck for the most composted, Jamie wandered into the barn and looked at the horses. She stopped near a dark brown horse with a white forehead. When she put her hand out, the horse nuzzled her flat palm.

"Looking for a treat, are you? I don't think I have anything to give you."

Rummaging through her pockets, she came up with a Lifesaver, fuzzy with pocket lint. "Next time I come, I'll bring you carrots," she murmured, scratching the horse between the ears.

"There you are. Consorting with the front end of the horse and leaving me to the tail-end business." Barbara pretended indignation. "Come with me so I can show you what well-composted horse manure looks like."

"Lord, you're bossy. Tell you what, I'll let you teach me about gardening if you let me teach you how to sew."

"You must be joking." Barbara shook her head in disbelief. "Any clothes I made would not be a pretty sight. Gardening is easy. I tell the yard man, dig a hole here, plant a bush there, and it's taken care of."

Jamie chuckled. "So gardening is a matter of being bossy."

"Maybe," Barbara said. "Now let's get back to your house and I'll let you practice bossing my gardener. We'll tell him where we want the beds dug, then we'll figure out what plants we need."

By late afternoon the yard had been transformed. A gold cup vine had been planted by the front steps, and a trellis installed on the end of the porch where climbing jasmine would twine with a deep pink mandevilla vine. On the other corner a magenta bougainvillea had been planted. A hedge of white and green variegated croton had been planted next to the house with cerise dwarf ixora at the front.

After paying the crew, Jamie and Barbara sat contentedly surveying the job.

"It will all grow together before you know it," Barbara said.

"How long before I have mangoes on my tree?" Jamie asked, indicating a two-foot-high twig with a few leaves which had been planted in the middle of the front yard.

"Three or four years. About the same time your orange and grapefruit trees start to bear. But you'll have guavas next year and passion fruit for juice."

Just then, Paul came home. He stood and admired the yard.

"Wow, when did you get all this done, and how much did it cost?" he asked as he walked past Jamie and Barbara, nodding hello. "Jamie, I'm gonna have a quick shower and then go over to Mick's. Don't wait dinner for me."

Jamie stared at the mango twig reaching skyward.

Barbara watched her.

"Don't look at me like that."

"Sorry."

"But you're not surprised," Jamie said.

Barbara slipped off her gardening gloves. "Brian mentioned it a couple of times - the drinking, I mean. My guy comes home, thank God. But remember what I said about this island, Jamie."

Jamie made a cutting motion with her hand. "This isn't about St. Lucia. This is about college and beer chugging at the frat house and not growing up."

Barbara looked at her gloves. They were heavily soiled. "I'm sorry."

"I'll be talking to him."

"Of course." She took Jamie's arm. "Anytime you need to talk. All right?

"Yeah, all right."

CHAPTER SEVEN

At twilight Andre and Taylor sat in large rocking chairs on the Jumeaux veranda. A quiet pause to savor their day.

"Enjoy the swim?" Andre asked.

"That was marvelous! I couldn't believe the water!"

"I know. I loved it as a kid. Still do. When we get the hotel up to speed I want to offer water activities, a dive shop. I talked to Emile about it. He's nervous about the environment, wants things done right."

Taylor leaned back, gently rocking. "I can understand that."

"So, what do you think of the place?"

"Here?" She smiled across at him, her hair still wet, pushed behind her ears. "It's a side of you, Andre. So different from New York. It's very natural here, rustic."

"And you like Manhattan. Deluxe apartments..."

"Jacuzzis, cold drinks..."

"I do okay in that department," Andre protested mildly.

She reached for his hand. "Yes, you do."

They sat quietly again, listening to the tree frogs, caressed by the gentle breeze.

The estate house was a rambling one-story, surrounded by a

deep veranda which shaded the rooms. One of the numerous outbuildings was the original kitchen. It now contained all the modern conveniences but was connected to the house by a covered walkway. Inside the house, the rooms had high ceilings and louvered doors which opened onto the veranda. No screens or air conditioning.

At first Taylor thought the netting draping the four-poster beds was romantic. Swatting a mosquito on her bare leg, she was, now a few days into her visit, aware of the net's true function.

Andre's voice interrupted her thoughts. "Tomorrow you visit my mother at her house in Castries?"

"Yes, she asked me to come about ten o'clock. Will you drive me up?"

"Actually, no."

She looked at him, startled. "No?"

"My mother wants to have you to herself for awhile. Probably wants to show you my baby pictures."

"And interrogate me."

Andre laughed. "She's a formidable woman. Frankly, she's had a difficult life. But you can get beyond the reserve. She's not cold so much as she cares too much."

"About what?"

"Family, heritage, the land. She deeply loves St. Lucia and all it means to our family." They watched a yellow breast darting after an insect and were silent for a moment, attending to their own thoughts.

"You said your mother had a difficult life?"

"Lots of things. Remember I told you she lost both her parents in a car accident. She was only twelve."

"I remember. A hard time for a girl to lose her mother."

Andre nodded. "My Tante Yve, her older sister, says she sort of closed in on herself. The first bout with depression."

"Difficult is too mild a word, Andre."

"Marcus and Bertille were there for her, then later for Emile and me..."

Taylor moved the talk in another direction. "Ah, yes, Marcus.

I think I'm bruised from that bouncy ride from the airport, between you and Marcus, talking away in...what is that language?"

"Patois. Bastardized French."

"Your closeness to him is obvious."

Andre leaned forward, his eyes intense. "He and Bertille were surrogate parents. I learned a lot about life and the way they see it...respect for the old ways. Bertille has wonderful stories to tell, handed down through the generations."

"And your mother? You said she married very young. What happened there?"

"Mother did marry very young. I suppose an analyst..."

"Might say a lot of things," Taylor said, dismissing the topic. She squeezed his hand.

"Anyway, when I was a small child and I hurt myself, or was upset about something, I went to Bertille. I'd sit on her lap. You know something, I can still remember that lap, the bigness and warmth of her, and something else."

"Something else?" Taylor regarded him quizzically.

"It's hard to explain. Things that happen here..."

"Andre, this is turning into some kind of island snobbery..."

"No, don't take it that way. I want you to understand. Being burrowed into Bertille took away all fear. Even as a child I could sense something extraordinary about her, a safety. This marvelous and a bit scary power about her. Marcus has it too."

Taylor laughed. "Must be why I thought maybe I should curtsy when I met him. Remember? You had to pull me along."

"They go well together. Marcus is her strength, I think, her protector. And Bertille is his mystery."

Taylor smiled. "I like that. Woman should be mystery."

"We may have different definitions of that word," Andre said.

"So I'm learning. Tell me more about your mother, I'm a little nervous about meeting her. I hope she likes me."

"You must understand that, for my mother, family comes before personal happiness. I think it's why she and my father never divorced. The idea of depriving children of their parents would be abhorrent to her." Andre paused in recollection.

"But you said they separated."

"They did. I don't think it ever registered with my mother that when she moved to Castries we felt abandoned. I was twelve, Emile just ten." His voice trailed away.

"I don't quite understand your mother's definition of family."

Andre didn't seem to hear. "A divorce would have meant dividing the estate. She views it as her children's rightful heritage. I think she'd do just about anything to keep it for us."

"What could possibly happen?"

"Probably nothing. She's just pretty intense about this. Don't be surprised if she raises the issue of a pre-nuptial agreement."

"Andre, we've never discussed a pre-nup..."

"If she brings it up, tell her politely to mind her own business," Andre said.

"Is a pre-nuptial something we should talk about?" asked Taylor, evenly.

"Probably, but not tonight. Let's enjoy the breeze and the tree frog's chorus."

"The Hallelujah Chorus!"

"They are loud tonight, aren't they," Andre laughed. "When I first went to the States, I had trouble sleeping because I didn't hear the night sounds I was used to. When I come home, it's like a familiar lullaby."

"You just used the word 'home.' Is this home to you, more than New York?"

"Yes, of course. This is where I grew up. But then I went off island for college, grad school. And the last few years I've spent most of my time in New York. I've been away for a long time. I'd like to spend more time here."

"Listening to tree frogs, sitting in a rocking chair like this?"

"It's not a bad life," Andre said, unsmiling.

Taylor twisted uncomfortably, then faced him. She turned the diamond ring on her finger.

"Would you? Really want to live here?" she asked, wondering why this was coming up now.

Andre watched the land, the dappling of grasses and leaf under the warm buffeting breeze. "The island is part of me, Taylor."

She said nothing, unwilling to press the issue.

The next morning, after an hour on the road, Taylor asked, "How long until we get to Mrs. Demontagne's house?"

"Another hour and we should be there," the driver replied. "There are some scenic turnouts ahead. Would you want me to be stoppin' so you can have a look at our beautiful island paradise?" he asked.

"No," Taylor said. "Just keep driving."

The taxi bumped along, something Taylor was getting used to, or at least expecting. Her linen slacks stuck to her, covering itchy red insect bites. God, she needed that cool ocean again, the sparkling spray and fun in Andre's strong arms, diving from his shoulders deep into the blue sea. Taylor wiped her forehead and clutched the damp tissue. Their talk on the veranda troubled her. Sitting there, gently rocking, this rift, this divide had appeared. Andre was actually thinking of living here - what was the description of the estate? - rustic. And insects galore that made it under the four- poster's mosquito netting. Taylor noticed sailboats on the sea. Maybe if Andre built the hotel they could build a villa on the island, live there when they visited. She needed New York. Their children would need good New York prep schools to get them into the right circles.

The thoughts wearied her. And now his mother. The Big Visit. The cold mother. Actually, in fairness, the emotionally injured mother. Andre had been forthright about that.

I wonder if she favors one of the boys over the other? Having Andre in New York gives her a base for her visits to the States. Perhaps it's better for her to have Andre in New York and Emile on the island. Emile is the one who is more interested in running the estate. Andre is more interested in making money, she thought, neatly compartmentalizing her future husband and brother-in-law.

Finally the driver turned into a lane lined with stately royal palms. Taylor, expecting another small wooden house with a veranda, was totally unprepared for the luxurious house crowning the hill. Constructed of coral stone with cool green shutters and accents, the house had breathtaking views overlooking the Castries harbor. Elaborate coral stone columns framed the arched doorway.

The driver honked. A housekeeper in a creole-style madras skirt and off-the-shoulder white blouse appeared and talked briefly to the driver, who took Taylor's suitcase and disappeared into the house.

"Mistress Demontagne is waiting for you in the sitting room. Please come with me."

Taylor was annoyed by her nervousness. She barely noticed the interior courtyard of the two-story house, a lush garden, open to the sky. *Will she like me?* she wondered as she followed the housekeeper. A formal dining room overlooking the harbor caught her attention. Everywhere she noticed elegant touches. A sumptuous fabric crowning a window, a *chinois* cache pot containing a blooming orchid, mahogany chaises with caned seats and needlepointed cushions. This house was light years away from the Jumeaux Estate house where she was staying with Andre.

The woman waiting for her was slender, of middle height, her graying hair cut unusually short. *A New York salon cut, I bet,* Taylor thought, noting the piercing blue eyes and beautiful skin taut over high cheekbones, the elegant dress.

"My dear, welcome to my home." Andre's mother embraced Taylor and kissed one cheek and then the other. "Would you like to freshen up after your long ride from the country?"

Taylor nodded.

"Natalie, please take Mistress Whitcomb to the Lotus Room. She will need a fresh juice." She turned to Taylor. "I've had your luggage taken up. When you are ready, please rejoin me here."

Taylor followed Natalie up an open stairway and around a balustraded veranda. Natalie stood aside and motioned Taylor into the room. Decorated in shades of lavender and cream, the head of the double bed was draped with yards of gauzy fabric gathered into a gilt crown. The tone-on-tone bedspread showed, on closer inspection, a design of large lotus flowers and pods woven into the fabric.

Glancing out the window, Taylor could see the cool green shutters flanking the bedroom windows, a green that cooled the eye and complemented the subtle variations of lavender and cream in the room.

Peeking into the bathroom, Taylor stepped down into a large bathing suite done in creamy marble with pale green veining. The tub area was obviously custom made, and she could see Jacuzzi jets inset in the sides. The walls of the tub area were glass with an unobstructed view down to the harbor.

It must be spectacular at night, Taylor thought, visualizing herself enjoying a whirlpool tub while sipping chilled Chablis from a crystal glass.

"Would you like me to unpack your things for you?" Natalie questioned.

"A little later, perhaps. Now I would like to freshen up. Thank you, Natalie."

When the bedroom door closed, Taylor ran a brush through her hair and looked at herself in the mirror. Her wrinkled outfit had to go. Changing quickly, she tucked a pale blue blouse into a matching long silk skirt, glad she'd made that recent trip to Saks. She gazed at herself in the mirror, evaluating. She was ready.

But first Taylor sat on the *chaise longue,* relaxing. She felt more comfortable in this setting. But even in a house like this, she wondered, could she live in St. Lucia?

Clarisse stood on the terrace while she waited for Taylor. She found it calming to survey the land, the lifeblood of her family, her very soul. And she would need to stay calm, because Taylor was patently one of the sleek ones, the Big City elite, totally unsuitable for Andre. She had dealt with the sleek ones before, had seen so many of them in the salon in New York where she had her hair cut. But each was different; she would have to tread lightly, offer no malice to alienate Andre. *What is it that these sleek girls want, over and above money and luxuries, and a living style that they may or may not deserve?*

Clarisse looked out over the harbor view, the sun offering its golden rays, a benediction to the island, whose history was so entwined with that of her family. Then she turned back inside. And Bertille and Marcus, of course. Not blood, but family nonetheless, welcomed and treasured, deeply loved for their caring of Andre and Emile. Bertille in particular had nourished Andre. Once she had seen her son burrow into Bertille's soft bosom and stay there, quite still, while she sang ancient songs to him. It had torn Clarisse's heart, and for that brief instant she had yearned for her own mother, some cracking of her inner ramparts against pain. When Taylor approached, Clarisse beckoned her back onto the terrace.

They watched as a cruise ship made its stately way into the harbor.

"We are seeing ships several times a week now," Clarisse said. "I quite like to watch them leave in the evening. Fairy ships, their masts strung with lights. Like Andre, I believe tourism will be St. Lucia's future."

Turning to Taylor, Clarisse asked, "Would you mind terribly if we lunched here? I very much want to get to know you, and we would have more privacy here than in a restaurant."

"No, of course not, in fact after the long ride I would love not to get into a car for awhile."

Clarisse smiled. "Yes, the roads are punishing. But better roads will bring more cars. The price of progress, I suppose. Let's sit here on the covered terrace." Clarisse motioned to a grouping of deeply cushioned, oversized rattan chairs. Taylor sat down, enveloped by the soft cushions, and ran her hand over the fabric, a nubby raw silk.

"Your home is exquisite, Mrs. Demontagne," Taylor said, wondering if this was the time when Andre's mother would say, *call me Clarisse.*

The moment passed.

"I'm glad you like it. It's a work in progress. I'm always hunting for island antiques, pieces of our heritage. It's important they're not lost."

Taylor pushed down her disappointment at the lost opportunity. "The estate house is charming, Mrs. Demontagne," she said, "but I must admit it wasn't what I expected."

"Oh?" Clarisse arched an eyebrow for effect and Taylor felt she had blundered. "What did you expect, my dear?"

"Andre called it an estate. I suppose I was thinking of Palm Springs."

"Estate refers to the land. I suppose in the States you would call it a farm. It is the land, not the estate house that is important."

"It does sound grander than farm and farm house."

"The Jumeaux estate house is authentic, you know. Of course, bathrooms have been added and the kitchen updated with new appliances. All cooking used to be done on coal pots. Bertille still cooks some of the classic dishes that way."

"It's very comfortable, beautiful antiques," Taylor said, hoping to remedy her previous blunder.

"Some are from the original Diamant brothers, the line I come from. The house is full of our family's history. I actually know who added what bedstead or sideboard." Clarisse paused. "I'd like to get to know you, Taylor. Tell me about yourself, your family."

Taylor had been expecting a question like this and launched into a brief synopsis. "My parents are from Philadelphia. Their families have been there for generations. My father's firm owns several department stores. My mother spends most of her time in volunteer fundraising for the Philadelphia Museum of Art. I have a younger brother. He's still in college. What else would you like to know?" asked Taylor.

"Do you love my son?"

Taylor was momentarily rattled by the abrupt, intrusive question. "Of course I love Andre. I wouldn't have agreed to marry him if I didn't love him."

"Do you really know him?"

"Of course. We want the same things, have the same goals."

"And what would those be?" Clarisse asked.

"We want a family. To raise our children in a certain lifestyle, so they can compete successfully socially and in their careers.

Andre and I love each other. We're way past puppy love, mindless infatuation. We know what we want."

Clarisse wondered whether Taylor recognized the passionate side of Andre, the West Indian cadence that resonated in his blood. "Would you be happy living here?"

Why are they all pushing for a decision about that now? Taylor wondered. "I can be happy wherever Andre is happy. He seems very settled in New York. That is where we plan to live."

"Andre is something of a chameleon," Clarisse replied softly, aware Taylor had evaded her question. "He takes on the coloration of his surroundings. When he is in New York he is a New Yorker. When he is on island, he is West Indian. I wonder if you know his West Indian side, Taylor?"

"Mrs. Demontagne, I believe I know Andre better than you realize. We've known each other for some time. The decision to marry was not impulsive. I hope you will come to know me and like me, but I am marrying Andre, not his family."

Clarisse stiffened, and Taylor sensed she had been too confrontational. "I apologize if that sounded rude. I feel rather like I am being interviewed," Taylor said.

"In a way, I suppose you are. Meeting you for the first time." Clarisse was quiet for a moment. "Andre must have told you that his father and I have not lived together for many years. This has been painful for both of us. I want my son to find joy in his marriage. I don't want him to come to regret what should be the strongest union on earth."

"And you think he would come to regret marrying me?" Taylor asked. She watched Clarisse, catching the strength of her, and something else, sense of mission, perhaps, something driving her blood.

"Andre is an adult, of course. He knows his own mind."

"Yes?"

Cool eyes fixed on Taylor, and she felt their raw power. "I'm just letting you know I wish more than anything for..."

"For Andre's happiness," Taylor smiled.

"Yes, child. His happiness. And I will do everything in my power to ensure it."

Taylor nodded. "Most mothers would. I can certainly respect that." Silence hung on the air, broken abruptly by a cruise ship's horn far below on the thick wedge of ocean.

CHAPTER EIGHT

"No way," muttered Paul. He opened the refrigerator door and took out a beer. "I'm not spending my day off tramping in the rain forest. It's what I do all week."

Jamie took silverware out of a drawer and began setting the table. "When Danielle called, I thought it sounded like fun. She said something about a picnic by a river."

"Couldn't you have run it by me first?"

"Look, we've been in St. Lucia for a while now and besides Barbara and Brian, we haven't met other couples," Jamie said. "They said they'd stop by for us Saturday about eight."

"In the morning! Jesus, Jamie, why so early?"

Jamie banged the drawer shut. "That's it! I'm fed up with you complaining because I'm not making an effort to get to know people and then when I do, you still complain. You can't have it both ways."

Paul looked chastened. "All right, sorry, you're probably right. But I'm telling you, being in the bush is no fun. Hot. Miserable. Buggy."

"I'm sorry, too. Look, next time I'll consult before I accept," Jamie said, hugging him, making an effort. "It'll be fun, Paul. You've seen a lot more of St. Lucia than I have, but I want to get to know the island, too."

"Hard to get used to, here. Strange place. Not like anything in New York, that's for sure."

Not for me, Jamie thought. *Familiar, comforting, like an old pair of well-worn jeans. Just fits.* Andre's face shimmered, smiling at her as they tied the tourniquet. So long ago, yet not really. *What was he doing now?*

"Okay, okay." Paul unwound Jamie's arms from around his neck. "What's for dinner? I'm hungry."

"Delia's special pumpkin soup."

Paul sat down at the table. "I'm getting into this creole cooking. Hey, and don't forget to check with Danielle about where we're going on Saturday. If we'll be in the bush, you'll need long pants and something with sleeves."

Jamie felt unsettled; the thought of Andre had rattled her. She turned to the stove and began ladling soup into bowls, bits of chicken swirling in the creamy orange broth.

The morning was still cool.

"My favorite time of day," Jamie said to Paul as they sat on their front porch waiting for Danielle and Jean-Pierre.

"I'd rather be in bed." Paul yawned and sipped his coffee. He shooed a bird from the railing. "Here they come. Man, wonder how they can afford that?" He motioned to the new Land Rover. "Omega must have given Jean-Pierre a big raise."

Jamie laughed.   "That or they're running drugs."

"Not the type."

"How do you know the type?" Jamie asked.

"I don't know, somebody willing to take big risks for a big payoff." He grinned. "Like me. Hey, I work with this guy. He seems okay. Maybe Danielle's the one with the money."

"'Ello," Danielle called out, her French accent apparent. Dressed in shorts and a brief top, the smart outfit set off her tanned skin and toned body. Jamie looked down ruefully at her legs covered in long, brown cotton pants. Taking Paul's advice, she'd called Danielle for guidance about what to wear, and Danielle had advised long sleeves and long pants. *Maybe I misunderstood her,* Jamie thought. *At least I wore my pretty parrot earrings.* The feathers fluttered, caressing her cheeks.

"We take the Land Rover, *d'accord,*" Jean-Pierre announced. He drove competently, but the continual swerving to avoid potholes did unpleasant things to Jamie's stomach. She foraged in her bag for a peppermint, her trusted remedy for nausea. Paul, who knew that riding in the back seat of a car was difficult for her, saw her pop the mint into her mouth and reached out and squeezed her hand.

"Can we pull over at the next convenient place? Maybe Jamie could switch places with Danielle."

"'Ave you a problem?" Danielle asked.

"Oh, I'm just feeling a little car sick. If we stop for a while and I can sit up front, I'll be okay."

"*D'accord.* Jean-Pierre, stop up there. There is the view out to the lovely sea, and we can stay for a few minutes. It is another half hour to the turn to the river."

"Thanks, Danielle," Jamie said gratefully.

"No problem, I will get better acquainted with Paul," Danielle said, taking Paul's arm.

The brief stop restored equilibrium to Jamie's stomach. From the front she had an even better view of the landscape as they wound through the countryside.

Lush green peaks cascaded into the distance. The deep mountain valleys gave Jamie a primordial feeling. She closed her eyes and drifted into a dream. The sea, the steady beat of a heart. Feathered wings enfolding, protecting.

"It is a beautiful island," Jean-Pierre said.

Jamie roused from her reverie. "What?"

"St. Lucia. It's a beautiful place..."

"Yes." Jamie fought hard to pull herself back to the present. "It is."

Before beginning the descent into Soufriere, Jean-Pierre pulled over so the foursome could get a look at the majestic Petit Piton on the south edge of the fishing village. The mountain was a remnant of the original caldera of the volcano that formed the island.

Pointing to a spot in the hills, Jean-Pierre indicated some wisps of smoke. "That is the famous drive-in volcano," he said, pointing out an area devoid of vegetation.

"It doesn't look very impressive from here," Paul said.

"It is very interesting. Hot springs and bubbling mud. Maybe later we can drive in."

"Drive into the volcano?" Jamie said, alarmed.

"Well, not drive into it, but you can get very close and then can walk into it."

"It is time to go ahead," Danielle said as she herded them back to the car. "We 'ave fifteen minutes to the river, and I am thirsty and hot and wanting food more each minute."

Following the rutted and potholed road, they ventured deeper and deeper into the rain forest. They drove through a ford in a small river, sun piercing the leafy canopy. Jamie saw women washing clothes, clean garments spread on rocks to dry. A picture to paint - some day.

The road continued through rusted machinery and remains of stone buildings. Trees grew through the ruins, reclaiming the earth.

"Here was the sugar cane mill of the Demontagne estate back in the 1800's," Jean-Pierre commented. "Much land was cleared at that time for the cane. When sugar was no longer profitable, the machinery was abandoned and the estate replanted in coconuts and cocoa. It is quite good cocoa. A Dutch candy company buys the entire crop every year."

"Jean-Pierre, you are surprising to me, so full of knowledge," Danielle said, a touch of sarcasm to her words.

"I find the island and the history quite interesting, *chérie*," Jean-Pierre replied evenly.

Jamie wondered about their relationship. They were both pleasant enough on the surface, but turbulent undercurrents eddied up from time to time, unnamed tensions that made her feel uncomfortable - as though she was observing something she shouldn't see. But then, how did she and Paul look to others?

"Put the Land Rover in over there," Danielle commanded. "There is a way down to the river. Paul, you and Jean-Pierre carry the cooler. Jamie and I take the blankets and chairs." Pulling a bottle of bug repellant out of her bag, she patted some on her arms and legs, then passed it to Jamie. "Do you wish some?" she asked.

"I'm so covered up, I don't know where they would bite me," Jamie said.

The path sloped gently down through the bush and ended in a clearing by a wide, shallow river full of rounded boulders, the clear water moving almost silently. On the other side, the forest vegetation was interspersed with clumps of flowering plants, which added bright accents to the dark greens of the foliage.

"Do you think we might see some parrots?" Jamie asked, following after Jean-Pierre.

"We might hear them. Not likely to see them. So few left," he replied.

Danielle led them upstream to a small area of sand. "The sand came in a recent flood. It will not last forever, but now it makes a place perfect for the picnic."

She snapped open the blanket and let it settle on the sand. "Put the cooler there, sand chairs here, here and here. I will be the hostess," she announced. Opening the cooler, she pulled out a bottle of chilled white wine, a bottle of *vieux rhum* from Martinique, cane syrup, a couple of limes and some cold beers. "This is the bar," she announced. "Jamie, what is for your pleasure?"

"A glass of wine, I think." Jamie smiled at Danielle, thinking how much she was enjoying the day, glad that Paul seemed to be having a good time as well. Danielle handed her the glass of wine and nodded to Paul.

"For you?"

"A beer for me," he said.

"And for Jean-Pierre as well," she said, handing out cold bottles of Red Stripe. "For me, a *petit punch*." She sliced a lime, squeezing its juice into a glass. "Some cane syrup for the petit part and old *rhum* for the punch. *Santé!*" She raised her glass to her companions.

"Now, let us see what special things my housekeeper has packed for us. Ah, here are some plantain chips to go with our drinks," she said as she passed a metal tin to Jamie. Reaching deeper into the cooler, she pulled out plastic containers and opened the lids. "Cold chicken, *salade avec avocat et tomate*. A little bottle of Dijon vinaigrette. Some Camembert...see the rind is like *la niege*, the snow, very fresh, the way it should be." She opened a large metal tin. "Ah, a mango tart. Quite tasty. *Maryanne est un bonne cuisiniere. Bon appetit, mes amis.*" Danielle laid out the food, then set out plates and cutlery so everyone could serve themselves.

The four talked companionably throughout the al fresco meal. Jamie was intrigued with Jean-Pierre's breadth of knowledge about the island. Later Paul and Danielle began climbing on the rocks, making their way up the river. Jamie, replete with wine and good food, found herself dozing off.

Jean-Pierre folded a towel for a pillow and handed it to Jamie. "I am going to hunt for *ecrevisse* near the rocks, just there. I think you call them crayfish. Have a good rest."

Jamie nodded and let herself drift away.

She was wandering in the forest, lost and afraid. She knew she was searching for something, but just what it was eluded her. A flash of white caught her eye. Caught on a branch, she gently pulled the cloth off and examined it. It was an infant's cap, linen with fine lace, the ribbons torn. The sense of dread increased and she stumbled forward, knowing she must be successful in her search or something terrible would happen. The brush closed in on her, scratching her arms and legs as she struggled on.

"Jamie, Jamie, wake up." Jean-Pierre was shaking her gently. "You have the bad dream."

"The child is lost, I must find the child. See the little cap? It's here in my pocket."

"Jamie, wake up." The shaking became more insistent. "Jamie, you have *le cauchemar*, the nightmare."

Jamie's eyes focused on Jean-Pierre's face. "It seemed so real. I was in the forest and I was lost, but I was hunting for something. And then I found a baby's cap hanging on a branch, and I knew it was a child I was searching for. The child was lost and would die if I didn't find it. But the forest was so dense and dark and I didn't know where I was. I still feel afraid." She shivered involuntarily.

Jean-Pierre sat next to her and put his arm around her to comfort her. "Nightmares seem so real. But you are here in a pretty place by the river. No one is lost, except perhaps my Danielle and your Paul, who have gone up the river jumping from rock to rock. No children are missing."

Jamie continued to feel oppressed despite the comforting words. There was something in the dream that was important to remember, but the details were slipping away. Something about the baby's cap, the lace... She tried to visualize it, but the picture faded.

Taking Jean-Pierre's hand, Jamie squeezed it. "Thank you for waking me up. I didn't want to stay in that dream. I felt desperate."

"We all have nightmares," he reassured.

"Yeah, but I seem to have more than my share of weird dreams. It runs in my family. But what was odd about this one is it was in the forest here. In St. Lucia. I've never been in the rain forest, but I know it was here. It was so familiar... trees like this, but a clearing with a waterfall..."

Just then Paul and Danielle reappeared. Paul took in the scene on the blanket. Jean-Pierre's arm around his wife, their two heads close together, obviously talking about something intimate. Anger surged through him as he watched Jamie take Jean-Pierre's hand.

"It seems your wife and my husband are better acquainted now," Danielle remarked. "Perhaps we have need to warn them we come before we see something we do not want to see." Danielle picked up a small stone and threw it into the water. "'Ello there! We discover a place to swim. Do you want to come?"

Jamie and Jean-Pierre looked up. Danielle noticed they did not spring apart, no guilty movements. Whatever had been going on, it had not been romantic. She glanced over at Paul, his jaw muscles bunched in anger. Intrigued, she stored the information away for future use.

"Do we all want to go for a swim?" Danielle asked again. "Paul and I have already been. It was agreeable."

"But we didn't bring bathing suits," said Jamie.

"*Ma chérie*, we have the suits God gave us."

Paul approached Jamie. "What is wrong with you?" he asked pointedly.

Jean-Pierre rose and moved away.

"I fell asleep after lunch and had a nightmare. I'm still feeling shaky."

"I'll just bet you are," he said under his breath.

"Paul," Jamie said quietly, "what's the matter with you? I fell asleep and had a bad dream. Jean-Pierre had to wake me up."

"Forget it. We'll talk about it when we get home."

Danielle and Jean-Pierre walked toward them. "Do we swim or do we hike a little?"

"I'd like to hike," Jamie quickly replied, instantly discarding the notion of skinny dipping with Danielle and Jean-Pierre. Later she'd ask Paul what had happened at the pool in the river. Always something to ask later.

Jean-Pierre pointed up the trail. "From the top there is a spectacular view of the Jumeaux Estate. There's even a cannon dragged there by the English. We're on estate land now."

"It is a hobby of Jean-Pierre to collect useless pieces of island information," Danielle commented, her disdain thinly veiled. "Is it not so, *mon joli?*"

Jean-Pierre's face hardened. "The old island families are quite interesting, and the Demontagne and Diamant families have been here from the beginning. The original Diamant land grant came from the King of France."

"I think hiking to the top of that hill sounds good. And I would love to hear more about the history of the island," Jamie said, wanting to move, to break the tension. The uncomfortable tensions she'd previously felt between these two had simmered to the surface. It was ugly.

Danielle motioned them off. "Paul, you can help me with the cooler before we start up the trail. The two historians go ahead."

Paul glanced at Jamie, resentment on his face. "Sure, let the historians go ahead," he said and turned his back on Jamie.

CHAPTER NINE

"Sorry to slow you down," Jamie said to Jean-Pierre as she stopped again to examine the ferns and orchids along the trail. "You know so much, and St. Lucia has such a fascinating history."

Just then Paul and Danielle caught up. Danielle was wearing a pair of jeans and a long-sleeved shirt. Jamie wondered, briefly, where she'd found a place to change.

"Are you feeling okay, Jamie?" asked Jean-Pierre as he whacked a hanging vine with his cutlass. "Another half hour and we arrive at the top."

"Does everyone on the island know how to use one of those?" Jamie asked. "Every man I see on the side of the road has one."

"It's a useful tool. Inexpensive, easy to sharpen. Most of the men you see carrying cutlasses are banana farmers."

"When I first came to the island, I was a little frightened that people carried weapons so openly."

"Does it frighten you to see a man carry a shovel?"

Jamie laughed, the oppressive feeling from her dream fading away. "Of course not."

"Men cut down large trees with cutlasses in less time than with a hand saw."

"I believe it. The guy who has been helping me with my garden uses his cutlass for all sorts of things. He digs with it, cuts, loosens the soil. You're right, it's very versatile. I tried using it one day, but it was too big and heavy for me. I tried to cut a limb and I felt the shock of the blow all day in my shoulder."

Jean-Pierre nodded. "From time to time I see a small one in M&C."

"I'll look. I'd like to learn to use one."

"But, Jamie, a fact of St. Lucian life. You should not be seen digging in your garden."

"Why ever not? I enjoy working in the garden."

"It is a matter of status. Your gardener would be embarrassed if his friends saw you helping him."

"Perhaps it's time St. Lucian men learned women are good for more than ornamentation."

Suddenly Jean-Pierre stopped and motioned the group to be silent. He indicated the top of a tree at some distance. "Parrots," he murmured. "Amazonia Versicolor, not many left. We are lucky to see them." Suddenly the parrot's raucous cries filled the air, and they took flight in a flash of green and gold.

"Look at them!" Jamie exclaimed, raising her hands in wonder.

Danielle looked puzzled. "Just parrots, *ma amie.*"

"Not just parrots," Jamie replied with heat.

Danielle glanced at her. "Oh? Why is that?"

"I don't know. I've always been fascinated by birds, but parrots are different. Smarter, they can communicate. Have a presence about them, a spiritual quality."

"You are becoming a real St. Lucian," Jean-Pierre remarked. "Some view the parrots very seriously. Have you been talking to anyone? Delia?"

"No, it's just a feeling." Jamie shifted uncomfortably. "But they belong here in this magical place. It's like a cathedral." She lifted her eyes. "All the high trees forming a canopy against the sky..."

"Forget the canopy, Jamie. Keep on truckin'," Paul said.

Danielle laughed. "Our Jamie is a romantic."

Jamie smiled, embarrassed.

"The air is close and *les moustiques*, bah," Danielle exclaimed. "I hope the view at the top is worth the effort."

As the others went on, Jamie stood and gazed into the distance. The cries of the parrots faintly resonated in the forest. Jamie touched the feather at her lobe, then started back up the trail.

Soon sweat was running down her back, and she was glad for the walking stick Jean-Pierre had cut for her. Her eyes burned as sweat dripped into them, and she brushed her arm across her forehead. If this is what Paul's days were like, no wonder he wanted a cold beer when he got home. If only he'd stay home to drink it.

The trees began to thin and Jamie felt a cooling breeze. The group walked into a clearing on the top of the mountain. The sun was hot, but the breeze cooled their faces. It felt heavenly. Jamie lifted her shirt and fanned her sweaty middle. In the distance she could see misty sheets of a tropical shower, and then, as the sun shone, a bright rainbow arching over the hills.

"I've seen more rainbows in our time on St. Lucia than in my entire life," said Jamie.

The experience of the grinding, humid climb slipped away as the small group stood subdued into reverent silence by the stunning vista before them.

The reverie was broken by a shouted, "Hallo!" coming from the edge of the clearing. Two men appeared, cutlasses in their hands. Paul and Jean-Pierre moved closer to the women as the men approached.

"*C'est* Emile," Danielle called out.

"And that's Andre," Jamie said, conscious of Danielle's sudden glance.

"Andre?"

"Jamie?"

"I didn't expect to meet you up here - or anybody, for that matter," Andre smiled. He grasped Jamie's offered hand. "You look a little the worse for wear."

"First time in the countryside. Should've brought a change of clothes. I'm sorry, I don't know..." She glanced at the other man.

"Emile Demontagne. You were expecting Dr. Livingston?"

They all laughed, relaxing.

"Paul works with me at Omega," Jean-Pierre said.

"Great job. Good people," Paul said. "Andre, I remember you from that truck accident the day we arrived. You and Jamie really took charge."

"More Jamie than I, Paul," Andre admitted.

"Ah, the accident!" Danielle said. "I heard about the woman who helped - that was you?"

"Fresh off the boat." Jamie smiled.

An imposing dark-skinned man drew forward. Jamie had not noticed him in the shadows at the edge of the clearing.

"It's good to have you on our island, Mistress. I am Marcus Deroche," he said, his dark eyes warm and supporting, probing her without causing offense. "You have a peaceful aura around you, child. Our parrots have marked you," he said, gesturing toward her earrings.

"Here we go again," said Paul, not quite hiding his impatience.

"What?" Andre asked, glancing from Jamie to Paul and back again.

"We've just got finished talking about Jamie's fascination with parrots."

"It wasn't quite like that..." Jamie protested mildly, looking at Andre, taking in the serious eyes, that cleft in his chin.

"The parrots are sacred," Marcus said.

Andre just watched her.

"So," said Danielle, wanting to recapture the limelight. "What is everyone doing here?"

Jean-Pierre interjected, "And it's okay for us, Emile? To be here, I mean. On Jumeaux land?"

"Of course. Actually Andre, Marcus and I are out to check on the crew cutting the boundaries for the estate."

Jamie barely heard him as she stole glances at Marcus and tried to control the turmoil inside her. *An aura? I'm marked?* She touched the feathers at her ears. Confused, her eyes settled on Andre. He smiled at her.

"We have a crew cutting boundaries. Thought we might be

able to see their progress." He pointed to a slight color variation demarcating a line in the foliage on a distant hill. "Over there, you can just make out where they have cut."

Paul said, "I know from what I'm doing for Omega what a job it is to clear a boundary. How much clearing will you have to do?"

"The estate is four thousand acres, and we must survey the lines. Ownership of land in St. Lucia has often been vested with the person living on the land, and with the island changing hands between the French and the British so many times, many titles are clouded."

Paul did a quick calculation in his head, "At 4000 acres, that might be ten miles of boundary to clear. If your land was square and flat it would be a major job, but in this terrain..."

Marcus interrupted. "Excuse me, sir. If you no longer need me, I will go back to the estate."

"Yes, of course, Marcus. Go on ahead. I'll be along in a minute," Andre said. Then he asked Jean-Pierre, "Where is your vehicle?"

"Parked by the river."

"Why don't you stop by the estate house on your way out?" Andre said. "Father is there and I'm sure he would enjoy seeing you."

Emile turned to Jamie and Paul. "Have you visited a working estate on the island?"

"No, we haven't," Paul said.

"Then I would be happy to give you a brief tour. After, we can sit on the veranda and have a rum punch. Or must you get back to the north?"

Danielle looked at the group questioningly. "We are not in a hurry. How about the two of you?"

"An estate tour sounds fascinating," said Jamie.

"And the rum punch sounds great," echoed Paul.

"Later, then. See you at the house."

Andre smiled at Jamie. "I told you it was a small island and we'd run into each other."

"In the rain forest, on the top of a mountain. It's a stretch..."

"Marcus would say there are no coincidences," Andre said as he turned and joined his brother on the other side of the clearing. "See you in a little while."

Jamie held Paul back for a minute. "This is turning out to be quite an adventurous day. Glad you came?" She smiled at her husband.

"You sure made yourself the center of attention," Paul said. "That Andre's got your number."

Jamie grabbed his arm. "What are you talking about?"

"That bit about auras and parrots. Too much. First Jean-Pierre, and now you're flirting with Andre. You haven't heard the last about this..." He shook her off and strode back down the path.

Jamie watched him go. She had been glad to see Andre. And she did think of him. Jamie caught up with the group.

At the bottom they piled into the Land Rover.

"I will sit in the back with Paul," announced Danielle.

Jamie slid into the front seat next to Jean-Pierre and fastened her seatbelt. Her hands clenched in her lap.

"Four thousand acres!" Paul said. "That's an incredible amount of land on this small island."

"They are original landowners," replied Jean-Pierre. "Of course, they pushed out the Caribes and the Arawaks, the original Indian population. But from the earliest days, the Demontagnes have owned a lot of the island. Marcus and his wife, Bertille, they own a large parcel of land next to the Demontagne estate."

"They own a lot of land, yet Marcus works for the Demontagne family?" Jamie asked Jean-Pierre.

"Andre and Emile's mother is a Diamant. Her family has owned this land since before the French Revolution. I do not know how Marcus and Bertille came to own that piece of land. It is quite remote. All cliffs and mountains. Worthless, really. The locals will not pass near it, I am told."

Danielle cut in. "*Mon chéri*, enough of the history lesson. We are almost there, and I must find a place to clean up a little and put on some other clothes."

Jamie looked down at her soiled pants and sweat-stained shirt. She should have planned better. Never again would she venture on an outing like this without bringing a couple of changes of clothes, a bathing suit and a towel, a wet washcloth wrapped in plastic, and her own bug spray.

The drive into the estate was lined with stately royal palms, the grass underneath cut short and the bush cleared back about thirty feet on either side of the drive. At the edge of the forest a jumble of bougainvillea spilled orange, cerise and purple as though splashed from overturned buckets of brightly colored paint.

"Les Jumeaux Estate?" Jamie questioned. "What does *jumeaux* mean?"

"The twins, *ma chérie*," Danielle said, "for the twin Pitons, I suppose."

Just then the estate house appeared. After the magnificent entrance, the house was just what Jamie had envisioned. A deep veranda, shutters to each room standing open, the porch columns decorated with hand-cut gingerbread trim. The old house was painted a pale yellow, the fretwork trim, white. Inviting rocking chairs, piled with bright cushions, lined the veranda. A huge tree, arms widely spread, sheltered the house.

"What an incredible tree," remarked Paul. "It's like the one in the square in town."

"Samaan, and probably three hundred years old," Andre said as he rounded the corner of the veranda with his father. "Welcome to Jumeaux. Please sit. Would you care for juice or a punch?"

"I would like to get cleaned up first," Danielle said.

"Of course. The guest bedroom and bath are around the corner and through the third door. Jamie?" Andre looked at her, the unspoken question in his eyes.

"Yes, thanks," she said as she watched Danielle disappear around the corner, "although the clothes I have on are all I've got, so perhaps you have something to throw over a chair for us. We don't want to muddy these lovely cushions."

"Let me see what the housekeeper can find. Can I offer you a rum punch or perhaps juice?"

"Have you any coconut water?" asked Jean-Pierre. "I will take my rum in that, please."

"I'll have a light punch," said Jamie.

"Same for me," replied Paul, "but it doesn't need to be light."

"Jamie," Andre said, "come with me. Maybe I can find a spare pair of shorts and a blouse for you."

Entering through the front door, Jamie was struck by the simplicity of the dwelling. The floors were unfinished wood, wide boards of local hardwoods. Some of the furniture looked as though it had been made by local craftsmen copying from pictures of finer English or French pieces. Other pieces appeared to be genuine antiques. The effect was charming, with a primitive note just right for the setting. A massive bureau placed against one wall and topped by an enormous tropical flower arrangement dominated that side of the room.

Poking his head into the kitchen, Andre gave the drink orders to Bertille, the housekeeper, and asked her to find some old sheets to cover the chairs where the men would sit. He then led Jamie into a front bedroom dominated by a four-poster bed with massive mahogany turned posts. Netting covered the top and fell on each side to puddle on the floor. Aside from a small table near the bed and one straight chair, the room was bare. The open shutters framed the view of the garden. A gold cup vine clambered up the posts, its exotic flowers like temple bells. *I wonder when my gold cup vine will look like that,* Jamie wondered.

Andre opened a door and walked into a large closet. "This used to be another, smaller bedroom, but my mother appropriated it for storage."

"I wish Danielle had told us to bring extra clothes."

"Surprised she didn't. She's been up that track before and knows how muddy it can be. Now, let's see. My fiancée left some things here on her last visit. Ah, here's a pair of shorts and a T-shirt. Why don't you see if these fit. Bathroom through there," he pointed. "When you're ready, join us on the porch for that drink."

"You're very kind," Jamie said, clammy in her damp clothes, the word fiancée smarting across her memory. She thought of Paul's comments, his accusations. In the bathroom Jamie finally settled for the tepid water which came out of the tap. As she dried herself on the towel hanging by the basin, she inhaled the fresh scent that comes only from line drying in the sun. The scent brought back a vivid memory of the line dried towels of her childhood, and she felt a pang of longing for her mother. *I'll call her tomorrow,* she thought. *Thank goodness the phone's finally installed.*

Finished with her cat bath, Jamie picked up the stylish shorts and T-shirt Andre had lent her. Curious, she peeked at the labels, wondering what they might tell about Andre's fiancée. The clothes fit just fine.

Pulling her hair into a French braid, she glanced at herself in the mirror, grateful to Andre for his sensitivity. It felt good to be clean and presentable again.

Taking the towel and washcloth she had used, Jamie bundled them and stepped into the kitchen to give them to the housekeeper.

"Mr. Demontagne was kind enough to let me use these."

Jamie stood rooted to the floor. The towel and washcloth slipped from her hands.

Bertille did not move. Instead, she offered herself in complete repose, her face as still as a carved African mask.

"I know you," Jamie whispered.

"Yes. And I know you."

"How?"

Bertille smiled. "How do you know me?"

Jamie licked her dry lips. "Something inside me."

"That is how it always is." Bertille remained quite still. As if bathing in quiet and touching something else, an ethos melted around her.

"I know your aura, child. Marcus mentioned it to me, but it was unnecessary. I knew you were coming."

Jamie felt pulled, as though time had shifted. Her vision grew dark around the edges. She felt hands on her shoulders, steadying her, as she was led to a chair. Gentle hands stroked her cheek and lifted her hair away from her neck.

Just then Andre entered the kitchen. "What's the problem, Bertille?"

Jamie smelled a strong, pungent aroma.

"Suddenly she began to faint. I put her in a chair and fetched some herbs. She comin' round now."

Andre chaffed her hands in his.

"Jamie, what happened?"

"I...I don't know. I came into the kitchen to give the towels to the housekeeper and suddenly...I felt like I was being pulled away. I thought I was going to pass out."

"Drink this." Bertille offered a glass of pale amber liquid.

"What is it?"

"Sugar apple juice," Andre said. "You need sugar and fluids now. You're not used to the heat. Same thing happened to you at the accident. Do you want to lie down, Jamie?"

"No," Jamie said, sipping at the juice. "I'm feeling better already. I'll just sit here a couple more minutes."

"I'll get Paul."

"No, don't. Please. I just need to sit for awhile. Please don't say anything to the others."

Andre glanced at Bertille, who nodded. "I will stay here with her. She'll be fine. No harm done."

Andre patted Jamie's shoulder, his touch gentle. "As you wish. We'll see you out on the veranda in a few minutes."

Jamie looked at Bertille. "Your name is Bertille?"

"Yes, always there have been Bertilles in my family."

"I must have seen you in town. You look so familiar. Oh, I know, my maid Delia said that Mama Bertille found her job for her. Are you that Bertille?"

"Delia is a cousin's daughter. Is she doing a good job for you?"

"Yes, she's wonderful except when she's bossing me around." Jamie smiled.

Bertille's face remained a mask, and Jamie wondered if she had said something wrong.

"I don't mean that in a bad way. It's just that she's taken charge." Jamie realized she was rambling.

"Bertille, thank you. I'm all right now. I think I'll go out and join the others." Jamie took the brown hand in her own and as she gazed into the dark eyes, the pulling sensation began again. Shaking her head to clear it, she pulled her hand free and quickly left the kitchen.

Joining the others on the veranda, she noticed Danielle's veiled look as she took in Jamie's smart outfit.

"*Ma chérie*, I thought you had not extra clothes with you?" Danielle commented.

"No, I didn't. Andre was kind enough to lend them."

"*Très jolie.* Do they belong to your mother, Andre?"

"No, not my mother's taste. They belong to Taylor, my fiancée from the States."

"I did not know you were to be married. Taylor, what an odd name," said Danielle. "Is this not a name for a man?"

"A family name. No more odd than Marie-Claude or one of those double French names, Danielle," Andre said.

They chatted for a few more minutes before Danielle stood. "We must go now, a long drive to the north. Monsieur Demontagne, Emile, Andre, *merci beaucoup pour votre hospitalité.*" She embraced each in turn, kissing one cheek and then the other.

"I'd like to say good-bye to Bertille," said Jamie. "I'll be right with you." She walked down the veranda and into the kitchen. Bertille turned from the sink where she was working. She again held herself in quiet repose, waiting.

"I've come to say goodbye."

"No goodbyes for us, child."

"Why do you say that?"

"Because we joined together in our spirits. It happens sometimes. It has happened to us."

"This aura...?"

"Yes, child."

"I don't understand? What does it mean?"

"Do not trouble yourself. All in good time," Bertille said.

"Is there, is there anything you can tell me?"

Bertille moved her hand along the edge of the sink. Laughter came from the living room, Paul's voice, a little brash. Bertille smiled. "One day, you will have a baby."

"But..."

"Life is a journey, child. We must guide ourselves and accept wisdom from others."

"You don't understand, my husband Paul..."

"I understand."

Jamie hung in the silence.

"You must go now."

Jamie started away and then turned back. "Why do I love the birds, the parrots?" Jamie managed, her throat dry.

"Because here on the island they are yours. You have dreamed them, yes? They are part of me as well. Our spirits be joined, you see. The parrots been waiting for your return."

"But..."

"They find you. You wear their feathers." Bertille motioned to Jamie's ears. "Do you feel frightened?"

Jamie hesitated. "No."

"That is good. There is no need for fear. In fact, you have cause for joy."

"But..." A horn sounded in the drive.

Bertille came to her and enfolded her to her bosom. "You must go now."

On the veranda, Andre was waiting. His dark eyes regarded Jamie.

"I told you we'd run into each other."

Lost in her own thoughts, Jamie didn't respond. "Bertille just said the oddest thing. That the parrots had been waiting for me."

Andre's face registered surprise. He reached out and gently touched the iridescent feather that hung from her ear. "Perhaps you have been waiting for the parrots."

CHAPTER TEN

The gold cup vine Jamie had planted by the front porch had grown three feet, its dark green foliage punctuated by showy bright yellow and cream blossoms. Jamie lifted one of the blooms and peered into the bell-shaped flower, its interior like a sensuous Georgia O'Keefe painting. Suddenly Delia tapped her on the shoulder, holding out a cup.

"Delia, will you stop making these disgusting teas for me to drink," Jamie instructed her housekeeper, as she took the pungently fragrant cup - an unknown herbal brew.

"This a tonic, Mistress. For energy."

"I'm not drinking it," Jamie snapped as she walked back into the house and poured the amber liquid down the drain. She wrinkled her nose as she sniffed the cup. *A tonic? A tonic for my marriage is what I need. Maybe Delia knows some spells that would make me more tolerant of Paul. Or better, would stop him from turning into his alcoholic mother.*

Jamie switched on the electric kettle and got a tea bag out of the cupboard. Her house, if not her life, was now neatly organized. She buttered a piece of bread and spooned on mango jam, then took her cup of tea and went out to the porch to sit. She thought back to last weekend and the chance meeting with Andre, the odd experience with Bertille.

She sipped the sweet tea, its familiar fragrance very different from the brew she had sent down the drain. The warmth of the cup in her hands was comforting. This island had tapped a part of her that had always shimmered just below the surface, an inner restlessness, a part she could never fully quiet. And she was dreaming again. Vivid, startling, sometimes frightening dreams, like the nightmare by the river. Sometimes simply beautiful.

She looked at her watch. Maybe she could catch her mom before she left for work. Jamie went into the house and picked up the phone.

"Mom, I hoped I'd catch you before you left for work," Jamie said.

"You okay? You sound..."

Jamie wondered how her mother could read her mood over the phone line. "I'm fine. Just missing you."

"You sound tired. Like you did when you were little and your dreams wouldn't let you sleep. You'd crawl into bed with Daddy and me..."

Jamie's throat tightened, tears pricking her eyes.

"And we'd tuck you between us and keep you warm until you fell asleep."

"I miss Dad," Jamie said.

"Me, too, Princess, me too. He's been gone for five years and I still expect him to walk in the door."

"Mom, I'm dreaming again."

"Ah..."

"You said Grandma dreamed..."

"She did. You're a lot like her."

"I wish I'd known her."

"You were just three when she died. I doubt you remember her."

"A little, maybe. Did she have birds?"

"She did. Parakeets. We took them after she died."

"Was there a big bird as well?"

"Odd you'd remember that. She had a parrot. We took it too, but it died a few weeks after she did. Heartbroken, I always thought."

"Maybe that's why I'm so intrigued with the parrots here?"

"Maybe. Your grandmother said when you were a baby that you had an iridescent aura that shimmered like feathers."

"Parrot feathers," Jamie murmured, stroking her earrings, wondering if the aura her grandmother had seen was the same Marcus had commented on.

"What?" asked her mother.

"Nothing. Mom...?"

"Yes?"

"How did you know when it was time to have me?"

There was silence on the line. "Are you thinking about having a baby?"

"Well, we've been married long enough. And you know I always wanted a big family."

Her mother chuckled. "No surprise there. You always envied your friends who had brothers and sisters and lots of cousins. But you didn't answer my question, Jamie."

"I'm not sure if this is the right time. Paul's been bringing it up." Now Jamie was sorry she'd opened this door.

"You'll know, Princess," her mother reassured. "It'll happen the way it's supposed to. Hey, I've got to fly or I'll miss my train. Love you. Bye."

"Bye." Jamie put down the phone and took a sip of her now cold tea. *I do want a baby, babies. That big family I've always dreamed of. But now? With Paul?* She shuddered, remembering his recent drunken advances, pushing him away.

"You'll never get pregnant this way," he'd said. "Isn't a baby what *you* want?"

"You never used to be cruel, Paul."

"You've changed since we came here, Jamie."

"What are you talking about?"

"You were always spacey, but here you're just coming unglued."

Jamie fought to stay calm. *Unglued! How dare he.* "What are you talking about?"

"Everybody here seems to know you. We run into some local in the rain forest and he carries on about your aura..."

"And that was my fault?"

"And this crap with the parrots..."

Jamie was indignant. "Paul, you're crazy."

"Those earrings you never take off."

Jamie's hand rose involuntarily to the feathers at her ears.

"See, like that. You touch them when you think no one's looking."

Jamie's hand fell back to her lap. "So you think we should have a baby?"

"Yeah, I do. You're acting like you're giving up on us. You push me away in bed. I'm saying maybe a baby would give us a fresh start."

"A fresh start was what I hoped this move would give us," Jamie said.

"And...?"

"And you're drinking more than ever, you're never home, always with your buddies. Should we bring a baby into that?"

Paul stood over her, his size intimidating. "And I go to work every day and bring home my paycheck. Don't I deserve some time with my friends? I even went on that hike last weekend, the one you didn't consult me about. How can you say I'm not trying?"

"You're changing the subject, Paul. We're married. We're supposed to do things together and..."

"Yeah, well..."

"And you need to look at your priorities. I don't think our marriage is high on your list. A baby, yeah, I want a baby, but we're going to have to be a lot better together before that happens."

"C'mon, Jamie. It's what we talked about before we came here. Maybe a baby is what we need."

Jamie wondered if she was in some upside-down parallel universe. Could Paul actually be thinking about them having a baby?

"We'd have to be better together, Paul. The way things are now - it wouldn't be fair - to me or the baby."

Paul looked away. "Maybe you're right." Then he reached out

for Jamie's hand. "I'll try if you will, Jamie. I'll try to be a better husband."

After he'd left the house, Jamie wondered where that left her. She wasn't sure she wanted to be a better wife.

Remembering the scene left her feeling worn out. *Maybe Delia's right. Maybe I am peaky. Maybe I need vitamins. I'll stop at Dr. Simpson's this afternoon while I'm in town and ask for some. And while I'm there, I'll ask about the birth control I'm using. Things are too unsettled now for me to get pregnant.*

A few blocks away, Paul pulled his truck into a driveway obscured for the most part by hibiscus bushes. He looked around. Not seeing anyone, he stepped out of the truck, walked to the side of the house, knocked, then let himself in.

"Oh, you are the stranger, Paul. I 'ave not seen you in four days," Danielle pouted.

Pulling the small, dark-haired woman into his chest, Paul nuzzled her hair, inhaling the musky scent. "Jamie's been on my case." *If Jamie gets pregnant,* he thought, *she'll be too busy to keep tabs on me.* He turned Danielle around and nibbled her bare shoulder.

"Why are we not in my bed?" Danielle pushed against him with slow, languid movements.

Paul withdrew slightly. "Not sure," he evaded.

Danielle ignored his uncertainty. "Does the island not make you, how do you Americans say, hot?"

Paul pulled away slightly, then seemed to make a decision. "Not the island. You, you make me hot." He captured Danielle's mouth in a bruising kiss. "Want to show me your bedroom?"

In town, Dr. Simpson's waiting room was full, but Jamie had learned to come prepared to wait. She pulled a sketch pad out of her tote, then closed her eyes and slowed her breathing, waiting for the rush of inspiration, remembering the night she had sketched the two parrots. She smiled to herself, knowing that sort of creative rush was not the way it usually happened. She laid one of her feather earrings on the blank sketch pad. The parrots. It always came back to the parrots. Bertille's voice whispered inside her head, "Our spirits are joined..." She could feel the safe warmth of being enfolded in Bertille's arms, could hear the great, calm, beating heart, could see Bertille's face, the wise dark eyes, the full nose, the high cheekbones and generous mouth. Her pencil flew across the page. Bold, abstract lines, distilling the essence.

The receptionist's voice interrupted her concentration.

"Mrs. Elliott, we are ready for you now."

Jamie followed her into the examination room and sat on the end of the examination table while she waited for Dr. Simpson.

"What brings you here, my dear?" asked the doctor, entering and closing the door behind him.

"Feeling tired. Thought maybe I needed vitamins..."

"Are you sleeping soundly?" he asked.

"I fall asleep, but sometimes my dreams wake me up."

"Perhaps a sleeping tea..."

Jamie grimaced. "My housekeeper keeps trying to give me that stuff. I keep pouring it down the drain."

"Let's have a look," Dr. Simpson said. He had listened to enough patients over the years to know there was more. "So your housekeeper is giving you bush medicine?" He sounded amused.

"Is there anything to it?"

"Oh, absolutely. Many bush remedies are quite powerful. I don't know what was in the drink your maid prepared for you, but I doubt it would hurt you."

"What's in them?"

"Your housekeeper can tell you the Patois names. Write them down and I'll tell you if it is all right to drink it. Some of these remedies are very helpful. Full of vitamins and trace minerals."

"So it would be all right to drink this stuff?"

"As I said, find out what's in the tea and give me a call. I've made a study of local remedies. In past times, many in St. Lucia had to rely on bush medicine. Much is harmless, even beneficial. However, there are some strong enough to cause a miscarriage, some even poisons, so it is wise to be careful..."

Jamie mulled over Dr. Simpson's comments as he proceeded with the examination.

"As for you, you seem to be in good health," Dr. Simpson said when he had finished. He wrote a few lines in Jamie's chart and then sat back, waiting.

Jamie sat silently for a full minute.

"My husband is talking about having a child."

"And...?"

"I really want a baby, but..." Jamie's voice trailed away.

Dr. Simpson waited patiently.

"Since we moved here my husband has been drinking more and more. His mother's an alcoholic," Jamie said as if to explain Paul's behavior.

"Does he think he has a problem?" the doctor asked.

"Of course not. Just tells me to stop nagging. He's never home."

"Do you think this is a good time for you to have a baby?"

"Paul says it will help. That if I don't, I'm giving up on our marriage."

"Do you think he's right?"

"I'm...I'm confused. He's mean and then apologizes. He's never home, but then he wants to work on the marriage and have a baby. I don't know..."

"You should not be pressured into something that doesn't feel right to you."

"I know. It's just that I don't know if this marriage can get better unless Paul stops drinking. What if he doesn't? I may lose my chance to have a baby."

"You have a lot to think about, my dear. Do you have a friend to talk to, your mother, perhaps?"

"I don't want to worry my mother. She's in New York. Nothing she can do."

"Then perhaps a friend. I think if you have someone to talk

to, you may start sleeping better, be less tired. And while you are here, let's talk about the kind of birth control you are using." He consulted the chart. "A diaphragm, correct?"

Outside Dr. Simpson's office, the humid air enveloped Jamie. She would be glad to get back to her house in Rodney Bay and the breezes coming off the ocean. Putting the bag containing her sketch book under her arm, she started off toward the market to find a transport bus. Lost in her own thoughts about her conversation with Dr. Simpson, she didn't hear the car honking.

"Jamie, hey, Jamie!" Barbara's voice finally penetrated her concentration. Jamie climbed into the car. "What in the world is on your mind?" Barbara asked. "You were a million miles away. No wonder Paul calls you spacey."

"No, he tells me I'm coming unglued," Jamie shot back.

"Oops, sorry. Hey, you know I'm just teasing..."

"I'm in no mood. Can you just take me home, please."

They drove out of the city. Jamie glanced at Barbara as she turned the car into the Vigie Airport road and pulled under an almond tree by the beach.

"What are you doing?"

"We are going to sit in the shade and talk," Barbara announced as she pulled the lever and popped the trunk. "I've got a couple of sand chairs in the back."

"You're being bossy again."

"Friend's prerogative."

Jamie looked at the stuff in the trunk. "Are you always this prepared?"

"I learned early on that I never knew when I might want something to sit on. And I always carry water and some car food."

"Car food?" Jamie asked.

"Food you carry in your car, hon! I never know when I might need something." Barbara sat down and opened a package of McVities fruit bars. "Now, tell me what's going on."

CHAPTER ELEVEN

Sunlight pierced the trees, gilding the forest canopy like a cathedral, shafts of light illuminating the fern- covered cliff like an altar. A waterfall fell from the top of the cliff, cascading into a pool below. A parrot swooped, fragmenting the mist into prisms of color, before disappearing into the dark foliage. The drone of insects diminished and the birds fell silent, as if hushed in reverence. For the few who knew this place, the silence was familiar - a waiting - known only to this sacred site.

Marcus sat on a boulder near the pool and removed his shoes, then his clothes. He stood for a moment, naked, an almost primordial being as he gazed around him. Already he was preparing his mind and heart for what was to come.

Using a calabash, he poured the pure cold water over himself, then used fragrant leaves to cleanse his body. The musky scent of the patchouli enveloped and soothed him. Revived from his day, cleansed of spirit, Marcus gave thought to the upcoming rituals. Already he was mouthing names, almost as if he held prayer beads, each bead a chief from long ago in their history.

Bertille had laid out a towel and a pair of clean shorts for him. As he dressed, he looked up at Bertille. They regarded each other, each aware of their burden, each aware of the honor. Marcus waited as Bertille bathed and purified herself. He watched her as the waterfall cascaded down, splashing on rocks, crystal in the waning sun.

Once finished she wrapped herself in a length of cloth and padded barefoot into the little daub and wattle house, its construction a reverence for the old ways. There she was joined by Marcus. She pliantly allowed Marcus to settle her on the soft mattress filled with sea grass. He covered her with a thin blanket and gently kissed her forehead. "I am always here," he said.

"I know, husband."

Bertille lay still with her eyes closed, cocooned in Marcus' presence. "My strength," she whispered.

Marcus waited, staring at the floor. He listened to Bertille's breathing, marking its quiet descending rhythm, the inward collapsing of all her faculties of mind and heart into some profound repose. Then she was gone...

Marcus kissed her gently on the forehead. Then, satisfied with Bertille's surroundings and her safety, he made his way out of the little house. He tried to quiet his mind, quelling thoughts of the day, the uneasiness of the men on the cutting crew as their work brought them close to the Deroche land, the conversation he had overheard.

Etienne had been reassuring one of the crew. "Marcus tell me he leave signs in the bush to mark the Deroche land."

"What kind of signs? If it be things wit' feathers 'n stuff wrapped in little bags, I go back down the cut," the workman had replied.

Marcus sighed. He knew the local people relied on him and Bertille for bush medicine remedies. He also knew they were feared. *It is better so,* he thought. *To protect this place, this legacy. Important they not come near.* He focused his breathing, pushing aside the intrusive thoughts.

Marcus made his way to steps cut in the cliff, dampened by the mist from the waterfall. Carefully positioning his bare feet, he counted his steps as he always did, noting the marks in the ground from his journeys. And those of the keepers before him. *Who will tell the stories after me,* he wondered? *It is time to find the one who will come after, one who can bear the honor and the burden.* He pushed aside the hanging ferns and entered the darkness. His hand found the flambeau and he lit it with a coal from last night's fire, a coal he had in the hollow of a rock. The small torch partially lit the interior of the cave, which stretched back into a plumbing darkness. Marcus made his way deep into the earth.

When he arrived at the most sacred place, Marcus stopped. Flame licked on small eddies of air, and shadows danced on the walls. He began his ritual. His voice resonant, his words sounding from the walls as they had done since ancient times, caressing the dank quiet. There in that hidden place, Marcus gave his support and full faith to his people. Sometimes his voice rose then fell away, like the waves lapping the shore. He stood in the flickering light deep in the bowels of the earth, chanting as he remembered.

Even after they were made slaves, the knowledge of this place was passed from generation to generation and the royal lineage known, passed down by oral tradition from time only remembered now by the stories. Both Bertille and Marcus were direct descendants of Caribe ancestors, the royal line, the keepers of the cave and its traditions. They listened to the spirits who had protected this place since the parrots dropped the seeds from which sprouted the land. And some day, they would be laid here to rest in the breast of their island mother.

The stories also told of other times when the caves had harbored other fugitives, and Marcus thought about the information in the stories that pertained to the Diamant family, to Clarisse's forebears. He thought that someday, to protect this place, he might have to tell what he knew. But that time was not yet. The spirits would guide him. His voice echoed in the shadows. "Wise ancestors, reveal to me your design."

Marcus knew the name of each chief in each generation, the story of each one's life and accomplishments. Some had been good chiefs, some weak, some cruel. But the cruelest of all, he judged, was the chief who had given his daughter to the French when they first arrived on the island, welcoming the whites and thinking to gain their allegiance by the union of his royal line with those who came in the ships with white wings.

The Caribes fought their new masters but were quickly enslaved. The union of the princess and the French settler produced children who were of Caribe and French lineage. Marcus knew from the begat stories that in his family's blood both these strands were joined.

The children of the princess and the French settler entered the blood lines on the island, then co-mingled with the blood of the Africans brought to work the cane fields and others who came later. *We are truly a people of the world,* thought Marcus, but he knew they had not yet gained true acceptance from the whites or their due in ownership and development of their island home.

Much later, Marcus made his way out of the cave, pausing only to make sure the ferns were replaced and hiding the entrance. He was weary, his throat parched from his chanting. He knelt by the pool and lifted the cold water to his mouth, then sat back on his heels, breathing in the stillness of the evening before he returned to sit by his wife. When she returned they would break their fast together.

Bertille was free, pure spirit, flying high over the twin peaks of the island. She flew in feathered flight across the timeless planes that had no past, no future, no beginning and no end. A panorama of images offered themselves, surging across her wings, and now she paused, dipping toward ethereal mists, and she was afraid.

She was not alone. A soaring parrot now swooped down to fly beside her, eyes gleaming in the translucent light. Bertille flew on as images formed in the mists; suddenly hardened edges of St. Lucia appeared, and flames, great flames sucked and flattened in vile winds, laying bare the verdant growth. Currents swept her up on a beat of wings, then both birds were flying together, turning away into a gossamer veil and away from fire and smoke. Only words followed them, and they tore at Bertille's heart: *Find the lost ones...*

She was tired now, and the words sapped her spirit. If the lost ones were not found, the forest would disappear forever, and the island would die. Bertille flew through veils and thinning mists, her strength ebbing. When she closed her wings and fell, she looked for her companion, but its feathered spirit was gone.

When Bertille awoke on her bed of sea grass, she was panting, gulping in drafts of air. It was twilight, forest sounds were returning, the wild buzz and click of insects, the raucous tree frogs. "Marcus..." she whispered. He reached out for her hand.

Later they sat quietly beside the coal pot, watching its glowing coals in the evening dark. Marcus looked carefully at Bertille. She was very tired, as he was.

"Who will come after us?" he asked.

Bertille shook her head as she picked up a basket containing some freshwater crayfish, found earlier under rocks in the river. She wrapped each in a piece of banana leaf, making a small bundle.

"All our rituals, Marcus," she said, laying out the crayfish to steam over the coals. "These rituals of our everyday life, feeding ourselves, the way we build a shelter...they connect us to the old ways, to the spirits of those before."

"But these rituals will be lost if we do not soon choose those who will take our places," Marcus said simply.

Her eyes watched him, like black glass in the firelight. "We are not so old yet, but you are right. It takes years to learn the stories."

"It is a heavy burden. To be a keeper is an honor, but the young ones do not seem so interested in the old island ways."

"Times change," Bertille said. "By the way, how did you get the crew to cut on the boundary of our land?"

"I marked the edges. Andre and Emile will be satisfied."

"These workers are from the village, you know how frightened they get when they come near this part of the rain forest."

Marcus nodded. "For generations the keepers of this place have made sure that strangers do not enter."

"It is so. The village children learn at their mother's knees not to come this way."

"The crew will soon be gone." He watched her again, poking at the steaming crayfish. "Bertille?"

"Yes, my husband?"

"This last dream of yours, I..."

"It was bad."

Marcus watched the flames and savored the tangy aroma of the steaming fish. His mouth watered as he waited on Bertille.

"It was a bad dream, husband. Our island was on fire, all was being lost."

A piece of charcoal broke, sending up a tiny plume of sparks.

"What else?" he asked.

"I was told to find the lost ones."

"Ah." Marcus' breath left him.

"As our people scatter they forget the old ways." Bertille pulled a breadfruit leaf off a nearby tree and rinsed it in the pool. Then she collected cold water from the waterfall. They would drink from the same gourd and eat from the same pot.

She continued. "This island will always be here, but if our heritage is lost, our people will be lost. If they forget how we came to be here..."

"The outside world diminishes us," Marcus said, as she joined him.

"Yes. But more, I sense the spirits around us are vexed."

"We are safe, Bertille. We have been safe for over three hundred years. It will not change..." Marcus said. "Here, let me peel a crayfish for you." His big hand reached into the coal pot.

"I am afraid."

"The spirits will not abandon us, Bertille. The cave protects our beginnings." He looked at her with love in his eyes. Its abiding goodness was caught in the firelight.

"It will take years to train a new keeper," Bertille said simply. "Someone to keep our secrets, someone to carry on the begat stories of our people and all our knowledge."

"Someone who must have courage to know the stories," Marcus added, biting into his crayfish.

"Who can be custodian to the healing and other gifts?"

"...And your dream world."

Bertille hesitated. "During my feathered journey there was another parrot."

Marcus looked at her sharply. "That has never happened before."

"No."

"What does it mean?"

"I don't know. But I wonder if I was in *that* spirit's feathered journey."

"Ah."

"Marcus?"

"What?"

"The parrots are disappearing. People catch them to eat or to sell their feathers. Soon they will be gone from this island."

"Emile talks about a sanctuary for them. And our Jack, perhaps his knowledge... and Andre will help - if he gets his hotel."

"That depends on his father."

Marcus shrugged. "As you say, times change."

"About us, who can we choose to use our gifts and knowledge wisely?"

"Perhaps our son, our Jack?"

Bertille ate slowly, thinking. "Do you think he has the courage?"

"Courage, yes. But going away from the island draws him. Leaving draws everyone. It's difficult."

Bertille picked up a mango, using her thumb to test its ripeness. "I told you about this Jamie."

"Yes. She is unusual."

"She is a woman of dreams. But I don't like her marriage to that man, it drains her strength." Bertille used her teeth to pull a piece of skin from the fruit, then held it out to Marcus.

"Paul?"

"He is a weak man. Not a bad man, but weak."

Marcus bit into the juicy mango. "I too wonder about Jamie. I told you of my talk with Andre. I told him he had a new aura. I wonder if it comes from Jamie - did you see the way they looked at each other?"

"But she is married. It is not a good thing."

"Andre is a man of honor, but..."

"But what?" Bertille asked.

"This other feathered spirit from your dream travel. I wonder now..."

Bertille smiled. "Her influence on me was profound. But she is from New York, far from our ways."

"Perhaps in her heart she has room for our ways."

Bertille stood and gently massaged Marcus's powerful shoulders. "I have asked Delia to bring me something of hers."

"Perhaps you will learn something."

"Also, something that belongs to this Paul, her husband."

"Ah."

Marcus and Bertille completed their quiet ritual of putting out the fire and storing away the charcoal. They moved with the pure essence of all good rituals: quietly, kindly, each with gentle support of the other.

CHAPTER TWELVE

"*Sa que fait?* What's happening?" Delia called to the housekeeper next door as she stood in the yard shaking a mat braided from couscous grass. Her small frame belied the strength in her sinewy arms, and she shook the mat vigorously again and again, dislodging the last persistent motes of dust. Hoop earrings and cornrowed braids danced in syncopation with her efforts, and her brown face bloomed into a big grin. She was pleased with her find: Paul Elliott's cufflink, now safely in her apron pocket.

"Your Mister and Mistress goin' up the hill tonight for the party?" she asked her neighbor, already knowing the answer.

"Eh, eh, the Mistress, she been crying all this week. No invitation be comin', and she with her dress hangin' in the closet."

Delia smiled smugly as she returned to the house and positioned the rug near the side of the bed. She pulled up the sheets and plumped the pillows. An invitation to a government minister's party at one of the big houses up in Cap Estate was prized, and as far as she knew the only other people in the neighborhood to be invited were the Careys.

"*Woy, woy, woy,*" Delia muttered as she began ironing a length of gauzy hand-painted fabric. The pale green material, patterned with hibiscus flowers, was lovely, but the wrinkles were stubborn. She flicked water on an especially stubborn spot and wondered whether the Mister would get home in time for the party.

"Delia," Jamie called. "I'm back from town. I did the usual park and run on the square and went over to M&C's to see if they had the paint I've been needing for the porch." Jamie paused and smiled at Delia.

"Oh, thank you for ironing my dress for tonight. I'm going to go soak in the tub and relax. Castries always wears me out. Has Mr. Elliott called?"

"No, Mistress. No calls this afternoon." Delia hung the fabric on several hangers in the bedroom. "I be leavin' after I finish the ironin' if that be all right with you. The floors mopped and dinner in the cold box. If you want me stay 'til the Mister get home, I can." Her eyes narrowed, just for a moment revealing the strong woman within. Then she was smiling again.

"You're a sweetheart for offering, but I want you to catch the last transport this afternoon and get back to your man. I'll see you on Monday and tell you all about the party."

"I be lookin' forward to that, I can tell you. You and Mr. Elliott lucky to get that special piece of paper invitin' you up the hill."

"Go on now, Delia, and let me run my tub. See you on Monday."

Jamie padded into the bathroom and began to fill the tub. As the water rose she swirled it with her hand, anticipating its therapeutic effects on her tired body. This was going to be a lovely evening, but what if Paul... She had to face it. He could come home drunk. Jamie swirled the water fiercely. No problems would spoil this evening. "I'm going to a party," she said out loud, "and I'm going to have a good time."

She secured her long dark hair on top of her head and climbed into the tub. She groaned as she immersed herself, shedding tensions and soothing muscles. Paul...

He came back to her as her first thought. It had to be. What was happening with him? And her talk with Barbara about Paul and the baby. That had been exquisitely embarrassing, but Jamie was glad she'd opened up to her friend. There was real support there. But the talk had reinforced some hard realities. Things with Paul would have to change before she could bring a baby into their world.

Perhaps tonight he wouldn't drink too much. After all, this invitation was really his: he had been singled out by the Minister of Development. Maybe Paul was right, his way of doing things, man talk, the guys after work having a beer... Her eyes moved to her arm and the faint bruise half hidden in the soap bubbles, the place where Paul had grabbed her last time they'd argued. *He didn't mean it,* she thought, uneasy at the unpleasant reminder of the new threshold of their relationship. She would need to apply some makeup to cover it.

She closed her eyes and thought of brighter things. She would look good in her dress, a celebration of self and her creativity. When the thought came she half expected it. She allowed it to linger. Would Andre be there tonight? Would he have Taylor with him?

And what did Taylor look like? She had to admit she was curious. Perhaps she wouldn't be there. Jamie smiled. *I've worn your clothes, Taylor,* she thought. *And I don't know what you look like.* How odd. Jamie sank sumptuously into the water. God, that felt good...

Andre. And Bertille and Marcus. The water stilled over her suddenly quieted body. She had almost fainted during the meeting with Bertille. And Marcus had had an impact on her. Both of them had touched her deep inside, enhancing the colors and echoes of St. Lucia itself. It made her uneasy, all the talk about parrots and how they were waiting for her. The thoughts broke free from where she had hidden them, surfacing and disturbing her. But she had known too Bertille's warm enfolding embrace, the softness of her maternal bosom. She knew instinctively there could be no danger there, no - she searched for a word she did not use - wickedness. Cause for joy, Bertille had said. And last night's dream. A parrot flying, and she was a feathered companion, trying to keep up with the more powerful bird.

Abruptly, Jamie got out of the tub, responding to deep yearnings of the child within her. She needed to talk to her mother. She wrapped herself in a large towel, then settled into a cozy rattan chair. Quickly she dialed her mother's apartment in New York.

"Hello?"

"Hi, Mom!"

"Jamie!"

"I'm so glad I caught you."

"So how are things, dear?"

"Going well."

"And Paul?"

She missed a beat, and she knew her mother would catch it. "He's fine. He likes his work. Mom, in fact I called because we're going to an important party tonight. I wanted to tell you about my dress." As Jamie described her dress, her mother oohed and aahed, just as Jamie had known she would. She felt better already.

"How will you wear your hair? Will you put it up?" her mother asked.

"No, I'm going to pull it over one shoulder and wear flowers in my hair. I think I will be quite stunning, if I do say so. Wish you were here to see me, Mom. I really miss you. You would love the flowers here. I go to sleep at night smelling the jasmine outside my bedroom window."

"It all sounds just lovely, princess. You'll look beautiful. Do you have a tan?"

Jamie laughed. "You know me too well, Mom."

"A tan always enhanced your green eyes."

"Mom?"

"Yes?"

"You remember my dreams as a child? You'd console me, help me get back to sleep."

Her mother laughed. "I'd read to you at two in the morning."

"Cinderella."

"Right. You always liked the classics."

"Mom?"

"What?"

"I'd dream about birds, remember? Parrots. Did you ever have dreams like that?"

The line went quiet for a moment.

"It was your grandmother who was the dreamer."

"It's odd," Jamie said, her heart skipping a beat.

"You probably don't remember, but we were concerned enough about your dreams to take you to see a therapist when you were small."

"I sort of remember that. What did he say?"

"Nothing that made much sense to us. Said you were extremely creative. I've got the report somewhere. So we made sure you had music and dance lessons. It was art where you bloomed."

"But what did he say about my dreams?" Jamie persisted.

"That they were the mind's way of releasing the tensions of the day."

"Oh, well, that's probably why I'm dreaming of parrots so much."

"Are your days tense, princess?"

"It's not that, it's just very different here, Mom. Everything is different, unexpected. But I really love the island. More than I thought."

"And Paul? Does he like it?"

"I think it's harder for him to adjust to change. He thinks my parrot dreams mean I'm coming unglued."

The silence was too extended. Her mother filled it. "I went for my annual physical today."

"You okay?"

"Doctor told me I'll live to be a hundred. You know all the Jenkins women do - live to be a hundred - then we die of sheer orneriness."

Jamie laughed.

"Well, dear, I know you're getting ready for your party, so I'll let you go. I promise to write, although nothing's really happening here. I'm trying to houseclean a bit."

Jamie smiled into the phone. "Lots of luck. I've unpacked everything here but can't find Grandma's lace handkerchief. The one she gave me to carry at my wedding. Well, it'll turn up."

"Of course it will. It's there somewhere."

"Love you, Mom."

"And I love you. Have a good time at the party."

Jamie hummed to herself as she brushed her hair and pulled it to one side. A little foundation and blush, some shadow and pencil to accentuate her eyes. She picked up the jasmine perfume she had found in a little shop near Castries and touched it to her pulse points. *Pencil, where's the eyeliner pencil?* Irritated, she poked around and found a spare. Standing in front of the large mirror, clad only in strapless bra and panties, she held the long rectangle of silk behind her back with her arms outstretched. She wrapped the painted silk around her, crossed the ends over her breasts, reveling in the sensuous feel of the fabric. Pulling the two ends behind her head, she tied them behind her neck and let the remainder flow down her back. Pearl studs in her ears and she was finished.

She stepped back and looked at herself critically. "Not bad," she said with a satisfied smile.

An hour later, when Paul came through the door, she was no longer smiling.

"Paul..."

"I know, I know. I just need a minute. Got my shirt and stuff laid out?"

"Everything's ready." She watched him walk to the bedroom. No stagger, thank God, but she could smell the beer.

"A quick shower and that's it. Won't be a minute."

Jamie stood there holding her clutch purse. She listened to the shower and rambling muttering.

He came out wet and smiling. "Forgiven?"

"Please hurry, Paul."

He waved a wet arm around. "So where's my socks?"

"Paul, it's all laid out on top of the dresser. Look, I'm going to sit on the porch and wait for you."

"One goddamn cufflink. What am I supposed to do with that? Cut one of my arms off?"

"Paul, just get ready, it must've rolled somewhere. Use another pair."

"Okay. See how easy I am to get along with? And remember, that Minister of Development wants me. Company shirts'll be there, but the only engineers invited were Brian and me. Howzabout that?"

Jamie clenched her fists, hating the slur of his words. She went out to the porch and sat. The little bullfinch joined her.

"How do I look, Rufous? Not that my husband would notice." Only later, when there had been too much quiet, did she go to investigate. Paul was passed out on the bed.

"Oh, dear God..." Jamie poked him in the ribs. He snorted and turned over. Cold fury swept through her.

She picked up the phone and dialed, but Barbara and Brian had obviously left on time.

Well, I'll just have to make a solo entrance, Jamie thought as she left the house. *And try not to get too sweaty walking to the St. Lucian Hotel to get a taxi.* At the edge of the porch she picked a sprig of jasmine to enhance her perfume and tucked it behind her ear. She stood for a moment inhaling the scented air, hoping the fragrance would calm her racing heart.

CHAPTER THIRTEEN

The taxi labored over the rutted roads as it ascended into the hills of Cap Estate. Formerly a sugar plantation, the land had been subdivided ten years ago. Now magnificent villas hugged the cliffs, the local bush transformed into lush, tropical gardens.

The driver needed no directions to find Minister Desmond Xavier's huge villa perched on a bluff overlooking the Caribbean sea. The lights of the house could be seen from almost everywhere in Cap. Jamie had heard Paul talk about the flamboyant Minister of Development, rumored to have grown wealthy over the years because of his insider's knowledge about projects to be funded by foreign aid. Barbara said the Minister and his wife, Julita, gave memorable parties.

Even from a distance the villa seemed huge and opulent. Inhaling the fragrance of the jasmine pinned in her dark hair, Jamie allowed the perfume to calm her anger at Paul and her impatience to get to the party. At this rate she would certainly make an entrance. The transport van finally stopped after negotiating a long drive through a row of towering palms.

Putting the fare and a generous tip in the driver's outstretched hand, Jamie surveyed the villa. Flickering torches and lighted candles beckoned to paths winding through the gardens. The front entrance was flanked by enormous bougainvilleas growing out of huge metal cauldrons left over from sugar cane days. Lighted from below, the bougainvilleas threw shadows over the stuccoed walls, cerise flowers covering the outstretched vines.

Jamie took a deep breath and entered the open front door.

Smoothing her gown, she stood alone for a moment, taking in the pale marble floors and high ceilings. Columns of coral stone lined the entrance foyer, directing her eyes to wide steps leading down into the living room. Everywhere were large bouquets of the tropical blooms she had come to recognize, ginger lilies, torch flowers, anthurium. "I wish Mom could see this," she murmured.

A servant in creole dress greeted Jamie. "The party has moved out by the pool. Would you like me to take your wrap?"

"Thank you, no, I'll keep it with me," Jamie responded as she began descending the broad steps into the expansive living room. Comfortable couches upholstered in a heavy cream silk had been gathered into four separate and inviting seating areas. The highly polished travertine marble on the floors reflected the lights of countless candles, flames protected from the breeze by hurricane shades in many sizes.

It was a beautiful room. Calm and neutral, a perfect foil for the daytime brilliance of the turquoise sea and bright blue tropical sky. Jamie followed the sound of voices and music until she stood, framed by two coral stone pillars, surveying the party in progress around the lighted pool.

"Jamie, you're like a fair flower among all the dark- skinned beauties here tonight. Will you come and dance with me?" Henry Wilkerson slipped his arm around her waist and pulled her to his side suggestively. Paul's boss on this project, and the man who'd rented their house for them, Henry was a notorious womanizer. But Jamie knew she could not jeopardize Paul's job by being rude. She had handled passes before and knew Henry would be an annoyance, not a real problem.

"No," she replied, "not until you get me a drink."

"Of course, my dear. What will it be?" Henry asked.

"A rum punch will do nicely, thanks. And have them make it a light one, please."

"Coming right up. Now don't go away, because after your drink I'll claim my dance. Where's Paul, by the way?" Henry questioned. "I saw him this afternoon and made it clear this was not a party to miss."

"He was tied up and asked me to come ahead," Jamie evaded. "He'll be along soon."

"I should hope so, it would really be quite rude not to make an appearance."

"As I said, he should be along shortly. Now, Henry, the sooner you get that drink for me the sooner you'll get your dance." Jamie masked her irritation with a light bantering tone.

Henry winked at her and set off for the bar. She watched him talking to the bartender as he gathered her rum punch and what looked like a larger snifter of cognac, not his first or second by the look of him. She then saw the bartender look in her direction and recognized James, the bartender from Mick's.

Often she saw James walking to work in the late afternoon. She nodded and smiled when he caught her eye.

"Here, my dear," said Henry, putting a glass in her hand. "You know all you have to do is come by my house some evening and I'll make you a rum punch from my own recipe. It's all in the sugar syrup, you know. Secret ingredients I'll never divulge."

Henry put his arm around her waist again. "Ready for that dance now?" Jamie set her glass down and turned into Henry's outstretched arms. The steel pan band was playing "Unchained Melody," the melody incongruous with the steel drums, but the music certainly fit the setting. *Like so many of the colors,* thought Jamie. *They'd seem garish in New York, but here they look just right.* She let herself drift as Henry, an excellent dancer, moved her gracefully about the floor. When she found herself looking for Andre, she checked herself.

"Will I get to meet the host and his wife?" she asked quickly.

"He was here earlier, but I haven't seen him for the last half hour, probably in a corner with his mistress of the moment. He has a taste for young flesh, you know. That's his wife, Julita, over there."

Jamie turned to see a slender woman with elegant bearing and regal African features. Her pale yellow silk sheath was accented by strands of antique amber beads. Jamie thought she looked like an African queen, hair cut short in a natural style, heavy gold tugging at her earlobes. Julita saw Henry's glance and walked toward them.

"My dear," she nodded in Jamie's direction, "and Henry, welcome to our home."

"Thank you for inviting me, Julita. May I present Jamie Elliott. Her husband, Paul, works on the water project. He was detained but will be here shortly," said Henry. "The Elliotts arrived just recently."

"Your home is exquisite," Jamie said, smiling into Julita's amber eyes.

"Yes, it is all we had hoped it would be. How do you like St. Lucia? Are you acclimating to the climate? We who are born here are used to the heat, but sometimes it is difficult for people not used to tropical weather."

"Actually, I've found the weather very pleasant. There always seems to be a breeze off the ocean. Of course, today when I was in Castries, I couldn't wait to get back." She sipped her drink.

"Yes, anywhere you are away from the breeze can be very hot. Just building up the hill a little, as we did here, means we always have the trade winds to cool us. Well, I am so glad you could join us, Jamie. I must compliment you on your dress. It is exquisite." Julita reached out and briefly touched one of the hand-painted hibiscus. "You must have found it in one of those wonderful boutiques in New York. Oh, excuse me, I see someone I must greet."

She turned imperiously to Henry. "Take Mrs. Elliott to meet the others, Henry." With that she departed, a musky evocative scent lingering in her wake.

Henry steered Jamie toward a group at the far end of the pool terrace.

"Rumor has it this house was Desmond's way of holding onto Julita. Apparently she found out about an affair he was having," Henry whispered. "He wanted to build down by the water. There's a spectacular little cove at the bottom of the hill. Quite romantic, although there's a wicked undertow. Anyway, Desmond was in no position to have it his way. So the villa is on the hill."

Henry pulled Jamie toward the music. "Come on, you promised to finish our dance. Then I want to introduce you to some of the others in the gang." He breathed into her neck as he slid an arm around her waist. Jamie clasped his hand and gently undid his arm. She put her arm through his elbow and smiled up at him.

"Henry, don't be pushy," she said in a teasing fashion.

"Well, you can't blame me for trying, can you? And where in bloody hell is that husband of yours? He will really embarrass the company if he doesn't put in an appearance. The Minister has a long memory. You should have made sure he got here."

"Me?" Jamie shot back. "Since when is it my responsibility to get him to a party? He's the one who works for Omega, not me."

If he were here, she thought ruefully, *I wouldn't have to put up with you pawing me.* She smiled at Henry and said, "You can chew him out when you see him. Let's join the rest of the party."

"Let me get our drinks topped up first," Henry said, and left Jamie leaning against a balustrade at the edge of the terrace. She could see the lighted paths that wandered off into the gardens surrounding the villa. A cruise ship moved slowly in the distance, the strings of lights on its masts looking for all the world like it was celebrating Christmas. Down the coast she could see the glow of the lights of Castries and the pinpricks of light dotting the receding hills, each point of light a dwelling nestled in the tropical vegetation.

The terrace, also decorated with groups of candles, glittered with reflected light. It was a magical setting, complete with fragrant gardenias floating on the pool.

Wonderful smells of spicy roasted meat wafted toward her, and Jamie realized she had not eaten anything since a hot dog in Castries eight hours earlier. She was famished.

I'd better see what there is to eat, she thought, *or another drink will put me to sleep.*

She saw him first, across the music and flow of voices. He was watching the stars and shadows. She found herself waiting for just a moment, savoring him, before calling to him. "Andre?"

He turned quickly, which pleased her in some indescribable way. "Jamie!"

"I was wondering if you would be here tonight," she said, then quickly tempered it. "I thought perhaps I could meet Taylor. I feel I ought to know her after wearing her clothes."

Andre smiled down at her. "She's in New York."

"Ah."

"What, ah?"

"It's hard to take New York out of a person."

His eyes darkened. "You seem to manage. In fact, more than manage. Say, what happened with Bertille in the kitchen at Jumeaux? She has her ways, but I've never seen her as deeply moved as that. Wouldn't say much when I asked her."

"Who knows? She held me to her bosom - can you imagine? She's so warm and caring." Jamie pushed away the rest of it, the pulling away into darkness, the odd talk of parrots.

"I did that as a child. So did Emile."

"What?"

"Hug into her, press against her bosom. All was right with the world then. No child's problems, nothing." He hesitated. "What do you think of Marcus?"

"They go well together. They must be very happy."

"Yes, they are. And very special. Look, there's the Careys, and Jean-Pierre and Danielle. Like to join them?" He took her hand.

Barbara beamed at Jamie. "What a gorgeous dress. Where's Paul?" Her eyes fixed on Jamie's hand still grasped in Andre's, then darted away.

"Here's Emile, and you know everyone else from your outing the other day."

Abruptly Jamie's arm was captured. "Ah, fresh blood. My dear, I'm Connie Clark." A short, round-figured woman of middle age pulled Jamie away from the group. "We are such an incestuous bunch. Fresh faces are always welcome. Now let me tell you about all these rogues. George is not my better half although he may think so from time to time. Of course, I put him in his place constantly." She smiled at her husband, who returned her smile with a placid patience.

"Liz, over there, is a dear but long suffering. She's quite a loner. Paints and reads in her spare time. We don't see much of her except at parties where she is obliged to show up. Her husband used to work for Omega, but left the island with a local beauty and sailed to Tahiti. Can you believe it! Liz didn't have anywhere else to go, so she stayed on. And that handsome young fellow over there is Nate. He gets invited to all the parties because he's unattached."

She continued non-stop, waving to a man seated near the pool, who waved back. "That's Ian Danville. One of the head honchos at Omega. Take my advice and don't get yourself in a corner alone with him. Our Henry can be a friendly nuisance who sprouts an additional arm with each cognac, but Ian can be a mean drunk. Of course, we all love Henry, but he loves all us ladies a little too much. It didn't used to be so bad before his wife left a year ago, but since then he's, well, I think he's really lonely, and we all look out for him, but he can be something of a boor when he's had too much. Word of warning. Don't ever take him up on his invitation to sample his rum punch recipe."

Connie paused to take a breath as Jamie wondered if she wanted to hear more. She glanced longingly back at Andre, who caught her glance and grinned. She was definitely stuck. Just then Henry approached the two women.

"Henry, I was just telling Jamie to watch out for you." Connie captured Henry's arm affectionately. It was clear that although Henry might be a bit much at times, Connie was fond of him.

"She's always telling the new, young ones to watch out for me. But I'm really quite harmless." He put his arm around Jamie's waist and began pulling her toward the dance floor. Swaying with the music, he spun her around.

"You really are lovely," he whispered.

Jamie pulled away slightly. "Henry, you're sweet, but let's not forget you're my husband's boss."

"Yes, that's quite right, and perhaps you ought to remember that when you push me away." His teasing had an edge to it.

"If that's a threat, I don't like it at all." Jamie's back went rigid.

"Excuse me, you don't mind my cutting in, do you, Henry?"

Andre's arm slipped around Jamie's waist and gently swept her into a cluster of dancers.

"Thank God," Jamie said, needing to say something but thoroughly lost in Andre's arms.

"He's a lech."

"Connie did warn me."

Andre laughed. "Good old Connie. I saw you trapped with her."

"She goes on and on without stopping."

"I think she acts on the principle that she has to get it all out before you are whisked away - like just now."

"He tried to come on to me, Paul's boss."

Andre's face hardened. "Did he now."

She was dancing then, feeling good in Andre's arms. She liked the way he didn't get too close, instead allowing her to move and sway gently to the music, yet guided by his lead.

Then everything shattered.

There was angry shouting first, emanating from the top of the stairs. All eyes watched as a slender young girl flung herself down the elegant staircase, a harsh and ugly contrast. Trying to hold the pieces of her dress together, she ran for the door.

"Pauline, come back!" shouted the man who started down the stairs after her.

"Stay here," Andre said quietly in Jamie's ear. Then he was making his way towards the stairs.

Jamie watched him go, his journey quiet and unobtrusive as he made his way through the guests now standing in shock.

Then Julita was on the staircase landing, a shimmering rage of yellow and amber, gun metal gray glinting in her hand. "You bloody bastard. With guests in the house! In our bed with a fifteen-year-old."

The Minister stopped halfway down the stairs.

Jamie watched as Andre smoothly interceded, escorting the minister back up the stairs.

"I told you to be discreet - is that too much to ask? You think with your lulu instead of your brain," Julita hissed.

Jamie felt herself being pulled back into the shadows. "Ian…"

"Just want to get you out of the line of fire. Julita has finally caught Desmond in the act, and she may actually shoot him this time." Ian pulled a bottle of rum off the bar and took a long swallow. He kept his other hand around Jamie's wrist.

Jamie pulled away but stayed in the dark corner. What had Connie said? A mean drunk - but what could happen with all these people around? He couldn't be that dangerous. Julita with a gun might very well be.

"Actually, she's an excellent shot," said Ian as if reading her mind. "She practices weekly at the gun range. Desmond should have known better when he married her. Of course, the island roro is that she forced his hand as she was only seventeen herself, fresh out of the convent school. It seems Desmond has always had a yen for young flesh."

Desmond and Andre started up the stairs toward Julita. The Minister's hands were outstretched in supplication, talking to her softly, hoping to distract her.

"Put the gun down, pet," Desmond crooned as he watched a man silently approach Julita from the rear.

"Don't 'pet' me, you lecherous old fool. When I think of all the young girls you've molested, I'd be given a medal if I castrated you."

Julita was so enraged she did not see the dark hand that suddenly grabbed her arm.

"No!" Andre said, taking the last few steps two at a time. But he was too late.

Julita struggled, and as the gun was forced down, she fired. The man fell to the floor clutching his foot. Julita looked down at him with contempt.

"Archie, what the hell did you do that for? You've gone and shot yourself in the foot again."

"Oh, my God," said Jamie. "She actually shot that man." She watched Andre disarm Julita.

"Well, my dear, you've now had a proper introduction to the cream of St. Lucian society. The wife of the Minister of Development has just shot the Chief of Police in the foot. Last time he did it himself."

"Shot himself in the foot?" Jamie's mind was reeling.

"He did. Look, this will blow over. No one will press charges. Julita will go to New York and buy herself some presents, Desmond will find another fifteen-year-old to suck his dick, and the Chief of Police will shoot anyone who reminds him of this debacle."

"But he's hurt."

"Somebody will put Archie in a truck and take him to hospital," Ian said, steering Jamie away from the terrace.

"Let's walk down to the cove." Ian pointed to a torch-illuminated path. "I saw the Careys go down a few minutes ago. Barbara can give you all the local gossip. It's best to stay out of the way for awhile."

Jamie's heart was still hammering. Who knew if Julita would reappear and start target practicing on her guests. "I guess we'd be safer down below..."

Behind her Ian Danville lifted the rum bottle to his mouth.

CHAPTER FOURTEEN

The path switched back several times, and Jamie's fragile heeled sandals were not the best footgear for the coarse gravel. She stumbled along, still shaken by the shooting and ugly scene. She wished Andre was with her as she felt a sharp stone press into her toes.

When the path opened onto a level area with a wooden bench flanked by lighted torches, Jamie sat down. "I have a stone in my shoe."

Ian lifted the bottle of rum to his mouth, then held it out to her. Jamie shook her head and rubbed her foot, unaware her dress had fallen open up to her thigh.

"Lovely." Ian reached out and stroked her knee. Jamie swatted his hand away. He grabbed her forcefully and began to pull her toward him.

"Ian, you're drunk."

Suddenly he put his hand into her dress and fumbled with her panties. Jamie pulled away and thrust a bent elbow into his mid-section. He exhaled sharply and she knew she had winded him.

"Get out of my way," she screamed as he blocked her escape to the house. "Okay, I'll let Brian deal with you." Jamie pulled her dress together and started down the path to the cove and the safety of her friends.

The small cove at the bottom of the hill, illuminated by torches set up for the party, was empty.

"You're a sweet dish, y'know." Ian's voice behind her was ugly. "You like me, don't you?"

"Ian, leave me alone. I'll tell Paul."

"Yeah, where is he, anyway?" He brushed his hand over her breast.

Jamie scratched at his face, her nails drawing blood.

"Oh, you're a hell cat. Like it rough, do you?"

Their struggle took them closer and closer to the waves crashing on the shore. Jamie twisted her body, trying to push him into the water. A wave crashed around her feet and she stumbled and fell into the surf. Ian lurched away on all fours and crawled crab-like up to the dry sand.

"You bitch. I'll make your husband's job at Omega hell." Ian stumbled up the path.

Jamie's breath came in ragged heaves. The water chilled her. She started to get to her knees, already concocting a story about her wet, bedraggled condition. But before she could stand, a large wave crashed around her and began sucking her down into cutting stones and sand with incredible force. She grabbed at the sand, sharp coral rocks tearing her hands and abrading her knees and arms.

"Ian, help me. Ian..." But her cries for help were lost in the crash of the waves and she suddenly remembered the undertow.

She clawed at the sand bed and rocks as she was tumbled cruelly down, down. When she could hold her breath no longer, sea water filled her lungs.

Then strong hands were pulling on her, dragging and half lifting her onto the sand. She felt herself being rolled over and a sharp thrust to her back made her retch. Seawater spewed out of her mouth, and she dry heaved as those same hands turned her to her side.

When she opened her eyes Andre's face was just a few inches above hers. He pushed her hair away from her face.

"You're all right," he reassured her. "You're out of the water and away from the waves. You're safe." His voice calmed her and she felt herself let go, her body shivering uncontrollably.

"Can you walk just a little?" he asked a few minutes later as he helped her to her feet and supported her to dry sand away from the waves.

"I, I need to sit for a minute," she said, then went limp. When she came to, she found herself wrapped warmly in a jacket with strong arms around her. She startled.

"Hush, it's all right. You're safe. Are you warm enough?"

"How did you find me? I was under the water, I didn't know which way was up. I was drowning." Jamie gave in then, crying, shaking in reaction.

"Shhh," Andre soothed, holding Jamie in calming arms. "I went looking for you after the Julita fiasco. I saw you with Ian going down the steps. He's got a bad reputation, so I followed a few minutes later. Ian passed me as I came down. You almost got pulled out by the undertow. I'm surprised someone didn't warn you."

Her teeth were chattering. "Henry mentioned it earlier in the evening. But I wasn't planning on going in. Ian got really out of line and I tried to push him into the water, to get away. I could have died."

"We've got to get you warmed up," Andre said.

Jamie nodded. He held her more tightly, a friendly gesture to warm her, could smell her faint jasmine scent.

"But I don't understand. If you pulled me out of the water, why aren't you wet? Your jacket is dry."

Andre laughed. "I'm not the hero. Actually, by the time I got down here someone else had pulled you out."

He looked around. "Marcus, where have you got to?"

Marcus came out of the shadows. "Sir, I am here. I have leaves to ease the hurt on the Mistress's knees and hands."

"I heard you scream, but by the time I got here Marcus had pulled you out." Andre squeezed the leaves, releasing a viscous liquid which he stroked onto Jamie's abraded skin.

"What were you doing here anyway, Marcus?" Andre asked.

"Listening to the sea, sir."

"Do you understand that, Jamie?"

"No, am I supposed to?"

"Not really," he said, then gestured to Marcus. "I envy the way he is connected to the island, the sea."

"Well, he knew what plants to get. Whatever those leaves were, my hands and knees feel much better," Jamie said with a grateful look at Marcus. "And I'm really glad you were listening to the sea just then, just here."

"I will go now, sir, unless you require anything else."

"No, Marcus. Thank you."

"Marcus, how can I ever thank you?" Jamie reached out her hands and Marcus took them. Constantly she felt some strange current emanating from this man. His eyes were warm and supremely gentle.

"You have no need to thank me, Mistress." Marcus turned to Andre. "She has an aura, and you have it too. Now I know where it came from."

Andre nodded. "Going to tell Bertille?"

"I have no secrets from Bertille."

"Remember, Jamie is a married woman."

"I remember." Marcus melted away into the darkness to the rhythmic crash of waves.

Andre smiled down at Jamie. "You've stopped shivering."

"I feel better." Jamie watched him carefully. "Do you know why I almost fainted that time in the kitchen?"

Andre shook his head. "Bertille. But I don't know why."

"She, she tells me I have returned, that I was expected."

"Does that frighten you?"

Jamie twisted in his protective arm. "A little. Apparently it doesn't bother you."

Andre looked off into the night. "Marcus and Bertille are gifted in the old ways, the old traditions. They practically raised me, so I'm not surprised that Bertille said something like that. She has a way of looking around the edges of the future."

When he was about to stand, Jamie stopped him. "No, please,

please can't we stay here a few more moments?" Jamie managed to say, clutching his hand. "It's just I'm so relieved to be all right. I thought I was going to die. And I thought of all the things I wanted to do and the life I'd hoped for and the children that would never be born." Her voice became very quiet. "I really thought I was going to die. And I knew I didn't want to." When the sobs came they racked her.

Andre held her.

When her sobs subsided she asked, "Do you have a handkerchief? My nose is running." Andre laughed and searched his pocket.

"You're in luck," he said as he pulled a handkerchief out of his pocket and began to wipe her tears away. He was struck again by the contrast of her pale skin against the dark hair and the dark lashes surrounding her very green eyes. He stroked her cheek and pushed her wet hair away from her face. She closed her eyes and burrowed into his warmth.

She seemed to sleep for a few minutes, then opened her eyes and looked at him. She touched the cleft in his chin, the dimple intensely familiar. "Thank you for being here just when I needed you."

"That honor goes to Marcus," Andre answered.

"But it all seems of one piece. I can't explain it. You were here and you let me get my bearings. I won't forget," she continued as she gazed at him. "I know I must know you. You are so familiar. So comforting."

"Perhaps we should talk to Bertille sometime."

"Perhaps we should." She looked at him, not wanting to hold back but afraid how he would take it. "Andre, Paul was supposed to be here tonight. In fact, the Minister wanted him here, although I wonder just how much of an honor that is now, after seeing him assault a child."

"Desmond's behavior is well known. Try not to think about it."

"But Paul, he was supposed to be here and he got drunk. He passed out. I had to come alone."

"You made a lovely entrance." Andre smiled.

"You watched me?"

"The whole place was watching you."

Jamie smiled. "What you said to Marcus, about my being married..."

"Yes?"

"It's not, not going well."

A large wave combed in from the darkness and struck the shore.

"It was a wave like that that almost got you," Andre murmured.

"I don't know what to do."

"I'm very sorry, Jamie. Perhaps you need to talk with Paul and..."

She clutched at his arm. "Oh, God, Andre, I've said too much, made you uncomfortable..."

"It's okay. I'm glad you can talk to me. Marcus is right. There's something between us. I suppose aura is as good a word as any."

"Yes."

"We'd better get back, explain your wet dress..."

"Oh, no. I can't face that."

"Well, then. There's a back way out of the cove. I could take you home. No one at the party will notice. They'll think you left in the confusion. Please trust me. No one will hear of this incident from me. And Marcus keeps his own counsel."

"All right," Jamie said. "Which way out?"

"The track is rough. Will you jump out of your skin if I need to hold on to you to get you over the rough spots? You've lost your shoes. I may even have to carry you."

"What if Paul came to the party? I can't let him see me like this or with you."

Andre took her hand again. "Let's see if your husband is at your house in Rodney Bay. If he's not there, I'll leave you at the house and come back to the party and see if he's here. If he is, I'll tell him you had an accident in the cove and I thought it best to take you home directly."

"He'll know something happened from my scraped hands and

knees. But you don't understand. I don't know what he'll do if he thinks you and I were in the cove."

"Will you please stop blaming yourself? You could tell him the truth - up to a point," he added ironically, thinking about Ian. "So, are you ready?" Andre grabbed one of the torches near the bottom of the path and pulled it out of the sand. It flared briefly.

"I'll never smell kerosene again without remembering tonight," she said.

CHAPTER FIFTEEN

Mick's Place was bubbling with its regular crowd. Occasional laughter gusted. Out on the beach terrace Jamie and Barbara leaned against the rail.

"I like your wrap, Jamie. One of your designs?"

Jamie nodded. "I made the blouse, too."

"Pretty. You smell good, too."

"Isn't it a nice scent? Jasmine - from that little shop near town."

They watched the coconut palms, dark silhouettes against a fiery sunset.

"Look at the patterns from the palms, Barbara. They shape and reshape themselves in the breeze."

"They're pretty all right," Barbara said.

Jamie looked at her. "Something wrong?"

"I saw the abrasions on your arms when your wrap slipped." Barbara scanned down to Jamie's legs. "Knees too. Everywhere. Is that all from what happened at the cove?"

Jamie stared and smiled ruefully. "So you know."

"Small island, Jamie. Actually I'm more concerned about that bruise you had before the cove."

"It was nothing, I banged my arm..."

"Looked more like a grab to me. Is Paul hitting you, Jamie?"

"No!" Jamie's face flamed hot.

"Grabbed you, then?"

"Well..."

"Arguing and he grabbed you - hard?"

Jamie looked back into Mick's at Paul and Brian having a drink. He seemed so relaxed, almost like the old Paul.

"What do you know about the cove?" Jamie asked, changing the subject.

"That lech Ian was after you. You got into a tug of war and got dragged out on the undertow."

"Almost. Marcus Deroche saved me. And Andre was there."

"Oh, yeah?"

"Don't say it like that. He helped me, got me home."

Barbara swirled her drink, then sipped it. "All that baby talk the other day, Jamie. Tell me you're not considering having a baby after all you're going through."

"Absolutely not." Her words were too strong, and she reached out and took Barbara's hand. "Really, we're okay in that department. No baby."

Barbara covered Jamie's hand with her own. "This hand holding is nice. I noticed you held Andre's hand..."

"He held mine, he was escorting me to be introduced..."

"At the minister's party." Barbara finished, words tumbling over each other.

The silence was broken by the sound of music from the bar.

"Down at the cove Andre reminded Marcus I was a married woman. It was all above board."

"But you wished it wasn't."

Jamie glared. "I can't deny it. To you, that is. No one else."

"Oh, Jamie. You know about Taylor..."

"I know."

When an angry shriek came from the bar, both women turned to look.

"Danielle on the warpath," Barbara said as they watched her poke a finger into Jean-Pierre's chest. "She's something else. Fireworks like nothing I've seen. Poor Jean-Pierre, he's in for it now."

"She does seem to pick at him and down him."

"But Danielle needs him, like having an umbrella handy, or the faithful outfit you wear in a pinch. Or just someone to take her moods out on."

Jamie stared. "You really don't like her a whole lot. This is a side I haven't seen, Barb."

"What, no cheery Barbara with mop and gardening tools?"

"Frankly, yes."

Barbara relented. "Island living. Brian keeps me sane at times. Danielle had a go at him, but my Brian is rock solid."

"You're a great couple."

"Hon, I'm your friend, right?"

"Yeah?"

"Watch out for Paul."

"Look, Barbara, we have our problems, we..."

"There's talk."

Jamie felt sick. "Oh, God."

"Jamie, ultimately it's none of my business, but don't take abuse, and for God's sake don't get pregnant."

"I've got that under control. Stop worrying." She smiled encouragingly at Paul as he waved from the bar.

"They want us to play a game of darts."

Jamie nodded. "Fine with me."

As they walked back into Mick's, Barbara said, "Do you just rattle around in that house all day?"

"That's one way to put it, but yes."

"Working on those super dresses?"

"Yes, what about it?"

"Later. Let's beat these guys at darts."

Near the sacred cave the moon touched the hillside and caught the sparkle of the waterfall. Leaves wafted on the same breeze that caressed the palm fronds at Mick's.

Bertille's eyes were closed. She sat quietly by the pooling water, the moonbeams bathing her eyelids. In one hand she held Paul's cufflink. In the other she held the lace handkerchief.

"The handkerchief is powerful, my husband. But it is not Jamie's. It belongs to a forebear. Strong feelings there, but not Jamie."

"What does it tell you?" Marcus asked.

"That Jamie and her forebears are powerful in their spiritual ways."

"They are our ways."

Bertille's brow furrowed around the question. "I want to say yes. I have held her, Marcus, close to my bosom. I know her spirit."

"And I have felt the aura around her - and Andre."

"Marcus?"

"Yes?"

"I believe she is the parrot who now flies with me."

"Then she is of us!" Marcus said with force.

"There's something else..."

Her husband waited, delicately attuned to her trance.

"This Paul, her husband..."

"Yes?"

"I see death."

As she spoke the moon faded behind a cloud, trailing a remnant luster across the sky.

In New York Andre watched Taylor, catching her profile as she observed the theater audience.

She felt his eyes on her, then smiled and pressed his hand.

Andre watched her, thinking she looked pre-occupied this evening. Her features were perfect, and her profile was breathtaking with its classic nose and mouth. She was lovely. And cool, sometimes detached.

Taylor gathered her thoughts and returned to Andre. She smiled. "Update me about the hotel, Andre. How are the plans coming?"

"Everything is always slower than you wish. I should know better than to be impatient."

Taylor studied his face for a moment. "But it's about more than a money-making venture. It's about the future of your country."

"That's very perceptive of you, Taylor." He hesitated, then forged ahead. "You've had some time to digest your impressions of St. Lucia. What do you think of it?"

"I...Oh, the lights are dimming. Let's talk later." Grateful for the diversion, she squeezed Andre's hand. "I love *Showboat.*"

Andre watched the curtain go up to an orchestral crescendo, into the introductory bars of "Old Man River." He found himself wondering at the irony of it. Taylor so far removed from St. Lucia, so careful about proper family bloodlines, and yet loving a show like this. As the performance began he found himself thinking about Jamie, arms and legs raw, cradled in his arms as the seductive waves crashed and slid back in their undertow. Bertille claimed she belonged to St. Lucia, had in fact returned. But he reminded himself of what he had said to Marcus. *She's married.* Andre forced her from him as he returned to Taylor and the theater.

Later, Andre guided Taylor through the milling after-theater crowd toward the waiting limo. "I guess you'll be humming 'Old Man River' for days now."

"I do love it, Andre. My parents took me to see *Showboat* when I was a child."

"Did you understand the implications back then - about someone with Negro blood passing for white?"

"No. To be honest, though, I find the idea disturbing."

"That's a little strong, isn't it?"

"Strong?" Then she grinned. "Ah, your own heritage."

"I might have a few drops, you know. Mother says no, but Bertille says yes."

"And of course you believe Bertille over your mother." Taylor's voice carried a petulant edge.

"I face facts. You know about Mother, how we tend to be distant. Emile and I learned so much from Bertille and Marcus."

"Yes, I know, Andre. I'm sorry. I said it badly. I'm sorry."

He smiled, shrugging it off. Taylor was all about proper northeastern families, not Caribbean kings.

"Feel like something to eat?"

"Yes."

Later, after a light meal of seafood crepes, they lingered over a bottle of Pouilly-Fuisee.

Taylor kept the talk light, dreading the moment to come.

"About St. Lucia," Andre began.

Taylor sighed. "Yes, St. Lucia."

"What?"

"We do need to discuss it. The island is incredibly beautiful, I do love it - although I could do without the bugs and mosquito netting over the bed." She smiled, softening her criticism. "But you must know the island and its exotic ways are foreign to me. I really need more time to think...about the possibilities and implications."

"You've always assumed we'd live in New York."

"Well, yes."

Andre nodded, signaling the waiter. "A Grand Marnier petit for the lady. I'll have a Remy Martin VSOP." After the waiter had gone he said, "I think I'm partly to blame here. I presumed a lot."

"Please don't think I'm inflexible, Andre."

"No, I don't think that."

Taylor covered his hand with hers, watching the candlelight cast prisms of fire from her diamond ring. "Must this decision be made now? I want to give St. Lucia a fair chance."

"I appreciate that. When can you come back?"

"Well, there's the Gala for the Children's Museum...I'm committed...but as soon as that's over, I'll catch the first plane down. How's that?"

Andre nodded. Jamie's face flashed before him and he felt a deep sense of uneasiness.

CHAPTER SIXTEEN

Jamie lay still, feigning sleep. She clutched her pillow as Paul climbed into bed beside her, smelled cigarette smoke and alcohol. In the dark she could see the illuminated bedside clock: 3:15 in the morning.

"Jamie?" He waited.

She shrugged and moved away.

"Jamie!" He brushed her shoulder, soft, caressing.

She stiffened at his touch. "What?"

"S'been awhile," he slurred.

"Sleepy. Not now."

"C'mon. Been a long time and..." His hand dropped to her breast.

"No!"

He sat up, angry. "Whadda ya' mean - no? Jus' like that, no? Where d'you get off, Jamie..."

"Just leave me alone, Paul. I'm tired."

"Yeah. Been gettin' it on with Ian. He told me about the cove."

Jamie reared up in outrage. "Paul, you're disgusting! The man attacked me..."

"Not what he said. Said you like it rough. I didn't know that about you, Jamie." He pinched her thigh - hard.

She slapped him, with more force than she had intended, driven by anger and a deep sense of loss.

"So that's how you want it..."

"No, Paul!"

"I'm your husband, dammit. Got rights. Who're you putting out for, you bitch - that Andre guy, too? Everybody gets a piece and not me?" His hand tightened on her upper arm.

"You're hurting me!"

"Maybe s'what you need. Knocked around." Paul sneered in the dim light. "Knocked up, maybe. Baby keep you busy, outta my hair."

"Paul! No!" she begged as he pinned her to the bed and used his knee to open her legs.

In the morning light Jamie stared at her face in the bathroom mirror, thankful it did not show the bruising hurt inside, unaware her eyes showed a palpable look of despair. She examined the fast healing scratches from the cove, but there was a fresh bruise on her thigh, another on her arm. A deep ache constricted her very center, the bruises on the outside just a shadow of the pain she felt within.

She filled the tub. The water soothed, like warm oil on shattered nerve ends. Jamie lay still and thought of her mother. Even on Jamie's wedding day she had tried to dissuade her. God...

"I'm getting outa here!" Paul called. "See the guys."

"See Danielle, why don't you," she muttered to herself, pressing deeper into the water.

The sun moved along its path, leaving her in faint shadow. The water in the tub had cooled and been replenished several times when Jamie heard a knock on the door.

"Hey, Jamie, you home?" It was Barbara.

"In the tub. Be out in a minute," Jamie called back.

When she felt ready, she got up, dried off, and pulled on old shorts and a T-shirt.

"Hot in here." Barbara had filled a metal bowl with ice cubes and put it in front of the fan on the table.

"Yeah, I guess." She looked at the fabric she had been working on, her carefully laid-out designs, now trashed in the corner.

Barbara looked at her, the sadness in Jamie's eyes apparent. "You okay?"

Jamie shook her head as she sat in front of the whirling fan. The coolness struck her. "Nice," was all she could manage.

"Where's Paul?"

Jamie shook her head again.

"Anytime you're ready," Barbara said, her voice gentling down.

Jamie waved a hand. "We had a fight last night. Said I'd asked for it down at the cove, even accused me of putting out for Andre. He was disgusting."

Barbara said nothing. She waited, noticing the fresh bruise on Jamie's thigh.

"He said...he said, if everyone else was getting a piece why shouldn't he, and maybe he should knock me up and I'd be too busy with a baby to nag him." When they came, the tears were hot, only to be buffeted by the cooling fan.

Barbara went to her and put her arms around her.

"He didn't use to be like this, Barbara."

"You wouldn't have married him, hon."

"I thought I could lean on him." Shame swept through Jamie as she remembered last night, the feelings too raw and shameful to share. Oh, God, he'd given her no time to put in her diaphragm.

Barbara let her sit. "Okay, okay," she soothed. "It's going to be okay." She kissed the top of Jamie's head.

"Oh, God, Barbara. Why do I feel so ashamed?"

"Don't know, hon. You didn't do anything."

Outside, grackles set up a raucous chatter. Insects droned as the sun rose in the sky.

"I need to talk this out."

"Okay."

"Need to get things moving again. Function. Does that make sense?"

"That makes a lot of sense."

Jamie took a deep breath, putting aside the ache in her chest and the profound sense of violation. She talked about her mother and what a good person she was, and how her father had died from cancer, and how they had ended up with no money and Jamie had taken a job in a dress shop and gone to night school, where she had met Paul.

"I really thought I could lean on him," she said again. She pointed at the bruise on her leg. "I won't let him do that again."

"Do you want to come stay with us?"

Jamie didn't seem to hear. "About Danielle, do you think..."

"What? That he's sleeping with her? I don't know, Jamie. Brian hears talk, that's all I know."

"I suppose the whole island knows," Jamie said.

"Not unless Paul gets tanked and brags about it." Barbara felt Jamie stiffen and quickly said, "But I don't see that happening. There's his job at Omega, the whole image thing."

"I don't think he can hold that up much more."

"Probably not. But when it hits, let it be his own damn fault, his own dumb actions. Don't let him have a chance to point a finger at you."

"But I haven't done anything."

Barbara sighed and looked at the fabric in the corner. She pulled a piece out and began folding it, smoothing out the wrinkles, wishing she could smooth out her friend's life as easily.

"These your new ones?"

"Ummm. What do you think?"

"Beautiful as always. You really have a gift."

"But they won't make me rich. When I divorce him I'll blow whatever savings I have. Paul will be a bastard."

"You'll file for divorce?"

Jamie looked at her, resignation etched on her face. "It's not working. Do I have a choice?"

"I suppose not," Barbara said quietly. "It's just the words spoken out loud sound so final, that's all."

"I'm not telling him yet. I need time to think. Probably have to go back to New York - right?"

"I don't know, Jamie. I'm no lawyer."

"I really hoped St. Lucia would give us a fresh start."

"I'm sorry it didn't."

"Anyway, I need time. But I won't let him hurt me again. If he comes near me again I'll call the police."

"I wouldn't count on much help there, Jamie."

"What do you mean?"

"They'll see it as a family matter, won't want to interfere."

"So I'm helpless?"

"Call us. Even if it's in the middle of the night. Brian will come."

Jamie squeezed her hand. "Thanks."

"I'm spending the day here," Barbara said, leaving no room to argue. "Have you had anything to eat?"

"Not hungry."

"Okay...I'm clueless. But I'm not leaving you to sit here and stew. Want to teach me how to sew?"

"It's okay." Jamie managed a first smile. "We're both winging it." As she said it, she thought about the odd choice of words, her dreams, flying with the parrots. Bertille. What would she think of all this?

Barbara picked up one of the designs. "Remember at Mick's, I asked you about if you were rattling around in this house, needing something to do?"

"Yes, I wondered..."

"There's someone I want you to meet."

Jamie nodded, going along. "Okay..."

"I want to introduce you to Andre's mother."

Jamie stared.

CHAPTER SEVENTEEN

On Monday morning Barbara arrived early, enjoyed some coffee, then stared critically at Jamie in her new sun dress. "Have you seen Paul?" she asked.

"Yes, I told him if he forced himself on me again I'd phone the police and the president of Omega. He'll leave me alone."

"Oh, God, Jamie. He forced himself on you?"

"Yeah. I didn't tell you that part. Too awful..."

"I'm so sorry. Why don't you stay with us?"

"No. He's given me the bed. He slept in the rattan chair last night."

"You're sure?"

"Yeah. I have to get on with my life. Does the make-up cover the worst of the scrapes on my arms? And there?" She gestured to her shoulders.

"Mostly. Maybe you've got a scarf or something."

Barbara followed as Jamie walked into the bedroom and rummaged in a drawer. "I'm glad you wore that sun dress. The abstract parrots are brilliant. Clarisse is going to love it."

"Thanks. I hope so. I really need a job, Barbara."

Barbara patted her hand. "It's all going to work out."

Jamie draped one of her hand painted silk scarves around her shoulders. "How's that?"

"Perfect. Let's go," Barbara said, gathering up sample dresses.

"What's Andre's mother like?"

"You'll see." Barbara's eyes were bright. "She told me to bring you to the factory, first floor. Wait 'til you see the antiques she stores there."

When they arrived Clarisse was not to be seen. While Barbara went looking, Jamie gazed at the elegant antique furniture. A mahogany headboard leaned against one wall, primitively carved pineapple finials an interpretation of Sheraton design. An armoire stood against another wall, the wood exhibiting an astounding display of graining. But it was the mahogany cradle sitting in the corner that drew her attention.

Barbara's next call was cut off as she said, "Oh, good morning, Mrs. Demontagne. I've brought my friend to see you, show you her designs..." Her voice trailed off as Clarisse stared at the parrot design on Jamie's dress.

No one spoke.

Jamie waited, feeling her cheeks grow hot. She could not take her eyes from this elegant woman, so poised, whose blue eyes offered both quiet decorum and - to Jamie - a touch of melancholy.

"This is Jamie Elliott," Barbara said finally, her usually breezy manner subdued.

Clarisse did not take her eyes from Jamie. "That parrot design, is it yours?"

"Yes, usually I do leaves and flowers..."

"Why did you choose a parrot design? It's unusual."

Jamie hesitated, thrown off by the directness of this powerful woman and the very piercing eyes. "I like parrots, always have," she said, feeling foolish at her response. "And the design just came to me..."

"It came to you."

"Yes." Uncomfortable, Jamie walked over to the mahogany headboard, her delicate touch tracing out the primitive carving. "This is exquisite."

"It's exquisite because it comes from the soul. Your parrot design also comes from the soul."

Outside a transport honked its horn.

Clarisse came forward and took the samples Barbara was holding. "I gather these other dresses are your designs as well." Her smile lightened the mood, and Barbara spoke into it.

"Like I told you on the phone, Jamie is looking for work. I thought if I brought her by..."

"Yes, indeed. I'm so very glad you did, Barbara. I wonder, dear, if you would mind leaving Jamie and me alone for a while? I'd like to talk to her."

"Not at all. I have some errands to run."

"Look, I'll catch a transport when I'm finished here."

"Okay. Call me when you get home." Barbara smiled cheerfully and left.

Clarisse's eyes were warm as she spoke. "We must talk, you and I. Do you like tea?"

"Very much," Jamie said, allowing her to take her arm.

"We shall have lemon or milk, whichever you prefer. Forgive me, but I can't help but notice you're favoring your arm."

"Yes, I hurt myself, unfortunately."

"I heard about the nasty incident at the cove, of course."

"Living here is worse than being in a small town," Jamie said. "No privacy."

"Yes, at times. But in other ways islanders are family. We help one another..." The blue eyes darkened with a memory. "Now, come into my office."

Handsome paintings of local scenic spots decorated the walls. Jamie recognized the open air market in town and the Pitons near Soufriere. A large work table was covered with lengths of fabric, large sheets of paper with bold designs.

"I'm usually in my office upstairs. This is where I escape when I want no distractions - does that seem odd to you, my dear?"

Jamie hesitated. "Not at all. Being creative is sometimes like being in a trance. Like when I did these parrots. Better to work without interruptions."

"Yes. Perhaps that's why your designs are so wonderful."

Jamie smiled and watched a small twinkle appear in Clarisse's eyes, then it was gone.

"Now let me fix the tea for us. I was just about to have it when Barbara let out her cheerful bellow." Clarisse's eyes glanced at Jamie.

"She's my best friend," Jamie said.

The eyes held hers for a moment. "Loyalty in this day and age. It's most becoming."

They sat at the work table and Clarisse arranged lemon, milk and sugar on a tray. "If you look behind you, you will see photographs of my family."

Jamie turned and studied the stern, posed portrait of Auguste Demontagne. Beside it were several casual photos of Andre and Emile, as small boys, with Bertille and Marcus. They were smiling in the sun. Jamie wondered why there were no pictures of Clarisse with her sons.

"I met your husband and your sons - and Bertille and Marcus Deroche."

"Oh?"

"Yes, we ran into Emile and Andre while hiking. They invited us back to Jumeaux. I like that picture of your sons with Bertille. That's on the Jumeaux veranda, isn't it?"

"Yes. The boys spent their childhoods there. I have the pictures there so I can see them from my desk."

Jamie saw the melancholy again. Then it was gone.

"There now," Clarisse said. "The tea is ready. Let me pour you a cup."

They sipped tea in silence for a moment.

"Andre favors you," Jamie said.

Clarisse smiled, pleased. "Yes, he has the Diamant chin. It shows up now and then. Emile favors his father. They are good boys." She picked up one of the sample dresses. "Tell me about this design."

"It's a hibiscus and I put a yellow breast there - flitting across the shoulder."

"A few strokes of paint. You've captured the essence of our little banana bird. As you did with the parrots on the dress you're wearing. Parrots are meaningful here, you know. Just ask Bertille sometime. She believes they are the spirit of the island."

"Well, as I said, I like parrots."

"You must have had one, to capture them so well."

"No, but I had a parakeet named Snoopy."

At that Clarisse laughed. "Jamie, my dear, you're absolutely charming."

Jamie reddened. Perhaps in some self defense and in small rebellion against Clarisse's slight condescension, she said, "I've always dreamed about parrots. Odd, isn't it?"

Blue eyes darkened. "Bertille wouldn't think so."

The mood changed, and Jamie sensed a withdrawing of Clarisse.

"Well, we need to talk business, Jamie. Are you currently working?"

"No, I..."

"Tell me more about your design background."

"I had some design classes in college, but I didn't finish my degree. Since coming to the island, I've been inspired by the tropical flowers, leaves, the birds. In terms of clothing design, I'm self-taught. I've managed an upscale ladies dress shop, which gave me an opportunity to examine expensive clothes and how they were made. I've tried to incorporate many of these details in my designs."

Clarisse held out a plate to Jamie. "Biscuit?"

Jamie took a thin ginger wafer.

When Clarisse spoke again her voice was clipped and efficient. "What I am intrigued about is whether some of your designs could be modified for the new batik line I'm planning. The hand painting is too detailed, but I think if the designs were simplified they might be wonderful."

"Is there someplace I could go to see the batik process?" asked Jamie. "That would help me determine how the designs would need to be modified."

"Yes, of course, I could set that up for you. In fact, I have one woman working in a corner of the sewing factory. She's very good at the batik process but is not creating the kinds of designs I have in mind. Again, I must caution you, I can't promise you a job. If some of your designs are suitable, I might buy them from you. Of course, you would have to sign a contract giving me exclusive use of the designs."

"Yes, of course. But I don't know anything about exclusivity contracts. I'm just glad you like my designs."

Clarisse stood and walked to her desk. Taking a pen in hand, she turned to Jamie. "How can I reach you?"

A few minutes later, back at the corner by the market, Jamie waited for a transport. She felt mystified by the meeting, which had gone from a personal warmth and expressed confidences to a sudden withdrawal. And then there was that melancholy. But why?

At the corner of the turn into Rodney Bay, she flagged the driver to drop her off and began the short walk home. An odd morning, but she had a job of sorts. And she'd had a small window into Andre's life, meeting his mother. How would this cool matriarch feel about Bertille, who had such warmth, who drew her sons to her bosom and offered nurturing through a child's fears and hurts? It would, Jamie realized, be very hard to bear. She would have to talk to Andre about it. If the opportunity arose. Her spirits fell at that thought. Even now he was on his usual commute to New York. And Taylor.

Jamie examined her arms, now almost free of scrapes from the cove and its ugly tide, and make-up was doing its job. When she suddenly remembered Barbara, a smile came. She would have to steel herself for a barrage of questions. Jamie realized she owed Barbara a lot, the very expanding of her world. Things were looking up. Her smile faded as she recalled the mahogany cradle. When Andre filled her thoughts again she welcomed him. Gladly.

Bertille washed the dishes in her sink and glanced at Marcus. Marcus picked up the eyebrow pencil. "So what is this?"

"It's an eyebrow pencil. Delia got it for me from Jamie's house."

"Can I use it to make notes?"

Bertille laughed. "What am I going to do with you, my husband! No, it must be returned to Jamie. Give it to Delia. She's already returned the handkerchief and her husband's cufflink."

"And she was careful about it?"

"The handkerchief will just look mislaid. The cufflink is under the bed."

Marcus put his strong weathered arms around his wife's shoulders. "What did you learn this time?"

Bertille shook her head. "Nothing, except she is a chosen one. We will have to see."

"I could use this pencil for figuring the land boundaries. It looks waterproof."

"Go!" Bertille laughed, flicking soapy water at him.

CHAPTER EIGHTEEN

It was more than Jamie had hoped. Clarisse bought a few designs and then offered her a job. She actually had an office on the second floor of the Jumeaux Designs factory. From her big work table she could look through the open wooden shutters and see the activity in the harbor: the graceful curve of a sail, the constantly changing clouds, palms on a far hill - all providing inspiration.

Perhaps Clarisse could not pay her much, but the opportunity to have her designs featured by Jumeaux Designs was a morale boost. Critically she examined her new batik design, the curved petals of a ginger lily.

One thing she had learned from her visit to the batik section was that good designs came from an artist's physical movements. She had watched Janette, the almost balletic quality to her movements, as she flowed molten wax onto the fabric. Jamie had known instinctively that she would have to capture that wonderful dance in her own designs. It felt good to be learning and contributing.

Idly her eyes wandered to the several parrot designs laid out on a chair. Clarisse's face came back to her, the quiet words...

"These are my own parrot designs, Jamie, but as you can see they are not so inspired as yours."

"Would you leave them with me, Clarisse? Perhaps I can add a touch here and there."

"Why thank you, my dear." For a moment Clarisse's pervasive melancholy had left her, then she had retreated, returned into that formal self which kept Jamie out.

She shrugged, the ginger lily petals recapturing her attention. *Just a bit more curve here...* Engrossed, she startled at the knock on her door.

"Come in."

Clarisse opened the door. "There's a call for you in my office."

Jamie didn't look up from her design table. "Who is it? Just getting this detail..."

"You'd better come. It's a hospital in New York. A Dr. Linden. Asked for the daughter of Janine Jenkins."

Jamie stood up, her design sliding to the floor. "That's my mom. She can't be sick. I was just talking to her."

"Hurry."

Jamie ran to Clarisse's office and picked up the phone.

"This is Mrs. Elliott. Janine Jenkins' daughter."

A female voice responded. "Dr. Linden, here. I'm calling from Columbia Presbyterian. Your mother was admitted last night."

"What's wrong?"

"I admitted your mother with a bacterial infection. Something she must have picked up while in the hospital recently for surgery." Dr. Linden's tone was professional but kind. Jamie listened incredulously. "We have her in the CCU. Her vital signs are good, and her condition is currently listed as stable. She asked me to call you and explain. I need to advise you that her other health problems are compounding her body's ability to fight off the infection."

"What other health problems?" Jamie asked. "She didn't tell me about other problems or surgery."

"I assumed she had..."

"Told me what? Please, it's my mother. Do I need to come to New York?" Jamie waited through a long pause for Dr. Linden's reply.

"Your mother was diagnosed three months ago with breast cancer. She had a lumpectomy and has been undergoing chemotherapy. We seemed to be winning the war against the cancer, but the chemo left her immune system compromised, and this infection, which might be less problematic for someone in good health, is potentially dangerous."

"Do you mean she might die?" Anguish shaped her words.

Clarisse moved to stand beside her.

"We're treating her with all the weapons in our medical arsenal but, yes, it is possible she will not be able to fight off the infection."

Jamie struggled to think as her world came crashing in. "Tell her I'm coming as soon as I can catch a plane. Please tell her I'm coming."

"Certainly. Family is sometimes the most powerful medicine there is, Mrs. Elliott."

Jamie's hand was shaking as she hung up the phone.

"We'll call your husband," Clarisse said.

"No! He's in the field. No way to reach him. Maybe I can get Barbara at home."

"Call her from here. Tell her I'm sending you home in a taxi."

"But..."

"It's the least I can do. Now call her."

Jamie reached for the phone and began dialing. The phone rang and rang.

"Where will you stay in New York?"

"At Mom's apartment in Bronxville."

"Good."

Jamie looked at Clarisse. "Thanks for your help."

Clarisse waved a dismissing hand. "And you must not worry about your work. It can all wait. Take care of your mother. I would like to be able to reach you, though. In case you need assistance?" Jamie gave her the name and address and phone number. "Now, go downstairs. I'll call for the taxi and keep trying to find Barbara."

After Jamie had gone, Clarisse picked up the phone and dialed New York.

The jetliner shuddered as its wing flaps dug into the air and its speed lowered for landing at Kennedy. The jarring shook her already upset stomach as Jamie adjusted her seatbelt and shoved the magazine in the pocket in front of her. She could not recall anything in it. But it had engaged her senses; she was able to turn pages and keep her hands busy while she worried.

Clarisse had reached Barbara, who had met Jamie at her house and helped her pack some sensible changes of clothes. And she had money, pressed into her hands by Clarisse as she pushed Jamie out of the office. She had time only to catch the tears in Clarisse's piercing blue eyes. *Later,* Jamie had thought desperately. She would try and take it all in later.

Right now, as the runway came up to meet them beyond her window, she gathered her strength and her faculties to help her mother. She was trudging up the carpeted exit to the terminal when it happened.

"Jamie! Jamie!"

She stopped and looked around. When she saw him she just stared.

"Here, Jamie. Let me have that bag. I'm so glad you got here so quickly. Mother said you would be on this flight."

"Andre..."

"And this is Angel Deroche. Angel, meet Jamie Elliott. Jamie, you have luggage, don't you?"

"Two pieces." She stared at Angel, tawny and beautiful, clad in jeans and an NYU windbreaker.

Within half an hour they were on their way to Columbia Presbyterian, Angel behind the wheel of the limo.

Andre pressed Jamie's hand. "So how are you bearing up?"

"Numb, really."

"That's understandable."

"How did you...?"

"Mother called my office." His face was grave. "This was important."

"You didn't have to..."

"Hey, you jumped in and helped your first day on St. Lucia.

You're almost one of us. I'm glad my mother called."

Jamie nodded. Her muted response revealed her tension.

"Maybe you should just close your eyes for a while," Andre said.

"No, I had enough of that and staring at magazines on the plane."

"A rough flight?" Angel asked from the front seat.

"Awful. Every minute felt like an hour." She looked from one to the other. "I can't thank you enough for..."

"Besides, Angel's mother-in-law would want us to help," Andre said, rolling right over her words.

"Oh?"

"Angel's married to Jack Deroche. Marcus and Bertille's son."

"We're in New York while he's in graduate school," Angel said. "Doing his doctoral dissertation on the Amazonia Versicolor."

"The St. Lucian parrot? I love those parrots."

"The same." Andre smiled.

Jamie studied Angel. "Then you're family?"

"Oh, yeah. When I married Jack everybody adopted me. Including Andre. He got me a job as a paralegal with his firm."

"And then I found out she had her limo license. I request her when I can."

"Then I'm even more grateful you've come out so late," Jamie said.

"I know how I'd be feeling if it was my mother..." Angel regarded Jamie in the rearview mirror. Her eyes darkened. "My mother-in-law is right, Andre. This one fits right in, even if she was born in New York."

Andre pressed Jamie's hand again. "Columbia Presbyterian's only ten minutes from here."

CHAPTER NINETEEN

The nurses' station on the critical care unit was brightly lit. Jamie approached the desk, Andre at her side. Her wrinkled blouse and skirt spoke of the hours of traveling from St. Lucia to New York.

"I'm Janine Jenkins' daughter. Dr. Linden called this morning and asked me to come. Can I see my mother?"

"Dr. Linden is with your mother just now. Please have a seat in the lounge," the nurse said, motioning to a small waiting room.

"Can you tell me my mother's condition?"

Consulting a patient chart, the nurse replied, "Critical."

"How could that be? This morning Dr. Linden told me my mother was in stable condition."

"Your mother's condition deteriorated over the course of the last six hours. I'm sorry. Dr. Linden will be able to give you more information. I'll let her know you're here."

Andre steered Jamie into the lounge. Table lamps lit the dim space. The clock on the wall, next to the muted television, read 11:35.

"I don't understand what's happened," Jamie said, tears welling hot.

"Look, Jamie," Andre said. "Your mother is in one of the best hospitals in New York. The doctor will be here shortly and then you'll know more."

Just then they heard soft footsteps and looked up to see a doctor standing in the doorway. Her pale pink scrubs were wrinkled, her face fatigued. Her hair was pulled back in a ponytail, which she was just liberating from a pink cap.

"Mrs. Elliott, I'm Dr. Linden," she said, stretching out a hand with short, unpolished nails. "Mr. Elliott?" she asked, turning toward Andre.

"A family friend," Andre replied.

"Good. I'm glad you have someone with you, Mrs. Elliott. Your mother's condition worsened rapidly today. We've tried the most potent antibiotics available, but she isn't responding. I'm so sorry."

Jamie turned white and sat down suddenly. She seemed to be in a tunnel which was turning blacker by the second. Dimly she heard, "Get her head between her knees."

When her head cleared, Jamie stared at the doctor. "What has happened to my mother? Is she dying? Was she this sick when you called me this morning?"

"No, she was very ill but stable this morning. She seemed to be responding to the antibiotic drip, but suddenly the infection overwhelmed her system. Her kidneys have shut down and she is conscious less and less. Be assured that your mother is in no pain. But as her body continues to shut down, she will become less able to communicate. I think it would be wise for you to see her soon."

Turning from Jamie, Dr. Linden spoke to the nurse in the doorway. "Gretchen, please see that Mrs. Jenkins is ready to see her daughter. Then take Mrs. Elliott to her."

The nurse nodded, turned and left.

"I'll be in the nurses' station. If you have any questions, don't hesitate to ask," said Dr. Linden.

Jamie sat numbed. "I can't do this."

Andre took her hands in his. "Jamie, your mother needs you now. She may be waiting to see you so she can say good-bye."

Jamie nodded and stood up.

"Does your mother attend a church in Bronxville?"

"Yes, St. Peter's Lutheran."

"While you are seeing your mother, I'll call and talk to the minister. He'll be able to help with any arrangements that have to be made. Do you know the minister?"

"Yes, Pastor Andersen. He married Paul and me. I grew up in that church. Ask him if he would come. My mother might want to talk to him, if there's time."

Andre looked up to see the nurse standing in the doorway.

"I can take you to see your mother now," she said. "Because of the type of infection, I need to ask you to gown before you go in." She handed Jamie a stack of paper scrubs, hair cover and booties. "There's a ladies' room just outside the lounge."

Andre walked her to the door of the rest room. When she came out, she was covered from head to toe in blue paper clothing. As they walked down the hall, Jamie was dimly aware that her gait felt uneven, as though she had forgotten how to walk. She barely noticed the bright orange "Quarantine" sign on the door.

She entered the room.

Her mother lay very still. Her breathing was shallow and uneven. Jamie thought how frail she looked against the white hospital sheets.

"Mom, it's me, Jamie," she said, reaching through the bed rails to take her mother's hand. A thrill of relief flooded through her as her mother grasped her hand in return, opened her eyes and smiled.

"Jamie, is it really you?"

Jamie struggled to hear her mother's whispered words. "I'm here, Mom."

"I'm so glad, Princess."

"I got on a plane this afternoon, as soon as I could after Dr. Linden called me. Oh, Mom, I wish you had called me to tell me you were sick."

"Honey, I was fine. I don't know what hit me. I started feeling really bad yesterday afternoon, so I called Dr. Linden. She told me to come...right away...so glad you're here..." Worn out, she seemed to slip away for a time. Jamie smoothed her mother's hair away from her face.

"I love you, Mom." Then Jamie sat quietly, conscious of the coolness of her mother's hand, the frailty of it. She watched the monitoring machines.

A light knocking at the door roused her. "I was able to reach Pastor Andersen," Andre said. "He's on his way. How's your mom doing?"

"I don't know. She seems to be sleeping. But she recognized me, and I think she knew what I was saying to her."

"What can I do for you? Get you something to eat or drink?"

"If you could get me some milk and maybe cheese crackers out of the vending machine, I'll see what I can get down."

"I'll be back shortly, then."

Jamie resumed her vigil. As the hours stretched out she occasionally stepped out of the room, grateful that Andre was still there.

It was almost dawn when her mother lightly squeezed her hand and opened her eyes. "Jamie?"

"I'm here, Mom."

"Jamie."

"Yes, Mom?"

"You must see my attorney."

"Mom..."

"Let me talk. He has something for you."

"Mom, I..."

"Promise me."

"I promise."

"Those dreams."

"My dreams?"

"When you were a little girl. And now they are back."

"Hush, Mom, let's not talk about..."

"There is a package for you in my bedroom. Treasure it. And see my attorney. You must promise..."

"I promise, Mom. Please don't worry. I love you, Mom. I'll love you always."

When she turned her head, her eyes found Jamie's, and for a moment overcame great tiredness with an inner warmth. "I'll be seeing your father."

"Yes, Mom. And tell him I love him too."

Jamie held the hand, but already she felt her mother leaving her. She sat resolute, guarding her mother, loving her, filling her with every iota of love she could summon. When the monitor alarm sounded, in that one precious last moment alone, she whispered, "Goodbye, Mom."

Later, in the waiting room, Andre sat on a couch with Jamie. The minister had come and gone, and some of the difficult decisions about planning the funeral had been made.

"I'm glad you got to say good-bye. Not everyone has a chance to do that."

"That's true. I didn't get to say good-bye to my father. He died suddenly one day while I was at school."

"I called Angel. We're going to take you to the Plaza. I've reserved a room for you. It's around the corner from my apartment. I didn't think it would be such a good idea for you to go back to your mother's apartment just yet. You need to sleep, and Angel will be available for as many days as you need a driver. I'll be only a phone call away. I don't want to hear any arguments about this. You need to sleep. You have some difficult days ahead."

"Is Angel here now?"

"She's waiting by the nurse's station."

The limo was in the parking garage, and they were soon in front of the hotel. All the arrangements had obviously been made, as Andre simply picked up a key at the desk.

When they got to the room, Jamie fell across the bed and Angel got her under the covers. "Don't worry about clothes. Sleep."

"What about you?"

"I'll be here. Sleep."

"Tell Andre I needed him."

"I'll tell him."

"And you."

"Go to sleep."

Angel emerged from the bedroom.

"She was asleep as soon as her head hit the pillow. Asked me to say she needed you...and me."

"Angel, I wasn't even thinking about Jack. Do you want me to call him?" Andre asked.

"No, I'll call. Hey, you're family, Andre. I'm glad to help out," Angel replied, giving him a hug.

"I want you to keep in touch with me by phone. I'm going back to my apartment to see if I can get a couple of hours of sleep before the meetings this afternoon. And if I'm not at my apartment, my secretary will know where I am. Thanks again, Angel. Jamie, Mrs. Elliott, is a very nice lady. Take good care of her."

"I gathered," Angel replied. She had worked with Andre on family business affairs and had met Taylor. She wondered how Taylor would feel about Andre's obvious emotional involvement, his protective stance toward Jamie. Angel had only just met her and could understand Jamie's appeal. The unstudied candor, the emotional openness. So different from Taylor's studied reserve. I wonder how this will play out, she thought as she retrieved a pillow and blanket from the closet and stretched out on the couch. She pulled the blanket around her and drifted off to sleep.

CHAPTER TWENTY

Andre set aside the projections and analyses for his venture capital meeting that afternoon and picked up the list of donations and flowers sent to Jamie's mother's funeral. Angel's handwriting was neat and precise.

The phone ringing on his private line broke in on his thoughts.

"Andre?"

"Taylor?"

"Andre, where are you? I'm at the restaurant."

"Oh, God. I'm so sorry, Taylor. I totally forgot."

"I talked to your secretary. She said something about funeral arrangements. What's going on?"

Andre rubbed the bridge of his nose. "My mother asked me to help one of her designers. Her mother lived in New York and died last week."

"Look, Andre. That's fine, but we had a date. I came in from Philly."

"What can I say? I forgot. I'm really sorry."

"Something's not right here, Andre. Your fiancée trains in from Philadelphia for a prearranged lunch date and gets brushed off, is that it?"

"You could have reminded me..."

"Honestly, Andre, you've been distant and distracted for weeks."

"Business..."

"I'm beginning to wonder how important to you I really am." Anger spun down the line as Taylor overrode his explanation. "Maybe you ought to think about why it's so easy for you to forget about me."

"Taylor, I'm truly sorry, but I've been preparing for an important meeting this afternoon about the hotel in St. Lucia."

"Maybe I'll just get back on the train and go home."

"Taylor, it was unpardonable..."

The line went dead.

Andre rubbed his temples and sat quietly for a moment. He looked from the venture capital proposal papers to Angel's list of donations and flowers. He picked up Angel's list.

Jamie rocked in her mother's rocking chair surrounded by boxes. Some were old, filched by Angel from supermarkets. Some were brand new, crisp and clean. She rocked back and forth, feeling the comfort of the chair, the soothing of its embracing rocking movements. Mom's chair. Where Jamie had cradled in her arms, where bad dreams had melted away. *How about a nice fairy tale, Jamie? What about Cinderella?*

Boxes all around her. Thirty years and more of a good life. She opened the high school yearbook held in her lap. She found her face: so very young, none of life's lessons yet imprinted on it. The small quote under her photo was from Thoreau: *Dreams are the touchstones of our characters.* Her mother had helped her find it. A small, private joke about the dreams which shaped her creativity.

The rocking chair creaked out its solace.

Through the bedroom door she could see her mother's bed, where she had been sleeping, trying to get close to her mother by taking in the perfume fragrance on her pillow, so different from the jasmine scent outside her island bedroom. Now all the linen had been washed.

She caressed the arm of the rocking chair in search of her mother.

The attorney. Jamie's brow furrowed. Mom had been so insistent. See her attorney. And yet, apart from an insurance policy of $25,000, there had been nothing unusual to report. But he had said he needed to get to the safety deposit box. Perhaps that would have some answers...

Jamie let the yearbook slip to the floor. She leaned back in the chair and closed her eyes. When the door buzzer rang, she startled.

"It's Angel. Jack's parking the truck."

"Come on up."

Angel steamed into the apartment inspecting the pile of boxes. "We did a good job here. Jack'll be up in a minute."

"*You* did a good job here. Six rooms and over thirty years."

"Yeah, and endless trips to the Salvation Army by Jack."

"Thank goodness for his truck."

"Well, so you don't have to decide about everything just yet. Will you stay in St. Lucia, do you think?"

"I really don't know. I've nothing to keep me here, and my job at Jumeaux Designs is a chance I'd never have gotten in New York."

"Big frog in a little pond."

Jamie laughed. "Don't you mean big frog on a little island? I hadn't thought of it that way, but it's true."

Angel smiled. She fell into a chair and blew hair from over her eyes. Her dark eyes studied Jamie as she rocked. "Nice chair."

"Soothing."

"Yeah."

"I have a lot to thank you for, Angel. Checking with the landlord, getting me that dark suit for the funeral, listing donations and flowers..."

"Hey, I was glad to help. Besides, you're practically family."

"Oh, come on. I'm not. Now Mom's gone, I don't have any family."

"Not to hear Bertille talk about you. Says you're one of her pretty parrots."

"You know, this parrot stuff is getting a little old. I like the birds, okay. You all act like they're some mystical force..."

"So how come you're wearing those parrot feather earrings?"

Jamie put her fingers to her ears. "Habit, that's all. And they remind me of St. Lucia."

They heard the front door open.

Angel called out. "Hey, Jack, we're back here. Don't trip over anything."

"Wow, more boxes. Where did all this stuff come from?"

Jamie stood and gave him a quick hug. "What would I have done without you both?"

"How are you doing?"

"Getting through okay, Jack. Thanks for asking."

"Good."

"Jamie flies back to St. Lucia in a couple of days. I was about to invite her over to my parents' tonight. Mom is making her Cuban specialities."

"Hey, good idea." Jack's eyebrows went up. "Come on, Jamie. I'll pick you up. You shouldn't sit in this empty apartment."

"Well, I don't want to intrude..."

"She's coming," Angel said.

"Will Andre be there?"

"Oh, yes. Andre'll be there."

"And Taylor?" She watched Jack and Angel exchange looks.

"No, Taylor won't be there. Listen, how's things with Paul and the divorce?"

"Angel," Jack protested, "you've the diplomacy of a Mack truck."

"There's been no time, Angel." Jamie waved a hand at the boxes.

"What does Andre think?" Angel asked.

"I - I haven't told him everything." Jamie was beginning to regret an earlier sharing with Angel. But pressures had built, she had needed relief.

"Good thing," Angel said. "Andre would have had a talk with him - and if more was needed he would've taken Emile and Marcus with him. Especially Marcus."

Jack smiled, trying to lighten the tone. "Yeah, Dad can be intimidating." He gestured to the closet and some items on the bed. "Is this what's left?"

"Yes."

"Why don't you go through it?"

"Okay." Jamie let out a breath, emptying her lungs.

"Almost through," Angel said softly, putting an arm around her.

Jamie opened a small box from the pile on the bed. Her breath caught when she saw her name in her mother's handwriting on the folded piece of letter paper. It had been placed on top of the tissue-wrapped contents.

Angel and Jack watched as she unfolded the letter. They waited.

Jamie's fingers trembled. She began reading.

My dear Jamie, This box contains your family inheritance. The psalter and child's cross have been passed through the generations. You know I always told you that you were descended from royalty. The family legend is that this book and cross belonged originally to a child (of French nobility). I've never been able to verify this, although lately I thought my genealogical research was getting me closer to the original owner.

A museum curator verified the book is written in French from the eighteenth century and the binding and style are consistent with the kinds of small books owned by the wealthy of that period. The small gold and diamond cross was also identified as from that period, and the fleur-de-lis design points to a French origin. I had hoped to give them to you when you had your first child and that by then I would know more about the owner. But just in case something happens, I'm writing this knowing you'll find it. Regardless of whom your ancestors really were, you have always been our princess. Love, Mom.

The small book was only a little larger than her palm. The smooth leather covering was heavily embroidered, the design ornamented with small pearls. Once white, it was now yellowed with age. The silk thread of the embroidery on the water-stained book's cover was missing in some places. Inside, vellum pages revealed hand lettered entries with illuminated first letters.

"It must have been exquisite when it was new..." Jamie said. "Want to see it?"

Angel carefully took the leather-bound psalter from her.

"It's really old. Is it a family heirloom?"

"That's what the letter says. Wonder why she never told me about it." Jamie took something else from the tissues inside the box. "Look at this. It's the cross Mom mentions in her letter. It must have been for a baby."

"May I see it?"

"Of course." The small cross, gold with tiny pavé-set diamonds, hung delicately in Angel's hand. "Angel, my mother's note talks about genealogy charts. Did you see them when we were packing?"

"No." Her dark eyes moved from the cross to Jack. "Look at the fleur-de-lis. Sure looks French."

"They must be around here somewhere," Jamie said. She took the tiny cross back from Angel and folded her fingers around it, then closed her eyes.

"What are you doing?" Jack asked.

Her fingers opened. "Oh, I don't know. Trying to make a connection, I guess. Hoping to get some sense of who this belonged to."

"Sounds like something my mother would do," Jack said. "It can get irritating. Mothers can be such a pain..."

Jamie's eyes glistened.

"Oh, God, Jamie. I'm sorry." Jack tucked his chin into his neck and mumbled. "Guess Angel's not the only Mack truck around here."

"It's okay. You just don't know how lucky you are to have big families. I'm the only one left in mine."

"Well, we've adopted you, Jamie," Angel said, giving her a reassuring hug.

Jack filled the gap. "You know, my parents say that families have connections that go beyond the physical senses. They're probably right, even if I try to push that off as mumbo-jumbo."

"It's not! I know what they mean, Jack. Dreams. I've had them since childhood. And connections on St. Lucia that don't make sense. Stuff like that." Jamie glanced at the empty rocking chair.

"Yeah, well," Jack said. "I'd get hold of those genealogy charts, see what your mother discovered. Maybe you're not the last."

Angel sought to break the mood as they stood surrounded by boxes, the empty rocking chair a silent presence. "Okay, then. About my parents tonight. Nothing fancy, just good folks. You're coming, right?"

"Sure. You guys are so good to me."

"We're your family, remember?" Angel hugged her again. "It's not good for you to be alone."

CHAPTER TWENTY-ONE

The windows of the second floor apartment were open to the mild evening. A hot salsa beat filled the air, and Jamie was happily in the middle of Angel's family and friends, trying out her poor Spanish long forgotten from school. She cast her eyes around for any sign of Andre, but he wasn't there.

"Give him time, Jamie," Angel said above the noise and music.

"I'm not..."

"Yes, you are."

Jamie gave in. "Okay, I am."

She didn't see him enter the room. He stood and watched her.

Then Angel saw him and gave Jamie a little push. "Go on."

"I'm..."

"Go! And if he asks you out to have time alone with you - go!"

His dark eyes found hers. His smile warmed, then he was coming towards her.

"Hi. Jack said you were coming."

"Yes. It's good to be with them. It's good to see you too, Andre, especially after all you've done..."

"I can't get over you."

"What?"

"Sitting there, trying to communicate in..."

"Fractured Spanish." Jamie overrode him. "Why wouldn't I?"

"Not everybody is as adaptive as you." He thought of Taylor's last visit to St. Lucia. "Hey, I need a drink to celebrate, let's get out of here."

"Leave? But you've just got here..."

"Come on. Look at Angel staring at us with that look of hers."

"It's not polite to leave like this..."

"Sure it is. This is family. We all relax around here. Come on." He waved a hand at Angel, who raised her rum and coke to him.

"No, Andre." Jamie grabbed his hand. "It would be rude to Angel's mother and father. I'm here for another day. Maybe tomorrow night?" The disappointment on his face inexplicably pleased her.

"Okay, you're probably right."

"But it has to be an early evening."

"Oh?"

"I leave the next morning to go back to St. Lucia. Five o'clock taxi pick-up."

Andre held up his palm. "I promise to get you home early. Scout's honor."

Jamie laughed. "You were a Boy Scout?"

"Sure. Where do you think I learned to use a tourniquet?"

A spoon tapped against a glass.

"So tomorrow night. Early dinner."

Jamie's eyes warmed to his. "Great," she whispered as the room grew quiet.

"*La comida está lista,*" Angel said. "Come and eat."

Angel's father stood at the head of the table and bowed his head.

The guests grew silent.

"Thank you, Lord, for the food on our table, for the hands that prepared it and for the family and friends gathered here by your grace. Amen."

Chairs scraped across wooden floors, creaking with diners settling in. Napkins rustled as Angel and her mother brought bowls of rice, beans, roast pork and paella. Conversation lulled as people filled their plates, talk punctuated by the click of serving spoons against china.

"Any hot sauce, Angel?" Andre asked.

"Hot, hotter or hottest?"

"Hottest you've got."

Angel returned from the kitchen and handed Andre a bottle. "St. Lucia Hot Sauce. Bertille sent it back with Jack."

"Perfect." Andre shook it on his rice and beans, then passed the bottle to Jack, who liberally dosed his plate.

"Jamie, you're practically a St. Lucian by now. You should try this." Jack held out the bottle.

Angel glared at him.

"Come on, it's part of our heritage. And this is Mom's special recipe."

Jamie looked dubious, then picked up the bottle and shook a few drops on her food.

"Whoa!"

"What?"

"It's hot, Jamie," Andre said.

"Come on. How hot can it be?" She took a big bite.

Angel looked alarmed.

Jack and Andre were smiling. "One, two, three..."

"Not so bad," Jamie said just before the burn kicked in. "Water," she croaked. "Water."

Andre and Jack were laughing.

"Honestly," Angel said, putting a tall glass of water in Jamie's hand. "You two ought to grow up. It's not funny."

"More water," Jamie croaked, her eyes streaming.

Andre was beginning to look worried.

"I'm sorry, Jamie. I thought you knew how hot it was."

She wiped her eyes with her napkin.

Angel gave her a clean plate. "Start over, Jamie," she said, cuffing Jack on the shoulder. She grabbed the hot sauce off the table.

"Is this what's in those bottles at the market?" Jamie asked, her voice still husky.

"Ahhh, Jamie, I'm really sorry," Andre said again.

Jamie dabbed at her eyes. "Maybe I'll create a T-shirt for Jumeaux Designs - for the tourists. 'I survived St. Lucian Hot Sauce.'"

"Where are we going?" Jamie asked the following evening when Andre picked her up.

"To Martine's. A tiny place someone told me about. I think only ten tables. Country French. I've been meaning to try it."

Ten minutes later they pulled into an alley. The windows supported flower boxes overflowing with a mixture of pink, purple and salmon petunias.

"Reminds me of St. Lucia bougainvillea," Jamie said.

"Does, doesn't it."

"You said something last night about celebrating...?"

"My latest venture capital deal," he said, aware he really wanted to spend time with her. "And the St. Lucia venture. It's really coming together, but there's still one major decision."

"Oh?"

"Deciding on the site. Near Soufriere or at Grande Anse."

"I'm happy for you, Andre."

He squeezed her hand. "I know you are. Here's the door."

The hostess greeted them. "Would you prefer to sit inside or in the garden terrace?"

"Terrace, no contest," Jamie said, swept along on Andre's buoyant mood.

They were led across flagstones to a corner table. Sprays of fragrant roses traced their way through trellis work.

Jamie suddenly felt a trifle nauseous. "Oh."

"Oh, what?" Andre said as they were seated.

"The flowers, a bit strong."

"Really, we can move..."

"No, it's going away now. Had the same reaction to my shampoo. I think it's all the tension of the last few days."

Andre looked at her. "You've been through a lot. I'm just glad we were here to help."

"Speaking of which..." Jamie delved into her purse and pulled out an envelope. "For you."

"What is it?"

"Paid back expenses."

"Jamie, for Pete's sake..."

"The five hundred is reimbursement to your mother. The balance is for the hotel room you got for me."

Andre stuck his chin out, a startling gesture which highlighted the distinctive cleft. "My mother gave you five hundred?"

"She was very kind."

"I'll say."

"You sound surprised, Andre."

"Well, it's just that mother's so...dignified. It comes across as distant even. I'm glad she did this, Jamie."

"She's distant with me too, of course, as with everyone. But sometimes she breaks out, breaks free. She certainly reached out for me last week, calling you and all." She hesitated. "I sense a sadness to her, Andre, some deep melancholy..."

"Yes. We can talk about that sometime. I'm glad you can see her in that light. Compassionately, I mean."

"She's helping me a lot. I have an office, did you know that?"

Andre lifted his eyebrows in mock surprise. "Have you now."

"Low pay, big office with great views," she finished.

"Will you go right back to work when you return?"

"Yes, I think so. Get back into routine. Also there's Paul..."

"Ah, yes. Paul."

"Andre, I want to talk about all of it, but later, all right? It's so lovely here..."

"Sure. And I should talk about Taylor. She's supposed to fly down to St. Lucia."

Jamie changed the subject. "Andre, I need your advice."

He looked at her, startled. "Sure. How can I help?"

"This morning I found some of mom's personal belongings. A small book, a psalter actually, and a small cross, a child's cross. They're both very, very old. Part of the reason for Mom's genealogy search, I'm sure." She looked at him. "What is it?"

Andre paused for a moment. "Both Angel and Jack mentioned them, the cross and the book. Sounds like your mother thought they were important."

"She said they'd been in the family for generations. I'm surprised I didn't know about them."

"Probably an interesting story there, maybe some mysterious ancestor."

"Jack said something about old families having connections that go beyond the physical..."

"You must understand that on a small island like St. Lucia people know who they are related to, can go back many generations. It underlines a great respect. My family - and Bertille's and Marcus' - place high value on heritage and ancestry." Andre thought briefly of Taylor, her own impeccable lineage, her comment that she had been expected to marry one of the DuPont boys. Jamie's voice recaptured his attention.

"So the genealogy..."

"Ask my mother. She's into that. Maybe she can help you solve the mystery." He smiled.

"Andre?"

"Uuumm?"

"When I came to the island, it all felt familiar. Even when I met you at the truck accident, even you looked familiar."

"So you've said."

"But at times it gets to be a bit much. Like Bertille, like she wants to suck all the New York out of me, turn me into a Lucian."

Andre nodded. "I'm not surprised. She's taken you under her wing."

"That's another thing. The parrots. You all act like I belong on St. Lucia just because I've always dreamed about parrots."

"Maybe you do, Jamie. You must admit it hasn't been hard for you to adapt to St. Lucia, accept the culture. But I didn't know you dreamed of parrots. Now, that's a Bertille thing." He reached across the table and touched the iridescent feather dangling from her ear.

The waiter handed them menus. "I'm surprised Bertille didn't say something to me." He picked up his knife and made creases in the table cloth, thinking. Then he opened a menu. "Now, what are we going to eat?"

They ordered a light meal of country soup and crusty bread.

"Andre?"

He smiled. "More questions?"

"Angel says things are a bit rocky with Taylor."

"Then she should mind her own business."

"No! I don't mean that, please. I mean with the loss of my mother, the things I've had to do up here, your wonderful help - I just couldn't have gotten through it without you and Angel and Jack - I just hope I haven't been the cause of the problems with Taylor."

"You haven't. I've been busy. Still am, with the follow through on a couple of venture capital deals and the hotel project. As for helping you, I wanted to do that. I feel a connection, too."

"And Taylor?"

He paused, waiting, as their soup, thick with vegetables, was placed in front of them. "She's not really comfortable on the island," he said finally.

"I'm sorry, Andre."

"We'll see how things go when she comes down." He waved his spoon, dismissing it. "Speaking of Angel minding her own business, she told *me* things weren't going well for you and Paul."

Jamie toyed with her bread. "I said we shouldn't talk about it, but here we are."

"Yes, here we are. So?"

"We'll probably get divorced, and please don't ask..."

"It's a small island, Jamie," he said gently.

"Anyway, with Mom's death, it's all had to wait."

"He didn't come to the funeral, I noticed."

"No. Another disappointment."

They ate in silence, then made small talk, trying to bridge the serious issues that had been raised. It would take time.

Andre took her home, allowing for a soft kiss on her cheek, that held just a little longer than it should have. He noted the soft jasmine scent she wore, a fragrance that reminded him of the island.

So different from the strong fragrance Taylor chose.

Jamie watched him drive away. On her way in she checked her mailbox. She tore open the package from her mother's lawyer. Inside were the genealogy charts.

CHAPTER TWENTY-TWO

In Clarisse's downstairs office Jamie sat quietly in her chair and watched as Clarisse prepared their tea with lemon. The ginger lily designs she'd brought to show Clarisse lay on the work table. Clarisse had the lights low, leaving the paintings on the walls in shadow. Jamie waited while Clarisse got comfortable, her tea in front of her. Clarisse looked tired, fragile, she thought.

"My dear, I trust you are feeling better after New York."

"Yes, I am. It was difficult, of course, but Andre was there - and I do thank you for calling him - and Angel and Jack. They were wonderful."

"I'm so sorry for your loss, Jamie."

Jamie nodded. "It was so sudden, that was the worst part."

"Did you get to speak with her?"

"I did. We were lucky. To have that time, those last moments, together."

Clarisse looked at her tea cup.

"Are you all right, Clarisse?"

The groomed gray hair and taut profile came up. "I, why yes, child."

"You left me for a moment," Jamie said, then wondered if she had been too frank.

"Yes, in truth I did. I was thinking about my own parents. I lost both of them in a car accident. I was quite young."

"With no chance to talk, to have last moments," Jamie said quietly.

"But I have my mother's ring as a remembrance. A small stone, but it holds my parents for me." Clarisse held out her hand.

"It's lovely," said Jamie. "I've always liked those old style settings."

Clarisse sipped her tea. "Andre told me you had dinner with Angel and her parents, and Jack, of course." She smiled.

"It was wonderful. They are all so warm. And Andre took me to dinner the night before I left to come back. He's been very kind."

"And you had some good talk?"

"Yes. I - I enjoy Andre's company very much."

Clarisse nodded, her blue eyes steady on her. "We talk, Andre and I, but mostly about the family, the island. Yet I sense he enjoys your company as well."

Jamie hesitated. "We are both contending with difficult decisions right now."

"Ah, yes. Life can hold difficulties."

Jamie tried to brighten the mood. "Did Andre tell you about the family treasures mother left for me?"

"He said a little gold cross. Is it the one you're wearing?"

Jamie fingered the cross at her throat. "Yes, I had a jeweler add some chain. It must have been for a baby, the chain was so short."

"Come closer so I can look."

Jamie went around the desk and bent forward. The light from the desk lamp illuminated the small cross, the tiny diamonds sparkling in the light. Clarisse's hand trembled as she touched it, her breath released in a deep sigh.

Jamie did not notice the color draining from Clarisse's face. "Yes, and a psalter, a little book written in old French. Andre's encouraged me to check into our genealogy, carry on my mother's research. He said you might be able to help me. I don't mean to presume, Clarisse...I already have a good start, thanks to Mom's hard work."

Clarisse sat back in her chair and stared at her tea cup.

"Clarisse?" Jamie waited for a long moment.

Clarisse managed a smile, lost around hidden thoughts. "I'm afraid I'm not feeling too well, Jamie. I hope you will forgive me and perhaps we can look at the ginger lily designs tomorrow... And perhaps you'd bring the psalter. I'd love to see it as well. Family heirlooms are precious."

Jamie stepped quietly around the desk to her chair. "Of course. I'm afraid I've been bothering you with all these personal things..."

"Not at all. I'm glad that all is well with you. But if you would excuse me?"

"Of course."

As Jamie left she glanced at the photographs of Clarisse's family. Emile and Andre...caring Andre. And Marcus and Bertille. Part of her life now, too. As was Clarisse.

Clarisse put her head in her hands. There could not be another cross like this, a twin to the diamond cross on a fleur-de-lis chain she owned, passed down in her own family which descended from the younger of the twin boys born to Anne-Cecile de Roche and Jean-Clair du Diamant.

Was it possible that the cross Jamie wore was from the lost twin?

Not after two hundred years! The family had searched for some trace of this child for generations. Clarisse's own efforts to trace the child using modern search methods had proved no more fruitful, and she had long ago decided the child had perished, putting to rest any concerns about what would happen if this branch of the family surfaced.

She was aware her family's interest in tracing the child was not just a matter of curiosity. It was, rather, based on the possibility of claims descendants of the elder twin might make on the original estate.

How much does Jamie know? she wondered. Clarisse had worked all her life to protect her children and secure their future. She knew too many secrets and had carried their burden for too long. There had been a time when she could not protect her children. Now nothing and no one was going to get in the way. The ugliness of the thought drained her, but she admitted to herself that the whole responsibility of the family heritage was a rack on which she had suffered for most of her life. Nothing, not even this blessed and vulnerable child, Jamie, could stand in the way.

CHAPTER TWENTY-THREE

"How're you doing up there, Jamie?" Barbara asked. "I've got peppermints if you're getting car sick."

Jamie looked back to see Barbara tucked in among beach towels, coolers and tarps. "I'm fine. You've been on a Grande Anse turtle watch before so, knowing you, you've everything we might possibly need."

Brian swerved around another pot hole.

"I like that outfit, Jamie," Barbara said. "Pretty."

"It's a Jumeaux Designs creation using a Jamie Elliott original fabric design. Coming to a store near you."

"Wow, I'm impressed," Barbara said.

"Me too." Jamie patted herself on the back. "But I've brought other clothes. Learned my lesson on that first hike with Danielle..." She stopped, pushing away a painful thought.

"I'm so glad I ran into Emile in town," Barbara said. "It'll be fun for all of us to camp together. And the turtles, if we're lucky enough to see some, are amazing."

Jamie had almost turned down this invitation when Barbara said Andre would be there with Taylor, but it was a small island and she couldn't avoid them forever. Besides, she really wanted to see the big sea turtles come ashore to lay their eggs.

"Why are we stopping?" Jamie asked as the beach unfolded before them, the edge of the sand thick with sea grape and coconut palms. Rolling surf pounded the shore.

"Four-wheel-drive," Brian said as he changed gears. "Once we start down the beach we have to make a dash to the campsite."

"Why?"

Barbara laughed. "So we won't get stuck in the sand like we did last year."

Brian got the gear to engage. "As I remember, you weren't laughing when we had to dig the jeep out." He shaded his eyes and gestured. "I see some campsites down there, already set up. Isn't that Emile's red truck?"

Jamie tightened her seat belt as Brian drove at a steady pace, around holes in the sand left by sand mining, crossing irregular rows of flotsam cast away by the receding tide. He finally stopped the jeep at the far end of the beach near the red pick-up.

"Welcome," Emile said as they piled out of the jeep.

"What do we do first?" Jamie asked. "Do we watch for turtles now?"

"No, they come ashore at night."

"I really hope I get to see one," Jamie said. "I've seen the parrots. Turtles would be so perfect."

Barbara was pulling stuff out of the back of the jeep.

"Here's your cutlass, Brian," she said.

"I'll help Emile and Andre cut tree branches to support the tarps. Give us a place to sleep under, get out of the sun. Jamie, you've got coconut duty."

"Coconut duty?"

"You collect dry coconut husks for a fire. Dry cow pies are good too."

"Think I'll stick to coconuts."

"Hey, Jamie."

She turned to see Andre and a lovely blonde woman approaching.

I'd better get this over with, Jamie thought, glad she had on her pretty blouse. *My design,* she reminded herself. *Original design.* She took a calming breath.

"Andre. Hello." Jamie hated the flush that crept up her neck.

"This is Taylor." Andre put his arm around Taylor's shoulders. Jamie locked her knees to keep from running away. "I was hoping you'd arrive before Emile and I hiked up the bluff."

"Oh?"

"We'll be gone a couple of hours. Thought you and Taylor could get to know each other. Say, how are you doing?"

"Okay. No, better than okay. Some days are still hard."

"Sure, I'd expect so."

Taylor watched the interchange, puzzled by something she couldn't put her finger on. Something about the way Andre's face changed, grew softer on seeing Jamie, something about the way Jamie had stiffened. Little things, but Taylor had noticed. "I think I told you this is one of the areas we are considering for the hotel."

"Yes, you did."

"You okay with staying here, Taylor?"

"Fine, darling. I may go for a swim. Water looks glorious."

"Not by yourself. There's a nasty rip tide at this beach." He glanced at Jamie, remembering that night at the cove, Jamie wet and shivering. How he had put his coat around her, warmed her with his arms. Now, Taylor's pale elegance a contrast to Jamie's dark hair and tanned face.

Jamie filled the gap. "I have to finish collecting stuff for the fire. Taylor, want to help?"

"Sure."

"Thanks, Jamie," Andre said. He pulled Taylor close and kissed her. "See you later, darling."

Jamie averted her eyes.

"You're going to ruin that beautiful outfit." She surveyed Taylor's clothing, more appropriate to cruising than a weekend camping in the sand.

"Isn't this okay?"

"Look, I'll share some of my stuff with you. We're about the same size. I think we may get dirty before the weekend's out."

"Jamie, Andre told me of your recent loss. I'm really sorry."

"Thanks, Taylor," Jamie changed the subject. "This is my first turtle watch. How about you?"

"Andre was so excited, I couldn't bear to turn him down. Do you know what we do?"

"Only what my friends told me. We take turns after dark, walk up and down the beach looking for turtles that need help."

"At night," Taylor said.

"That's what they told me. Let me see what I can find for you to wear." Jamie began rummaging through her duffel of clothes. "I really hope I get to see a turtle." She pulled out a pair of shorts and a T-shirt, some jeans for later. "Here you go."

"Where do I change?" Taylor asked.

"There's the bathroom." Jamie's smile was rueful as she pointed to the grove of palms and seagrape.

"Taylor. Wake up," Andre said. "It's our turn."

"Hmmm. Take Emile," she said, glad her warm covers cut the stiff breeze off the water.

Andre shook her shoulder. "Come on, Taylor."

Taylor sat up, envious as she watched Brian and Barbara crawl into their sleeping bags.

"How many times do we have to do this?" she asked, putting on a wind breaker.

"Every six hours, so twice tonight." Andre handed her a can of insect repellant. "Sand flies," he said.

"As if they could land on me in this wind." Taylor took the can and sprayed.

"Ready?" he asked. The half moon gave just enough light for them to see shapes, vague outlines.

"Use the flashlight, Andre," Taylor said.

"Can't. Light might scare the turtles. That's why we had to douse the fires so early. And why no music."

They'd been walking for half an hour when Taylor grabbed Andre's arm.

"I see one."

"Where?"

She pointed.

"Shhhhh. If it hears us coming it'll go back in the water."

They crept closer. It wasn't a turtle, just a box trashed on the beach.

"Do you always get to see turtles?" Taylor whispered.

"No, not always. But I love coming anyway. Marcus and Bertille brought us as children. Lots more turtles then. They're an important part of the island's..."

"Heritage, I know. Andre, I said I'd give it a chance."

He ignored the bait. "Meant to ask you. Where'd you get those clothes? Not quite your style."

"Jamie lent them to me. It was nice of her."

"Yes, she is. Nice." He thought of the rumors about Paul.

Andre heard a muffled cry and then a thump.

"Taylor. Where are you?" he whispered.

"Down here."

"Wait a minute. Let me put the torch on." He turned around but didn't see her. "Talk to me so I can find you."

"Down here. Fell in a hole." Andre shone the light on her.

"God, Taylor, are you all right?"

"You didn't tell me there were holes."

"Forgot to mention the sand miners. They're not supposed to take the sand, but it's a way for a man to make a few dollars." He reached down, clasped her wrist and helped her out.

"Andre, can we sit for a few minutes?"

"Okay." He sat beside her on the sand.

"Cold?"

"No. Frustrated."

"Oh?"

"Andre, I can tell you love this. It's part of your, oh, I'm beginning to hate the word, part of your heritage. But it's not me."

"You just got off to a bad start, stepping in that cow pat when you and Jamie were collecting coconuts for the fire."

Taylor shuddered. "Andre, you're not listening. You want to be here. I don't."

Andre reached out for her hand. Taylor pulled it away.

"You stay and have fun with your friends. I hope you get to see lots of turtles, but I want you to take me home."

Andre sighed. "I really hoped you'd enjoy it, Taylor."

"I know, darling, but I'm not. I know you want to share your island life with me, but could you just take me back to Jumeaux." She swatted at a cloud of sand flies.

"Can't until daylight."

"Why not?"

"Because the noise of the truck would scare any..."

"Turtles. The precious turtles."

"Right. Look, I'll take you back to Jumeaux at first light."

"I'm sorry, Andre. This just isn't me."

Andre was silent, not wanting to say the words out loud. *But it's me, Taylor, the part of me that belongs to St. Lucia.*

"Where's Taylor?" Emile asked as Andre joined him on the Jumeaux veranda.

"Turned in early," Andre replied, his face glum as he settled into one of the big rockers.

They sat and rocked, hearing faint sounds coming from the kitchen where Bertille was still working.

"Sorry Taylor didn't like the turtle watch."

"Me too."

"Jamie and I found a turtle. You should have seen her, Andre. Jamie, I mean." Emile chuckled, remembering. "Lying on her belly digging in the sand to help the turtle. She was so excited."

Andre tried to rock away his disappointment. "Let's talk about the hotel. Do you agree now the Grande Anse site won't work?"

"Yes. You've convinced me. Bad rip tide, wind, snakes."

Andre looked at his brother. "Right. So we're back to the site here, between the Pitons."

"There's the problem of the access road to the site. Really need to go through Marcus' and Bertille's land. I doubt they'd give us a right of way."

"I've discussed this with the lawyers."

"And?"

"They said we've got to have that land. Said maybe the title wasn't clear."

Bertille had just lifted a stack of dirty plates from the dining room table when she overheard. She stood quietly. Listening.

"I told you at the beginning this project might divide the family."

"It gets worse. The lawyers were definite. Said they had a group of investors ready to invest forty million dollars and no locals would get in the way."

"I suppose their solution is to throw money at the problem."

"Exactly. Said everybody has a price, told me not to get too ethical."

"They don't know Marcus and Bertille."

"And there's no reasonable alternative access."

Bertille put the rest of the dinner dishes in the sink and began washing them, lost in her own thoughts. It was impossible to think that the land which had belonged to the family for generations might be taken from them.

Evil flying round this place tonight, she thought.

Speaking out loud, she said, "Go back to bush, go back to ground, go make mischief somewhere else."

Quickly finishing her kitchen chores, Bertille went in search of Marcus.

CHAPTER TWENTY-FOUR

Jamie stood in front of the full-length mirror and eyed herself in the new Jumeaux sun dress. The ginger lily design was graceful and accented the simple cut of the dress. There would be no other like it at tonight's Bastille Day party.

She stood quite still, imagining Andre seeing her, feeling that familiar trip-beat to her heart. But he would be there with Taylor, and if he was there with Taylor, then it meant things were better between them. The whole thing at Martine's, lingering over dessert, the tentative, almost awkward sharing of problems, skirting around unspoken attractions - none of it counted now. After meeting Taylor at Grande Anse, Jamie could see why. Taylor was cool elegance, controlled reserve. If he brought Taylor tonight it meant things were better for them, and even if Taylor wasn't up for turtle watching, she had obviously made the case that she could adapt to island life.

Jamie hugged herself, remembering Andre's soft kiss on her cheek. He had held it too long, the touch intoxicating, then gone. There had been *something* there! Even Angel had sensed the connection and had given tacit support.

She smoothed her hands down her thighs, then critically examined her arms. She thought briefly of Paul. That difficult night.

She hadn't talked to him in weeks, stepped over him sleeping on the living room floor when she went to work. On the nights when he came home.

Idly Jamie went to her small desk and fingered the genealogy records. She still had to decide if she would stay on St. Lucia, but for now she would lose herself in work, number one; and number two, find out how to get started on divorce proceedings. Somehow she would manage, and meantime there was a party to go to, and Barbara and Brian. She glanced at her watch. They would pick her up in a few minutes.

"This place always looks better at night," Barbara said, as they walked towards the restaurant and the marina beyond. They could hear the party as music swelled across the night, lively and with a driving calypso beat.

Jamie looked out at the moorings, the glow from the restaurant glinting off the masts which rose like pale threads from the dark water. "You're cynical. I think it's beautiful."

Barbara squeezed her hand. "You're a romantic."

"I hope Ian Danville won't show up."

"I don't think so, but it's always possible. If he does, just stay by us. He probably doesn't remember that night in the cove."

"I'll never forget it," Jamie said. "Will Emile be here?"

"You mean Andre?" Barbara said softly.

"Yes, of course I mean Andre," Jamie snapped. "But he's not available, Barbara, and is probably coming with Taylor, so..."

"Oh, hon. Sorry. It's an occupational hazard..."

"Bossy meddler?"

"Ouch. Maybe I could hang out a shingle."

"Barbara, if Andre and Taylor, I mean if they...I might have to... I mean, Hell, I don't know what I mean. Could you stay close? I guess that's what I'm asking."

"Sure. As long as I can have a couple of dances with this handsome stranger." She took Brian's arm as he joined them after parking the jeep.

"You mean the drill sergeant?" Jamie said.

"Who, me?"

"Yeah, you. No coconut or cow pie duty for me tonight. I'm determined to have fun."

"Good for you, Jamie," Brian said warmly. "But I might have to boss Barbara around just to keep in practice."

Barbara poked him. "There's only one boss in this family."

"She's an acquired taste, like olives," Brian said.

"See how he puts up with me, why I love him so?" Barbara kissed him.

Palms in pots fluttered in the breeze off the water, and candles in paper bags lined the boardwalk entrance. A railing separated the restaurant from the water and the boats moored there. Bare bulbs with woven basket shades cast swaying shadows on the tables. Music and laughter lifted the party, already in full swing.

Jamie looked around for Andre and Taylor.

"Not here yet," Barbara said, reading her thoughts. "Brian, some drinks for your lovely women folk."

"Coming right up."

Jamie and Barbara scanned the room. "There's Emile over by the bar," Barbara said.

"Who's the woman?"

"Not sure. Emile plays the field."

"Different from Andre."

Barbara looked up at her.

"He's really quite shy. And not to knock Emile, but Andre has quiet values, he moves gently," Jamie said.

"Jamie, I swear. What the hell happened in New York?"

"I took care of my mother..."

"Oh, Jamie, I didn't mean that, I could bite my tongue. I mean with Andre."

"Andre helped. So did Angel and Jack."

"I know that. I pumped you dry when you got back, remember? I know about the cross and the psalter. They're exquisite, by the way. But it's something else..." Barbara's intelligent eyes peered up into Jamie's.

"Here we go," Brian said. "I settled on margaritas."

"Brian, your timing stinks."

"And I love you madly, too, hon."

Jamie smiled at them, just for a moment envying them what they had. That was when she saw Andre and Taylor. "Let's move," Jamie said, suddenly uncomfortable, watching Andre's easy grace as he greeted friends, and Taylor looking cool and devastatingly blonde in tailored slacks, a matching pale ecru shell with spaghetti straps, her slim waist set off by a magenta sash. Jamie knew a moment of doubt, looking down at her ginger lily design.

"Flashy blonde," Barbara said loyally. "You're classy in a different way, that's all." Barbara smiled up at her.

"Thanks for staying close. I may bolt again," Jamie murmured. They leaned on the railing, looking out over the water, looking down at moored sailboats. "This is nice. You can see right down to the boats."

Barbara nodded, swaying to the music.

"Andre and Taylor are coming over," Brian said. He tucked Jamie's arm into his elbow and discreetly led her away to examine a flowering plant.

Jamie's heart skipped a beat.

"Jamie?" Taylor's modulated voice tore into her. "How lovely to see you tonight. I was hoping you'd be here. Emile told me you got to see a turtle."

"I did. I'm sorry you missed it. I'm still excited about it. I've offered to go back and watch again."

"It's good to see you again, Jamie," Andre said, taking in her enthusiasm. "All settled in at work?"

"Yes, thanks. We're almost finished with the new designs for the Tropical Flowers collection."

"If that's one of them," Taylor said, "you outdid yourself. It's absolutely lovely."

"If you don't mind excusing us," Andre said, "I want to introduce Taylor to the Clarks over there. She'll enjoy Connie." His dark eyes twinkled.

Jamie turned back to the railing.

"You survived, hon."

Jamie took a drink from her glass, the salt on the edge of the glass focusing her attention. She licked her lips. As she glanced down at the boat below, she noticed the hatch was open, soft lights emanating from the berth. Jamie watched in voyeuristic fascination at two entwined bodies, surging and thrusting. Body contours glistened with sweat, the pulsing lights from the dance floor revealing hypnotic flashes of the raw sexual scene.

Pulling her eyes away, she gazed back at the crowded dance floor, vaguely troubled but unsure why. A sudden sound from below recaptured her attention. Looking back down at the boat, a head of dark curly hair appeared for an instant as the strobe lights pulsed, and Jamie recognized Danielle. Jean-Pierre was on the dance floor, so the other body in the boat could not be his. Jamie glanced from the dance floor to the boat below just in time to catch a glimpse of Paul's face. *Oh, God, had Barbara seen too?*

Anger surged through her. Without thinking she picked up her glass and threw it at the boat. Then another and another. As the glasses shattered, Paul reared up and yelled.

Barbara's hands reached out to her.

Jamie ran, evading her, knocking over a chair, brushing through small gatherings who shifted, startled, as she went by them, not noticing the concerned faces of her friends. She plunged across the dance floor, tears blinding her as she hunted for a way out.

"Jamie!" Andre called after her.

Then she heard Taylor's voice calling after Andre, a modulated command.

When Andre caught her at the door he turned her, looking into her eyes, his own filled with concern.

"Go back, Andre," she said.

"What's wrong? "

"Please, go back." Jamie urged. Andre did not loosen his grip on her arm.

"Taylor needs you," Jamie said.

"You must tell me what's wrong. Is it Paul? Your mother, what is it?"

"Go back to Taylor."

"Jamie..."

"Please..." Jamie wrenched free and ran.

When she finally slowed, her breathing was ragged. She gulped in the sweet tropical air, could barely hear the music and laughter of the party. Like the glasses she had thrown, any unacknowledged hopes for a reconciliation with Paul had shattered back there. His philandering was old news, but such a public display was humiliating. In front of her friends. And Andre. His embrace as he caught her at the door. How she had wanted to let him hold her. The tears, the blinding tears that came now were not for Paul.

At home Jamie locked up the front door and checked the back. Paul had a key, but she doubted he would come home. Tomorrow she would get the locks changed. She opened both bedroom windows for cross ventilation and crawled into bed, still wearing her designer dress. She willed herself to be still, taking deep breaths of the scented jasmine planted under her window. She reached for her cross and psalter and gathered them to her. "Mom..." was all she said.

She was still awake when Paul turned his key in the lock and stepped inside.

"What do you want?"

"No problem, Jamie, absolutely no problem. I just need a couple of things and I'm outa here."

She followed him as he moved around the house.

"How come you're not yelling?"

"You just did me a huge favor, Paul. You just set me free."

"What're you talking about, Jamie? You been talking to those parrots again. You're sick, you know. Oughta see a psychiatrist."

Jamie wondered why she wasn't feeling angry any more.

"Okay, I got my passport, all right? And a little cash I stashed away. And I've already got most of my clothes. Shit, I'll be glad to get out of here. No more time in that stupid rattan chair or pillows on the floor."

She listened as he spoke, relieved. The sleeping in the chair and on the floor was over. He was welcome to go to other women's beds

- or boats. She really didn't care.

"Okay, that's it. If you want to throw something, now's your last chance."

Jamie felt curiously detached. *Why don't I care?* she wondered.

"I'm heading for Martinique with Danielle. And while we're on the subject, what the hell did I do that was so wrong? You practically threw me out, you cut me off from a love life - what's a guy to do?"

The cross was warm in her hand. She brought it to her lips.

"I guess that's it then."

She listened.

"Aren't you going to say anything?"

Jamie was silent.

"Some of it worked, Jamie. Give me that."

She stood in the doorway and watched him walk away.

CHAPTER TWENTY-FIVE

At Jumeaux the sun was high in the sky by mid-morning, hanging full against a clear sky. The day would be hot. On the veranda, Andre sat in one of the big rockers, deep in thought, his chin resting in his palm, his mug of tea grown cold.

"Good morning, Andre," Taylor said, lightly touching his shoulder.

"Good morning. Can I get you something? Juice, perhaps? Tea?" He motioned to his cup.

"No, I'm fine. Where is everybody?"

"Father left early for Castries, and Bertille isn't coming in today."

"Ah."

"Why ah?"

"Because I need to talk to you."

"Of course, Taylor. You know I'm always available."

Taylor decided not to remind him of the missed lunch in New York, his preoccupation, the distance in their relationship. What she wanted to say really wasn't about that.

"I didn't sleep well last night."

"We put a coil in your room. Were the mosquitoes bad?"

"No, it wasn't that. I just was doing a lot of thinking."

Andre shifted in his chair. "About what?"

"About us, our lives."

"And..."

"Andre, please. I love you, probably always will in some way. But our lives together..."

"Taylor, I'm sorry about the turtle watch thing. I realize I shouldn't have pushed you to go. I just thought that..."

"No, I'm glad you pushed me to go. It made things clearer for me."

"Things?"

"You told me that I needed to know the part of you that belongs to the island. You were more right than you knew. Your roots here are a rich heritage, Andre, but it's a heritage I can't embrace."

"Can't or won't?"

"Please don't be contentious, Andre."

"I wanted you to love the island."

"I know. I hoped I would, but for me it would always be a beautiful place to visit. I said I'd give it a chance. Now I know I could never live here."

Andre rubbed his temples.

"Headache?"

He shook his head. "Taylor, I know I've been distant..."

"I tried to tell you, but you couldn't hear me. And then last night it all fell into place. Something about the way you looked at Jamie, the despair in your eyes when she ran from the party."

"You're the one I was at the party with, Taylor, you're the one here at Jumeaux." Andre shifted in his seat, clearly uncomfortable.

"Shhh, Andre. Let me give you this gift. Don't you see it, feel it? I could sense a connection between you and Jamie at Grande Anse, but last night..."

"She was distressed, Taylor. Something had obviously upset her and..."

"Other people were around, Andre. Barbara, Brian." She fingered her diamond engagement ring. "Andre. Let me help you here. I think there's more to your feelings about Jamie than you realize."

"Now wait a minute, Taylor…"

She blinked back tears. "I saw some of it at Grande Anse. She's more beautiful when she's with you, Andre. She glows. And so excited last night, telling about helping the turtle."

"I care for Jamie."

"My woman's intuition tells me it's way more than that, but you'll have to find out for yourself." Her hand came across to grasp his. "I know you care about me, Andre. In fact, you're the most thoroughly decent man I've ever known."

"Taylor…"

She took off her engagement ring and pressed it into his hand. "Neither of us is the bad guy here, Andre. And this isn't even about Jamie. Maybe I'm wrong about that. But I'm right about not marrying you. I'm not right for you. You need someone who can love the island the way you do." Her hand came up towards the land. "All of this, the island life, the family heritage, the responsibilities…it's more than I can handle. Truth to tell, I don't want to handle it." She managed a smile. "This is not your fault, Andre. We both tried."

She watched Andre stare at the ring. They had bought it together in New York. So long ago, it seemed.

"You need a wife here on the island. Someone to raise your children here, to raise them to love this place the way you do. I can't be that wife."

Taylor could see the anguish in his eyes.

"I'd want to be in the States. Bertille would raise our children, like she raised you. It's not what you want, Andre."

"No," he admitted.

"You love this island, but the world will pull you out. Your deals and hotel projects, your corporate side. You need a wife who can anchor you here. If we married and lived in New York, you'd never forgive me."

"I've done this badly, Taylor."

Taylor stood up. "No, both of us tried. And now we've made a good decision. Go after Jamie, Andre. Find out if she's the one. Before she has to swat you with a two-by-four to get you moving."

Andre smiled. "She likes you, you know."

Taylor kissed him, her lips cool and soft. Andre looked into her eyes, great affection there. He pressed the ring back into her hand.

"I want you to keep this. Have the stone reset. To remember the good times."

"When we went swimming that time? I'd dive off your shoulders into the blue, so blue waters?"

He nodded as she slipped the ring into her pocket.

"We'll both remember those times. And if I'm right, Jamie won't mind."

She walked back into the house.

Jamie sat on her couch and looked out the window. No shadows. Could it already be noon? She picked up a smiling photograph of her mother and father, which she had brought out from the boxes in New York. They smiled into the lens, their eyes watching her. They were obviously happy. It had been taken about a year before her father died. That was the marriage she had wanted.

Her fingers found the cross at her throat. The genealogy charts lay on the couch beside her. The little psalter next to it, tucked in white tissue. Her heritage.

With a conscious effort she thrust Paul from her. *Got to get moving, get organized.* She made a cup of tea, grabbed a couple of tea biscuits, picked up her sketch pad and went to sit on the porch. The little bullfinch came and sat on the railing.

"There you are, little guy."

The bird cocked its head.

"You're such a good listener." She broke off some crumbs for the bird, then picked up her sketch pad. Idle lines, clearing her thoughts.

"You know," she said, "my husband's left me." She put more crumbs on the page where she was drawing. The bird came and sat.

"I'm glad he did, but now I have to decide what to do." She put a few crumbs on her finger, and the little red-breasted bird perched there, unafraid.

Jamie sat very still. *What do I want?* Unbidden, the answer came into her head. *Stay here. Stay on this island. I have friends here, I have a job, no ties in the States. And something more, the connections I feel.* Relief flooded in.

"So," she said aloud. The finch startled, flitted to the railing. "I'll stay." Her fingers found her pencil and she began drawing as she gazed at the little bird. What else?

The biggest decision made, she began a list on her page.

1. Divorce. *Maybe Mom's lawyer in New York can tell me what to do,* she thought. She gazed at the sketch of the little bird, her hand moving across the page. The crook of a tree, a nest with fledglings. Parrots. Those odd dreams of flying with another parrot. *Why am I thinking of that now?* she wondered. *Maybe with Paul gone those unsettling dreams will go away.*

Okay, she said to herself. *Concentrate. Get organized.* She wrote a number two and added embellishments. Like the script in the psalter. Okay, that's a direction.

2. Genealogy. Ask Clarisse if she will help me.

Maybe not, Jamie thought. *She's pulled back. Don't know why.* She flipped her sketch pad back to an earlier page. The page where she had sketched Bertille's face. Wise eyes stared back at her, the high cheekbones, the full mouth. She remembered that day in the kitchen at Jumeaux. There was a connection there that needed to be followed. She wrote a numeral three.

3. Explore connection with Bertille. *But how can I do that without running into Andre and Taylor? Have to stay out of Andre's way.*

4. Stay out of Andre's way.

The bullfinch hopped onto her sketch pad. Wanting attention. "Stay out of Andre's way," she said aloud. "Might as well say, don't think about living, don't leave the house. On this island I'll never be able to avoid him - or Taylor."

The phone rang and the bullfinch took flight. She rose to answer it, then halted in the doorway. Paul, wanting something. New York, hospital bills. It rang five more times before she picked it up.

"Hon, where were you?"

"Hi, Barbara. I was on the porch talking to my bullfinch."

"You okay? After last night, I mean."

"I'm okay."

"Honestly, Jamie. Paul's an absolute louse and so is Danielle. God, right under your nose..."

"He did me a favor, Barbara. Any doubts I had... It's all over now but the paperwork."

Jamie listened to the silence as Barbara geared up for her Big Question.

"What did you say to Andre when he ran after you?"

"He didn't run after me exactly, he was concerned. Wanted to know if I was all right."

"I've got news!" Barbara said, not succeeding in keeping the triumph out of her voice.

"What news?"

"Taylor's going back to New York."

"So?"

"Alone. Permanently."

"How in the world do you know that?" Jamie asked.

"Jennie Gibbs, who works at the airlines desk, is a friend of Connie Clark's. Said Taylor and Andre were supposed to go back to New York next week, but the tickets were changed. Taylor's going back tomorrow."

"So?"

"By herself, Jamie. And Jennie said she wasn't wearing her engagement ring."

"Your point is?"

"Are you dense, hon? Island buzz is they've broken off the engagement."

"Honestly, Barbara. You've lived here long enough to know how unreliable the roro, the gossip, is. And Jennie Gibbs and Connie Clark should mind their own business," she added, realizing as she said it that Andre had used a similar line at Martine's.

"I thought you'd be happy to hear it?"

"It's gossip, Barbara."

"But..."

"No but. Paul's gone. If Taylor and Andre have broken it off, the next move is up to him." Jamie's hopes and fears twisted inside.

"But you could…"

"What? Show up at his office? Say 'I heard Taylor dumped you. Wanna hang out?'"

"I just want you to be happy," Barbara said.

"I know, I know." Jamie paused. "Barbara, as Paul left he said something troubling."

"What?"

"He said, 'Some of it worked, Jamie. Give me that.'"

"More than some of it is supposed to work," Barbara replied angrily.

"I know. But he got me thinking back. The good things…"

"You're not thinking of…"

"No, I'm not. Just want to get some balance, some perspective." Jamie slumped into a chair. "Look, I'm really tired."

"Didn't sleep so good, I guess."

"No. Paul came in around three, said he was going to Martinique with Danielle."

"Bastard. I hope their boat sinks. Now will you get the locks changed?"

"He got his passport and some clothes and left. I think I'm relieved. And yes, I'll get the locks changed."

"He's going to call you, you know."

"Paul? I doubt that."

"No, you dodo. Andre."

"Barbara, give it up." She couldn't let herself hope. "I'm going back to bed. I'll call you later." Jamie hung up the phone and opened the sketch pad to her list. *Stay out of Andre and Taylor's way.* If the gossip was true she could cross that one off. If the gossip was true.

Her garden was now always in bloom. The mandevilla vine by the front door opened its pink blooms to the afternoon air, taking in its sustenance. Jamie dug in one of the flower beds on the east side of the house where there was some shade. Using a hand trowel she loosened the soil around the jasmine under her bedroom window, her hands in the dirt healing, the calming fragrance of the flowers a renewal. In the days since Paul had gone Jamie had gone back to work, walked on the beach, dug in her garden. And waited. For the call Barbara had said would come. The call she was beginning to think wouldn't. She was wiping soil from her gloves when she heard the phone. Its sound carried out from the open windows. She took off her gloves as she stood up.

"Hello?"

"Jamie? It's Andre."

Jamie's breath caught in her throat. "Andre."

"I've been wanting to call. See how you were after the..."

"Scene at the party. Really, I'm okay. More embarrassed than anything."

"It'll all die down."

"I suppose."

Jamie watched a yellow breast swoop across her garden, then disappear into some foliage.

"Look, Jamie. I was wondering if we could talk, maybe do something."

"Do something?" She held her breath.

Andre cleared his throat. "Why do I feel like I'm fourteen?"

"I don't know. Why do you?" *Andre,* she thought, *tell me what's happening.*

"Look, Jamie. Taylor has left St. Lucia. She and I have broken off our engagement."

"Oh, Andre, I'm sorry to hear that," she said, knowing it was the most hypocritical thing she had ever said in her life. "Actually, I heard."

"Oh?"

"Jennie Gibbs called Connie Clarke, who called Barbara, who called me. Like you say, it's a small island."

"Coconut telegraph. I heard that Paul has gone off with Danielle."

Jamie waited, biting her lip.

"Look, I'm suggesting we talk. Like at Martine's. Nothing more."

Jamie hung there, remembering his kiss on her cheek. That was all she had...

"Are you crying?"

Jamie managed a chuckle. "No, I'm not crying."

"Oh."

"Now don't sound disappointed."

Andre laughed, then. "Talk, Jamie. That's all."

"Talk, like on a date?" Jamie asked.

"Yes, like a date. Now I really feel like I'm fourteen."

"We're both out of practice, Andre."

"Look, I'm off to New York tomorrow but will be back at the end of the week. Can I call you then and we'll make plans?"

"I'd like that, Andre. I'd like that very much."

Jamie held the receiver against her cheek before she replaced it. She looked at her open sketch pad, the list. 4. *Stay out of Andre's way.* And now? Now her world had taken some huge emotional seismic shift. She felt she should welcome it, but it was all too new; did she dare to hope? She watched her parents smile at her.

Bertille clucked under her breath as she mashed soursop through a strainer.

"What is wrong, Bertille?" asked Marcus, concerned.

"I dreamed this afternoon. The spirits flying, all twined together around Mr. Andre and the pretty parrot, that Jamie. The colors bright, but dark strands pulling on that lady." She poured the soursop juice into a pitcher and added milk and sugar.

Marcus held out a glass.

"Oh, Marcus, I am afraid." Her mouth set in a hard line. "Pain and suffering coming for these children."

CHAPTER TWENTY-SIX

Andre expertly steered the rental car through the quaint French village. Jamie snuggled into her seat next to him, loving the adventure.

"This is amazing, Andre. Martinique is so much like St. Lucia."

"The mountains, the vegetation. But with French detailing and character."

"And better roads," Jamie said.

"Martinique is a department of France. They pump a lot of money into infrastructure."

"Andre, it's been nice."

"Me, too, Jamie. Getting to know you."

"You're more complicated than I'd dreamed. And especially your family."

"It's why I'm glad you agreed to come to Martinique with me. To Tante Yve's. So much I want to share."

"It was a short flight."

"Island hopping can be fun. So many cultures so near to each other." He hesitated. "Jamie, I hate to bring this up, but have you heard anything about Paul?"

"Not much. Brian said he got fired from Omega. And apparently Danielle dumped him."

"Yeah. I heard that too. He's been hanging around the marina. With a bad crowd."

"I'd rather not even think about him, Andre."

Andre reached out and pushed her hair back from her cheek. "I'm glad your husband is a fool. Hey, where are your parrot earrings?"

"Worried they'll get damaged. Saving them for a special occasion." Jamie changed the subject. "Tell me about your aunt."

"Tante Yve is my mother's older sister. School breaks we were like a tribe moving from her house out to one of the small islands inside the reef. Always in the water or playing in a boat of some description."

"Sounds like she doted on you." Jamie pictured Andre as a boy, his compact little body, brown as an acorn, glistening as he frolicked in the water.

"Tante Yve married into one of the Béké families on Martinique and has lived here ever since."

"Béké?"

"The original planter families," Andre said as he turned off the highway. The road now wound through fields of bananas, cultivated in long mounded rows. Shortly Jamie began to see glimpses of the Atlantic.

"Is the Atlantic side of Martinique rough like the beach at Grand Anse?"

"Some places, but much of the coast is protected by coral reefs. I'll take you to Josephine's Bath."

"Josephine's Bath?"

"Shallow water near the reef. It's a tradition to take your boat there, anchor and sit in the water drinking a *petit punch*."

"That sounds like an island tradition I could endorse," Jamie laughed. "How many *petit punches* before one can't climb back into the boat?"

They chatted comfortably as they drove, exchanging histories, memories, filling in the gaps. Jamie regarded Andre's face, its easy familiarity. Different from that first day on the road...at the accident.

That had been a startling familiarity, troubling.

Andre stopped in front of a gaily-colored creole-style house overlooking one of the small bays on the convoluted Atlantic coastline. Jamie could see a dock at the bottom of steps leading down the hill and a sleek runabout anchored there.

"Here we are," Andre said.

"She's expecting us?"

"Of course. I phoned her. Oh, there she is."

A woman came around the side of the house, her arms full of orchid sprays. Obviously she had been gardening, and Jamie thought only French women could garden in such style. She had gray hair, like her sister Clarisse, and there was a strong family resemblance although she was shorter than Clarisse and rounder. Andre embraced his aunt and kissed her on each cheek. She handed him the orchids as he introduced her to Jamie.

"*Très jolie*, Andre. Where did you find this morsel? Are you going to keep her?" Tante Yve asked as she and Andre chatted in French. "You are going on the boat, no?"

"Yes, I want to take Jamie to Josephine's Bath. Did you pack a lunch for us?"

"*Mais oui.*" She motioned to a wicker basket on the terrace. "And the ingredients for *petit punch.*"

"Thanks, Tante Yve."

As they started down the stairs, Tante Yve held Andre back.

"I make both the guest rooms up for you and Jamie. I am still old fashioned that way."

"Two rooms is just fine." He hugged her. "She's special, Tante Yve."

"I can see the way you look at one another." She handed Andre the keys to the boat.

"We might be late," Andre said as he started down the steps.

"She's adorable," Jamie said as Andre joined her. She waved to Tante Yve from the dock. "How is it French women always look so stylish?"

"I hope you've noticed I am quite attracted to your forthright American style."

"Forthright. Hmm." Jamie laughed. "Is that a compliment?"

"Tie your hat on or you may lose it," he called to her as he revved the engines and they maneuvered away from the shore.

Her artist's eyes drank in the colors, the thousand shades of blue depending on the depth of the water and the shadows of the clouds.

"The light on the islands is truly amazing, it's...I don't know how to express what it is, solid, luminous. But it makes me want to paint."

"Another day you will come with your painting supplies. Today I'll show you where I spent school holidays with Tante Yve's family. We'll have lunch at Ilet Oscar, where there is a tiny beach. If we're lucky we might find a fisherman to catch something for our lunch."

"Are your mother and her sister close?"

"Mother, as you know, keeps to herself for her own reasons. Tante Yve is more open. Close? They share the bond of caring about the Diamant history and heritage."

"Clarisse keeps to herself because she's been hurt. Sounds like your Tante Yve has weathered life a little better."

Andre glanced at her, his face serious. "I'm learning quite a bit from the women in my life these days," he said.

"Your women!"

Andre laughed. "Score one for you."

"You sound better about it."

"I am." He reached out and pressed her hand. "I am."

The salt tang of the sea air drifted over them as they sat on the blanket, shaded by the fronds of a coconut palm. The picnic hamper was open, remains of bread and cheese spread about on paper plates.

"I'm surprised Tante Yve didn't pack china," Andre said, catching a paper plate lifting in the breeze.

Jamie watched a freighter far out to sea. It shimmered in the rising heat.

"See that fisherman over there?" Andre said, suddenly.

"Where?"

"Look, I'm going to see if I can buy some fish from him. We can light a fire, stay for awhile."

"But we're full of cheese and baguette."

"We'll just have to make room." He captured Jamie's hand. "I'm not ready to leave yet."

"We'll be late getting back."

"I said we might be. Late, that is."

Jamie listened to the soft sound of the waves curling into the shoreline as she watched Andre bargain with the fisherman.

When he came back he was smiling. "He cleaned them for us."

"Don't you know how to do that?"

"Of course, but it helps to have a sharp knife. Which I don't."

Jamie just laughed.

"Are you having fun with me?"

"Who, me?" Jamie stared, wide-eyed.

"Go find some driftwood for the fire. Make yourself useful, woman."

"Coconut duty again? What are you going to do?"

"Me? K.P. I'm going to find some banana leaves to steam the fish in. Now get moving."

Jamie walked the shore picking up pieces of driftwood, twisted shapes bleached silver by the salt water and sun. In a few minutes a fire was going, and Andre had found an old grate he propped on some stones. While they waited for the fire to burn down to coals, he laid the fish on some banana leaves. Then he rummaged in the hamper.

"What are you looking for?" Jamie asked.

Wordlessly he held up a lime, halved it, then squeezed the juice over the fish. "Now watch this," he said, tossing the limes into the fire. They burned brightly for a moment, perfuming the air.

"Smells nice," Jamie said.

Andre dotted the fish with a little butter, folded the leaves around it and laid it on the grate over the coals. "Ever done this?"

"We didn't often see fishermen on the streets of Bronxville."

His dark eyes watched her, brimming with humor. He tore off a piece of fresh baguette. "For you," he said.

"Andre?"

"Uummm."

"This is so nice."

"A change of pace."

"More than that."

He looked across at her and reached for her hand.

When she wrapped his hand in hers, she said, "We've been going slow."

"Your pace. I haven't wanted to rush you."

"I know."

"If you let go of my hand I can open the banana leaves, we can have some fish."

At that she was on him, rolling around, laughing. When they stopped, looking at each other, enfolded in each other's arms, the exquisite unplanned moment cloaked them to the sounds of the sea. "Jamie," was all he could manage. Then she felt herself gathered up, his mouth gently kissing her face, her eyes, then finding her mouth. She cradled in his arms, taking in the warmth and touch and taste of him.

"Oh, God," she said.

"It's all right. We'll go slow."

"Andre, no more slow."

"You're sure?"

"Yes, I'm sure."

"Tonight we will be in two rooms at Tante Yve's, but then I will take you to L'Habitation."

"What's that?"

"A small inn, a restored planter's house. It's magical. I want to share it with you."

Jamie put her hand on his lips.

"One room," she said. "One room."

CHAPTER TWENTY-SEVEN

It was late afternoon when they turned into L'Habitation. Vines, which overhung the drive, stroked the car as it bumped up the cobblestone road. Around a corner, the restored eighteenth century planter's house rose before them, poised on a small rise. Wide verandas shaded the windows on the first floor, and Jamie could see comfortable wicker chaises set outside each room.

"We begin here, Jamie."

"I know," she said, suddenly nervous.

Jamie wandered around the reception area as Andre registered. He turned to watch her and she smiled, held up one finger. *One room*, she mouthed.

Through tall doors in the antique-filled reception area, Jamie saw broad steps leading down to an oval swimming pool, the quiet water reflecting the colors of the late afternoon sun. In the distance geometrically arranged banana fields marched up the slopes.

Andre came and stood beside her.

"It's magical, isn't it? I've been fantasizing about bringing you here." He breathed in her soft jasmine scent.

"I'm not sure if the magic is the place or being with you."

"Maybe both. Let's go get settled. We have time for a swim before dinner, if you'd like that."

The mahogany steps were covered with a coir runner, the wooden banister smoothed by years of passing hands. At the top of the stairs, Andre turned the key in the mahogany door.

"I didn't see anyone else around. Other guests," Jamie said.

"There are only twelve rooms. We may be the only ones here."

Jamie entered the large bedroom and sat on the edge of the draped four-poster bed. She fingered the sumptuous fabric, an oriental design of Chinese red and yellows, and ran her hand over the sheets on the turned-back bed. Linen. The windows, framed by the same fabric that draped the bed, were open to the tropical air and the rain forest view beyond. Broad swaths of heliconia bordered the edge of the forest, and purple bougainvillea climbed into the trees.

"There's even a good place to curl up with a book," she said, opening the tall doors onto the veranda and the twin chaises she had noticed from below.

"Did you bring a book?"

Jamie blushed.

"So, what do you think?" Andre asked.

"Like you said - magical." Jamie smiled at him. She paused. "I don't want to know who else you've brought here." Quickly she covered his mouth with her hand. "I'm sorry, Andre. That was out of line. None of my business..."

He folded her into his arms. "I've never brought anyone else here. It's been a dream, one I was saving."

"I'm glad."

"Jamie, you're trembling."

She nestled into his warmth. "We needed to start someplace that doesn't have other..."

"Memories?" he finished.

"That but more. The outside world seems far away."

Her faint jasmine scent hovered.

"Time for us..."

"Yes." She pulled away. "Now I'm feeling fourteen. Want to try out the pool?"

They sat in the shallow end of the pool, waist deep. Twilight shadows flickered through the low palms as they sipped their Ti Punches.

"Is this like Josephine's Bath?" she asked.

"More civilized." He set his glass on the edge of the pool.

"No worries about getting back in the boat." Jamie's eyes teased him.

"Do you know how sexy that is?"

"What?"

"That mischievous glint in your eye."

"Paul used to hate it."

He brought his fingers to her lips. "Shhh. No talk of history right now. Only this new beginning."

"It's hard..."

"I know..."

"...the past."

Andre pulled her onto his lap, the water on their bodies warm as the soft, sensuous air. He touched his thumb to her lower lip.

"Jamie, I want to love you properly in a wide bed. On linen sheets."

"I want that too, Andre. I'm just feeling..."

"Frightened?"

She pulled back a little. "How did you know?"

"Don't you think I'm a little scared, too? We've had our disappointments. Taylor broke it off..."

"...and Paul left me for another woman." Jamie was briefly quiet. "But I'm glad. I'm glad Paul's gone and Taylor left you."

"We can be together with..."

"No guilt," Jamie finished. She took a deep breath. "I don't want you to be disappointed. What if..."

"Jamie, if you're not ready, we'll wait. We can start over. Get to know each other. Date like other people..."

Jamie put her arms around Andre's chest. Her fingers caressed the ripple of his spine. "So much of our dreams... No, we've waited so long, it seems. Linen sheets...and that wide bed upstairs. That's what I want."

In their room the windows were open to the gentle breeze. The heavy fragrance of the rain forest mixed with jasmine as Andre wrapped a soft towel around Jamie, lifting a corner to dry her hair.

"I don't think you know how lovely you are."

"I like to hear you say it."

"I want you to believe it."

"Me, too."

Andre patted the towel down her back, pulling her close.

Jamie tilted her head up, reaching for his mouth. Their kiss tasted faintly of rum and lime. And then they were on that wide bed, on the cool linen sheets. Abandoning hurts, risking vulnerabilities, finding joy in one another. Passion, then peace.

Later, at dinner, they were the only couple in the dining room. Tall doors stood open to the tropical night.

"Same night sounds here. The tree frogs, the cicadas. I've grown used to them."

He touched her hand across the table.

"Did you arrange this?" she asked.

"What?

"For us to be the only ones here. Did you rent the whole place?"

His eyes twinkled. "Why didn't I think of that!"

Jamie was horrified. "Oh, tell me you didn't spend a fortune..."

"I'm teasing you, Jamie."

"Then this is serendipity, us being the only ones here?"

His thumb stroked her palm. "The Gods of Love indulging new lovers."

She pulled her hand away. "You'd better stop that or..."

"Or what?" He continued stroking.

"Or we'll have to forget dinner and…"

"We have time, Jamie. The wide bed, the rumpled linen sheets. It all awaits. Just up the stairs."

She tucked a stray curl behind her ear and looked at him boldly. "For dessert."

"God, but you're sexy."

Suddenly she stood.

"What…?"

"I don't want to sit across from you. I want to sit next to you." She slid into the chair.

The waiter appeared, silently moved dishes and cutlery, then withdrew.

"This is much better," she said.

"I like you close." He reached out and touched her earlobe. "You're wearing your parrot feathers."

"It's a special occasion."

He raised his glass. "To discovering who we can be together."

They touched their glasses and a crystal note, bell like, shimmered into the tropical air.

In the morning they had breakfast in the open sided pavilion, taking crumbs from their plates, feeding the birds.

"That little red breasted bullfinch is a twin to the one who shares my breakfast every morning in St. Lucia," Jamie said.

"Did you sleep well?" Andre asked. "During the night you cried out, but when I held you, you quieted."

"An old dream."

"A bad one?" He reached out and took her hand.

"Sort of. I'm in the forest, hunting for something. Mist, hard to see." Jamie shook her head as if to clear the fog.

"Then I'm glad I was there to hold you."

"Andre? …You weren't disappointed?"

"No. Loving you was lovely. We were lovely."

"We were."

"We'll wipe away your hurt, Jamie. Erase that sadness I see sometimes in your eyes."

"My hurt and yours. They're part of us, Andre. Part of who we'll be together."

"I want to make it all right."

"Being with you is making it all right."

"Jamie, would you like to stay here a couple more days?"

"In the wide bed? Making love..."

"Sleeping after...

"Waking to find you next to me..."

Her eyes told him everything.

CHAPTER TWENTY-EIGHT

The Castries market was already bustling by seven-thirty in the morning when Barbara and Jamie arrived. Barbara expertly parked the car between a battered pickup truck and a small blue sedan. They grabbed rattan shopping baskets out of the trunk and made their way into the noisy marketplace. It was already hot, and the ground was littered with coconut husks and vegetable trash. Jamie purchased lettuce from a vendor with a large rattan basket stuffed with glistening green heads. A heap of seasoning peppers and a couple of mangoes were added to her basket as they made their way through the market.

"Okay," Barbara said, stepping around crates full of live chickens. "Where have you been for the last few days?"

"Oh, I just needed some time away."

"By yourself."

Jamie smiled. "Well..."

"And where were you by yourself?"

"Martinique." Her smile broke open, radiant.

"Andre! You were in Martinique with Andre!"

Jamie just stood and grinned.

"I can't believe you didn't tell me. I tell you the gossip about

Taylor leaving, minus her engagement ring, then you disappear."

"I didn't disappear. You just didn't know where I was."

"I'll be mad for twenty seconds that you didn't tell me. Oh, God, Jamie. That's wonderful. I mean it, I really mean it. I stopped by the house, you were gone..."

"You should have checked with Jennie Gibbs at the airport charter desk."

"So, you went to Martinique?"

"We needed time by ourselves. Someplace without nosy neighbors," Jamie said, twitting her friend. "I even got to meet Andre's aunt, Tante Yve. She's lovely, Barbara."

"Jamie, my nerve ends are screaming here. Forget meeting his family. What..."

"We went out on a boat."

"Forget the boat."

"Barbara, you're relentless."

"So he brought you home, you invited him in..."

"It wasn't quite like that. Come on, Barbara, give me a break."

"And..."

"Look, we went to bed. Okay. It was wonderful and that's all I'm going to share with you right now."

Barbara hugged her basket, leafy greens damp against her arms, her eyes teared.

"Does Clarisse know?"

"I don't know. That's for Andre to take care of. I haven't seen her much. And when I do she's oddly distant, distracted."

"What's wrong with her?"

"I don't know."

"Anyway, Andre's aunt, Tante Yve that you liked so much. Is she Clarisse's sister?"

"Yes."

"I didn't know she had a sister."

Jamie smiled. "A hole in your intelligence gathering system. Andre adores her."

"Not a brooding sort, like Clarisse?"

"No. Odd in a way, since both Clarisse and Yve lost the same parents. But Yve seems to have weathered it better."

Barbara's mouth firmed into a line of concentration. "Perhaps there's more to it."

Jamie stopped walking and touched her stomach. "Barbara, do you have a peppermint or something?"

"Ah, all this new excitement in your life! Your stomach's in knots again."

Jamie popped the peppermint into her mouth. "Come on, let's finish before it gets even hotter."

It was ten minutes later when Jamie stopped walking again and steadied herself on a pile of crates.

"Jamie?"

"I'm going to be sick."

"The gutter," Barbara said, taking her arm. "Over there." Barbara held her shoulders. "So much going on for you, Jamie. Losing your mother, Paul, Andre..."

"Let's get back to the car, please..."

In the car Barbara found a bottle of water. "Don't drink it, just sip it. Freshen your mouth a little. You'll be okay."

Jamie took the water gratefully, then stared into Barbara's worried eyes. "Why are you looking at me like that?"

"It's nothing, you'll feel better in a few minutes..."

"What is it, Barbara? What?" Jamie gripped her arm.

"Hon, before Paul left, that time when he forced you..."

Jamie retched as the words registered. "Oh, my God."

"Look. It could be tension, just tension. But Dr. Simpson's office is close by, we could..."

"Andre. Oh, God. Andre." She slumped into the seat.

Barbara shook her. "Now listen to me, Jamie, listen to me. Don't lose it. First things first - and you could have some medical problem, a medical thing that needs sorting out." Barbara bit down on the words as she voiced them. "It doesn't necessarily mean you're pregnant."

Jamie stared at the car floor mat, her face pale. She rotated the water bottle in trembling hands.

Wordlessly Barbara started the car.

Jamie and Barbara sat in Dr. Simpson's waiting room. Jamie stared unseeing at some posters for immunization shots, smiling children's faces.

"Shouldn't be long," Barbara said.

Jamie's mind was filled with thoughts of Andre. It had been wonderful after that first night. Not just the love making, although that had been nothing short of magical, lost in each other's arms. But it was the rest, the getting to know each other, a grounding, a sense of completion she still could hardly let herself believe. All so new, so fresh, so fragile.

"Andre wants me to come to Jumeaux," Jamie said. "To spend a few days, I mean, when he gets back from New York."

Barbara's eyes watched her. "That sounds nice, Jamie. It really does."

When her name was called Jamie got up. "This shouldn't take long."

Barbara watched her go into Dr. Simpson's office.

CHAPTER TWENTY-NINE

Andre stood at her front door, grinning. Before she could speak he swept her into his arms, and Jamie was swept up in her own joy in spite of herself. She savored him, his spicy cologne. Remembering Martinique.

"Andre!"

"Got back early from a bunch of lawyers. Working on the hotel project, I'm afraid. It'll put a crimp in our time together. God, it's good to hold you again. I've missed you."

"I've missed you, too. Where's Emile? I thought he was picking me up?"

"I had to come, Jamie. Be with you."

She kissed him and gently edged towards the red estate truck. She hoped yesterday's news didn't show in her behavior, or in her eyes, now clear after yesterday's tears. "Was New York okay?" she asked as he put her case in the back of the truck.

"A bunch of lawyers carrying on about land titles." He pulled her into his arms again.

"Missed you. Tried to call you yesterday."

Jamie nestled in his arms for a moment.

"Come on," she said, pulling away. "I'm anxious to get to Jumeaux."

The truck threaded its way through the tourists walking along the road, enjoying ice cream cones or coco water in the shell, looking in the souvenir shops for gaudy T-shirts to take home. Once on the main road, Jamie sat quietly, staring ahead. In Castries the central market was still crowded. Jamie could see where she had stood in the gutter, Barbara hugging her shoulders. *How can I tell him? When? I'll have to talk to Andre, release him. He could go back to New York, even Taylor. She would want him. But what if he still wants me?* Jamie wondered. *And what will Clarisse say? Auguste?* She forced herself to relax, to talk.

"Andre, have you seen your mother? She hasn't been at the office..."

"That happens sometimes," Andre said, steering around a hole in the road. "Actually she's at Jumeaux right now. When she gets under the weather, she comes out until things don't overwhelm her anymore. I don't know what's on her mind this time, but she should've left a note at work, or called you."

Jamie watched a small fishing boat pulling into shore. She rummaged in her pocket for a peppermint, tried to focus on making conversation. "I'm sure she's interested in the hotel plans, too."

Andre's face grew serious. "The hotel project has some problems to solve, especially with an access road through Bertille's and Marcus' property. Mother is very concerned about that, as I am."

"Why? Can't they give you a right of way?"

"Bertille's very upset. She's tense, talks quietly with Marcus. We see them with their heads together. It's tense."

"But you aren't going to build the hotel on their land?"

"No. It's the access road to the hotel that needs to go through their land. There's an alternative, but it costs much more. And the lawyers, they just look at the money angle."

Jamie looked out the window. A large cruise ship in the harbor was a majestic presence. "I don't envy you this problem."

Andre looked at her. "I want to share it with you. Jamie, I love you. I want you in on everything that concerns me and my family."

"Clarisse..."

"Look, I intend to tell Mother and Father about us on this trip. They have to know, right?"

Jamie's stomach churned. All the times she had given herself to Andre, knowing the joy of it, her love for him, and all the time there had been this life inside her...

"You'll just have to trust me, Jamie," he said, reaching for her hand. "I'm doing this for us."

"I know. Look at the cruise ship." She had to change the conversation, get away from the hurt. "I'm seeing the big ships more and more."

"Tourists. That's where the financial future is, Jamie. And why we need the hotel. Right now, though, the money stays on the ships."

"What about Emile and his parrot habitat idea?"

"We go around on it, but frankly it's a good idea. We need to save the parrots. And Jack's almost finished his report on a habitat — Emile and Jack are in cahoots, I think. But they should know I support them. We've got to get past a decision on the access first, though."

"When we get to Jumeaux, I want to spend some time with Bertille and Marcus. Is that all right?"

"Of course. They care very much about you, have a deep interest in you, as a matter of fact. Remember when you first met Bertille?"

"How could I forget? It was very powerful."

"She's onto us, y'know," Andre said.

"Who?"

"Bertille. She suspects, anyway. But she keeps her own counsel. Won't say anything until we're ready."

"Maybe it's better if we are discreet. Just for a few days." *Just until I can tell you...* she thought. "Andre, if your mother knew, would she be upset?"

"Just leave that to me, Jamie."

"I'm just a little uncomfortable. You're free, but I'm still married - at least on paper. I guess that's where it counts."

Andre reached out and took her hand. "You're nervous, aren't you? Look, I promise we'll be discreet. They'll put us in separate bedrooms, anyway. And we won't tell anybody until you say it's all right. Now relax."

CHAPTER THIRTY

When they entered the long drive into Jumeaux Estate, Andre honked the horn. They watched Auguste and Emile come out to greet them. Bertille stood silently to one side.

Jamie returned Auguste's greeting, thinking about how little he had changed from the photograph in Clarisse's office. It was as she embraced Emile that she felt the strange and unpleasant feeling cloak her. It was like a pall over her, and it disturbed her. When she went to Bertille, she found her embrace stiff and reserved. Jamie looked into her eyes. Something was out of place, something was wrong, she could feel it in the air around her, some malignant presence.

"Andre," Auguste was saying, "you are in your old room, next to Emile's. Jamie, we have a lovely room for you."

Jamie managed a smile. "Thank you." As she mounted the steps to the veranda a sudden cold chill ran through her.

"You okay, Jamie?" Andre asked, holding her small suitcase.

"Yes. Yes, I'm fine." But as she glanced around, she saw Bertille watching her. Her face was a mask, her body rigid.

"Bertille has made tamarind juice," Auguste said, "and there's also some coconut water. Please come and sit. Relax. I will join you in a few minutes."

As Andre settled into a rocker, a shadow crossed his face.

"Something wrong?" Jamie asked.

"Truth? I said goodbye to Taylor sitting here."

"I know it wasn't easy."

Andre nodded. "No regrets, Jamie."

Her stomach knotted up again. She looked around at the activity: Bertille and Marcus, Auguste issuing orders to a field supervisor, Emile moving the truck. When Bertille came to them with juice, Jamie said, "I'd like to have some time to talk to you, Bertille."

"Of course," Bertille said, preoccupied, starting away.

Andre looked up. "Bertille. That's not like you."

"I'm sorry, Andre. I'm concerned about your mother, that's all."

"It's a bad headache, isn't it, a migraine?"

"Perhaps."

"You'll fix one of your magic potions. That'll fix it!" Andre said.

Bertille's stare was cold. "Do not condescend to me, Andre. I raised you, did I not? Show some manners."

Jamie sat uncomfortably. Andre blushed as Bertille left.

"What was that about? I feel like a little boy," Andre said.

"She's worried about your mother. You and Emile are very lucky to have had her to help raise you."

He looked at her, his dark eyes reflective. "You're right. I need to think on that more often." Andre rocked in the chair for a moment. "Is it just me, or are things tense around here?"

More than tense.

"Yes, I've noticed. Probably the lawyers." Jamie managed a small smile, trying to keep things light.

"Yes, you're right! You'll get to meet them later, you know." Andre stood up, came over to kiss her. "I'd better go see them."

"Will Clarisse attend the meeting?"

"She's welcome. Depends on how she's feeling, I guess. But she will be kept informed."

Jamie lifted her book. "I'll relax with this, I think."

Andre kissed her again. "Don't tell me how it ends. I want to read that one."

She watched him go. Then she was alone in her rocking chair, still disturbed by a pervasive unease around Jumeaux. How would she tell Andre about the baby? When would the moment present itself? Would there ever be such a moment? Jamie set the book aside and went to the kitchen to see Bertille. She took the empty glasses with her, a pretext.

Bertille glanced up from her work. "What do you feel in the air, child?" she said, without any small talk.

"It's tense, whatever it is."

"More than that. Much more. I sense - evil." Bertille lifted a whole red snapper onto her cutting board. "The spirits swirl and dance. Undercurrents of pain and suffering. All is malignant. Marcus knows. He detects the spirits through me." She scraped at the scales, a harsh sound.

"Evil? What do you mean?"

"Loup garou, the man who is not man. He is out there."

"I don't understand."

"You are pregnant, Jamie." Bertille's words were harsh in the bright kitchen.

Jamie did not hesitate. "Yes."

"But it is the wrong child..."

"How can you say an innocent child is the wrong child! Shame on you!" Jamie's fears burst loose, her words tumbling out in shock and reaction to Bertille's unerring insight.

"Sometimes evil can overpower innocence, child. Have you told Andre?"

"I haven't found the right time yet."

Bertille came to her. "Don't tell him. I sense that..."

"What?"

Bertille shook her head as she turned the fish over, scraping scales from the other side.

Jamie averted her eyes. "I have to tell him. He needs to know."

"Then Clarisse and Auguste will know too."

"And Emile," Jamie said vehemently. "And Jack. And Angel."

Bertille stared at her fingers, as if reading them for answers. "Everyone is in rebellion today. Spirits fly."

"I mean no disrespect, Bertille. I just have to handle this myself."

For a moment Bertille's eyes warmed, then fell back into a brooding dark. "Listen to me. Stay close to the house. Do not go out."

"Don't go out? But it's lovely here. I brought my sketch pad..."

"No!"

Jamie froze in shock at the power emanating from this woman's spiritual core. She looked at the kitchen door as Marcus entered, his face grave.

"Our concern is for your safety, Mistress," he said as she went toward the door. With Bertille and Marcus together in the room, the kitchen held overwhelming energies. Jamie brushed past. She sat rocking, trying to sort out the tumbling images, the confusion, the emotions. Growing unease filled her. Then anger. *My child is not a wrong child!*

She got up and returned to the kitchen. Marcus was gone. Bertille looked up from cleaning the fish. She said nothing.

"Bertille?"

"Yes, child?"

"You say the spirits are vexed, angry."

"Yes. There is evil around us. Can you not feel it in the way people are acting? Andre condescends to me, you challenge me rudely in the way you speak to me. I myself am rude and sullen." The knife flashed in the sunlight as she gutted the fish, sending entrails into a waiting container.

Jamie pushed down her nausea. "And Clarisse?"

Bertille sighed, almost a soft cry of despair. "I am concerned. Something is wrong." Her eyes found Jamie's. "And it concerns you."

"Me? Not you and Marcus? Concern for your land and property rights?"

"Clarisse is concerned about that, as we are. She will talk about our concerns with Andre and Emile. But she is struggling with something else - it plagues her."

"What is it?"

The knife stopped, held still in Bertille's powerful hand. "She is in anguish. I've seen it before, but not in many years. It's from before..."

"Before what?" Jamie stepped closer, studying Bertille with some alarm.

Bertille put down the knife. She wiped her hands as she gathered her thoughts. "You have met Tante Yve?"

"Yes. How did you know?"

"No matter. How did you find her? Friendly, kind, humorous?"

"Why, yes."

"Different from Clarisse."

Jamie hesitated. "Yes."

"What does that tell you?"

"Tell me? I don't know. They're different."

Bertille poured a small glass of coco water and handed it to Jamie. "To settle your stomach." She sighed deeply. "Perhaps this is the day to tell you. Perhaps it will placate the spirits."

Jamie licked suddenly dry lips. She sipped her drink.

"First, before there was Andre and Emile, there was a daughter."

"A daughter?"

"Her name was Elizabeth, but Clarisse called her Lilibet." Bertille smiled, remembering. "A beautiful child."

"What happened?"

"Meningitis. She became brain damaged by the terrible fever. Doctors did all they could, I did all I could." Bertille's eyes carried a deep anguish.

"I'm so very sorry, Bertille."

Bertille shrugged her big shoulders. "I tried to help Clarisse and Auguste. Marcus helped me. In any case, they took Lilibet to the States for consultations, but it was no use. When Lilibet was found trying to suffocate a visiting friend's baby, they knew they had to institutionalize her for her safety and care."

"Oh, Bertille, how awful."

The shoulders shrugged again. "Lilibet died soon after in the institution. Clarisse changed after that. She brooded, losing interest in life, withdrawing to her room. It was difficult for Auguste. And the boys."

"How old were they when this happened?"

"Andre was twelve. Emile was ten. Difficult times."

"And you raised them?" Jamie said.

Bertille dabbed at her eyes. "Even before that. I raised them for Clarisse, who could not reach out. I took them to my bosom, child. I did what I could. They were good boys."

"And Clarisse?"

"There is never a day she doesn't think about Lilibet. The grief has taken her from her family. She lives separate from Auguste, she is withdrawn from Andre and Emile. It has been bad," she finished simply.

"For years Clarisse prayed, saying her rosary, offering novenas. I prayed in my way to the spirits of my world, but nothing helped her." Bertille drank down her tamarind juice as if to slake some deep unquenchable thirst. "Eventually, she abandoned God."

"But her business, it does so well..."

"She found her sanity in business, in Jumeaux Designs. She poured herself and all her energies into it from dawn light until dark. It has saved her, I think, from suicide."

Jamie wrapped her in her arms. "Thank you for telling me, Bertille."

"I too might have collapsed but for Marcus." Her tears were salt on Jamie's cheek. "Marcus is my strength."

"I understand."

Bertille gently broke free of Jamie's embrace. "Secrets, child. So many secrets, and so many responsibilities..."

"I'm glad you told me."

Bertille looked at her, surprised. "You think this is all, that you know it all now?"

Jamie stared, watching as Bertille picked up the snapper and began rinsing it in the sink.

"You must go now. I must do things for our guests - these lawyers!" She spat out the word.

Jamie walked to the door.

"Child."

"Yes?"

"Clarisse will know about you and Andre. Nothing escapes her. This baby..."

"I'll have to talk with Andre, Bertille. It's the only way."

"Your baby is doomed."

Jamie stood in the doorway, stunned by the ugliness and violence of Bertille's words. "Never, never again talk about my baby like that! Never!"

Bertille's eyes were intense, trance-like. "Do not go outside. Stay in the house."

Jamie walked from the kitchen feeling sick. From the far reaches of the house she heard loud laughter as the lawyers and the Demontagne family found a brief common ground. Jamie wondered if Clarisse was there with Auguste, Andre and Emile.

CHAPTER THIRTY-ONE

"You know," Auguste said, offering Cuban cigars to the lawyers and family members, "we should have held this meeting at night. In the evening we could have lit torches around the gardens. It's quite lovely."

"We're from New York, Auguste," one of the lawyers said, smiling. "We go more for the Friday night fights or catching a Broadway play."

"Ah, yes. A different world. Andre knows more of New York than I do."

"Andre fits in. A talented businessman." The lawyer waved his cigar at him.

"Thank you," Andre said. "We are pleased to share our island with you."

"And we've done well on the island, right?" The cigar wagged again. "We've seen a couple of solicitors who can handle legal details, the government officials are open to waivers of duty on materials and supplies - I'd say things are going well down here."

"Not to mention the tax incentives," Emile said.

The lawyer winked and the cigar did its dance.

"But we have this matter of the access," Auguste said.

"Yes, Auguste. The access road must be rerouted. The route in the preliminary plans will cost many times what a more direct route would cost."

Andre's words were measured. "The access road on the preliminary plan is the only access there is."

"Not necessarily. Look at the elevations. Here's a much more sensible entrance." A stubby finger pointed on the map.

"More sensible perhaps, but that land doesn't belong to us," Auguste interjected. "It's owned by Marcus Deroche's family. It's been in their family almost as long as Jumeaux has belonged to the Diamants and the Demontagnes. I seriously doubt they would sell it."

"Everybody has a price. And perhaps there's some other bargaining chip. Perhaps the title isn't clear. If there's a cloud on the title, they can't refuse a reasonable offer. We've got to have that piece of land. This project will never get off the ground if we can't get into the forest some other way. Before we go back to New York, I want to meet with our people here. I want the title to that piece of land researched."

Bertille came in quietly and attended to drinks and ashtrays, her face a mask as she worked.

"Perhaps the family never really had a claim on the land. Maybe they think they own it because they've been living on it so long. If the title isn't clear, it might be possible to buy them out. Anything is possible if you throw enough money at it," the lawyer said, tapping white ash into the clean ashtray.

"Marcus and Bertille are like family." Andre bristled. "I will not have them defrauded or harmed in any way."

"Who said anything about defrauding? Don't get too ethical on us now, Andre, you have a group of investors ready to put up close to forty million dollars. They aren't going to be nice about some locals standing in the way of this project."

"Let me speak with them," suggested Andre, trying to buy time. "And perhaps the engineers could revisit the subject of the access road. Let me see if there is an alternative solution."

In her room Clarisse heard voices rise, but then the meeting had quieted again. She wondered how Auguste was doing. But she had full faith in Auguste. And Andre, and Emile. Her sons. All of what she was suffering, all of what she carried on her conscience in indescribable torment, was for them. For a moment she held her head in her hands, then she went to her traveling case.

From a small frayed pouch she withdrew a fine chain and tiny diamond encrusted cross. She laid it in her palm. It gleamed even in the dim light of the shuttered room. She set the old papers aside and grasped the psalter. She should pray, she knew. But prayer had long since left her.

As the cross warmed in her hand, Clarisse asked the question for the thousandth time: *Could Jamie be a descendent of the lost twin?* But she knew the answer. And she knew the consequences, far graver than those being discussed over cigars and drinks. Somehow she could provide for Bertille and Marcus if they lost their land. In a generation, with money wisely invested, they could be wealthy. No, the profound problem was that Jamie, as descendent of the lost twin, could lay claims to the Diamant property she had brought to her marriage to Auguste. They could be tied up in court for years.

Clarisse turned her attention to the parchment. All had been built on this: the family heritage, its history, its magnificent successes and triumphs. And now...

She watched the sun trying to penetrate the shutters. Just like her ground floor office in Castries - where she retreated, shutting out the world to stay sane. Except for her work. And now, with bitter irony, Jamie was key to its success. Her exquisite designs.

Jamie. She cared for her. She could not help it. In spite of the threat she now represented to the family, Clarisse cared for her. So many echoes of Lilibet. Would Lilibet have grown up to be like Jamie? Jamie, the lost twin. She would have to keep this secret close to her breast, be very careful if Jamie researched her own heritage. What could she find? Yes, she must hold the secret to her bosom, just as Bertille held her precious sons to her bosom when Clarisse could not.

When the tears came they ran silently down her face to drop onto her hand, wetting the child's cross. How could Anne-Cecile have sent one child off to safety, only to find she had abandoned and doomed that child - all because of her choice of whom to pick up and carry?

And now, centuries later, Clarisse Diamant Demontagne was being called to account.

CHAPTER THIRTY-TWO

Jamie looked up from her rocking chair as Andre bent over her. When he kissed her she held back, startled by his sudden appearance and intrusion on her thoughts.

"Sorry I've been tied up. How's the book?"

"I'm not really reading it. I've been thinking about things."

"That sounds ominous." Andre smiled, looking down at her.

"Look, Andre, I don't think I'm going to have a convenient time to talk to you, so I'd better just get it out."

Andre slowly squatted down beside her chair. "Okay."

"I've got something I must tell you."

"Okay."

"You know, I've been feeling sick lately. I thought it was just tension. But I was out with Barbara. We were at the market..."

Andre watched her, waiting.

"I threw up. In the gutter. Barbara said I should see Dr. Simpson. She took me to his office." Jamie watched the concern change his face.

"Oh, Jamie. Are you sick?"

She shook her head, not trusting herself to speak.

Andre waited.

"Jamie...?" he asked, unspoken fear in his voice.

"I'm not sick. I'm pregnant." She searched his face. "It's Paul's."

"Oh, Jamie..."

"I think I should go back to the States, not hold you to anything. Start again."

A silence stretched awkwardly.

"I've got to find him and tell him. He has a right to know."

"Will you go back to him?"

"Oh, God, no!"

"Then don't talk about cutting me loose."

"Andre, you see how it is. How can I face you, your parents?"

"You're already facing me." He touched her cheek. "It's not too bad, is it?"

She watched as he tried for a smile, but it dissolved slowly back into concern. "You deserve better than what I can offer, now," she said.

He kissed her then, warm and exquisitely tender. "Let me be the judge of that - as long as you want me, that is."

"Oh, Andre! It's what I wanted to hear." She buried herself into him across the rocker arm. "But I couldn't allow the hope."

"And the answer is yes," he said, caressing her hair.

"Yes, to what?"

"Your unspoken question. Yes, I can love another man's child. Your child. It will be our child."

Jamie clung to him, staring into the shadows.

"What is it?"

"Bertille. She says the child is doomed."

"Doomed?" Andre stiffened in anger. "That's outrageous, she's overstepped her bounds this time..."

"She's just agitated, Andre. Please. She's saying the spirits are vexed and the loup-garou..."

"Loup-garou?"

"The man who is not a man. She says she feels his presence."

Andre puffed out his cheeks as he exhaled around his anger. He rubbed the bridge of his nose as he looked at her. "Is there anything else this family and St. Lucia can throw at you, Jamie? This is just too much. Look, first things first. Paul. You must tell Paul."

"And what about us, your parents?"

"We love each other, we'll love the child. I'll talk to my parents after you've had a chance to talk to Paul. How do you want to handle it?"

Jamie bit her lip. "I think I need to go back to Rodney Bay, just for a day or two. Talk with Barbara and Brian. He seems to have a finger on the pulse of what goes on in town. Then I can check with the Omega Company - find Paul and tell him." She sagged under the weight of all of it. "Then begin divorce proceedings. I'll have to go back to New York to do that."

"Leave some clothes here."

"What?"

"Leave some clothes here. So I know you'll be back."

"Just a couple of days, Andre."

"I know. Can I help? The Demontagnes have connections, you know."

"I know. And what you offer is logical, but I can't do it that way." Jamie fumbled for her words. "When I come to you I want to come to you with all this behind me. It's something I must handle. Does that make sense?"

Andre nodded. "It does. But phone me, right? Maybe ten times a day?"

"And you phone me." Jamie smiled, hugging him. "But I'm dreading how Clarisse and Auguste will take all this."

"That's for me to handle - you have things you must do by yourself, I have mine. So, how are you feeling now? What did Dr. Simpson say?"

"He says I'm fine. He gave me vitamins."

"Are you taking them?" he asked, kissing her nose.

"Andre..."

"I can drive you back, make the necessary excuses."

There were no words. Jamie just clung to him.

Outside, the uneasy air over Jumeaux surged against scudding clouds.

Barbara stared out the windshield at the sea and beach near Vigie. The parked car's hot engine ticked in the heat. A breeze wafted through the open windows. She smiled at Jamie. "Good a place as any."

Jamie nodded.

"So, you taking care of yourself?"

"Of course."

"I tried the house."

"I told you I was going to Jumeaux for a few days."

Barbara's eyes brightened. "So Andre knows? Because if you didn't tell him..."

"He knows."

"And?"

"He loves me, Barbara. He wants me and the baby. It's more than I could have hoped..."

"You're a good person, Jamie. Don't go selling yourself short. You're gutsy, loyal, talented - all the qualities a good man wants and for a couple to have - Andre's a lucky guy."

"And pregnant, you forgot that."

Barbara's hand came out. "Listen, you two are big enough for this."

"Yes, yes we are."

"Has he told Clarisse and Auguste?"

"We're waiting. First I need to find Paul. I thought you and Brian could help."

"We'll try, sure. Brian's pretty good at things like this."

"He knew about Paul and Danielle."

Barbara winced. "That's over. One more notch on her lipstick."

"Odd he hasn't returned to the house, pick up some remaining things."

"I don't think he'll do that, Jamie. I have to tell you, Brian says Paul is running with a bad crowd."

"How bad?"

"Drugs. Smuggling. Word is Customs has their eye on him."

Jamie was quiet.

"What?" asked Barbara.

"Just remembering something he said once, that he had the personality of a risk taker, somebody willing to risk all for a big payoff."

"Well, if there's anything to what Brian's been hearing, he's taking some real chances."

"I wish you'd told me."

"Would have. You weren't home, remember?"

Jamie's eyes softened. "And I didn't call, did I."

"What can I do for you, hon?" Barbara smiled.

"So what about Omega? I'm thinking of going over there."

"He got canned when he went off to Martinique with Danielle."

Jamie watched a bird hover on the honing edge of the breeze, its eyes black and greedy. "He had such promise."

"No. Like you said once. A frat house kid on an endless party. He never grew up, Jamie. And now he's out there somewhere, screwing up. How do you plan to tell him about the baby?"

"Straight out, no point in a confrontation."

"He might like the idea of a child."

"He might, for a few minutes. Then he'll be off on some grandiose venture."

"And the divorce?"

"He'll go along - provided I do all the work, pay for it."

Barbara grinned. "You've got him pegged."

Jamie nodded. "Everything but where he is."

CHAPTER THIRTY-THREE

Delia stood in the doorway, her hoop earrings dazzling in the sun. Her eyes were watchful as she waited on Jamie. Jamie wondered if she had been talking with Bertille.

"I won't need you today, Delia. You can have the day off."

"But I prefer to stay and work, Mistress."

"I'll pay you for the day. I just want to be alone, okay?"

Delia shrugged and turned away.

After she had gone Jamie looked around her at the house. Then she got out cleaning supplies and a palm broom, attacking the already clean house with a vigor coming from frustration and anger. She'd watched Brian's face, his averted eyes, as he told her the new talk about Paul. Just a matter of time before he'd be arrested. Some drug gang. She and Barbara had just sat there. For once her friend had no words of solace or encouragement.

Jamie swept out the kitchen, cleaned the bathroom and checked for scorpions. She paused, remembering their arrival, the luggage and boxes, no plug for the percolator, the truck accident, Mom still alive, meeting Andre. Worlds away now. When she cleaned the bedroom she found Paul's cufflink under the bed. "Paul..."

When it came it was a foreign sound, a huge sullen rumbling that shook the house. Crockery rattled. The floor vibrated beneath her feet. Then it faded, subsiding, leaving once again a quiet day of sunlight and trees and gardens. Birds, one by one, resumed their song, the grey grackles their harsh clamor.

Jamie went to the phone. "Barbara? What was that?"

"Sounded like an explosion, something big. Sounded like it came from the marina."

"Want to go and check?"

"No. Best let the locals handle it. We'll all know soon enough."

"Coconut telegraph."

"Right. So what're you up to?"

"Just cleaning the house, working off stress."

"You're supposed to let Delia do that. You should be taking your prenatal vitamins and sitting with your feet up."

"Cleaning gives me something to do, takes my mind off trying to find Paul. Actually, I feel good. Energetic."

"Say, want to go over to Mick's later for a drink?"

"Barbara, I'm pregnant. No alcohol."

"Sorry. That was dumb. Unless I can convince you to have a tonic water. Maybe with a slice of lemon?"

Jamie smiled. "Thanks, Barbara. I'll let you know."

"Are you going to the marina later?"

"Yeah, *Cathay Queen* is supposed to come back in later today. Brian thinks Paul's on it."

"Better wait until they've cleared whatever happened over there."

"Okay. Hey, I'll call when I'm ready to go. If Paul's there I could use some moral support."

When she heard the knock Jamie thought first that Barbara had come over, then she wondered if it was Andre making a surprise visit, ready to gather her up in his arms. She could use that right now. Andre...

The police constable stood at the door, his bulk an ambiguous presence on her threshold. Starched white shirt, knife pleats in his dark slacks, epaulets at his shoulders, his face expressionless. Jamie's stomach tightened.

"Mrs. Elliott?"

"Yes?"

"I have some bad news..." he began solemnly.

That's how she would always remember him. Solemn. Performing his duties.

"It's my duty to tell you that your husband, Mr. Paul Elliott, has been killed in an explosion."

Jamie stepped back, her face grey.

"The *Cathay Queen* blew up in the harbor this morning. Your husband was on board. Investigations are being made, of course. I am very sorry to bring you this news. Your husband's body..."

Jamie made the dress she wore to the funeral. She felt she owed Paul that. For the good times, the early times, when his hair had gleamed in the sun, and his boyish smile had captivated her. She worked through the night, pressing back the ugly images of a dead Paul, the viewing that had been necessary for identification purposes, cold and ultimately meaningless.

The memorial service was small. Andre sat beside her, as did Barbara and Brian. Several of 'the guys,' Paul's drinking buddies, were there. The minister's words were fine but generic, uttered about someone he never knew and was now gone.

Outside the small Castries church Jamie squinted in the sunlight. Her eyes were dry. Her grandmother's lace handkerchief, taken up for the occasion, was unused. She felt Andre's arm go around her shoulders. Barbara and Brian stood in silence, a discreet distance from them.

"You say you're sending Paul's body back to the States?"

"Yes. To his parents."

"Will you tell them about the baby?"

"Not yet. It's too early. But soon. It's their grandchild. They have a right to know about the child."

"Are you coming back to Jumeaux?"

"Yes. I can be ready in an hour. The house is the way I want it. Paul's things are boxed up."

Andre kissed her cheek. "And your room's ready at Jumeaux, and the lawyers are gone. Everything's ready for you."

"We need to talk to your parents."

"Give yourself time, Jamie."

She pressed his arm. "I'm walking away from an old life, Andre. One that had some good, but mostly bad. I don't need time."

Jamie unpacked her small overnight bag of its few personal items and laid them on the guest bed at Jumeaux. She was glad she had left the funeral dress. It had no place here. She sat on the edge of the bed and spent a few moments collecting herself, gathering her poise, getting back her emotional balance. A soft knock at the door surprised her. "Who is it?"

"Bertille. I've come to talk."

"I'm not so sure that's a good idea right now, Bertille. Could we wait and..."

"I need to apologize to you. Please allow me to talk."

Jamie got up and opened the door. "Come in, Bertille."

Bertille entered the room and, by some indescribable power to her presence, shifted the mood, imbuing it with mystery and a sense of foreboding. She stood quite still, her rounded figure caught in slanting sunlight, her eyes quiet and watchful.

"Your road is not an easy one to travel," Jamie said.

"That is true. It is both curse and blessing."

Jamie waited.

"Andre has talked with me. He is angry with me. I have never known him to be so angry."

"You said terrible things, Bertille, frightful things..."

"But I spoke the truth. My fault was in speaking at all, and not keeping matters to myself and Marcus."

"That's not much of an apology."

"I do apologize, child. I did not mean to hurt you or frighten you. I foolishly relied on my sense about you, my instincts about you that I've had since we first met. You are different, you see, and I know you feel it too."

Jamie sat down on the bed. "That's true."

"So I am sorry. But I want to ask you - when you returned to Jumeaux, did you feel the atmosphere here?"

"Yes."

Bertille waited, her fists clenched by her sides.

"What is it? What are we feeling, Bertille?"

"The loup-garou. The man who is not a man."

"So," Jamie said slowly, "why is he here - if he is here?"

"He is here. I wonder now if he will leave, that his presence has to do with the violent death of your husband, that your baby will be safe."

Jamie forced a smile she didn't feel. "Let's hope so."

"You told me when you first came here about your dreams of parrots."

"Yes, I love the parrots."

Bertille nodded. "Do you fly with your dream parrots?"

"Dream parrots? That's an odd way to put it."

"Do you?"

Jamie thought about it. "Yes, I think I do. I have this free feeling of being at a great height, looking down."

"Looking down on what?"

"Oh, different things," Jamie said, suddenly uneasy and wanting to dismiss it. "Land. The sea."

"Other parrots?"

"Sometimes."

"Do you dream of anything else?"

"Bertille, this is making me quite uncomfortable."

"Please...anything else?"

"Well, sometimes I have nightmares. A dream about a lost child."

"And what do you experience in your dream?"

"I'm lost in a forest, like the forest around here, actually. And I'm looking for this lost child."

"Is that all?"

"That's all except for the feeling that if I don't find the child I'll die."

The words fell into the silence of the guest bedroom.

"Maybe you are the lost one? Maybe the dream is about losing your mother, or losing your marriage, or more."

"Maybe." Foreboding gripped her. "Bertille, I don't wish to talk about this any more, I've just come from my husband's funeral, it's been a bad day."

Bertille walked slowly to the door. "I understand."

"Bertille, can you give me a hand with this chain? I don't wear it as a rule. I wanted it for the funeral and now it's caught somehow."

When the cross slipped into Bertille's waiting palm, she gasped and stepped back.

"Bertille, you okay?"

"The lost diamond."

"What lost diamond?"

"Nothing, nothing. The cross is very beautiful." Bertille held Jamie's chin in her palm and said soberly, "Take care, my child, there are those who would not want this diamond found."

"Why would anyone want to take this family heirloom?" Jamie asked, misunderstanding Bertille's words. "The cross is precious only for sentimental reasons. The stones are tiny and it can't be that valuable."

"Troubled spirits 'round you, my child. Flying like angry birds. Beware they don't make you fall."

CHAPTER THIRTY-FOUR

It was cool in the forest by the waterfall. Bertille and Marcus sat by the pooling water, preparing to bathe and cleanse themselves for their ancient rituals.

"I must calm myself, Marcus. Calm my spirit."

Marcus waited, as he had done on many such occasions.

"I went to talk with Jamie. I went to apologize because I had said too much. I frightened her."

"About the baby?"

"More - about my sense that the baby will die."

Marcus shook his head.

"But then, Marcus, as I was about to leave, she asked for my help with her necklace, a cross and chain."

"Yes?"

"Marcus, it was a small cross, a diamond cross - a child's cross. Its effect on me was so great I cried out." She grabbed his well muscled arm. "It is like the cross in our ancient stories. The cross you sing about in the ancestor's songs."

"Bertille, you don't know that."

"You don't trust my powers? You don't trust my powers after all these years together?"

"I trust them, Bertille. But for days you have been distressed about the spirits."

"Yes, and rightly so."

"Your senses are heightened, perhaps distorted..."

Bertille's eyes wetted with tears. When Marcus reached for her, she pulled back.

"Tell me what you need," Marcus said at last.

"Prepare me. When we are cleansed, place me on my bed of sea grass and assist me."

Marcus nodded.

As they bathed in the crystal cool waters, Bertille and Marcus moved slowly.

"Our burden is heavy, Bertille."

"Prepare me."

A flock of parrots flew together searching, hunting for one of their own, one lost long ago. Their green and gold bodies flashed in the sunlight, a vivid contrast to the blackened earth beneath them. No trees welcomed them to stop and rest; no cool, clear streams invited them to dip their beaks and quench their thirst. They could hear the earth rumbling beneath them. Beating their wings faster, they flew to an ancient mahogany tree in the island's sole remaining patch of green.

On the topmost branch was the missing parrot, hungry and thirsty, near death from exhaustion. It had been lost for a long time and was now too weary to fly anymore. The flying parrots surrounded the weary bird, some dripping water and placing food into its beak, sharing their meager stores.

The flock sat in the branches of the enormous mahogany tree and gazed at the devastated landscape surrounding them. The newly found parrot began to weep.

"What will become of us and our children? How can we bring the trees back? Will we ever see a green blanket of trees covering and protecting our once beautiful island? Where will our chicks live?

Where will they fly? What can we do? We are only parrots."

In great sorrow, the parrots folded their heads beneath their wings, pondering the impossibility of what must be accomplished to save their island home. The claws on their feet dug into the mighty branches of the mahogany tree. Beneath them, the earth rumbled and shook.

The weeping parrot took wing, then tumbled toward the earth, its skin and feathers burned away by the fires on the ground, until only its bones remained, white as coral from under the sea.

As though one wing, the flock flew down to their fallen brother. Turning and turning, they drilled a shaft in the earth, a resting place for the bones of their brother. Then they flew to the sea, spinning together faster and faster until they pulled a slender spout of water from the surface, maneuvering it toward the shaft in the parched land. They could hear the earth as its depths were filled, its thirst quenched. Slowly pale green appeared on the landscape and then darker areas as trees sprouted and reached toward the sky. Gold and magenta flowers bloomed and perfumed the air. On the spot where they had buried their brother, a samaan tree now stood, its branches spreading a great distance, protecting all beneath.

When Bertille's breathing changed and he knew she was now sleeping, no longer flying, Marcus left her and went to prepare food.

"Are you all right, Bertille?" he asked his wife when she joined him by the coal pot. "You know I worry about you when you are away."

"Marcus, the flock must turn together as one, the place of the bones is the way to keep the island alive."

Marcus spoke slowly, mindful of the import of what he was to say. "Bertille, do your parrot eyes say it is time to tell what we know about the resting place of our ancestors?"

Bertille did not reply. She was tired, concerned about something else. "The pretty parrot, Jamie, that child is in danger, Marcus.

The mountain cannot be revealed if the parrots are not turning together. Dark forces twist around that pretty bird. The whites do not understand the dangers twining, twisting faster and faster. One parrot falls and all fall."

They sat together listening to the waterfall. From somewhere in the darkening indigo sky, a parrot screeched. "She also dreams of a lost child," Bertille said, watching her reflection in the cool water, trying to read its mysteries.

CHAPTER THIRTY-FIVE

Jamie stepped from the Jumeaux veranda and stood savoring the air. Sunlight bathed the line of trees marking the edge of the rain forest. Birds offered their familiar songs while parrots swooped, green and yellow arcs across the sky. She breathed in the air, checked her sketch book and pencils, her notes on the bird-of-paradise flower, and walked off down the trail.

The sun was warm and she felt glad to be free of the house, the faint smell of cigars smoked by the departed lawyers, and worrying about the closeted Clarisse. But Andre was always there, helping her shed old anxieties about Paul, helping her look to their future together. If there was one drawback it was the lack of privacy, not being able to share a room, to have him so close he was part of her. But they could talk in the brief time they had. They could discuss their future together. Even now, when he'd had to fly back to New York, they spoke daily on the phone.

When she came to the bench she sat down and opened her small snack. She had been lucky, she mused, nibbling on one of Bertille's homemade ginger cookies. Bertille had not been in the kitchen when she'd grabbed them. Jamie listened to the forest sounds. There was no evil here, no anxiety, just warm sun slanting through the foliage. And the songbirds. She picked up a second cookie.

Bertille looked up in surprise when Clarisse entered the kitchen. "Good afternoon, Clarisse. I was just preparing some juice for you."

Clarisse managed a smile. "My headache's finally gone. I'm fit for human companionship."

"Then come and sit down."

"I will."

"It's mango."

Clarisse watched as Bertille set the glass in front of her. "Is Andre back?"

Bertille sat down, her powerful arms on the table top. "No. Tomorrow. More lawyer talk about our Deroche land and access for the hotel. Those lawyers hunt for loopholes. They want us off our land."

Clarisse sipped her drink, the glass refreshingly cool on her dry lips. "It need not be a bad thing, Bertille. You and Marcus could become very rich from the sale of your land and investing wisely. Andre could help you."

Bertille stood up. "Clarisse, how can you say such a thing! The Deroches, the Diamants, the Demontagnes - all of us are families with heritage going back. We will never sell and dishonor our people."

Clarisse nodded, taken aback by the force of Bertille's statement. "Forgive me, I wasn't thinking. I have a lot on my mind these days."

"Me too. There are secrets that are about to come out, Clarisse."

Clarisse put down her glass as a shudder ran through her. "Secrets, what secrets?"

"Family secrets. We both have them. We have kept them for hundreds of years."

Clarisse's voice turned cold. "Old families have a right to secrets, to protecting the welfare of their families."

"Yes, but sometimes there are new happenings in life that upset the old ways, our old secrets."

"Nonsense, Bertille," Clarisse said, her voice rising. "I do believe..."

Bertille's hand suddenly came up, silencing her.

"What is it?"

Bertille stood as stone, her eyes closed.

"Bertille? Bertille!"

"Jamie. Jamie has gone into the forest. I feel her there."

"Well, it's a nice day, she probably wants to sketch..."

"No! No! Evil is out there! Evil, Clarisse." Bertille hurried from the kitchen. "Marcus! Marcus!"

Jamie brushed a crumb from her mouth and gathered up her sketch book. Her head jerked up at a sound, strange and violent, an anguish on the balmy air. "What?" she murmured. It came from inside the tree line, beyond the lush foliage, the spikey leaves of the bird-of-paradise. A cry. A woman's cry? A child's cry? The only sound in an eerie silence. Clear, pure tones, a desperate need. Jamie did not hesitate; she ran toward the sound. The forest was dense, disorienting. Then suddenly quiet.

She stopped and looked around her, panting and scratched. All was still. No birdsong. No buzz of insects. She listened, but there was no further crying out. As she stood poised, listening, an odd mist curled from the mossy, dead-leafed earth. It coiled and twisted, formless, then shaping, then formless again. A cold damp touched her skin and she shivered. "Andre," she said, fear inundating her, assaulted by lost child images from her nightmares. "Andre," she said again. The malignant cold embraced her, an evil she recognized from deep within. She stood paralyzed as the mist twisted into a man's head and torso, then fell away into the convulsing wreaths dancing before her.

Jamie ran. She ran on energies summoned from primal fear. Cloying ugly silence, a suffocating presence enfolding her. Still she ran, crashing, bruising, bleeding through the undergrowth. When she hurtled into the dark earthen pit she fell unconscious.

Auguste, Bertille and Clarisse stood back as Marcus lit the first of the flambeaux. He addressed the men, lifting his cutlass and the oily smoking torch. "I will lead one search party, Auguste the other. We know the trails. It will be our best chance of finding her. If you find anything - anything - blow your whistle. Understood?"

The men nodded.

"She wanted to draw pictures of the bird-of-paradise. They grow best by the bench on the old trail," Bertille said.

"Then we start there," Marcus said. He looked at Clarisse, his cutlass reflecting the firelight. "Clarisse, it will be dark soon. You must stay here."

"You must stay, Clarisse," Auguste murmured.

"But I will come, husband," Bertille said. Her voice rang out and there was no denying her.

Wordlessly Marcus turned towards the old trail and tree-lined fringe of rain forest. Auguste, Bertille and the men followed, their flambeaux leaving oily smoke trails in the late afternoon sky.

Clarisse watched them go, her heart pounding. "Fire fends off evil," she whispered. "Dear God, keep her safe..."

Marcus could hear Auguste's group hacking through the forest. He looked at the remnants of the sketchbook in his hand. It was now in tatters, smeared and wet. He tossed it aside, then swung his cutlass like a pointer. "That way."

"Are you sure?" one of the men asked, his face etched in shadows from the firebrand.

"Bertille?"

Bertille closed her eyes and lifted her scratched and bloodied arms. They waited, some of the men uneasy and looking around. When her eyes opened she looked at Marcus and nodded decisively.

They hacked and moved and searched. Darkness closed in and the flambeaux cast flickering shadows across tree limbs.

"Bertille?"

Bertille stopped, her arms coming up in supplication, then she cried out, the images searing her. "There! There!"

Marcus' cutlass swung at the branches and vines, moving forward with every breath remaining in his gasping lungs. Bertille called out again and again, but there was no answer.

When they reached her Jamie lay still and silent, the rotting leaves at the bottom of the pit rank and foul. Marcus climbed down and gathered her into his arms as the whistle blasted the night.

Clarisse hastily pulled down the light bed covers and watched as Marcus and Auguste laid Jamie down. "I shall prepare herbs," Bertille said. She hurried away.

Jamie spoke through the fever that gripped her. "Cold...cold...evil..."

It was Clarisse who now drew Jamie to her bosom.

CHAPTER THIRTY-SIX

Dr. Simpson stepped back from Jamie's bed and looked around at those gathered there. Andre, now back from New York, carried a special anxiety, and the doctor noted it. He glanced around at Auguste, Clarisse, Bertille and Marcus. Only Emile was missing. He looked again at Bertille. Something there too. In all his years of practicing medicine in St. Lucia, he had come to respect and even support the use of some island bush medicine. She was an ally. Abruptly he pushed his folded stethoscope into his jacket pocket. "Andre," he said. "I wonder if I might have a word with you in private?"

Andre followed him and they stood in the door of the bedroom. "Yes, Doctor..."

"I sense your caring for Jamie. I see the concern in your eyes. Her situation is complicated." He paused.

"Because she's pregnant?"

"Ah, so you know."

"Yes, Paul's child." Andre glanced back at the group. Bertille's face was unreadable. "Yes. We've talked about it. Jamie and I will raise the child, we love each other, the child is a blessing."

Dr. Simpson studied Andre's face, the fatigue there. "Have you talked with members of your family?" A slight nod of his head indicated the gathering at Jamie's bedside.

"No, not yet. Mother, I think suspects I'm in love with Jamie. But neither of my parents knows about the baby. I had planned to talk with them when I got back from New York, but this happened..."

"Andre, I'm going to assume you are the responsible party for Jamie..."

"Of course, I'll pay her bills."

The doctor dismissed the comment. "Andre, I have known your family far too long to be worried about that. Jamie told me she has no family, her husband is now dead. I need to know who is responsible for her..."

"What are you saying?" Andre's face registered his concern.

"Look, she will be all right. She is a lovely young woman and I am happy for you, Andre. But your family will need to know. Their response is unpredictable. Your mother..."

"I know, and now is not a good time. She seems to be in one of her downswings."

"Yes, but I see the way she is responding to Jamie. Perhaps there is healing for her there."

"We'd better get back," Andre said.

"What is going on?" Clarisse asked. "You're worrying me, Doctor."

"Will she recover?" Auguste asked.

Dr. Simpson nodded. "She will recover, but it could take some time. There's mental trauma here, along with fever and some heart arrythmia, which I believe is temporary. In layman's terms, Jamie has been frightened out of her wits -literally. She needs rest and quiet." He pulled a prescription pad from his pocket. "I'm prescribing these for her. Just follow the instructions. I'll be back tomorrow, and please phone me if there is any change - good or bad."

His words hung in the room as his wise eyes sought Bertille's.

"Bertille, may I consult with you." They stepped to the door.

"The bush medicine you used when the worker was hurt using an axe, when he was poisoned and delirious?"

Bertille nodded and spoke quietly. "That tonic will not hurt the child."

Dr. Simpson's face showed relief. "It's always good to work with you." He grasped her arm. "Give Jamie that. But only once a day."

Bertille looked around, her eyes challenging and proud. She would fight the wolf fever.

Dr. Simpson headed out the door. Andre followed.

"Speak to your parents."

"I'll take care of it," Andre said.

For the first time since he had arrived, Dr. Simpson allowed a small, wry smile. "I don't envy you."

With Jamie sleeping soundly, Andre gathered the four of them into the dining room. Clarisse chose to sit down. Auguste stood by the window, distanced from his wife. Bertille and Marcus stood behind their chairs at the table.

"What about Emile?" Clarisse asked.

"He's out checking on the surveying crew," Auguste said. "Whatever this is about, we will tell him later."

All eyes turned to Andre.

"You saw what happened," he began. "Dr. Simpson called me away to speak in private. It concerns us all."

"What do you want to tell us, son?" Auguste said.

Andre took a breath. "First, I am in love with Jamie. And Jamie is in love with me." He listened to his words. They sounded so simple, yet meant so much.

"That is good news, Andre," Clarisse said, brightening. "I did suspect, of course, and when Taylor left..."

"What is the bad news?" Auguste asked abruptly.

"There is no bad news, Father, unless we count Jamie's illness and the way she's had to deal with her husband's death."

"Then what news is it?" Auguste's voice rose in impatience. "Is it some secret between you?"

Clarisse and Bertille looked at each other.

"Yes, it is - was - a secret. I had planned to tell you all this when I got back from New York." Andre looked around at them. "The fact is, Jamie is pregnant with her husband's child. It's been very difficult for her, as you can imagine. When she told me, confided in me, I could see the anguish. She said she thought she should go back to New York and start again."

"And you said no, because you love her," Clarisse said, her eyes bright with tears.

"This child is innocent," Andre said, smiling at his mother, "and we shall raise him - or her." His smile faded as he looked at Bertille. "Every child is innocent, and this one will be part of the goodness of Jamie."

Bertille met his gaze.

"I must get back to her," Clarisse said, getting up from the table.

"Mother?"

"Yes?"

"I'm touched more than I can tell you at the way you have ministered to Jamie. It - it surprised me, a little, if you will forgive my saying so."

Clarisse stopped in the doorway. "A child is innocent. And Jamie is innocent, too."

Andre's brow furrowed. "Innocent of what?"

"I must go," Clarisse said. "Andre, get those prescriptions filled at once." She turned then, quite suddenly, caught in mid-stride. "Bertille? Aren't you coming?"

Moments later Clarisse and Bertille began their vigil.

The next day was cloudy, a wash of grey applied to sky and sea. Andre got up from Jamie's bedside and walked to the window. Clarisse and Bertille watched him.

"She seems a little better, Andre," Clarisse said.

"The medicine from Dr. Simpson, and my tonic," Bertille said.

Andre turned to them. "Perhaps you should both try and get some rest. I'll stay with her."

"No," Clarisse said, "both of you go and get some rest. Andre, what are those papers you have?"

"Records on the land owned by Bertille and Marcus."

"Title searches?"

"Yes. But they still can't refute ownership by Bertille and Marcus. The land is theirs, and I don't think anyone will be able to prove otherwise."

"We will not grant access, Andre," Bertille said.

Clarisse looked thoughtful. "For the Deroches, just as for the Diamants and Demontagnes, the land is everything."

Andre rubbed his temples.

"I'm sorry if you have a headache," Clarisse said. "Mine lasted for days."

"Andre?" Bertille said.

"Yes, Bertille?"

"Marcus asked me to send you to him. He wants to speak with you."

"Where is he?"

"In the storage shed."

"Call me if she wakes up."

"We shall," Clarisse said, patting a fresh damp cloth on Jamie's forehead.

Andre found Marcus working on the wheel of a tractor. Grease smeared his cheek. His beard needed attention.

"Is that the same tractor you were working on before?"

"It is." His eyes held an irony. "We have had distractions."

Andre embraced him. "I must thank you again for all you did. Without you perhaps Jamie wouldn't have been found."

"It was Bertille, her instincts, her spiritual powers."

"She told me to come and see you, Marcus. Is it about the access to the hotel site?"

Marcus shook his head. "There's something I need to show you."

"Something here? Now?"

"No, in the forest. Tomorrow morning. You and Emile."

Andre held back his questions. "Very well. What time?"

"Eight o'clock."

Andre knew Marcus as a man of honor, of good balance and judgement. His questions would have to wait.

Clarisse allowed herself five minutes to sit in a chair in her room and rest from the tension of ministering to Jamie and worrying about her. And in that same concern she thought about Andre, his helplessness as he sat by her side. So many constraints on emotions, and how much was caused by her? Secrets, Bertille had said. Clarisse knew all too well the staggering burden of her own secrets, but what of Bertille's? What could they be?

Bertille, who had raised her children for her, who had sustained her through the loss of her daughter Lilibet. Bertille, who had provided her with a chance to heal from that grievous wound. And she had been there when she had deliberately estranged herself from Auguste, her nerves raw, and finding no consolation with Auguste and his strict, insular ways.

But it seemed Andre had more than that, far more than that, with Jamie. It was as if they were soul mates. Soul mates, and all that implied. Clarisse opened her eyes. Soul mates and faded psalters.

These past days and nights, sitting by her bed, worrying as Jamie's fever rose and broke again and again - she recognized she had come to love Jamie, too. That in caring for her there was a healing of old hurts, a time when she was not the one to sit by a sick child's bed.

It was time to stop hiding in darkness. It was time to bring all secrets into the light. She nodded to herself, a decision made. When Jamie was well again, she would bring them all together.

CHAPTER THIRTY-SEVEN

Andre came to sit by his mother at first light. "Still asleep?" he whispered.

Clarisse nodded as Andre put his arm around her shoulders. "Thank you."

"I love her too, you know."

Jamie stirred, opened her eyes and smiled up at them.

"Well," Andre said. "That's more like it."

Wordlessly she reached for his hand.

"How do you feel, child?" Clarisse asked.

"Tired. Washed out. I don't remember much..." Jamie suddenly heaved upward, gasping.

"Easy, easy," Andre said, gently pushing her down. "It's okay now."

"Bertille, where's Bertille?"

"She's working in the kitchen. But she has been here with you..."

"I know. I sensed her here. I sensed all of you here."

Andre kissed her cheek and she gripped his arm. "Marcus wants to show us something in the forest today. I don't know how long we'll be."

"You're not chasing that, that - thing!"

"No, no. Calm down. It's all right."

"Does Bertille say it's all right?"

Bertille came in and smiled when she saw Jamie talking to them.

"Ask her yourself," Andre said.

Bertille stood by the bed and nodded with approval. "You look better now."

"I'm very tired."

"I gave you one of my tonics. Good for fever."

"And Dr. Simpson was here, he's coming again today," Clarisse said.

"Dr. Simpson?" Jamie's eyes widened.

"It's okay," Andre said quickly. "I've told them everything. They know. About us, about the baby, everything."

Jamie's eyes found Clarisse. "I'm sorry about..."

"Don't you worry, Jamie. We are all here to take care of you. Don't worry."

Jamie exhaled and fell back into the bed.

Bertille felt her brow. "She's hot again."

"It's time for her medicine," Clarisse said.

Jamie held on for the medication, then fell into a fitful sleep. Only then did she let go of Andre's hand.

By eight o'clock in the morning the slate grey of the previous day had cleared. A hot sun gathered strength as Andre went to meet Marcus. "Jack. This is a surprise!" Andre shook hands, glad to see him.

"How's Jamie?"

"Much better. I think she's over the worst. So how goes grad school, your parrot study?"

"Finished. All set. All I have to do is convince some skeptical professors that my dissertation passes muster."

"Then will we have to call you Dr. Deroche?"

"Absolutely," Jack said. "Do you know where we're going? Dad's being mysterious."

Marcus interrupted them. "Here's Emile. I think we should start now."

"So how do we go, Marcus?" Emile asked. "Do we walk?"

"No, it is best if we drive to the beginning of the track. Can we go in your truck, Emile? Bring your cutlasses. The forest is thick where we are going."

Andre and Jack vaulted into the bed of the pickup. Ten minutes later the truck was halfway up a mountain near the proposed access road. Marcus indicated a dirt track, and Emile turned left. Bumping down the rutted road, not much more than a path, Emile soon had to shift into four-wheel-drive to navigate the washed-out gullies. Finally Marcus indicated a place to stop.

"From here we walk," he said, taking his cutlass from the back of the truck.

Andre and Emile followed with Jack not far behind. It was not until they topped the first ridge that they would see where they were. Through an opening in the trees they could look down into the Soufriere valley, the Jumeaux estate below them. They could still see the faint boundary lines cut months earlier, now almost erased by the rapidly growing tropical vegetation.

Marcus led them up the mountain following an almost invisible track. Then another ridge and down into a high walled valley. It was almost an hour later when they entered the clearing near the waterfall.

Andre and Emile were surprised to see Bertille, her arms crossed over her chest, standing in front of the little house, her face somber. When she saw the men, she turned and went into the house without speaking.

Marcus motioned for Andre, Emile and Jack to sit down on boulders near the pool. "I will get Bertille. Part of the story is hers to tell."

"Well, my parents are acting truly mysterious," Jack said. "Isn't this a beautiful spot? I thought I'd been all through this forest. How did I happen to miss this?"

"Odd, I think I've been here. Do you remember, Emile?"

"No, I don't," Emile said. "And I'm not so sure Marcus didn't bring us by some circuitous route so we wouldn't be able to find it again. How do you suppose Bertille got here? I saw her in the kitchen at Jumeaux earlier this morning."

They heard Marcus and Bertille approaching. Marcus spoke first to his son. "Jack, the stories we are about to share belong to you and the other young ones in the family. Many of them you have already heard, but not in just this way. What we are going to show you would have not been revealed to you until later in your life, perhaps never. Only time will show if your mother and I have made the right decision."

He turned to Andre and Emile.

"Sirs, before I show you what I have brought you here to see, Bertille and I must tell you the story of our people who came from the big island to the south." Marcus looked at the waterfall as he composed himself. "We know that the people who came here first made their way up the island chain from South America. Our people, the Arawaks, were a gentle people. We lived near the beaches, the ocean and land providing us with food and shelter. We prospered here for thirty generations before the warring Caribe came. Some of us fled to the forest; many were killed. But eventually the Arawaks and Caribe combined, and it is from these people that Bertille and I are descended."

Marcus looked at Andre and Emile.

"When the whites came, they enslaved us and took our land, even this land sacred to our people. Those brought in chains from Africa mixed with our people, as did other races. But always there were those chosen to keep the stories and to remember the ancestors. In this generation, Bertille and I are the keepers. We know the stories and the ancestors back many, many generations until the first ancestor on the island. Only in this generation have the stories and family lines been written down. In times past all was committed to memory and passed from one generation to the next. We knew we would not always be slaves," Marcus said, pride evident in his voice.

"In olden times," Bertille said, "special children would be identified to be future keepers and would start learning the stories when young. But now our children go off island and there have been none that we thought would want this burden. So Marcus and I have written the stories out so they would not be lost.

"It would take hours and hours for us to tell you of the ancestors. So I will begin with B'til and Makus, who saved your ancestors," she nodded to Andre and Emile, "during the time of the brigands."

Andre and Emile glanced at each other, fascination evident on their faces.

Andre said, "Mother told us our families have been connected for many generations."

"It is true," Bertille continued. "B'til and Makus were slaves belonging to your ancestors who came from France before the revolution. During the brigand uprising the family of Charles du Diamant, the Diamant brother who lived on the estate, was killed. Charles was badly wounded. He and his sister-in-law and her small son were hidden here in the forest by our ancestors for almost four years. When peace returned to the island and they could return to Jumeaux, they freed us and gave land to our family in gratitude. They were surprised that this is the land we chose, but they did not know of its importance to our people."

"You are talking of Anne-Cecile Diamant and her son, Louis? But they are buried in our mother's family plot," Andre said.

Marcus and Bertille looked at each other. Bertille continued, "This land is sacred to our people. As the keepers of the ancestors and their stories, Marcus and I come here often. But the importance of the land is more than the history."

She motioned to Marcus, who stepped into the edge of the pool and splashed water on his legs, torso and arms. He then lifted his hands in supplication.

Marcus' face was grave. "What I am about to show you has been secret, the knowledge passed in our family since the ancestors first walked the island. Bertille's parrots have prophesied that for the land to survive, the secrets must be revealed. Follow me."

Jack caught Andre's eye. "Prophesied?" he murmured.

Marcus began the climb up the face of the cliff to the top of the waterfall. Stepping behind the waterfall, he pulled back a curtain of ferns and Andre, Emile and Jack entered the darkness, followed by Bertille, who carried a flambeau torch. Lighting torches around the perimeter of the cavern, she nodded to Marcus.

"Only the keepers have been allowed to see what I am about to show you. We have signs the ancestors will understand if I break this taboo as a way of saving our history and culture." His gaze fell lovingly on Bertille. "My life's partner talks to our ancestors."

Marcus stood quietly for a moment. "Now I sing the song of the ancestors. Bring a torch and come behind me."

Marcus began a recitation in a language neither Andre nor Emile understood. It was not the commonly spoken Patois. They glanced at Jack, who seemed as puzzled as they were, but his scholar's instincts showed a gathering excitement. Grabbing the torches Bertille handed them, they followed Marcus until he disappeared from sight around a sharp bend in the wall of the cave.

They started down a gently sloping tunnel and several more times Marcus disappeared from view, his chanting voice leading them. There seemed to be a current of air moving in the tunnel, for their flambeaux flickered and the air supply seemed good. They moved deep into the earth and walked for what seemed a long time. Finally Marcus stopped in front of a wall of stone and ceased chanting.

"The ancestors' resting place begins here. Bertille will give you fresh torches."

Andre and Emile turned to Bertille, who lit fresh flambeaux from those they carried. Only Jack saw his father face the wall and place his hands on it. When they turned back to Marcus, there was an opening in the wall.

"I begin with my father," Marcus said and continued to recite as he walked. He stopped beside a niche in the wall. Placing the torch so the others could see into the niche, Andre and Emile observed two skeletons lying side by side.

"My father and his priestess wife," Marcus said, and to Jack, "Your grandfather and grandmother."

"But Grandfather was a Christian," Jack said. "He and Grandmother are buried in the cemetery by the church. I remember going to his funeral."

"It was what he wanted others to see. He was buried there but was brought here later. It was his wish. When I die, I will be buried also, but later my bones will rest here, as will Bertille's some day." He pointed to an empty niche.

"Come, I show you my father's father and his father's father and so on." Marcus began the singsong recitation which Andre and Emile now understood to be the history and stories about the occupants of these catacombs.

Jack was dazed at the implications of what his father was revealing.

And Andre was astounded by what he was seeing. A subculture of which he had been totally unaware and a cave system like none he had ever seen. The island was volcanic, not limestone. There were no cave systems he was aware of. Just then Jack voiced the same thought.

Marcus' reply was simple. "There is much that is hidden." He continued to stand for many minutes by each crypt as he sang the story of the ancestors who rested there. Finally his song ceased.

"These are the bones of Makus and B'til," he said.

"But I see three skulls. Are there three skeletons in this crypt?" asked Andre.

"Yes, the other is that of Anne-Cecile de Roche du Diamant."

"That can't be. She's buried in the family plot," Emile said.

"Yes, that was where she was laid, but this is where she rests. Next to the people who saved her, next to the man who fathered one of her sons."

"What, what did you say?" Andre's head reeled with the implications of Marcus' statement.

"The ancestors' song tells of a son born to Anne-Cecile during the time of hiding. The child was fathered by Makus. When the whites were able to return to the estate, B'til and Makus came back with the Diamants, and the child was raised on the estate as the child of B'til and Makus."

"This is preposterous," Emile said. "Forgive me for saying so, but it is. You have no proof of such a relationship. Why, this would mean that we're all related."

"Just so," Marcus said, picking up a small metal box resting in the crypt. Pointing to the continuation of the cave system, he said, "The ancestors continue back to the very first king and his priestess. There is no need for us to go further."

He turned and began to make his way back up the tunnel, occasionally stopping to caress a skull or thigh bone, to straighten a feather or small clay pot.

It was clear to Andre that Marcus knew intimately the life of each of these ancestors as though he had lived during their time.

When they returned to the entrance cavern, Bertille spoke. "This was where Makus, B'til and the others hid during the time of the brigands. Master Diamant was wounded in the head. He survived, but his mind was no longer good. When they returned to the estate, Anne-Cecile ran the estate. Makus helped her. Anne-Cecile is responsible for freeing our people and giving us this land. The ancestor's song says it was her wish to rest here." Bertille paused. "Husband?"

Marcus took up the tale. "Anne-Cecile raised her son, Louis, and he inherited the estate when his uncle died. Louis' twin, Philippe, was lost in the uprising and believed dead. It is from Louis' line that your mother descends." He gazed at Andre and Emile. "Both Bertille and I come down from the son she could not acknowledge. He was the first Marcus."

Andre fought back his fatigue. He could not take it all in. As stunned as he was by the revelation of the intertwined bloodlines, he was even more awestruck by the historical significance of the cave. Marcus retraced their passage back to the clearing. They could hear Jack barraging his father with questions. When they reached the bottom of the cliff, they sat on the boulders rimming the pool below the waterfall.

"Sirs, I have taken a great chance to show you the caves of our ancestors. I hope it was the right thing to do. Now perhaps you can understand why it is not possible to permit you to build a road here."

Andre nodded.

"Marcus, your trust in us is not misplaced. I've always admired you, and I'm honored we share the same blood. This sacred place represents the heritage of not just your family but the whole island. It's a national treasure, symbolic of all the families on the island." He gripped Marcus' shoulders.

"I swear to you no harm will come to this place, even if it means we do not build the hotel."

Marcus and Bertille stood off by themselves for a moment while Andre, Emile and Jack began the long walk back to the truck. Bertille spoke first.

"You were wise not explaining that Jamie is the lost twin."

Marcus nodded. "I did not feel good about it. You saw how upset Emile was at the knowledge of our connected families."

"All in good time, my husband. Jamie's place in our joined histories will be known."

Marcus studied her face but could not read her expression. "How will that be?"

"I'm not sure, it is not yet clear. But I think the answer lies with Clarisse."

"They are waiting," Marcus said, gesturing toward the trail.

On their return to Jumeaux, Andre was alarmed to see Clarisse standing on the veranda, waiting for them to pull in. He jumped down from the truck. "Mother?"

"Andre, Dr. Simpson is with Jamie..."

"What's happened, what's happened?"

As he tried to get past her, Clarisse held him with surprising strength. "Jamie has had a miscarriage. No! Stay with me, all of you stay with me!"

She held on to Andre until he quieted. "Jamie is all right. In fact, the doctor says perhaps it is a good thing this baby was not born. There were some...difficulties...with the fetus."

Andre gently pushed past his mother. He walked slowly into

the house. Everyone else waited outside. They watched as Bertille moved to the tree line at the edge of the rain forest and lifted her arms. They could not hear what she was saying.

CHAPTER THIRTY-EIGHT

Jamie sat comfortably in her rocker on the veranda, a light blanket over her knees, her mother's genealogy charts in her hands. Andre sat across from her in his chair, one he had pulled into position so they now had this loving routine. As usual, he kicked off his sandals and pressed his toes against hers.

Jamie smiled. "That's nice."

"Find anything?" Andre asked.

"Nope. Looks like Mom got back to family in New York in 1860, but then it's a dead end."

"Disappointed?"

"Not really. I don't know what I thought she'd found. Maybe someday your mother can help me see if I can find more." Jamie relaxed into the chair, rocked quietly for a moment. She looked out to the hills, as she had done for several days, enjoying the flowers, the ever-changing light in the forest and swift darting color of the birds.

"Look how beautiful everything is, Andre."

"It is. And so are you." He reached out and took her hand. "So how goes it?"

"Depression has lifted, thanks to Dr. Simpson. It was natural to experience it, he said, given the circumstances. Right now I'm feeling pretty good, Andre. I'd like to talk with Clarisse about going back to work..."

"Whoa! You're not quite ready for that yet."

"I mean here. I can work here."

"You haven't put this idea to Mother yet, have you?"

"Well..."

"Jamie."

"She agrees with me."

He wiggled his toes against hers. "Agrees about what?"

"Therapy. Help me recuperate by keeping me involved and busy. No pressure, Andre, no deadlines."

Andre knew when he was outnumbered.

"So," Jamie said. "What's going on? Bring me up to speed."

"Good stuff is happening. You'll be pleased. First, Jack has finished his parrot habitat study. We're talking about a sanctuary for them, before they get killed off. You should see Emile. He's a driving force, really pushing Jack."

"And the hotel?"

"We're going to use the other access - keeping out of Bertille's and Marcus' family land. The Deroche land is clearly sacrosanct."

Jamie nodded. "Emile and Jack told me about the cave, the graves there. The Deroche ancestors."

"It'll become an historic archeological site, Jamie. Jack is planning a Heritage Center. With all due respect and reverence for what it represents to St. Lucia and all island peoples."

"Then I'm glad you're in charge. And the hotel plans?"

"The lawyers bitched, but they came around."

"They're probably salivating over all the profits that'll come in."

Andre nodded. "Yes, this hotel will be enhanced by the parrot habitat and a Heritage Center. But frankly, I'd like to see some of those profits go into cultural causes."

"Me too."

Clarisse called out, interrupting them. "Jamie?"

"Hi, Clarisse, Andre's here."

Clarisse smiled at both of them. "So I see. Jamie, you have more color in your cheeks today," she said, critically examining her.

"I feel pretty good, Clarisse. I need something to do."

"Try these." Clarisse handed her the sketchbook and pencils. "I got them from the office. I did an hour's work, got back into things." She smiled, a little embarrassed. "Have you heard from Barbara?"

"She called yesterday. She's a good friend."

"Yes, she is." The piercing blue eyes, now quieted, found her son. "Andre, I'd like to chat with Jamie for a few minutes - would you mind?"

Andre swung his feet down and slipped them into his sandals. "Not at all, Mother," he said, kissing Jamie.

Andre hesitated a moment, then he leaned over and kissed his mother. "Take your time, I have work to catch up on."

When he left, Clarisse slowly raised her hand to her cheek.

Jamie smiled. "I like it when he does that. He always holds it a little too long."

Clarisse's eyes glistened, catching the sunlight.

"Clarisse?"

"Silly of me. I'm getting sentimental in my dotage."

"No, you're not. You're allowing loved ones back into your life."

"You know what?"

"What?" Jamie stared at her, startled.

"When I get back to Jumeaux Designs I'm moving permanently into the upstairs office, opening all the windows."

"To let in the real world."

"I think it's time, don't you?"

Jamie studied her face. "Clarisse, what's wrong? We don't have to talk now if you don't want to."

Clarisse wadded a tissue in her hand. "I have some things to tell you, very important things."

Jamie waited.

"What I wish to tell you now, here, is something about me." She took a breath which pushed out the reluctant words. "I had a daughter, Jamie. She died."

Jamie reached forward to touch her. "Say no more, Clarisse. I know about Elizabeth - Lilibet."

"You do!"

"Bertille felt I should know. She loves you so. She hurts for you."

"Bertille hurts for everyone. It's something she must bear as a price for her spiritual gifts."

Jamie considered her thoughtfully. "I suppose so. I hadn't thought of it that way."

"That's why she needs Marcus." Clarisse selected a fresh tissue. "Jamie, do you remember when you came to my office wearing that little gold and diamond cross?"

"Why, yes. I'd just gotten back from New York - my mother's funeral. I wanted to wear it so I could feel close to Mom."

Clarisse nodded, her eyes wet. "You have no idea how powerful those words are, Jamie."

"What? Why?"

Clarisse reached into her pocket and pulled out a small cloth bag. Opening it carefully, she pulled out a fine gold chain with a tiny gold and diamond cross. It glittered in the sunlight.

Jamie's hand moved unconsciously to her throat. "Where did you get my cross? I have it packed in my bag."

"Not yours, my child, mine. It is a twin to yours. It belonged to the child of my ancestor, Anne-Cecile du Diamant."

"Let me see it." Jamie held it in her hand. It was the same yet different. A slight coloration perhaps. Then Jamie remembered the jeweler had cleaned hers when he lengthened the chain. "I don't understand," she said at last, placing the cross and chain beside her on the sketchbook.

"It's rather complicated."

"I bet it is," Jamie said, a faint unease stirring within her. She remembered running through the forest, the twisting malignant mist, then it was gone.

"Our ancestor, Anne-Cecile du Diamant, came from France with her twin sons. Their names were Philippe and Louis."

"She came alone, with just the children?"

"Her husband was to join her, but he never came. There was a slave uprising and Philippe was lost. It was presumed he died."

"A slave uprising?"

"Think back, child. We are talking centuries ago. Our history."

"So what happened?"

"With Philippe presumed dead, Louis inherited the Jumeaux Estate. If his brother Philippe had lived, he, the eldest son, would have inherited."

The room was very quiet. Motes of dust danced in the sun rays.

"I believe that you, Jamie, are descended from Philippe du Diamant. I knew it the moment you showed me your cross and told me about the psalter. I have one as well." Clarisse nervously crumpled her tissue. "The crosses were given to the Diamant twins by the King of France, Louis the Sixteenth."

Jamie stared. "The King of France?"

"Yes. He and Marie Antoinette stood as godparents to the twins, and the diamond crosses were christening gifts."

"And the prayer books - what about them?"

"They probably came from the De Roches, Anne-Cecile's family. I don't suppose we'll ever know what happened to Philippe..."

"Wait, now wait. Let me absorb all this. Kings and slave uprisings, crosses and prayer books." Jamie stared, the unease still within her.

Clarisse nodded. "I'm sorry. The story is so much a part of me, I just..."

"So slow down, let me understand this." Point by point Jamie repeated the history. Then a wave of anger washed over her. "Why didn't you tell me all this then, when I was wearing the cross in your office!"

"I was afraid. I didn't know you well, and I was afraid you would try and claim the estate."

"Claim the estate? Good God, Clarisse. Do you really think I..." Jamie caught herself. "How would I do that after all these years?"

"You might have tried. Even if unsuccessful, the whole matter could be held up in the courts. Legal matters are very complicated here."

"I might've kept you tied up in the courts for years?"

Clarisse looked at the floor.

"Oh, Clarisse. How could you think I would do such a thing? I was totally alone. My mother and father were dead. And after Paul died, I had no family. You could have reached out."

"I can only ask your forgiveness," Clarisse said quietly.

Jamie rubbed her brow, trying to take it all in. "So we're family, you and I?"

"And Andre, and Emile, and Tante Yve - and Bertille and Marcus, if you know about the visit to their cave of ancestors."

"Yes, I know. Andre and I talked about it."

Clarisse remained silent, waiting.

Jamie watched her, the thought coming to mind like a ray of warm sun. "When I first came to this island, it felt so familiar. Even Andre looked familiar. Everyone passed it off as island experiences. But it was deeper than that...and the parrot dreams, and the lost child... Clarisse! Bertille has seen my cross. She talked of the lost diamond. Diamant."

Clarisse looked up sharply. "How would Bertille know of these things?"

"Not by spiritual powers, not that." Jamie thought about it. "If I had to guess, I'd say the ancestor rituals handed down to Marcus and Bertille. The oral traditions."

"But when Marcus took them to the cave, he didn't mention you as family, from Philippe, the lost twin."

"No, he didn't, did he. Bertille and Marcus can be quite cunning when they want to be."

"Don't think harshly of them," Clarisse said quickly. "They were afraid of losing their land, their family heritage - far older than ours."

Jamie leaned back and closed her eyes. "You're right, of course."

"Listen to me," Clarisse said. "All of this misunderstanding, this ambiguous knowledge, must be made clear. I came here to talk about the cross and prayer book, and to tell you who you are."

Jamie stood. "Let me get my psalter. I have it with me."

When she returned she put the small book in Clarisse's hands. Clarisse opened it. She slid her fingernail along the edge of the first page, releasing a double fold. "See here, the old script is faded, but I believe it says Jean-Philippe du Diamant. Mine says Jean-Louis du Diamant." She closed the little book and handed it back to Jamie.

"We need a family meeting. I shall arrange it. We shall clear the air of this mystery which has been such a burden."

"Good, I'd like that. I know the others would too."

"I'll need to phone my sister, Yve. Bring her here."

"Clarisse?"

"Yes?"

"I wish you had known my mother. You would have loved her. And my father."

"I'm sure I would."

"And my grandmother. She was the one who had the parrot dreams. I guess I inherited it from her. My mom told me before she died that they took me to see a psychiatrist as a child, worried about my dreams. The doctor told them it was the mind's way of working out tensions from the day."

Clarisse stared at the floor. "Tensions from the day."

"What could he possibly have known about parrots and a child lost two hundred years ago." She handed Clarisse her cross and chain. She smiled impishly. "Why don't you hold on to this. I already have one."

CHAPTER THIRTY-NINE

It was two weeks later, with a clean bill of health from Dr. Simpson, that Jamie grabbed Andre's arm and pulled him onto the veranda. "Let's talk."

"Yes, let's talk. Tell me, why is Tante Yve here?"

"Wait for the meeting," Jamie said firmly.

"What are you and Mother up to?"

"Come on, Andre. Allow us this."

"I usually know what's going on around here."

"Let's go for a walk. I've been doing a little each day."

Andre smiled and hugged her. "You're in some sort of a mood this morning."

"Let's walk over to the back lawn."

"The back lawn."

"Yes, the bench near the ginger lilies."

At the bench Andre looked at her. "Jamie..."

"Now sit down." She playfully pushed him down and kissed him as she had been unable to for quite some time. "I miss making love to you."

"And I miss you! It's hard to concentrate on work."

She looked into his eyes, suddenly serious. "Andre, I have

something very important to ask you." She ran a caressing thumb over the familiar cleft in his chin.

"Make it quick, I'd rather kiss you."

Jamie pulled back. "Be serious."

"Okay, I'm listening. What is it you want to ask me?"

Jamie paused. "I've thought about this a lot, especially these last few days, these wonderful healing days."

"Yes? Come on, Jamie."

She laughed self-consciously. "It was easier when I was in bed thinking about you. Look, Andre. I love you more than I can tell you. I want to be with you when I go to sleep at night and when I wake up in the morning. I want us to have beautiful babies with my green eyes and your dimpled chin."

Andre started to speak.

"Don't you dare, this is tough enough. What I want to ask is," she let out the breath she had been holding, "is - will you marry me?"

He relaxed then, leaning on the bench in a way she would remember forever. "Yes, Jamie. I will marry you. And before you think this is totally your idea, I've just been waiting for the right time to ask you."

"I'm glad, because the time is right now. Say it again."

"Yes, Jamie. I will marry you."

"I like the way you say that. Clear and unambiguous."

"I don't joke around on something like this. Incidentally, shouldn't I have asked you?"

"I wanted it this way. I lay in bed wanting it this way. Okay?"

"Fine by me."

"I don't have a ring for you," she said.

"I think that's my department."

Jamie kissed him. "Let's keep this quiet for now. Until after this family meeting. Your mom has something important to tell the family."

"Are we heading for another Demontagne family crisis?"

Jamie playfully punched his arm. "Don't let Clarisse hear you talk like that."

"So what's the meeting about?"

"I know some of it, Andre. But please, give your mother some support. I suspect things will be difficult for her. I do know she's nervous."

"Okay. It's odd, isn't it. Remember when she was cold and distant, and very authoritarian? And now she's more open and showing nerves."

"She's on her way back from wherever she took herself, Andre. She just needs time and support."

They made their way back to the estate house.

When they entered the kitchen they were greeted by Marcus and Bertille. Jamie was surprised to see Marcus in his suit and Bertille in a "Sunday best" outfit. Marcus had his big hands clasped around the small metal box in his lap.

"I'm dressed for this occasion, Jamie," Bertille said, "but I'm still responsible for this kitchen."

Jamie laughed and made her excuses. "Andre, come for me in five minutes. I've got to change."

As she rummaged through the guest room closet where she kept some of her clothes, she pulled out a simple pale green sheath and a pair of sandals. As she bent over to slip on her shoes, she looked at her ring finger. What sort of ring would Andre choose for her?

Just as she stood, Andre came into the room.

"Do you like this green sheath?" she asked.

Andre enfolded her in his arms. "Anything with you in it."

Jamie kissed him back passionately, then adroitly slipped free. "We have a meeting to attend, and I've got to fix my lipstick."

"This is going to be quite a day."

"Going to be? Andre, a woman proposed to you this morning - you've already had quite a day." Jamie held up her small cross and chain. "Help me with this, will you?" She held her breath, waiting for Andre's reaction, but he gave none. Clarisse had kept her secrets well. For the first time Jamie got nervous about the meeting and what would come to light.

They had assembled in the living room. Auguste and Clarisse were standing together. Jack and Angel, with Angel obviously pregnant and sitting in a straight-backed chair, were talking with Emile. Tante Yve sat nearby.

Jamie went around the room hugging everyone with enthusiasm and warmth. She startled Emile, who looked puzzled. When Jamie got to Angel and Jack she hugged them and then patted the roundness of Angel's belly. "Glad you are here for this," Jamie whispered.

"I'm sorry about your baby, Jamie."

"Me, too. But there will be others." Jamie comforted herself with the words.

Clarisse's voice rose over the low conversations. "Where are Marcus and Bertille?"

"I think they're in the kitchen," Andre said. "I'll get them."

When Andre returned he was followed by Marcus and Bertille. All eyes found the small dark metal box Marcus was carrying. They stayed on it as he sat down and placed it carefully in his lap. His eyes turned respectfully to Clarisse.

Clarisse stood and cleared her throat. "Thank you all for coming. Yve from Martinique and Angel and Jack, we welcome you back from New York." Clarisse's voice trailed off as she looked around. Her gaze settled on Jamie, then she began.

"I've asked you here because it is time for me to tell you a secret I have carried for some time. It concerns all of us in this room." She paused for a moment, finding her words. "When I was a child I found some papers hidden away in my mother's bedroom. I still remember that day, I was on the bed with my story books... I didn't know what they were."

She glanced at her sister, Yve. "When our mother and father died I simply forgot about them - like children do. I forgot them until many years later. At that time I was old enough to understand what I had found, but I was afraid to tell anyone."

Jamie watched Andre lean forward in his chair, his dark eyes intent on his mother, a woman who had in the last weeks changed before his eyes.

"I have agonized about this for a long time, and I can't tell you how difficult it is to hold a dark secret, to have it rule your every waking moment so that you are never free of it..." She looked at her hands. "But something happened that made me realize I must disclose my secret." Her eyes found Jamie. "One morning at work I noticed Jamie wearing a small cross, the very cross she is wearing today."

Jamie felt Andre's quick stare.

"The very sight of it made me ill, and to this day I don't know how I managed to keep hold of my senses. That small cross literally changed my world as I knew it." Clarisse faltered then, eyes skittering around the gathering. When they found Jamie, Jamie nodded in encouragement and smiled.

"Jamie told me she had found the cross in her mother's belongings after her mother's untimely death. There was also a small book, a prayer book, she said. Very old and worn and faded..."

Auguste murmured something to Clarisse, and she continued in a firmer voice.

"I too have such a cross. I too have such a prayer book, a psalter. As I examined Jamie's cross I thought about my own, and I knew the crosses were identical, and that although I hadn't seen it, the prayer books would be identical too. In my case, the cross and psalter had been with the papers I had found as a child and kept so secret. Mine had belonged to Louis du Diamant. He was the younger of twin sons born to Anne-Cecile de Roche du Diamant." Her hand came up and pointed to Jamie's throat. "Jamie's cross, and also her prayer book, had belonged to Philippe du Diamant, the elder of the twins."

"The elder!" Emile exclaimed. Quickly he quieted and watched his mother, the worry showing in his face.

"Mon Dieu," Tante Yve said, her hand coming to her mouth.

Everyone watched Clarisse, then Jamie, who tried to smile and with great effort resisted touching her cross. Instead she held herself composed so that all could see it.

Marcus pulled uncomfortably at his tie, one big hand remaining protectively over the small metal box.

CHAPTER FORTY

"I...I am very ashamed of what I did next. I did nothing." Clarisse said, looking at Jamie as she spoke, almost in penitence. "I did not tell anyone about Jamie's cross and its significance. I can only confess I was afraid, more than I had been afraid at any time in what has proven to be a long and lonely life."

Auguste murmured his support, and Clarisse went on.

"It was wrong of me, and I have apologized to her. But that is not all. The rest of this secret I carried, and which I will be free of today, thank God, concerns Bertille and Marcus and their family." She managed a smile at Angel. "Which will soon be increased."

Bertille shifted in her chair, moving closer to Marcus, who sat in heavy silence.

"It was Bertille's and Marcus' ancestors who hid Anne-Cecile and her son for four years in the forest. Both families know that part of the history, and I'm sure that those here will share it with others." She nodded towards Jamie and smiled.

"But there is something you don't know... What you don't know, what I found in the papers with the family cross and prayer book, was that during that time of hiding, Anne-Cecile had another son, fathered by her slave, Makus. This child, the first Marcus, became part of the bloodline from which their family descends." She looked at Bertille and Marcus as if seeing them for the first time.

"So, you see, we are all related."

Emile and Yve shifted in their chairs, concern in their eyes.

"I...I don't know where this knowledge will lead us, but I am glad to be relieved of it, to share it openly with others. It has been nothing to me but a grievous burden. So this is another reason I speak today. When Andre and then Bertille told me that the hotel project might endanger the Deroche land, I had no choice but to speak out."

Clarisse stood there for several moments, trying to summon more words. But then she realized she had finished. She had emptied out the hidden events that had haunted and troubled her for so long. She sat down abruptly and looked around, some apprehension filling her eyes.

Andre spoke quietly to Marcus and Bertille, then went to his mother. "Emile and I learned this part of the story recently," Andre said, "but I can't tell you how important it is to me, Mother, that you had the courage to tell what you knew today. You did the right thing for the Deroche family. I am very proud to be your son - and I know Emile is, too."

Worry etched Emile's face. He looked at Tante Yve for support. "But if Louis is the younger twin, and what you say about Jamie's ownership of the other cross and psalter..."

"It's all true, Emile," Clarisse said.

"Then...then we have lost everything! Everything! Jamie could..."

Auguste spoke, raising his voice for the first time. "Let's wait, Emile. I have a feeling this meeting is far from over. Wait." He looked directly at Marcus. "Marcus, I believe you have something to say."

Marcus looked to Andre for support. "Sir, if you will explain..."

"What Marcus is asking me to explain is the special and unacknowledged labor he and Bertille perform on this island. Both Marcus and Bertille are their generation's keepers of the oral traditions of their family line. They are the keepers of the ancient songs, their ancestors' collective memories. These songs tell of Anne-Cecile and Makus, their son. Marcus?" Andre looked at him.

"Tell the rest," Marcus said.

Andre nodded. "Marcus and Bertille are also the keepers of their ancestors' resting place. This is what they showed us, had to show us, to make New York lawyers and me, with my own rather selfish business plans for a hotel, realize the folly and violence we were inflicting on sacred land." Andre looked around at the gathering, offering Marcus' worries. "The resting place of the Deroche family ancestors is of immense historical and archeological interest and value. It must be protected at all costs." He smiled at Marcus. "Now, dear friend, you must speak. I don't know what you have to say, and that box makes me nervous - but today is the day for sharing ancient matters between ancient families."

Marcus carried the small metal box to the front of the room where Clarisse had stood. Opening it, he lifted out a yellowed and stained piece of parchment. He held it in his big hands. He looked around the room, preparing for a role that was very new to him.

Jamie watched, fascinated by the uncommon grace of this big and powerfully-built man.

"This is the paper Madame Diamant wrote when she was in the cave, hiding during the uprising. Our ancestors' songs say it acknowledges the son she bore Makus, and gives us title to the land which contains our cave where our ancestors rest."

Clarisse's hand came up. "May I see it, please?"

The gathering waited as she studied it intensely.

"This is more than a document of lineage, it is a will giving the mulatto child - forgive my use of that word, Marcus, it is described here..." She hurried on. "It is a will giving the mulatto child an equal share of the Jumeaux wealth, to be shared with Anne-Cecile's other living children." She looked at Jack and Angel. "This means you, Jack, are to share equally with my children."

Emile stared at the floor.

"Auguste, will you read the rest, please." Clarisse handed him the parchment.

He went to the window and translated with difficulty the faded French script penned so many years before by Anne-Cecile.

No one spoke, and the silence lengthened.

It was Clarisse who stood then, and struggled to hold the families together. "I have always had need for my sons' approval and love. But truth be told, I placed higher value on protecting their financial holdings in Jumeaux. It has been a true folly. I've burdened my heart and soul with secrets that ultimately were not worth keeping. Look what has happened here today. Emile is upset, as perhaps we all are to some degree. In the telling of my secrets, other secrets have come out - and what does it all mean?

"I can tell you what it means to me: I've learned far too late that family - true family - means love and trust, not material things. We are all family here, including Jamie, whom I firmly believe is the descendant of Philippe, the lost Diamant."

Clarisse looked around. "And so, my last secret...the oral history that Marcus and Bertille report is true. Anne-Cecile did bear a son fathered by Makus. I have the document Anne-Cecile wrote prior to her death. This document speaks of the unbearable sadness Anne-Cecile endured when she could not acknowledge this son publicly. Don't forget, she had lost her husband. And her other son had disappeared and was never found. She did everything she could to protect both her remaining sons given the times in which she lived."

"Do you know how he was raised?" Jack asked, reaching for Angel's hand.

"Yes. He was raised in the house with Louis, her other son. He and his family were freed. He was educated with his brother by private tutors at a time when that was very rare. Eventually she sent him to the States. He was boarded with Unitarians in Boston and tutored privately. He was well educated."

Jack's eyes shone.

Clarisse looked at Marcus. "Do your sacred songs tell of this?"

"No, Mistress, they do not. They only tell he left the island and came back and fathered children. His bones rest in the mountain. The songs do tell of his love of island plants and animals."

"Plants and animals," Jack said.

Clarisse smiled at him. "Your love of the parrots has deeper roots than you knew."

Finally Andre spoke into the quiet. "So much to absorb. Why don't we take a break?"

CHAPTER FORTY-ONE

"Isn't life strange," Jamie said as they walked from the living room. "By a twist of fate I find myself on an island where I fall in love with a man who turns out to be a distant relative."

"Very distant, I hasten to add." Andre smiled. "Look, let's take a moment with Jack and Angel. I need to mention something."

"And we need to talk to Emile. He's not taking this meeting well."

"Emile will be all right. So will Tante Yve."

"Her '*Mon Dieu*' set a tone, didn't it."

Andre pulled her close as they joined Jack and Angel.

"Jack, when everyone gathers again, let's present the plan for the Heritage Center and how we'll protect the cave. There are some financial implications now, after what we've heard today. I think it would be good to let the others know our thinking."

"Sure thing." Jack smiled, glancing from Angel to Andre. "Anything for a relative."

"So this is what we're in for - relative jokes?" Jamie asked.

"Probably. But isn't it fascinating that I have an ancestor who was a half-brother to one of yours. That's something!"

Andre laughed. *It will all work out,* he thought.

"There's your mother," Jamie said quietly. "Perhaps you should..."

"I'll talk with her. Thanks, Jamie."

Clarisse stood on the veranda, her arms braced against the porch railing. She stared out over the green, cloud covered mountains. Andre stood quietly beside her. "This land, this Jumeaux. I once looked out like this in pride. Now, I wonder if any of it is mine," she said.

"You did the right thing in there, Mother. We'll work it through."

"I couldn't bear what you and Emile would think of me if you found out I'd withheld so much. And now Emile is angry."

"What Emile is angry about is loss of property in the sharing with others. But look at his work with Jack, his interest in the environment. Things will work out. He just needs a little time."

"I hope so."

Andre put an arm around his mother and gently steered her from the veranda.

"Jamie is wonderful, Andre. Such a fine young woman. We talked, you know."

"I know. She and I talked too. She proposed to me out on the back lawn this morning. Can you believe that?"

Clarisse stopped walking and stared in surprise.

"So we're engaged. I'll have to get a ring." He reached out and took his mother's hand. "You're the first to know."

"And she proposed to you? I like that. She's so right for you, Andre." Clarisse lifted her left hand. "Do you think Jamie would want my mother's ring? The stone's not very big. Or will she want a new, modern setting?"

Andre stared at his mother. "You just keep amazing me, Mother. I think Jamie would think it would be the perfect engagement ring," he said as his mother placed the ring in his hand. He gave her a long hug. "Come on, we'd better get back inside."

They found everyone gathered in the kitchen, with a formally attired Bertille serving tea and juice. Jamie was chatting with Angel and Tante Yve, Marcus was sitting quietly, still holding his metal box. The mood was lighter, more relaxed. Jack said something to Emile and he smiled. Andre escorted his mother to his father, then joined Jamie.

"Mother knows," he said.

"Knows what?"

"The back lawn thing."

"You call it a thing?"

"What thing?" Angel asked, instantly on the alert.

"Never mind that. We need to restart the meeting."

Bertille came over with fresh juice for their tall glasses and a big plate of her homemade ginger cookies. Her eyes beamed in delight at Angel, then she patted her stomach.

"Everybody's patting my belly," Angel said.

"'Twill be our first grand," Bertille said. "It's a boy, you know. You must stay in St. Lucia, learn our ways." Then she was gone, serving others, comfortable now in the group.

"Jack," Andre said, "this idea for the Heritage Center, what will be the cost of it, ballpark figure?"

"Depends on how elaborate we want it to be."

Andre thought for a moment. "The investors may be willing to fund part of it. I think I can make a convincing argument that the Heritage Center will help sell the hotel. We'll have something no other hotel in the world has."

Jack waggled his glass for emphasis. "Just what I told Emile - a major archeological site owned by the families, in addition to a rain forest sanctuary dedicated to the preservation of the parrot habitat."

"I saw him smiling," Jamie said.

"It's a winner all around, Jamie." Jack's face became serious as he looked at Andre. "One thing, how do we make sure the family keeps control of the cave? Will the Heritage Center be run by the family? Can you get funding, even, if it's not owned by the hotel group?"

Andre nodded. "Actually, we'll set it up as a family trust, a non-profit corporation. Non-profit will make it easier for us to get funding from all sorts of sources."

"The family will have to own the cave to protect it."

"And the Heritage Center?" Emile asked, joining the group.

"Like I said, we can set it up as a family trust, but we need some capital to get started. Probably a charity group from the States would support it. And the parrots? There'll be no problem getting funding to save them."

"Good," Emile said. "That's good."

"How are you, Emile?" Jamie said.

Emile managed a small smile. "Shook up, but okay." He glanced around. "I think I'll talk with Mother before we get started again."

"And I need to clear away a bit," Jamie said, sweeping up crumbs from the table. "I'll give these to the birds." As she maneuvered through the crowded kitchen she fell against Marcus, dislodging his grip on the metal box. The box holding Anne-Cecile's will tumbled to the floor. Everyone turned as it clattered and burst open, sending colored pebbles bouncing across the wooden floorboards.

"Oh, Marcus, I'm so sorry! I should've watched where I was going..."

Jamie got down on her knees and began picking up the pebbles. When Jack came to help he suddenly stiffened, swearing under his breath. "What's the matter, Jack?" Jamie asked, alarmed.

"Father, where did you get these?"

"They are the colored stones that Anne-Cecile and Makus used to play a game. I think now you call it Mancala." Marcus held out the box for the pebbles. "When they could not come out of the cave, it helped pass the time. The ancestors' song says the pebbles belonged to Anne-Cecile. See, they were kept in this pouch." His big hands held up the faded fabric, grown rotten with time.

"But do you know what these are?" Jack demanded.

"Son, why are you acting like this? They are stones from a game, a remembrance of my ancestors. Sometimes your mother and I play this game with these stones."

Jack quieted his voice and spoke more respectfully, pushing down his excitement. "Yes, Father. They are stones, but very valuable stones." He picked up several translucent pebbles. "Unless I'm mistaken, these are uncut diamonds. And this," he said, picking up a reddish stone, "is a ruby, and these - emeralds."

Clarisse and the others gathered for a closer look. "The lost diamonds," she murmured.

"What diamonds, Clarisse?" Jamie asked.

"The story was passed down that Anne-Cecile carried diamonds to the island, then lost them. We always assumed the story meant the Diamant child who was lost in the rebellion."

"But it's real diamonds," Jamie said excitedly. "And they've been on this island all these years?"

Andre looked at Emile. "When we were boys we hunted for these stones, digging holes everywhere."

Marcus nodded. He looked embarrassed. "I would watch you play, but my concern was always keeping you from the cave. I never thought..."

"What a strange day this is," Angel said.

Clarisse gripped Marcus' arm. "These stones belong to the Deroche family. You have guarded them all these years. And Jack, it is your family that should control them."

"Wait a..." Emile said.

Clarisse held up a hand.

Jack spoke. "If Father agrees, I'd suggest we use their value for the Heritage Center."

"I agree if your mother agrees," Marcus said simply. "But the stones really belong to all of us, don't they? We are all descendants of Makus, B'til and Anne-Cecile. In the past we were slaves and slave owners. That time is gone. Now we are only people joined by blood and history. What we make of that history is what's important. We must make our island people proud of their heritage."

Bertille stepped forward. As Jamie watched, she felt the old power emanating from her presence. "The parrots have told me that only by flying together can their island survive. Now we have three parrots, Jack, Andre and Jamie, who bring the family together."

Her eyes held each one of them to account. "You will protect the mountains so the parrots will fly free forever, and the ancestors' resting place will remain undisturbed. My parrot eyes see the future in you. Evil has failed. We have come together."

The kitchen was very quiet as Bertille delivered her solemn words. No one found them bizarre or disturbing. This meeting was the place for ancient rights and covenants to offer themselves.

Andre broke the silence. "I have one more secret to share." He reached out and took Jamie's hand. "Jamie proposed to me this morning, and I accepted." His wide smile evidenced the joy of sharing this news. Murmurs flooded the room.

"And I have something to give Jamie."

Jamie looked at him, puzzled.

He reached into his pocket and pulled out Clarisse's ring. Jamie's green eyes widened as she looked from Andre to Clarisse.

Andre gently lifted Jamie's hand. She looked up at him, love shining in her eyes. As he slipped the ring on her finger, he felt the sureness of an unbreakable connection.

Soul mates, thought Clarisse, moving to hug them both.

EPILOGUE

Jamie awoke to sun streaming into her bedroom window at Jumeaux. She lay still, listening to the peep of a yellow breast who had built a nest nearby. In the distance she heard the screech of parrots. *Fitting,* she thought. For her wedding day. And odd. No more dreams of lost children or parrots flying. She found she missed her dream parrots. Would they return, or would they leave her in Andre's care? She looked at her engagement ring, Clarisse's mother's ring, the one she had admired so many months ago. The love and history there pleased her more than she could say.

She should get up. It was her wedding day. There were things to do. She stayed where she was, listening. On the bedside table her mother and father smiled from her favorite photograph. "Thanks, Barbara," she murmured. One more quiet moment, cramming into it all her love for Andre, all the anticipation of the day, then she sprang from the bed and went to the closet.

It was still there, of course. Her wedding gown. She ran her hands over it, exploring the softness, the fine fluid silk of pale cream. She draped the fabric in her hands and critically examined the hand-painted tropical blooms and foliage in an exquisite mosaic of cream, some barely tinted with mauve, some hinting of the palest blue or green. It was lovely. A simple sleeveless sheath with a jewel neckline, long and slit to the knees in back. The fabric was elegantly delicate. She would wear her diamond cross and her engagement ring. She had debated wearing her parrot earrings. This was, after all, a very special occasion. But she had reluctantly put them away - they were getting tattered - in the little psalter, part of her heritage on St. Lucia. She would wear her little pearls.

Jamie slipped into shorts and pulled a T-shirt over her tousled hair. She kissed her fingertips and touched the photo of her parents as she left. From the veranda she walked around the house and into the kitchen. Bertille was already there, brewing coffee. "Hi, Bertille."

Bertille came to her, enfolding her in a warm hug. "'Tis a beautiful day for a wedding, my pretty parrot," she said. "How did you sleep?"

"Would it disappoint you if I said I slept fitfully, thinking about Andre, and that I didn't dream of parrots?"

Bertille's brow knitted. "Not even one?"

"Nope."

"I'm sure they have their reasons. All will be clear in good time." Satisfied with herself, Bertille went to the coffee pot. "Do you want some to start this wonderful day?"

Jamie shook her head. "Just this," she said, picking up an orange and heading for the door.

"Don't you wait too long to get ready, child! The morning's half over. You slept late!"

"I won't be long, Bertille."

"Mind yourself."

Jamie ran out onto the grass luxuriating in its coolness, the raspy texture under her feet. The sun was up and the sky full of those puffy, whipped cream clouds she loved. She hopped a little, enjoying the feel of the grass, then she bit into her orange to start the peel. *Wedding Day!*

As she bit into the succulent orange section the juice ran down her chin and she wiped it away on the back of her hand. Then she wiped her hand on her shorts.

"I love that about you," Andre said.

She turned to face him, waving the orange. "You're not supposed to see the bride until we're at the church."

"Let's get married right now, just the way you are." He had her then, tasting her orangy mouth. Her soft jasmine scent hovering around them.

"Sorry, but we have guests to consider. At the church..."

"Oh, I'll turn up."

She playfully punched his arm. "I didn't mean that, I meant at the church..."

"It's a beautiful church, it's Anglican, and it's in Choiseul."

"I know it's beautiful, but..."

"You do?" He nibbled at her ear.

"Of course. We met with the priest there."

"And a good man he is."

"Andre, you're goofy."

"A special day. And I finally get you in my clutches."

Jamie grinned. "It's been quite some adventure, hasn't it?"

"And it's just the beginning."

"Here we are at our bench."

"Where you proposed," Andre said.

They sat together in silence for awhile, savoring the morning and this last time together before they would be joined in marriage.

"Andre?"

"Uumm?"

"Your mother's making my bouquet. She's got Georges, your gardener..."

"Our gardener..."

"Cutting arm loads of pink and red ginger lilies and tropical fronds for the church. That's what I wanted to know about the church. Did you see what she's done? My bouquet is a secret."

Andre laughed. "We're not much good in the secrets department anymore."

"She's so wonderful, Andre. So light, accessible and loving." Jamie held up her hand, the small diamond sparkling in the light. "This..."

"No longer the matriarchal presence."

"She carries herself differently, too. A lighter step."

"Yes, I've noticed. I kiss her now, I make a point of it. Emile does too. And Father..."

"Your father what?"

Andre shrugged and slipped off his sandals. He sat there wiggling his toes, thinking. "I'm not sure, but I'm wondering if the two of them are getting back together again."

Jamie looked at him. "Are you sure that's not just wishful thinking? Auguste is even more reserved than she."

"Could be wrong. Let's wait and see."

"Andre?"

"What?"

"Good thing you'll be wearing long pants at this wedding. You really do have knobby knees."

He was on her in a minute, tousling her hair and kissing her neck.

"Andre!"

"Say I have nice knees."

"Okay, give up, give up."

They laughed in the morning sun as the birds sang and a parrot at the edge of the rain forest observed them.

"You have nice knees," she said solemnly. "I love your knees. In fact, I love everything about you."

He kissed her then, long and passionately. When he gently looked into her eyes he said, "I loved you from the first time I saw you, helping those injured men at the truck accident. I just didn't know it."

She burrowed into him. "A lot's happened."

"A world has changed. Families have changed."

"And today things change even more."

Andre cupped her face in his hands and kissed her eyes and cheeks and lips, feather soft. "I love you, my darling Jamie." He reached into the pocket of his shorts and brought out small dangle earrings, parrot feathers rendered in gold and emeralds. "Will you wear these today?"

The sun was higher now and bright. The little wooden church sheltered in a grove of trees.

Barbara was her usual inquiring self. "Clarisse is bringing your bouquet and her son, right?"

"That's the package deal," Jamie said.

"You sure don't sound nervous."

"Not when you're as happy as I am, Barbara."

"Are those beautiful earrings a gift from the groom?"

"He gave them to me this morning." Jamie touched the gold dangling at her ears. "These won't get bedraggled like the ones Serena gave me."

"And I'm stuck with rooster feathers. Oh, there's Clarisse's car now."

They watched as Andre got out. He was wearing white linen slacks and a collarless shirt that Jamie had fashioned for him of the same silk as her dress. They watched as he assisted his mother, then kissed her lightly on the cheek.

"Oh, hon, he looks good enough to eat," Barbara said, wickedly jabbing Jamie in the ribs. "Oh, my God, look at the bouquet."

Both women stared as Clarisse and Andre walked toward them. The bouquet of jasmine, orange blossoms and pale vanda orchids that Clarisse put into Jamie's hands fell almost to Jamie's knees in trailing strands of creamy silken ribbons and small blossoms. Jamie's eyes filled with tears at the love that had gone into its creation.

"Oh, Clarisse, this is exquisite. Thank you so much." Jamie leaned over the bouquet to kiss her. Andre handed his mother a circlet of creamy, fragrant frangipani blossoms, which she placed on Jamie's dark hair.

"There. Now, my dear, you look like a bride. So, it is time," Clarisse said. "I will signal them to start the music when I am seated."

"Don't walk too fast down the aisle," Barbara said.

"Bossy - even on my wedding day," Jamie said, laughing.

A minute later the sounds of the traditional bridal march began, interpreted by an island pan band.

"Andre, what a wonderful surprise!" Jamie said. "I thought there wasn't going to be any music. The church has no organ or piano."

"It seemed fitting, an island thing."

Taking his arm, Jamie looked up at him. "Shall we go get married?"

They entered the church holding on to each other, their love more than either had dared to hope for. A dream that had reached across generations and time. An unbreakable bond.

THE END

The Adventure from
A Dream Across Time
Continues

JAMIE DEMONTAGNE HAS IT ALL. Her family lives in a fairytale compound high above the seacoast on the tropical island of St. Lucia. She has found the love of her life in Andre Demontagne, has three darling children and a flourishing career.

Her children are beautiful and talented but her son is deeply troubled and Jamie fears she will lose him as events from two hundred years ago conspire to destroy his world. Can this child, this family, this marriage, survive the mysterious forces tearing them apart?

Turn the page and read the prologue and first chapter of *A Circle of Dreams,* AND meet Jamie's children.

Look for *A Circle of Dreams* in June 2006!

Sainte Lucie
1838

PROLOGUE

Anne-Cecile Diamant opened the door to the mahogany armoire. *As I did all those years ago,* she thought. *The day Philippe was lost. A day like today. The sun was shining, I could hear birds, see white clouds scattered across the blue sky. I thought we might have rain.*

Pulling a handkerchief from her sleeve, she touched it to her temples, damp with sweat. She reached into the armoire and pulled out a small white psalter, the little book given as a christening gift. Inside was a slender gold chain with a tiny diamond-encrusted cross. These belonged to her son, Louis, now grown with children of his own. There had been another cross, identical to this, which she had put on Louis' twin brother, Philippe, in this very room. On the day they had escaped with their lives, fleeing a slave uprising. The day Philippe had disappeared.

She punished herself with the thought. *He was so small, only four. He must have been terrified.* She remembered fastening the little cross around her son's neck and tying the psalter around his middle with a scarf before they headed down the track to Malgretoute beach to board a ship for Martinique and safety. She remembered her own terror at finding her brother-in-law grievously wounded, her sister-in-law and three children dead on the track. Remembered running across the dark sand, carrying Louis, brigands with cutlasses coming to kill them. She remembered Philippe being thrown into a boat and hearing the oars thrusting through the water as it made for the ship. And then she remembered nothing until later in the caves. The dark caves where they had hidden for four years until it was safe to come back and claim the estate.

She reached into the armoire again. A small baby's cap, handmade lace with ribbons that had tied under her little boy's chin. One of the few objects she had brought from France when they came to the West Indian island of Sainte Lucie, fleeing before the terrors of the French Revolution. She fingered the hand-embroidered "P" where the ribbon attached to the cap, remembering the dark curly hair of her infant son, the baby's cap the only tangible object she had that connected her to Philippe. Only the cap. All the rest were memories.

Yet she had never given up hope. She had gone to Martinique to search for him, only to learn that the ship had never arrived, was rumored to have been lured onto the rocks by pirates. All aboard had perished. *I would have known,* she thought, *if Philippe was dead. Even after all these years a mother would know. I am not so old, just sixty-eight. I can't, I won't die until I find him.*

Her heart tripped a beat and she was suddenly dizzy. Gripping the side of the armoire, she steadied herself before leaving the room through the door that opened onto the wide shaded verandah. *I'll just lie down for a few minutes,* she thought, her heart hammering. *Then I'll feel better.*

The dark-skinned woman stood in the shadows of the verandah, watching the old woman settle herself on a chaise pulled close to the house wall, well out of the brilliant rays of the late afternoon sun. *Not be with us much longer,* she thought, taking note of the swollen feet and ankles, the blue tinge at the edge of the pale lips. She shook her grey and grizzled head, her face suffused with sadness. *Searching,* she thought, *her spirit already searching.*

"That you, B'til?" the old woman called softly.

"Yes, Mistress Diamant, I brewed you some herbs. Help you feel better."

"Come and sit with me, B'til." She patted a space on the chaise. "I've been remembering..."

B'til sat next to Anne-Cecile Diamant and patted her bony hip. "We both are old now, Mistress. Much to remember."

"I've been thinking about Philippe." Anne-Cecile's face was etched with sadness. "Why couldn't we ever know what happened?"

"The spirits keep that knowledge from us, Mistress." She held up her hand, a faint bluish tinge rimmed her nails. "I been flying again. I know you have no peace until you know."

"You've taken the herbs that help you join the circle of women?" Anne-Cecile's face changed, hope evident in her eyes. "What did you see?"

"Like all the other times. I see the ship, the lights on the cliff top. I hear the waves, then the timbers splintering as the ship comes on the rocks. I feel the water in my lungs. Then nothing. I be sorry, Mistress." B'til clasped the pale, veined hand of the woman who had given her freedom, the woman who treated her as an equal, a sister.

Hope faded from Anne-Cecile's eyes, like a candle's wick flickering out. "I still remember the first time you made the circle with me, B'til. The time we both flew into the spirit world and searched. It took weeks for the blue to fade from my hands." She inspected her hands as if the blue tinge might still be there all these years later. "I would know if he were dead," she said fiercely. "I would know."

"Your other son gives you grandchildren. Can you not find joy there?"

"Of course, B'til. But every time I see Louis, I see Philippe as he would have been. It is the not knowing that pains me so. I had to give up Marcus, but I know where he is, that he is alive and well."

B'til was surprised that Anne-Cecile spoke of her other son, the child she had given birth to during the four years they had hidden in the forest, hidden from the brigands and the French army who sought to slaughter all the aristocrats. The child who was fathered by Makus, her former slave. B'til had raised him as her own, and he had been freed along with all the Diamant slaves as soon as Anne-Cecile could emerge from hiding. Marcus had been sent to Boston to be educated, boarded with Unitarian abolitionists. He was there now. They did not know if he would ever come back to the island where he was born.

Anne-Cecile continued, as if she could read B'til's thoughts. "It is enough to know he is alive. I have given him all I can. The world is not ready for me to acknowledge him. But you have the papers?"

"Yes, Mistress. The papers you gave us in a box in the caves. Before he die, Makus show me where they be."

"And you will share the secret with the next one after you?"

"It is done, Mistress. There are keepers who know the story."

"You have been a sister to me, B'til. A comfort through all these years." Anne-Cecile sat up and tried to stand, but was overcome with dizziness. "Something else I must show you, B'til. In my bedroom."

"Later, mistress." B'til helped Anne-Cecile back onto the chaise. "Lay back down now and rest. Sip the herbs I brewed for you. They are sweetened with honey from the orange trees. Plenty time to show me later. I sit with you a bit." She held the hand of the woman who had been part of her life for so many years, felt the reedy pulse, the occasional skipped beat. *Her spirit fly soon,* B'til thought, *but she still be searching. She walk this place until she know.*

St. Lucia
1986

CHAPTER ONE

An elegant woman stood waiting behind the chain-link fence, umbrella over her arm. She was concentrating on the small LIAT plane which had just arrived on St. Lucia from Martinique. As a gust of wind ruffled her salon-cut gray hair, her gaze flicked to the black clouds in the late afternoon sky. The bougainvillea by the airport entrance looked faded in the dim light, and streetlights around the small terminal did little to brighten the gloom.

At last she saw the couple for whom she waited, the woman carrying an infant. Her face brightened as she waved. "Andre, Jamie, over here."

Andre Demontagne waved back, calling, "Mother. We'll meet you in the terminal."

"No, Andre. I must see that baby right now."

Andre leaned over to his wife and whispered, "How like Mother. When she's impatient there's no denying her."

Jamie Demontagne smiled back at her husband. "Even through a chain-link fence."

"How are you, my dear?" Clarisse Demontagne's fingers reached through the web of the fence. "Can I see him?"

Jamie pulled back the blanket, proudly exposing the newborn's face.

"Clarisse, may we present Philippe Diamant Demontagne."

The baby was wide awake and looked directly at his grandmother.

"I think he has your blue eyes, Clarisse," Jamie said.

Clarisse tilted her head to get a better look. "It seems possible, Jamie, although you never know with newborns. But I think he did not get your green eyes." She lifted her head and looked at Andre steadily. "I think he looks like his father. Including the dimple in his chin." She chuckled. "He's absolutely beautiful."

An airplane roared overhead as she turned back to Jamie. "So you have named him Philippe, after the lost twin?"

"Yes," said Jamie.

"Let's hope you are not tempting..."

"Mother!" Andre interjected.

"We thought it fitting," Jamie said, "another Philippe after all these years. A return, of sorts."

There was a pause, then Clarisse spoke. "Well, it is lovely to have you with us at last, Philippe. We will not lose you."

Jamie's breath caught in her throat. "Of course not, Clarisse. This child will not be lost."

Jamie knew the history of Philippe Diamant, Clarisse's ancestor, a child lost in the terror of the French Revolution when it had come to St. Lucia, two centuries before. That Philippe had never been found. The family had learned of his survival only when Jamie was proven to be his descendant. The marriage of Jamie and Andre had brought the family together again.

Just then the dark clouds unleashed a torrent of rain.

Andre snapped open an umbrella, protecting his wife and child.

"Mother," he said as the rain intensified and Clarisse struggled to get her umbrella open, "go into the terminal. We'll meet you inside after we get through immigration and customs."

Inside the small terminal, Andre shook out the umbrella and they joined the end of the immigration line.

Jamie stood, slowly rocking Philippe. "I thought these tropical waves were farther apart. The storms seem to be moving faster."

"Nothing to worry about, Jamie. Just a sudden showery pocket." He changed the subject, an attempt to be reassuring. "I don't remember Yvie and Lissa ever having blue eyes. They were always green. Like yours," he said, touching his wife's cheek affectionately.

Jamie smiled. "His blue eyes are like your mother's, and let's not overlook all the other people mixed in over the generations since my side of the family left the Indies."

"Whatever got mixed in made you a wonderful blend. You really are lovely, you know, Jamie." His fingers moved down her shoulder-length dark hair.

Jamie's eyes were lively in the flourescent light. "I know that look. You'll have to wait a couple of weeks. I'm still sore from pushing this one into the world." She reached over and touched the cleft in Andre's strong chin.

"I missed you," he said. "Having you away from me."

"I know, but Martinique was a safer place for me to give birth, and Tante Yve took very good care of me."

The baby stirred, fussing slightly, his mouth rooting. He quieted then, his eyelids closing as he fell asleep.

The immigration and customs officials seemed anxious to get home, and things moved quickly. It was not long before the porter was hefting their luggage onto his hand truck and bursting through the door into the terminal. Clarisse was waiting impatiently.

"Enough is enough, Jamie. Now I must hold my beautiful grandson."

Jamie handed Philippe into Clarisse's outstretched arms. There was evident joy on her face as she drew Philippe to her. It took her back to the time with her own sons, Andre and Emile, when she could still mother them, before tragedy had caused her to withdraw from their lives.

Andre was growing impatient. "What vehicle did you bring, Mother?"

"The big jeep with the car seat," she murmured, her eyes transfixed on the baby's. "Obviously you are not taking the speedboat to Soufriere tonight. The seas are much too high. I think it will be a bad year for storms when we have this kind of weather in July."

Clarisse continued to sway with the baby, making occasional grandmother faces at him, then questioned Jamie and her son.

"Are you sure you want to go on? You could stay with your father and me tonight. We don't get down to Jumeaux much any more. Your father's not up to that long drive and the road is so rough. Are you sure you won't stay?"

Andre looked to Jamie, who shook her head.

"No, Clarisse, I've been in Martinique for three weeks. I need to get home and see our daughters. I'm sure we'll be fine. It's just a couple of hours. The next tropical wave is some way off, and I have every confidence in Andre's driving. We'll be fine."

"Speaking of Martinique, how is my sister?"

"Tante Yve's doing well. She's as full of energy as ever. I felt very welcome. And how are things at Jumeaux Designs?"

Clarisse smiled. "If you mean, did we miss you - yes, we missed you, but we coped. The latest designs for the blouses and dresses you approved are working out well. But there are plenty of things waiting for you."

"Ladies, enough of the chit chat. We need to get on the way to Jumeaux. You know how fast it goes dark. Do you want us to drop you at home on our way out of town, Mother?"

"No, there are plenty of taxi drivers who can get me home. Go on, I don't want to hold you up a minute longer."

"Jamie, sit here with Philippe while I get Mother on her way." Clarisse passed Philippe back to Jamie, a gentle relinquishing as the women exchanged kisses.

"You two, I mean you three, have a safe trip down to Jumeaux. Call me when you get there or I'll worry." She leaned down to kiss the baby's head and held Jamie for a moment. "I'm glad you are through the ordeal, child."

Jamie hugged her back, this imposing woman, once so cold and formidable, who had drawn her into her heart and her family.

Jamie watched her husband help his mother into a taxi and snuggled her son a little closer. *It's so good to be home. I can't wait to have all of my family around me again*, she thought, anticipating the reunion at Jumeaux. She had sorely missed her four-year-old twin daughters, Yvie and Lissa.

The wind gusted again, and the fronds of the coconut palms lining the nearby beach clacked in response. Jamie could hear the waves crashing against the beach. High surf, she thought. Must be some storm out there. She pulled Philippe closer as Andre pulled up with the big jeep.

Jamie strapped the baby into the car seat in the back of the jeep and slid in beside him.

"I'd rather you were up here with me," Andre said.

"I know, me too."

"Do you need to nurse him before we start?" Andre asked.

"No, he's still asleep. I'd rather wait until he wakes on his own. We can always pull over in one of the villages."

The rain subsided as quickly as it had begun, but the dark sky indicated more on the way as they headed out of the airport and into Castries, the capital of the small tropical island they called home.

"The traffic lights are out," Andre commented as he waited to make the right turn onto Jeremie Street, just past the central market.

"That's nothing new. I can never figure out when they're supposed to be working."

Just then all the lights in the capital went out.

"That's not a good sign," Andre said. "Storm must be intensifying."

"Maybe it's a planned power cut," Jamie said, trying to reassure herself.

From the center of town they turned up the winding road onto the Morne, then down into Cul de Sac valley, through its rows of banana plants, broad verdant leaves glistening with rain. It was near Anse La Raye that the wind came up and the heavens opened again.

Andre slowed the heavy vehicle and put the wipers on high.

"We may need to find a place to pull over."

"It's about time for the baby to wake up. Find a place to pull off and I'll nurse him while we wait for the rain to slack off. It's a shame we can't see anything. I had hoped to come home to gorgeous sea and mountain views."

"There's a scenic turnout up ahead. It'll do for a place to stop." Andre pulled the car off the road. Wind buffeted the vehicle, and the pelting rain intensified the afternoon darkness. They could barely see out the windows.

Jamie unstrapped the baby and lifted him out of his car seat. He started to cry as she opened her nursing bra.

"Three days old and he knows exactly what to do." The baby latched on and began to suck. Jamie leaned back in her seat and relaxed.

"Nursing the twins was much trickier," she said, thinking back to the first days with Lissa and Yvie. If it hadn't been for Bertille Deroche and her mother-in-law, she wouldn't have known what to do. "It's easier this time now that I know what I'm doing."

Andre laughed, watching her from the front seat. "We had to learn fast as first-time parents, and two at once."

"Thank goodness we had lots of support. Everybody wanted to help." Jamie listened to the pounding rain. "We are so blessed, Andre. We have two beautiful daughters, a healthy new son."

Andre turned on the demisters as the windows started to fog up.

"Don't forget our big family - all wanting to help and sometimes sticking their noses into our business."

"I know. But since I came from a very small family, I love having your family around..."

"And they've adopted you. For a transplanted New Yorker, you're more St. Lucian than I am."

"And you're spending more and more time in New York. I really wondered if you'd get back to see your son born."

"I did, didn't I? And I'm here now." There was a slight edge to his voice.

"Sorry. Just saying I was worried you wouldn't get there in time. But you are gone a lot. The girls miss you."

Jamie continued nursing in the awkward pause. They sat listening to the rain drum on the roof.

Jamie burped the baby and put him on her other breast.

Andre reached into the back seat and stroked her breast. "I miss you, too, when I'm gone."

Without warning, the wind intensified and the car rocked as rain thundered against the roof.

"How close are we to the edge of the turnout?" Jamie asked anxiously.

"Lots of room. Don't worry."

"It's just that there's been so much rain, and I don't want the hill on the other side of the road to let go and push us over the edge."

"Honestly, Jamie! You can think up more ways to get us killed. The hillside is fine, the turnout is solid. As soon as the rain subsides a bit we'll be on our way."

"Just feeling anxious. Must be the hormone overload after giving birth."

Andre watched as she put the drowsy baby back in the car seat and strapped him in again. "Whenever it lets up," she said, pulling her clothes straight.

"It does seem to be lessening. Why don't we make a dash for home." Andre pulled the vehicle back on the road, but their progress was reduced to a crawl by the torrents of water cascading over the road. Pot holes were full axle deep, and here and there small mounds of dirt had slipped off the hillside onto the road.

Jamie drifted off to sleep, secure in the knowledge that Andre would get them home safely.

She was jolted awake.

"Andre, what's happened?"

"Landslip on the road, pushing the car."

He was on the front edge of the slip, needing to get out of the mud. He jammed the transmission into the lowest four-wheel-drive gear. Jamie could feel the car slowly moving toward the edge of the road, watching as her husband backed up and tried to move forward. She had an odd image of herself as a child as her father tried to rock their car out of a snowdrift.

"Jamie, get the baby out of the car seat."

"Why?"

"Just do it. You may have to get out of the car."

"Andre..."

"Get the baby out of the seat. Scoot over to the door. Do it!" The intensity in Andre's voice terrified her.

Panic closed off her throat. Her fingers slipped as she tried to undo the harness buckles. Finally, just as she had the baby free, she felt the wheels grab the road and the jeep lurched ahead on revving the engine, out of the mud and out of danger. Jamie clutched her sleeping baby to her and stifled a sob.

"Got to keep going," Andre said, wiping at the condensation on the windshield. "Don't know how the rest of the road will be. Can't go back now."

"Should I put the baby back in the car seat?"

"Do you have the Snugli? Strap him in. That way he'll be right with you. The rain seems to be letting up but I need all my concentration right now."

Jamie listened to the keening of the wind. The tropical front had turned into a tropical storm ripping across the island. The sound reminded her of something, something she couldn't place but that filled her with dread. Then it came back. The night in the rain forest when she'd followed the cry of a woman and become lost. That same high-pitched tone of desperation and anguish.

"Andre, do you hear that?" she asked.

"The wind? It's really moaning."

"No, behind the sound of the wind. A woman crying? Don't you hear that?"

"Jamie, you've just been badly frightened. It's just the wind."

She allowed the soft warmth, the gentle rhythmic breathing of her child against her chest to calm her. She couldn't, wouldn't, let that other terrifying time intrude now. Now when her life was settled. Jamie forced herself to review the wonderful parts of her life as she tried to stem her feelings of panic. She was happy and content. Her four-year-old twin daughters were a handful, but absolutely darling. And now a new son. She loved her job at Jumeaux Designs. Andre's business travel took him away from the family for more time than she liked, but she knew it bothered him as well. She couldn't ask for a better husband.

Then she heard the woman's cry again. Her son stirred. "Be still, Philippe," she murmured, savoring the name. "We won't lose you."

Her thoughts turned to the anguish Philippe Diamant's mother, Anne-Cecile, must have felt when he had been lost. *Stop it*, she told herself.

"How are you doing, Andre? Do we need to stop somewhere?"

"We're committed now, Jamie. There's the danger of more landslips, and the villages are no safer."

"Why?"

"They're all built on the rivers. With this much rain there's the danger of flash flooding. We'll keep on going. We'll get through all right."

"Any way I can help?" She watched the steering wheel jolt in his hands, fear gripping her chest.

"Just hang onto Philippe and try to relax. It'll be fine."

Jamie didn't believe Andre any more than he believed himself. She concentrated on her son to divert herself from her fear. "Yes, I think Philippe suits you. We've all been waiting for you," she whispered to the baby who slept unaware.

The deluge had stopped by the time they reached Jumeaux, the Demontagne family compound high in the mountains above Soufriere. Jamie and Andre had built the house at Jumeaux Estate shortly after their marriage five years ago, locating the house just across the garden from the old estate house. As they pulled into the drive, lights on the verandah bid them welcome. Andre honked the horn.

"Andre, the baby," Jamie admonished as Philippe squirmed and began to cry. She unhoooked the Snugli and lifted him out.

"He might as well wake up, Jamie. We seem to have a large welcoming committee. There are his sisters and Marcus and Bertille with Delia trailing behind. There'll be a row about who gets to hold him first."

Andre opened the door and Jamie handed the baby to him. Suddenly two squirming four-year-olds were in her lap, hugging her, covering her cheeks with wet kisses.

"Mama, we missed you."

"Me too, Lissa," Jamie said, hugging her daughter, the quiet one. "But I'm home now."

"Why did it take so long to get our brother? I wore my new dress to church and you weren't here," Yvie complained.

Squeaky wheel, thought Jamie, grabbing Yvie's hand and smiling up at Andre, who was trying not to smile.

"If you let me get out of the car I'll introduce you to your new brother."

On the verandah of the old estate house others waited. Bertille and Marcus Deroche, a stately, regal couple, were descendants of Arawak and Caribe Indian chiefs and African slaves. Dressed in their Sunday best, they knew instinctively that the arrival of this child was an event of great import.

Delia stood to the side. The housekeeper in Jamie's first little house on St. Lucia, she now cared for the family in their home here on the Jumeaux Estate. Delia lived nearby with her son, Rodney. The smile on Delia's mahogany face gleamed as brightly as the gold hoops at her ears.

"Let me have him," Jamie said, taking the baby from Andre. "I will never forget how Marcus and Bertille welcomed me into their hearts. It's important that Philippe be presented to Bertille and that she hold him first. She's the thread."

Andre looked at his wife.

Jamie shrugged. "It's a woman thing." She might have been transplanted from New York, but her instincts and loyalties were from the island.

The walk down the path and up the two steps to the verandah of the old estate house seemed to Jamie a long way. *These are the people who raised Andre, who saved my life, who shared their ancestors' secrets so an important island heritage would not be lost,* she thought. They knew who I was before I did. It is right that Bertille hold *Philippe first.*

When she reached Marcus and Bertille, Delia stepped away, taking the hands of the twin girls.

Jamie offered the baby into the arms of Bertille Deroche.

"Our son," she said. "Philippe Diamant Demontagne."

Bertille's piercing glance unnerved Jamie.

"Is it wise to tempt the spirits?" Bertille said, even as she enfolded the newborn into her protective warmth.

Jamie's face was impassioned. "We have brought him home, Bertille." She thought back to her mother-in-law's comments. "This child will not be lost."

Bertille stood quietly, holding the baby as a sudden breeze rustled leaves, startling a flock of bananaquits into a burst of yellow flight.

Marcus and Andre exchanged puzzled looks as the silence

lengthened.

Yvie stamped her foot. "I wanted to hold my baby first. You said he was our brother."

The silence was broken as the grown-ups smiled at the insistence of the four-year-old.

Andre knelt down and gathered Yvie and Lissa into his arms. "First a hug for your father. Then you can both hold your brother." He lifted his daughters into his arms and carried them into the sitting room of the old estate house, where he deposited them on a large, cushioned settee. The little girls looked solemn as the baby was laid between them.

Lissa stroked his face. "He's very soft, Mama. Look, he's holding my fingers."

Yvie pulled away and got down out of the chair as Jamie helped hold the baby so he wouldn't fall.

"He's no fun. I'm going to go read a story." She stomped petulantly out of the room.

Jamie looked at Bertille. "Read a story? I've been gone for three weeks and she's reading? At four?"

"We aren't sure, but she is spending time with her books. We see her mouthing some words."

Jamie stroked Lissa's straight dark hair as the little girl calmly watched her brother.

"Both my girls are very bright, but I think they must be very tired. Lissa, you'll have lots of time to spend with your new brother in the morning. Now it's time for bed."

"All right, Mama. I'm glad you're home. Are we going to sleep at our house or in the old house with Grandmother Bertille and Grandfather Marcus?"

"We're going to our house. You can run across the garden in the morning to visit."

Delia stepped forward. "Mistress, would you like me to bring Yvie?"

"Would you please? I'm suddenly exhausted. We haven't had time to tell you about what happened on the drive down here, and Philippe will be hungry shortly. I'd love to sleep for awhile before he needs to nurse again."

"I'll bring Yvie. You and Mister Andre go on ahead. The nursery is all prepared."

Andre had been standing aside with Marcus and Bertille. Jamie knew from the looks on their faces that he had told them of their harrowing escape from the landslip.

Bertille stepped forward and picked Philippe up from the settee.

"We're all exhausted. Jamie, do you want me to drive you over to the house?" asked Andre.

"No, Lissa and I will bring Philippe. It's just a few steps through the garden. Why don't you bring the car around with all the baby gear."

Inside they could hear Delia bargaining with Yvie.
"If you come now without a fuss, I will make you waffles for breakfast."

Squeaky wheel gets the grease, Jamie thought again, looking down at Lissa. *The compliant one who minds will get waffles, too. But now I can't wait to get us all into bed.*

She turned to Bertille, whose face had softened.

"He is a beautiful child," Bertille said as she rather imperiously transferred Philippe to his mother's arms.

As Jamie turned away, Marcus caught Bertille's eyes. He saw Bertille take a deep breath, the look on her face part hope, part fear.

Steaming piles of fresh waffles greeted Jamie as she entered the kitchen the next morning, baby over her shoulder. She settled into a rocker in the corner where she could look out into the gardens between her house and the old estate house where Marcus and Bertille now lived, the helliconia and bougainvillea backlit by the sparkling Caribbean sea beyond. A small dark bird with a red breast landed on the windowsill.

"Rufous, you've come to meet my new son," Jamie said. The little bird cocked his head as if listening.

Jamie put Philippe to her breast, where he latched on and began to nurse vigorously.

"Delia, I'll have my waffles the way the twins like theirs, with butter and mango jam. And could you put a piece of waffle on the side so I can feed Rufous?"

"More," Yvie demanded from the table.

"What do you say?" Jamie reminded.

Yvie scowled mutinously. "More. Please, more."

"How are you doing this morning, Lissa?" Jamie asked, scattering waffle crumbs on the windowsill.

"I have a present for my brother, Mama."

"That's very nice of you, Lissa. Why don't you finish your waffles and then you can show him." Jamie put Philippe over her shoulder and took a bite of waffle between patting up bubbles and putting him to her other breast.

Yvie narrowed her eyes and looked at her sister and then her mother. She could tell her mother was pleased with what Lissa had just said. Who would want to give a present to the baby? All he did was sleep. She stuffed a big bite of waffle into her mouth.

"Small bites," reminded her mother.

Yvie chewed furiously.

"'Scused, please?" said Lissa.

"Me, too," Yvie echoed, halfway to the door.

"Of course, sweeties. Lissa, why don't you go get your present. Delia, where's Andre? He was gone by the time I got out of bed."

"Marcus came for him earlier. He was just finishing his breakfast and Marcus came. Something about a landslip."

"We barely got through one last night on our way home." Jamie shuddered at the recollection, the terror as the car was slowly pushed toward the edge of the road and the drop-off beyond. The keening of the wind. She pushed the memory away. *We're home. We're safe.*

Philippe let go of her breast and gave a sudden cry. As she gentled him in her arms, Jamie wondered if his upset was a reaction to her own.

"I heard it raining hard during the night. Has the tropical wave passed by?"

"It seems so. I listened to the weather on the radio this morning."

Their conversation was interrupted as the two girls entered the room. Lissa held a fistful of blue flowers and Yvie a jam jar with a lid.

"Lissa, these flowers are beautiful. Where did you find them?" Jamie asked.

Lissa patted her baby brother as he lay in his mother's arms. "He needs blue, Mama. I don't know if these are the right ones, but they were the only blue ones I could find."

"What do you mean, he needs blue?" Jamie asked.

"I just know, that's all. He needs blue," Lissa said.

Yvie pushed foward. "I have a present, too." She thrust the jam jar into Jamie's hand. Jamie could see the large spider inside, the furry legs, the malevolent eyes. She didn't know whether to laugh or cry, but she knew she couldn't be sqeamish.

"It's a lovely spider, Yvie. Where did you find it?" Jamie said, turning the lid to make sure it was on tight.

"Under the verandah. Rodney helped me. I was going to keep it for myself, but since Lissa had a present..."

"Thank you both for welcoming your new brother. Delia, can you put these lovely flowers in some water, please?"

I'll have to talk to Delia about her son, Rodney, Jamie thought. Some spiders are dangerous, and Yvie doesn't need any help getting into mischief.

"Yvie, I think Philippe might be too little to appreciate your gift. Why don't we go find Grandfather Marcus? He'll be able to tell us what kind of spider it is and how we should take care of it."

"Come on, Lissa. Don't be a poke." Yvie marched out the door, glad she could keep her spider.

Jamie and Delia smiled knowingly at one another as Jamie burped Philippe and rewrapped him in a lightweight swaddling blanket.

Jamie followed her daughters across the garden separating the two houses, the grass still wet from the rains the night before. The trees dripped with water but the bougainvillea sparkled in the sun, already high in the blue sky. The ominous dark clouds of yesterday had blown through with the tropical wave.

Jamie looked to the old estate house, remembering when Andre's father, Auguste, had lived here. Now elderly and frail, he lived in Castries with Clarisse, the two reunited after two decades of living apart. Only one of the healings in this family, she thought. Bertille oversaw the housekeeping duties for the compound, and Marcus managed the estate with Andre's younger brother, Emile, now increasingly off island investigating new crops, pond-grown crayfish, fish farming in the sea, even his latest, mushrooms grown in some of the island's cool, shady valleys.

Jamie could see Marcus, Bertille and Andre standing near the far edge of the garden, looking down the hill. The girls ran on ahead.

Yvie arrived first. "Grandfather, look at my spider. Mama says you know about it and how to take care of it."

"Indeed I do, Yvie." Marcus winked at Jamie as she approached the group.

Andre stooped and picked up the girls, one in each arm.

Jamie looked down the hill. "My God. What happened here?"

"A landslip during the night. Keep away from the edge, it's still unstable," Marcus said, motioning Jamie back.

"What an amazing tree," Jamie exclaimed as she saw the huge old samaan tree that had been revealed by the landslip. It stood at the bottom of a ravine, the soil having parted on either side of it before pushing through to another, deeper gully.

"It is one of the old ones," Bertille said. "A Father Samaan. See the thickness of its trunk and the reach of its branches? The one by the estate house must be descended from this old one."

"Father Samaan is blue," said Lissa.

Bertille and Marcus glanced at one another. Jamie laughed. "You mean he's sad?"

"No. Blue, see the blue light around him. Like the flowers I brought for my new brother."

"What blue light?" Jamie asked her daughter.

Lissa pointed. "Don't you see? There and there."

Jamie shook her head, bewildered. The baby books had warned the children might act out after the baby came home.

"Honestly, Lissa..." Jamie began. She looked to Bertille, then Marcus, wondering what she might be missing.

Marcus motioned her to be quiet, then took the child from Andre. "Show me, child," he said, his voice quiet as he walked closer to the edge of the ravine, apart from the others.

"You can see it, can't you, Grandfather Marcus?"

"Just a little, but I'm surprised you can see it, Lissa."

"I don't always tell what I see."

"Hmmmm..."

"Like the blue around my new brother. But a different blue. He needs more blue, Grandfather. I have to find the right blue."

Marcus turned to face the little girl, her green eyes earnest.

"That would be a very big job, Lissa. Perhaps too big a job for a little girl. Would you like me and Grandmother Bertille to help you?" He could feel the softening of the little body he held, the release of an unbearable tension; he could barely hear the soft reply.

"Yes, please. I think I'm too small to do it all by myself."

Come visit the Annie Rogers website at:

www.annierrogers.com

ALSO come visit the blog. It's all about romance, writing and publishing. Learn about the background of the Annie Rogers adventures, the characters, the settings, the experience of writing. You can make your thoughts known as we exchange views. Come join the fun!

http://letmedigress.blogspot.com

Special Offer

A Dream Across Time at 20% off list price
plus Free Shipping and Handling

Payment can be made by Visa, MasterCard or check. Make checks or money orders payable to Bivens and Jensen Publishing. Send checks to: Bivens and Jensen Publishing, PO Box 448, St. Michaels, MD 21663.

A $30.00 service fee will be charged on all returned checks. If you are ordering from outside the USA, please contact us first regarding shipping costs. If you have any questions, e-mail Annie Rogers at annie@annierogers. com or call 800-823-2002.

Please allow 2 - 3 weeks for delivery.

Name: _____

Street Address: _____

City: _____ State: _____ Zip Code _____

Daytime Phone: _____

E-mail Address: _____

Item	Price	How Many?	
A Dream Across Time	$12.76 (includes S&H)		
		Sub-total	
		Maryland residents add 5% sales tax	
		Order Total	

Check Enclosed_____   Pay by Credit Card_____

I authorize the above order to be charged to my credit card.

Visa or MasterCard number _____

Expiration Date _____

Name of Credit Card Holder _____

Billing address _____

Signature of Card Holder _____

Date _____

Please autograph my book and inscribe as follows: _____

_____